PART

THE CHRONICL

THE HEART OF FIRE

BY

J A CULLUM

EDGE SCIENCE FICTION AND FANTASY PUBLISHING
AN IMPRINT OF HADES PUBLICATIONS, INC.
CALGARY

Cinkarion - The Heart of Fire
copyright © 2010 by J. A. Cullum

Edge Science Fiction and Fantasy Publishing
An Imprint of Hades Publications Inc.
P.O. Box 1714, Calgary, Alberta, T2P 2L7, Canada

In house editing by Shoshanna Glick
Interior by Brian Hades
Cover Illustration by David Willicome

EDGE Science Fiction and Fantasy Publishing and Hades Publications, Inc.
acknowledges the ongoing support of the Canada Council for the Arts and the
Alberta Foundation for the Arts for our publishing programme.

Library and Archives Canada Cataloguing in Publication

Cullum, Janice A., 1944-
Cinkarion : the heart of fire / J.A. Cullum. -- 1st ed.

(The chronicles of the Karionin ; bk. 2)
ISBN 978-1-894063-21-0

I. Title. II. Series: Cullum, Janice A., 1944- . Chronicles of the
Karionin ; bk. 2.

PS3553.U34C52 2010   813'.6   C2010-900159-1

FIRST EDITION
(z-20100725)
Printed in Canada
www.edgewebsite.com

Dedication

To my husband David,
one of my better critics.

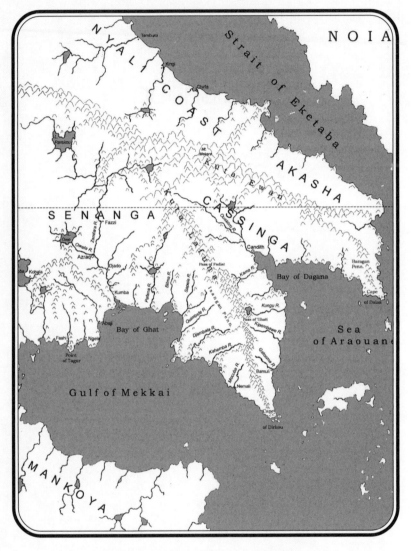

North Eastern Cibata

Book I

ROCKS
AND RIPPLES

"Certain events, like rocks dropped in still water, cause ripples in the stream of time."

— FROM VOLUME 3 OF "THE COLLECTED WRITINGS OF THE WIZARD CORMOR"

I

4624, 463rd Cycle of the Year of the Tiger
Month of Ingvash

> "Little I thought, when I was a lass,
> That I'd end up a whore in an alehouse,
> But times are hard and money's tight
> So I sell my body through the night."

— verse from "The Sailor's Lady"
from Songs of the Sea and Shore, edited by Bar Panyara, 4592

A WIDE, UNPAVED STREET RAN THE LENGTH of Nemali's harbor. Under the late afternoon sun it teemed with people. Merchants and planters, dressed in garments ranging from voluminous robes to tailored khaki, gestured and shouted. Nearly naked laborers led donkey or bullock-carts, pushed hand-drawn barrows, or carried hogsheads of oil and wine on their backs. The reek of rotting fish, copra and decaying vegetation wafting off the tidal flats mingled with a faint aroma of cloves.

Above the commotion, the sun scorched the arch of the sky and blazed down on the exposed brown mud at the mouth of the Mocuba River and on the gray coral and adobe walls of the town. There was no trace of the cooling fog that sometimes came in off the Gulf of Mekkai.

Morrien Songard wiped her forehead with her sleeve. Under a wide straw hat, her red hair was pulled back in a braid but tendrils had escaped. Heat, sweat and split ends made the loose hair frizz around her face. She had been pretty once, but now her face was lined and her body thickened. Her breasts sagged under her loose, faded cotton dress and her skin looked pasty. Only her eyes, large and green, retained their former beauty.

She shouldered her way through people and wagons, trying to reach a vantage point where she could see the length of the harbor. A cart piled high with copal and hides and another carrying kwaluccan, tortoise-shells and beeswax swayed past, both on their way down from the river landings to off load at one of the ships. Another string of wagons was headed the other way, carrying goods from the ships destined for inland plantations: bolts of machine-made cotton cloth, china, firearms and ammunition from Mahran or Ilwheirlane in the Northern Hemisphere.

"Move aside there!" a voice yelled nearby. Morrien stepped backward as a cart full of sacks of hunical, barrels of salt meat and fresh vegetables barely missed her on its way toward the boarding ramp of the ship on her right. "Don't plan on lingering this trip," the voice continued to some third party. "Loading my supplies and lifting anchor. Sooner I see the last of Nemali, the happier I'll be. Got any sense, you'll do the same."

Morrien looked around for the source of the voice and saw a burly sailor in scarlet and green, a captain's insignia on his hat. His companion, more soberly clad in brown, wore matching insignia. The second man said, "You hear something specific, Halev?"

Halev frowned. "Dekese has ambitions. Wants Cassinga right off the map so there won't be any human nation left in Cibata." He shook his head. "Nemali's just not a safe place, right across the river from tiger folk."

Morrien dodged through a gap in the stream of carts. She had covered almost the full length of the harbor and *Arroth* was not in port. She cursed. Three months, and still no news from her family.

Halev was right. Nemali was a ripe fruit waiting to be picked. The merchants had pled for more troops for years, since the region northwest of the Mocuba River had fallen to Senanga. But Njombe Isiro, the Ahar of Cassinga, was too busy with the pleasures of his court to heed them. Even when taxes were raised, Nemali gained only three dozen soldiers, though the increase should have paid for ten times that number.

Morrien sighed and headed back. She would have to hurry to make it to the tavern before her evening shift.

Though the crowd thinned away from the harbor, she was still late by the time she reached the Molting Griffin. The gray coral building had a thatched palm frond roof. From the narrow, raised wooden sidewalk outside the bar, Morrien could see down Anzib Street to the harbor where the tops of the ships' masts caught the last rays of the sun.

Inside, she blinked to adjust her eyes to the lack of light. The tavern was smoky from the fire in the open hearth. Years of that smoke had darkened the beamed ceiling to black. The heat was stifling, but the aroma of roasting meat almost drowned out the other, less appetizing scents coming from the river mouth and the harbor.

"Hey, Morrien! 'Bout time you got here. We need another round!" a heavyset man called from a back table.

Morrien took off her hat and grabbed her apron, yelling the order to the bartender, Erlen.

She took over from Kafir who had been basting a haunch of seral roasting on the spit in the hearth.

"Slowing down already, Morrien? Sure you don't need a rest break upstairs?" a customer asked, gesturing crudely. His friends laughed.

"Only if you're going to turn the spit for me in the meantime."

This sally was greeted with renewed hilarity. She thought she heard sounds from outside and the floor seemed to vibrate but she could not be sure over the noise in the tavern.

Pushing back her hair with a reddened hand greasy from the basting brush, Morrien crossed to the bar where Erlen had set a tray with six tankards of mead. She hefted the tray and carried it over to the men, thumping it down in the middle of the table. "Help yourselves, lesskan," she said, matching their vulgarity and swaying out of the way of their groping hands.

Suddenly a man threw the door open. Screams came from the street outside, followed by the sounds of gunfire. "Linlarin!" he yelled. "The whole cursed army of Senanga! They broke through the wall. They're taking the town!" As fast as he had appeared, he disappeared, turning and running toward the harbor. There was a loud boom in the distance and the floor vibrated as it had before. Morrien froze for a moment, then shrugged, put the tray down and went back to turning the spit as everyone except Erlen charged out into the street. At least it gave her something to do with her hands.

"You're not going to try to escape?" Erlen asked.

"What's the point? They'll have crossed the river upstream. They'll be all around the town by now. If Senanga wants Nemali, no one here's going to stop them. I'll take my chances as a slave. Better that than playing hide and seek in the jungle with a bunch of tigers."

The screaming had not stopped and the gunfire sounded closer. The cannon boomed again. Morrien waved her arm at the door. "They've broken through the wall. What're you waiting for? Get going, or all the ships will have gone."

"You're sure?"

"Yeah, I'm sure." Morrien turned back to the meat so he couldn't see her tears. She should have stayed in Candith, but in Candith she'd been an embarrassment to her family who had never understood why she wouldn't marry. They hated the way she lived. She let go of the spit and dug her fingernails into her palms to stop herself from crying as she listened to Erlen make his uneven way out onto the sidewalk. She should never have come to Nemali.

When Erlen had gone, Morrien wiped her face on her grimy apron and cleared the tables, piling the empty tankards onto the tray and dumping them out on the service table. Then she pulled the roast seral onto a serving tray.

She was carving when the Senangans arrived, pushing open the door, a wave of nearly naked figures, both male and female, with only brief leather harnesses to hold their weapons and equipment. Their skins were every shade of brown, from near black to bronze, and shiny with sweat. She had heard that tiger folk fought naked to facilitate their shape-changing, but the actual sight of them still shocked her. Except for their height and striped hair, their nudity revealed them as disturbingly human.

Morrien swallowed, then drew herself up and faced them. "The food's fresh," she said in Eskh, the trade language.

"You're alone?" one of the Senangans, obviously an officer, demanded in the same tongue. The only one fully dressed, he wore a scarlet uniform, the jacket decorated with gold symbols of his authority.

She took a deep breath. "Search if you like, but you're wasting your time." Walking over to the counter, she collected a pile of plates. One linlar moved to stop her, but the officer waved him back and gave a series of commands in his harsh, sibilant language. Four of the soldiers left to search the rest of the building.

"If they break things, I may not be able to serve your dinner," Morrien said.

The officer's face twitched in what might have been a smile. "Why didn't you run with the others?"

She shrugged. "Where could I go?"

"Humans aren't usually so sensible." His brilliant amber eyes examined her and she felt a momentary nausea, as though his eyes were seeing inside her. Then he laughed. It was a cruel sound echoed by more screaming and gunfire in the distance, this time from the direction of the harbor. There was another roar of cannon fire and the building shook.

The yellow-gold eyes were still fixed on her. She gestured to the roast. "You want some of this? There's fresh baked bread and a lorsk casserole in the back."

The officer said something sharply in his own language and all but two of the troopers left in the room filed out. The remaining soldiers positioned themselves on either side of the door.

"I think I will have something to eat. This is as good a place as any for my command headquarters." He sat down at one of the tables farthest from the fireplace.

"You want the rest of the food from the back?"

"Certainly." He gestured to one of the guards by the door. "Sathar will accompany you." He paused and again his eyes burned into her. "So you won't tamper with the food, I'll expect you to join me."

Morrien's eyes narrowed. "If I'd thought to have poison handy, that wouldn't have stopped me."

His amber eyes sharpened. "You don't care about your life?"

"Why should I?"

His expression was enigmatic. "Even slavery can have its compensations. It depends on the slave."

His eyes brightened and Morrien suddenly realized that he was extremely handsome. The tawny stripes in his black hair were the only alien thing about him. He had a high forehead and an aquiline nose above a wide, flexible mouth, thin-lipped but sensual. She turned her gaze away and hurried toward the back room, so aware of the eyes of the officer on her back that she hardly noticed the soldier a few steps behind her. Twenty years ago, even ten years ago, she would have been thrilled to meet a human man who looked like the officer, but he was not human. He was linlar; he could change into a tiger. Moreover, he was the commander of the Senangan army and she was a harlot several years past her prime.

She was about to pull aside the curtain to the back room when she heard the sounds of a struggle. The soldier behind her pushed her out of the way and the two who had preceded her emerged, dragging out a struggling boy.

"Kafir! I thought you left with the others."

The sound of his name seemed to snap something in the boy and he went limp. The two soldiers, one holding each of his arms, supported his weight.

"Stand up and come here, boy!" the officer commanded in Eskh.

Kafir stared at him, his body still, but his attitude expressing stubborn disobedience and contempt.

The officer studied the boy, then said something to one of the soldiers holding him. The Senangan dropped Kafir's arm and stepped back, his body melting, flowing toward a new form. Morrien gaped at the metamorphosing shape, both fascinated and repelled, as it resolved into a tiger with a high, domed head and fierce eyes. She observed, almost analytically, how the soldier's harness, which held his bow and arrows, a sword and a pistol, had been designed to fit the tiger form as well as the man.

The change took under a minute. Kafir had gone to his knees when the soldier dropped his arm. When the other soldier holding him also let go, he remained frozen in a position of supplication, his eyes wide with terror, fixed on those of the tiger. Then the tiger's front paw reached out and the boy's face disintegrated into a mass of blood and torn flesh. There was a snapping sound as his neck broke. Kafir was dead.

Morrien stared. She had seen men die before, but always in the heat of some sort of action or from disease. She had never seen a death quite so sudden or horrible. "Why?" she asked, tearing her eyes away from the red pulp that had been the child's face and turning to the officer.

"He was of no use to us. Too rebellious."

"And me?" Morrien swallowed. "Will you do the same to me when I've finished serving your dinner?"

"You needn't worry, I have no intention of killing you. You interest me." He gave a brief command for the body to be removed, then turned back to her. His thin lips stretched into a wry smile. "I imagine in some respects you'll even find life as my slave less onerous than the life you've known."

"Just a different class of customer."

He frowned. "Not quite. I'm ready for my dinner now." He nodded a dismissal.

Morrien fetched the rest of the food and served him. He seemed to have forgotten his earlier remark about her eating with him, for which she was grateful. She had no appetite. By the time he finished, several other officers had come to make reports and she served them as well.

By midnight she was exhausted. She gathered from the little she understood of their speech that the minor skirmish that had been the taking of Nemali was over. The Senangan forces were in charge. The surprise of their attack against the poorly armed city meant that they had met almost no resistance. The humans who hadn't escaped were either dead or subdued.

"I've finished," Morrien said. "Can I go up to bed, now?"

The officer eyed her and grimaced. "I'd prefer you to wash first."

"What do you mean?"

"I intend to employ your services but I find your current state repulsive. Correct it. You have fifteen minutes."

Morrien realized that she was staring at him again, struck dumb with surprise. She was thirty-eight and looked older. She had no illusions about her appearance.

His eyes met hers and she felt another wave of attraction, stronger than the one she had experienced earlier.

Too stunned to resist his power, she nodded stiffly and climbed the stairs.

Two soldiers carried up enough water to fill her old, wooden tub and Morrien bathed and washed her hair. She felt better clean; it had been days since she'd had such an opportunity. The bath couldn't ease her tension, however, and she realized that she was terrified. Earlier, she'd been too shocked to notice her fear. She shivered.

"I told you that you have no need to be afraid."

The voice of the Senangan commander coming out of the darkness startled her.

"I'm not finished."

"You've had enough time. I'll dry you." He held out the towel and Morrien had little choice but to rise and step out of the tub into it. She wondered if the sight of her body, the aging body that bulged in all the wrong places and sagged where it should have bulged, would make him change his mind, but it did not.

Instead his mouth twisted and he said, "Ironic, here you are, an aging whore, but if a wizard had discovered you when you were young enough to train, you might have been uniquely powerful."

While her mind reeled from his words, he dried her with the impersonal precision he might have used on a pet animal. When she was dry, he made her lie down on the bed. Then he undressed and lay upon her and coupled with her.

Morrien had feared he might maul her; the tiger folk often tortured human prisoners. She had expected the feel of his hands to revolt her and had steeled herself not to be sick. It hadn't occurred to her that she might enjoy his touch. It had been years since she had felt anything during the act of intercourse other than a mild distaste at being handled, yet every time his strange amber eyes met hers she felt drawn. With his eyes controlling her, his hands pulled responses from her body that she hadn't known even in her youth. What she had thought to endure became instead an experience so exquisite that it drowned out the horror that had gone before. She lost herself in the slow spiral of feeling, the fire that spread through her veins, until she was all fire exploding in ecstasy. When it was over, she lay panting and covered with sweat by the officer's side, her body relaxed in a way that she had never felt before. She was shocked back to reality by his expression of aloof disdain.

She reached out to him, but he rose quickly, avoiding her touch. His skin was dark and shiny, the color of the ancient wooden beams downstairs. "Enough," he said.

"What do you mean?"

"I thought my meaning obvious."

"But it was so..." Morrien could not find words.

He looked her over dispassionately. "Of course. I believe in rewarding those who perform their services well."

"But I..."

"I am Senrec Kamrasi, the commander of the Senangan army. My only marriage was a complete fiasco. I have need of a strong heir and you have great genetic potential. The possibility that you might produce such an heir was worth a few moments of my time. But now I have duties to which I must attend. I'll see you're dispatched to my home in the morning."

Morrien watched, stunned, as he dressed, his manner dismissing her as though she had ceased to exist. A sickness rose in her throat.

Everything had happened so rapidly, but she should have known. He was a linlar; he had were-sight, if nothing more. Furthermore, he was the commander of the Senangan army. Why hadn't she realized right away that he was a wizard? He had looked at Kafir and known Kafir would be rebellious, not because he could see that from Kafir's stance, but because he could look inside Kafir's brain. He had looked at her, but he hadn't seen what a man would see. He had seen inside her all the way down to the pattern of her genes.

She shuddered. He had manipulated her so easily. Press a button here and the whore will wiggle, she thought, but the button hadn't been a physical one. He hadn't raised those sensations in her by the way he had touched her with his hands. He had been inside her brain. She gagged, trying to choke down her nausea. The defilement was worse than physical rape, that mental invasion that had made her crave his touch, and feel emotions she had never felt before.

And she was impregnated with his sperm! Morrien trembled. Her body felt abruptly cold, despite the heat of the room.

The commander finished pulling on his scarlet pants and buttoning the shirt he wore under his jacket and sat back down on her bed to pull on his boots. He didn't look at her as he did so. She might as well have been invisible. She had served her purpose and now was not worth even the slightest attention.

Morrien felt a sudden, overpowering rage, a hatred as intense as the passion he had raised in her only minutes earlier. He had been inside her mind! She sold her body, but her mind was her own. She stared at his back, his broad, flexible back, and memory of the passion she had felt ripped though her. She hated him, loathed him, but her body still craved his touch and he couldn't be bothered even to look at her. He hadn't felt a thing.

But he would! He was so arrogant that he was paying no attention to her at all. She knew what it felt like now when his mind was inside her, and it was gone. Her hand felt under the mattress for her dagger. She had often found it useful to have a weapon handy.

The dagger came to hand easily. Morrien didn't think about what she was doing. She kept her rage and hatred in the still place inside her. She knew how to use a knife. She had carried one since she was nine.

The commander finished with one boot and was pulling on the second. She angled the blade upward to penetrate his ribs and drove it into his back with all her strength just where she knew it would reach his heart.

The linlar gasped when the blade struck. He started to rise and turn. She felt the knife try to force its way out and twisted the blade sideways as she shoved it back. His body convulsed even as his arm swung around and struck her on the side of the head. She lost her grip on the knife as she was knocked off the bed but the officer didn't follow her.

He tried to stand. She felt his fury like a wave of pain. She was afraid that he would cry out. Then he collapsed onto the floor.

Morrien climbed to her feet, her ears straining to hear if the sound of his fall had disturbed the soldiers below. When more than a minute passed and no one came, she looked down at the body, shocked by what she had done—and more shocked by the fact that, now that he was dead, she wanted to hold him, press herself against him, feel again that terrible pleasure. The thought appalled her but she couldn't avert her gaze from his tall, lean body. He had fallen on his face and the knife stuck up from his back. Blood saturated his shirt and formed a pool on the bare wooden boards of the floor.

She should try to get away from the tavern. His soldiers would kill her if they found her with him. She felt cold and sick and wondered if she had the strength to escape, or cared enough to make the attempt. Instead she sat down on the bed next to the scarlet jacket he hadn't had time to put on. It was almost the same color as his blood.

Morrien was still sitting on the bed in a state of numb apathy when an explosion rocked the building. The sound of shouting came from downstairs and then gunfire.

So, it's not over, she thought, and a stab of fierce gladness pierced the fog that had overcome her. Someone was fighting back, maybe sailors from the ships.

The thought prodded her into action. She found clothes in her chest of drawers and dressed. The floor felt warm under her feet and she slipped on her shoes, trying to make out what was happening from the confusion of noises below. It was only when she opened her door and smelt the acrid smoke in the hall that she realized the tavern was on fire.

One look at the stairs already starting to char told Morrien she could never get down them alive and her room overlooked Anzib Street. She was sure to be seen if she tried to escape that way. She turned and ran to the room across from hers, feeling the heat of the floor through her shoes. The window! She threw it open, climbed out onto the spiky thatch of the roof and slid down to the edge. The irregular surface tore at her clothes, but she just managed to catch the gutter. She dangled three meters from the ground, afraid of the drop, until her fingers began to go numb. When she let go, she fell in a heap in the alley behind the bar. The impact knocked the air out of her and bruised her hip.

She stood up slowly. When she looked around the corner, she saw a troop of Senangans rounding up prisoners. The air reeked of smoke and gunpowder. Over the roar of the flames she could hear screams and the staccato noise of gunfire.

She headed down the alley. She was bound to be caught, but she could put some distance between herself and the Griffin. That way at least she might not be associated with the commander's death.

The night was lit by the spreading fires, a chiaroscuro of shifting shapes and running figures. She was knocked down once and felt nearly too tired to rise. Sometime later she was summoned to halt. She turned and saw a troop of Senangan soldiers escorting some two dozen prisoners. There was no escape, not when any one of those naked, human-looking soldiers could turn into a tiger and chase her down. The one who bound her hands with a coarse rope and pushed her into the line had satiny flesh the same dark color as the commander's. She shivered when he touched her, welcoming the bite of the whip that reprimanded her for being slow when the line started to move again. The pain took her mind off her memories of the feel of a linlar's flesh.

The rest of the night was a blur of being dragged back and forth through the city amid a chaos of fighting and fires. Just before dawn Morrien found herself standing on a hill outside the town in a temporary holding pen. A wind had come up from the south, clearing away most of the smoke, and she could see clearly again. Nemali was blossoming with red and yellow fires, like flowers, as the sun turned the hazy sky pink with dawn. She wondered how horror could look so beautiful.

II

4624, 463RD CYCLE OF THE YEAR OF THE TIGER
MONTH OF CERDANA

> *"What constitutes abuse of power? Obviously, one who uses a
> public position to assist one's friends and damage one's foes is
> guilty of abuse. A public position requires an even-handed
> administration of justice, granting equal rights to friend or foe.
> Those in the private sector may grant favors. Public officials
> may not.*
>
> *"Any use of power to gratify personal desire must be considered
> abuse. The public official has no right to private purposes
> during his term of office. The ultimate good of all the people he
> serves must be his only consideration."*
>
> — EXCERPT FROM *THE ART OF GOVERNMENT* BY VYDARGA V OF ILWHEIRLANE

T HE PALACE OF NJOMBE III, Ahar of Cassinga, had thick, white-
washed adobe walls, mosaic floors, and high ceilings. In the
throne room children sat in corners pulling ropes to swing palm frond
fans. There Njombe sat and listened to a report from General Menkor
who had been, until the month before, commander of the Cassingan
forces in Nemali. One of the slim, brown boys pulling the ropes
listened too. Nathan Ouakoro was fourteen. At the end of the day, his
master would expect him to be able to repeat verbatim every word
spoken. A nearly eidetic memory was important to one who wished to
be a wizard.

"With no further reserves, there was nothing more we could do,
your majesty," the General said, his mustache seeming to bristle with
dissatisfaction.

"It was inevitable that Nemali would fall, your majesty," said Graff
Ulein, the Lord Chamberlain, from his position of honor at the Ahar's
side.

Nathan eyed the ahar. Njombe Isiro was forty-nine and had ruled
Cassinga for twenty-five years. A tall, heavy man with skin nearly as
black as his hair, Njombe looked deceptively impressive in his royal
blue silk robes. One needed to be close to notice the red-rimmed eyes
and faint muscle tremors of the long-term kufi addict.

A muscle in Njombe's right cheek twitched and he took another pull of the calming drug in his pipe before asking, "Why inevitable, Graff? We sent troops to reinforce the city, didn't we?"

"Of course, your majesty, but all support had to be sent by sea." The Chamberlain's body, swathed in red and gold silk, was rounded with the effects of self-indulgence and the hands that gripped his staff of office were soft. He gestured with them as he elaborated his point. "Senanga, as of course you remember, your majesty, has controlled both passes through the Kuta Lafuno, the Mountains of the Moon, for the past fourteen years." Graff paused, and Nathan watched as the information sank into the Ahar's drug laden brain. "When supplies have to be sent by sea, they're at the mercy of the Senangan pirate fleet."

"So there's nothing we can do?"

"Nothing, your majesty," Graff agreed, "except reinforce the Gatoomatam, the southernmost district still under our control. It, at least, is on this side of the mountains and can be supplied by land."

"Not true, your majesty." The objection came from a tall, lean man, as dark as Njombe, but dressed in plain white muslin robes, a stark contrast with the rich silks worn by the others.

Nathan, pulling rhythmically on the rope of one of the fans, eyed him warily. The Wizard Balek was angry and, as Balek's apprentice, he would have to deal with the effects of that anger. Balek would never strike him, but Balek often took out his anger in physical activity. Nathan did not look forward to climbing a mountain, or something equally as strenuous, at the end of the day.

But he would not complain, not even if Balek tried for the summit of Mount Agadem, the highest peak in Kuta Ewan. He had great admiration for Balek. Less than two dozen human wizards had survived from the time prior to the Wizards' Bane seven hundred years before, and Balek was one of them. He had been young then for a wizard, one hundred eighty-seven, and he still looked young, his skin sleek and unwrinkled, his muscles firm. Like many of those who survived, he had been in Cibata at the time of the Bane. Unlike most of them, he had stayed in the Southern Hemisphere and fought ceaselessly for Cassinga's survival. Moreover, Balek had raised Nathan, and looked after him as if he were Balek's own son.

"What do you mean? What's not true?" The hand holding Njombe's pipe jerked.

"There are a great many things you can and should do, your majesty." Balek strode up to the throne and glared at Njombe. "Send the army through the Pass of Tibati. Dekese stripped the Djambalatam of troops when he attacked Nemali. It should prove easy to take the pass and Panjara, as well. Even under Senanga, the area around the Wizard's Peace is thinly settled." His body leaned forward, as though by proximity he could force his ideas into the ahar. "If your forces float barges down the Djambala River, they can make much better time than Dekese's marching overland, even if he hears of the attack in time to meet your army before it reaches Korogwe."

"Your majesty, the wizard's suggestion is insane," Graff said, "Cassinga couldn't control the Djambalatam, even if by some miracle we could take it, and the attempt would leave the rest of Cassinga unprotected."

Balek glared at Graff. "I can muster a dozen wizards anxious to support your forces and a mind call from me to the Nyali Coast would bring twenty to thirty ships and at least three thousand men, perhaps as many as seven thousand, to rendezvous with the Cassingan navy off the point of Dirkou within two weeks time." He turned and gestured toward the window. "Ask General Menkor here if he doesn't think such a plan can succeed."

Menkor, who had retreated to the side of the room while the others argued, now found himself again the center of attention. He bowed to Njombe. "Your majesty, such a plan might work if it were put into effect immediately. The Senangan forces lost their general and chief strategist in the taking of Nemali and their casualties were much heavier than they had expected due to a counterattack from the crews of several of the ships in port."

Njombe hesitated, looking from one to another of the three men before him. He took a deep pull on his pipe. "I don't know what to do." He turned to his Chamberlain. "The wizard's plan sounds risky, but shouldn't we make an effort to do something?"

"Not just risky, your majesty, totally irresponsible," Graff said, making a sweeping gesture with his staff of office. "Balek has made no allowance for what the Senangan navy might be doing, much less for the weakness of our strategic position. Following his suggested course would jeopardize the safety of all the territory remaining under our control. You mustn't even consider it."

"Your general doesn't see it that way, your majesty," Balek said, turning back to Njombe, "nor will your troops. They'll think it a greater madness if you do nothing to avenge the dead. The tiger folk respect strength, not weakness. If you let them keep what they've taken without even a fight, then they'll attack again and again until there's nothing left to take."

"Your majesty," Graff said, stepping forward anxiously. "We have no hope of taking or holding any of the territory west of the Mountains of the Moon. We need to reinforce the land we still hold, not expend our forces on futile gestures."

Nathan's hand slipped on the fan rope as he felt his master's anger and, not for the first time, he wondered at the strength of the oath that kept Balek from simply forcing his will on Njombe.

Later, in Balek's own quarters, Nathan stroked his cat and watched while Balek paced. Nathan had never seen him angrier. "What will you do now, rai?"

Balek stopped pacing and turned to the boy. "Do now? I'll petition for aid from Ilwheirlane." He snorted. "Not that they'll send any, but it's a good idea for it to be on record that someone asked."

"Why, if you know in advance you'll be refused?"

"Politics, Nathan. Politics. Derwen will put a good case before Vanda, and Ilwheirlane is pledged to support all the human lands. They'll turn us down this time, but every time we ask for aid, it makes it a little harder for them to turn us down the next time." Balek took a deep breath, and exhaled. "Then we'll take a short trip to Awban. I want to examine the defenses in the Pass of Fadiat."

Nathan stifled a groan.

4624, 463RD CYCLE OF THE YEAR OF THE TIGER
MONTH OF ILFARNAR

THE WIZARD DERWEN, ESALFAR OF THE VARFARIN sat at his desk in Ninkarrak, trying to catch up on his paperwork while another wizard waited. He enjoyed the feeling of control that gave him.

"Well," Derwen said eventually, turning to the Wizard Ashe, whom he had summoned, "that's taken care of. Glad you could get here so promptly."

Ashe inclined his head. "Perhaps you will explain the urgency?"

Derwen rose and crossed the room to a table where a serving tray had been set out, pouring them each a glass of wine. "There's a meeting I want you to attend with me. It's always a good idea to have a witness when one makes a royal request, especially as I expect the petition to be denied."

Ashe looked startled. "What petition?"

"Balek wants military aid for Cassinga. What he really wants is for Ilwheirlane to come and fight his battles for him, which isn't going to happen. But I have to pass on his petition, and then I'll have to go to Cibata myself."

"Why would Balek want you in Cibata?"

Derwen snorted. "He says my presence will be a sign of the Varfarin's continued support of human rule there, which he feels is threatened. If Vanda doesn't authorize military aid for Cassinga, I'll have to sail within the week. And that brings up the other reason I summoned you."

Derwen had hunted for months for a wizard who could teach wizardry well, but had no current apprentice. As he was going to have to leave, he had to find someone to take over the instruction of his two students. The Wizard Ashe came highly recommended. The Wizard Kaaremin and his mate the Wizard Andamin had trained Ashe and insisted he was a superlative teacher. With that recommendation, Derwen had decided to ignore the fact that Ashe had qualified as a full wizard sixteen years before, but only recently joined the Varfarin.

So Derwen set himself to persuade Ashe to take over his pupils, which turned out to be not as difficult as he had feared. When Ashe agreed, Derwen thanked him and added, "I'm not looking forward to this trip to Cibata, but at least I'll have one less worry."

"I heard about the fall of Nemali," Ashe said, leaning back in his chair. "But did the loss of the Mocubatam truly put Cassinga at risk?"

"The human foothold in Cibata has been tenuous for years. There's always real cause for concern. And we lost four people," Derwen said, "two of them qualified wizards. The others promising apprentices. " He rose and began to pace.

Ashe swirled the wine in his glass and then looked up, meeting Derwen's eyes. "What does Balek expect you to accomplish that he can't?"

"I'm not sure, but Balek doesn't seem to have accomplished anything recently." Derwen paused and shook his head, unhappy with the prospect of dealing with Balek again. Balek always made him feel as though he had obtained his position under false pretenses.

He shrugged. "Balek says he thinks my presence will help to muster forces along the Nyali Coast. And, if nothing else, we hope to be able to rescue the wizards we lost." He took out his watch. "We'd better go now. The meeting's due to start and I mustn't be late."

Minutes later Derwen and Ashe were ushered into the elegant, sun-lit, sitting room of Vanda III, Estahar of Ilwheirlane, arguably the most powerful human being on Tamar, despite the fact that her wizard talent was weak.

Vanda sat at a marin wood desk in the only unpadded chair. A small woman, fair-skinned and pale-eyed, even her hair was a colorless blonde. Too small and too pale for such a lavish setting, Derwen thought, but she was a better ruler than her father had been. Vanda understood the deeper currents.

Derwen looked round, noting the presence of Admiral Emin Vordal, the Commander-in-Chief of Ilwheirlane's navy. He would not be an ally today.

General Palus Braydon, Commander-in-Chief of the army, charged in as Derwen sat down. Short and burly, he radiated an air of energy. There was no doubt of the intelligence in his eyes under their bristling hedge of brows. Still, he would be even less of an ally than Vordal. Derwen had been hoping he would miss the meeting.

"General Braydon," Vanda greeted him as he made his bow, then waited until he was seated. "The Wizard Derwen has a formal petition to present to my military council from a colleague in Cibata, requesting our assistance."

Derwen stood up and looked around. "You've all heard by now of the fall of Nemali. What you may not have heard is that Njombe has refused to authorize any retaliatory action whatsoever. If the human nations make no attempt to avenge Senanga's act of warfare, Cassinga is doomed. The Wizard Balek has formally requested that Ilwheirlane send troop ships to Cassinga, as Belisanne III did when human forces defeated the Senangans at the Battle of Tidjikja. For the sake of our own survival, we must support the other human nations against the aggression of the were-folk."

"Send troops halfway round the world to fight a battle even the locals refuse?" Braydon looked outraged.

"The army of Cassinga is willing to fight," Derwen said. "It's only Njombe and his Chamberlain who fear the outcome, and that's cowardice, not reason. How long do you think Cassinga can last, General, if we allow the Senangans to think that they can attack human lands without fear of reprisal?"

Braydon snorted. "Not going to last any longer making hopeless gestures. Look at the map, man. Nemali and the whole of the Mocubatam have been isolated and indefensible for years, ever since the Pass of Tibati fell. Njombe's doing the sensible thing for once, consolidating what he has left."

"Your majesty, we cannot afford such an expedition at this time. We already have more than we can handle with the piracy on our own coasts," Admiral Vordal added.

Vanda turned to Derwen and spread her hands. "As you see, my advisors feel that the action you've requested would be unwise. And I agree. However, I'd like to think that their answer, and mine, might have been different, if Njombe himself had requested aid in support of his own plan of attack. As it is, any action on the part of Ilwheirlane could be taken as interference with the internal affairs of another human nation."

III

4624, 463RD CYCLE OF THE YEAR OF THE TIGER
MONTH OF ILFARNAR

> "Okene: 'I shall take her to the empty country, the free
> holdings around Panjara.'
>
> Owerra: 'Beware the lands where wizards have waged war!
> Such ground is poisoned with a deep and lasting
> bane which rots the blood and twists the very seed of
> living things.'"
>
> — FROM ACT I, SCENE 2, OF *SHAN JERCET: THE TWISTED TREES* BY BERTOUA
> MANJACAZE

The territory taken by Senanga in the invasion of 4624 encompassed the land southeast of the Mocuba River and west of the Mountains of the Moon, all the way to the Cape of Dirkou, the southernmost point of the Isangan Peninsula. The center of government for the Mocubatam, as this newest district in the Senangan Empire was called, was the Kulhar's mansion in Nemali.

Situated at the north end of the town, the grounds around it abutted the eastern bank of the Mocuba River. Constructed to form three sides of a rectangle around a central courtyard, the mansion was a two story stucco building with a red tile roof. A high wall of adobe brick pierced by two gates guarded the fourth side of the courtyard, which was divided in two parts by an ornamental wrought iron fence. On the south side of the fence a row of orange trees grew amid plantings of jasmine, kaffirboom and fragrant ericala, effectively blocking the view between the two halves. The south court was set with mosaic tiles and held a fountain in the shape of a dolphin with water coming out of its mouth and falling into a pool of black and white marble.

No mosaics decorated the north court. Strictly a service area, it was paved evenly with blocks of stone, and delivery carts brought supplies there: sacks of rice and hunical, fish from the river or gulf, meat and vegetables of all kinds. They also brought slaves. Morrien was brought to serve here with many of the other women prisoners the second day after her capture.

Twice a week in good weather she helped the other slaves drag laundry tubs out of the scullery and set them up in the paved yard. Then they filled them with water that flowed through clay pipes from the river and washed the linens and clothes of their masters.

"Aren't you going to tell them that the father of your child was a linlar?" Jura Birao's voice was breathless. She was small and thin to the point of emaciation. It was a strain for her to lift and wring out the sopping wet sheet from the rack where Morrien had hung it after pulling it from the copper boiling tub. Her face paled as she tugged at the heavy, water-soaked material and forced it through the wooden wringer, but Jura always talked no matter what she was doing.

"Hush! Someone might hear you." Morrien looked around the open courtyard, but no one was paying attention to them. The boiling tub and wringer were set apart from the wash and rinse tubs where the other slaves were working. It was a brilliant spring day in the month of Ilfarnar with a brisk wind blowing off the Gulf of Mekkai, taking the heat away from the steaming tub and the fire beneath it. Looking out through the open gateway, she could see down to the river and the dom palms and clumps of laconica and tasseled papyrus on the bank. "Of course, I'm not going to tell them," she said sharply. "Do you think I'm mad?"

She looked better than she had the night Nemali had fallen. Her pregnancy was well advanced, but only apparent to a keen eye. She had lost weight doing the hard work required of a kitchen drudge in the new Kulhar's residence, and the telltale rounding of her abdomen had been compensated for by her loss of fat. Also, she had spent more time outdoors in the past months than she had ever done in her life before. She did laundry in the courtyard and if extra hands were needed in the fields or orchards, she helped out there too. The fresh air and sunlight had taken the pasty color from her skin and replaced it with a faint tan.

"But if the child's born with were-sight? I heard that sighted children are adopted and live as full citizens of Senanga. Daloa said her second child was born sighted and she pointed him out to me playing with the Kulhar's daughter."

"What happened to her first?" Morrien stirred the linens and pulled another sheet from the boiling water with a paddle, draping it over a rack to cool.

"What do you mean?"

"The were-folk test babies in their ninth month, before they're old enough to be taught were-sight if they're not born with it." Morrien paused as one of the other women came over with a bucket of wash, dumped the wet linens into the copper boiler, nodded briefly and went back across the yard. When she had gone Morrien stirred the new sheets vigorously.

"What kind of test?"

"They test to see if the baby has were-sight. If the baby doesn't pass, it dies."

"But why? Why don't they just leave them as slaves?"

"I don't know, but that's what they do." Morrien shrugged. "Old Erna told me when I first started to show. She's been a slave for twenty years, had five babes, but none of them lived a full year."

"None of them? But I'd think the babies would at least have a fifty-fifty chance."

"That's not how I've heard it. Erna's an extreme case, but only about one child in three is born sighted if one parent is fully human."

Jura slumped, dropping the sheet she was working on so that Morrien had to grab it to save it from the ground. "I better finish that before it has to be washed all over again. You stir the sheets in the tub."

"Thank you, Morrien." Jura's voice was little better than a whisper and Morrien was horrified to see that she was crying.

"What's the matter?"

"I'm pregnant," Jura said, her voice nearly inaudible and the tears streaming down her face. There were no sobs, only the tears welling up and flowing down her cheeks.

"Miune, guard us. You can't be pregnant. You've slept in the dormitory every night since I've been here."

Jura's face twisted in the travesty of a smile. "It doesn't have to happen at night, Morrien. You know that."

"Who was it? How did it happen?" Morrien wrung out the sheet, twisting it viciously, wishing that she could twist some linlar's neck the same way. Jura was little better than a child herself.

The tears stopped flowing and a strange expression crossed Jura's face. "We were out cutting back the kwaluccan," she said, her face rapt with remembered pleasure. "You remember the day, about two months ago, just after the Kulhar arrived."

"Yes, I remember," Morrien said flatly. "You weren't with the rest of us when we got back. You came in an hour late and the guard whipped you for it."

"Yes." Jura frowned, but another memory overpowered the recollection of pain. She smiled. "I met the Kulhar's son, Zezere Abandu, in the orchard. He said I shouldn't be doing such rough work, my hands were too refined." She looked down at her rough, reddened hands and spread them out as though she thought they really were smooth and delicate. "Then he took me to one of the barns and we climbed up into the hayloft and made love." She clasped her hands and pressed them against her bosom, hugging herself. "It was fantastic, Morrien, the most wonderful thing I could ever imagine."

"You haven't heard from him since, have you, you little fool?" Morrien turned away, grabbing the wrung out sheet to hang it on the clothes line. Her fingers slammed the pegs onto the rope to hold it.

"But he made love to me, Morrien. And he made me feel so beautiful. I'm sure I'll see him again soon." There was a note of bewilderment in Jura's voice.

"Don't hold your breath," Morrien said. She seized the paddle and lifted out another of the boiled sheets. "He's a wizard. He can make you feel whatever he wants you to feel. They like willing, eager sex partners. That's all there was to it. Believe me."

Jura looked up at Morrien, her eyes huge and pleading. "I don't believe that. I can't."

Morrien bit her lip and hung the second sheet on the rack. Then she took up the first sheet, even though it was still hot and shoved it into the wringer. "Have you told anyone else?"

"No. I wasn't sure, at first. But I've missed my second flow, so I must be."

"They're fertile, the linlarin, especially the wizards. I was always careful and Miune knows I had experience. In more than twenty years I never slipped, never got pregnant, but just one night with a linlar wizard and look at me." Morrien tapped her rounded abdomen. "They manipulate our ovaries as easily as our emotions." Her voice held a cold, iron bitterness that she could taste.

"What can I do?"

"Survive. That's all either of us can do." Morrien wrenched the sheet out of the wringer and struggled to peg it up beside the others flapping in the breeze.

Jura went back to stirring the sheets. Then she said, "What happens if your child is sighted? Won't they punish you?"

Morrien smiled, her eyes bright with mockery. "I was a whore, remember. How am I supposed to know if the father was part linlar? I'm not even sure who the father was." She frowned. "I can get away with it with most of them. Just as long as I don't meet another powerful wizard. They can read your thoughts."

"Then how did you manage to kill him," Jura asked, momentarily distracted by her curiosity.

"He wasn't looking."

"But they're bound to know with me, aren't they?" Jura asked after a pause. Her eyes were pleading as though she hoped Morrien would deny it.

"Considering how few human men there are left in Nemali, I'd say that's a safe wager." Morrien yanked on the wringer handle, glad of an excuse to look anywhere but at Jura.

"So my baby will die?"

"Think of it as his baby and be glad of it," Morrien snapped, finishing the sheet and lifting it up to hang beside the others.

Jura's eyes filled with tears again. "Would you be glad?"

Morrien's eyes were drawn back to Jura's and she knew that they were filled with her own pain. "Sometimes. Sometimes I hate them so much, I hate the child, too. But at other times," she paused and shook her head. "No. Then I think that it's a part of me now, no matter who planted the seed. That's why I go on lying."

IV

*"No person of mixed blood shall be admitted to membership
of this organization.*

*"No person of mixed blood shall be allowed to dance with any
group sponsored by this organization. If this rule is broken,
the offending group shall cease to be so sponsored and all of its
members shall lose their eligibility for membership."*

— EXCERPTS FROM THE CHARTER OF THE HAILARIN DANCER'S GUILD

L EAP AND SPIN. A GRACEFUL GESTURE of the arms, bend
and rise and leap again. The heat was oppressive. The air felt
heavy, dragging her down. A series of fluid pirouettes, another bend
and another leap through the thick, humid air. Her feet hurt. If she
looked down, she knew she would see her ballet slippers stained with
blood, but the dance was nearly over now. Another leap, the highest
she could reach, a series of other steps, less difficult, thank Jehan, and
then the final pirouette as she sank to the floor.

Silence. Her head came up, terrified that the audience had not
liked the dance, that this time they would boo instead of cheer. But it
was all right. They were rising now and starting to applaud. The hesi-
tation had been out of reverence for her artistry, the time it took for
them to come back to reality. Einara Hareel relaxed and bowed. Then
the other dancers came out on stage and they all bowed, and the audience cheered. She rose on the wave of applause, buoyed up by it, and
let the energy of the audience's approval carry her offstage.

The critics called her the greatest dancer on Tamar, but sometimes
she was still afraid. The deeply rooted insecurity came from the days
when she had gone hungry to keep her dream of dancing alive, when
no troop would hire her because of her height. The Dancer's Guild
had forbidden her membership, accused her of having human blood.
She had scrimped and saved, dancing in bars and at country fairs,
until she could afford to pay a wizard for a full genetic profile. Only
with that in hand had the Guild accepted her, even though no human

or hailar had ever before approached the elevation of her leaps or her incredible grace.

She was too tall. The hailarin, the eagle folk, were hollow boned and rarely as tall as even the shortest humans. Einara's feathered crest towered over others of her people. No wonder that all her life she had been considered a freak. Yet the strength of her legs could vault her to her own height above the ground. When she danced she was beautiful, so dancing was her life.

PERRIN TREVITH CLAPPED with the rest of the audience. As owner of the theatre, the size and enthusiasm of the crowd meant money in his pocket, but that was not why he applauded. He was simply awed by Einara's talent.

He had paid a great deal of money to bring Einara Hareel's troop all the way to Dandaburra. He had been concerned that ballet might be too sophisticated an entertainment for the people of the area: farmers, miners and herdsmen. He could see now that he need not have worried. Her first performance had sold out and no one could watch Einara without appreciating her artistry.

BACK IN HER DRESSING ROOM, Einara collapsed on the couch. Her maid Negene knelt quickly to remove her bloody slippers and make her comfortable. The room was small but clean and well furnished, a great improvement over many she had encountered on the tour. The cushions on the couch felt soft. The lighting around the dressing table was more than adequate. Einara sighed and laid her head back, closing her eyes.

"They loved you," Negene said. "They always love you."

Einara recognized that her maid had already picked up on her insecurities, despite having only been with her since the beginning of the tour. Her mouth twisted wryly. "Until I get too old and my jumps lose their height. Then they'll turn on me again. How many years do you think I have left? Three or four? Half a dozen? I'm thirty-three now."

Negene fetched a bowl of warm salt water, heated earlier on the stove in the back room, and positioned Einara's feet in it. "You'll always be great and they'll always applaud. When you're no longer able to dance yourself, you can teach."

Einara laughed but the sound was brittle, like breaking glass. "I'll never teach. When I can no longer dance, I'll die."

Negene looked up at her mistress with worried amber eyes. "You mustn't say things like that. You frighten me."

Einara's eyes narrowed and she felt the bronze feathers of her crest stand upright, a sign of temper. "I forget what an innocent you are. Dream of happy endings, if you like, but don't talk of them to me."

There was a knock on the door.

"Answer it, Negene, but tell whoever's there that I'm too tired for company."

Negene opened the door only a little, positioning herself to stop anyone from coming in.

Einara was surprised to see a human, the man who owned the theatre. She had expected another member of the troop.

"Mistress Hareel is too tired for visitors," Negene said apologetically.

"I expected that. I just wanted to congratulate her and to give her these with my compliments." Perrin proffered a huge bouquet of flowers. "She was magnificent."

"They're beautiful." Negene took the flowers in her arms, but did not move out of the doorway. "I'm sure she'll be pleased."

"I also want to invite her to lunch tomorrow afternoon. I realize that she must be too tired to dine with me tonight." He eyed Negene's position with a raised eyebrow. "I promise I won't barge in on her, if you'll convey my invitation."

Negene hesitated, then nodded. "Very well, Master Trevith."

She carried the flowers to Einara. "It's the man who owns the theatre. He brought you these and wants to know if you'll have lunch with him tomorrow afternoon."

"I heard him," Einara said, examining the flowers. She took a deep breath, inhaling their perfume. "Why not? His flowers are gorgeous. Tell him, I accept his invitation, as long as he understands that I must be back early to prepare for the evening performance."

Negene looked disturbed. "He's human, mistress."

Einara smiled. "I know that, Negene."

"Dariel won't like your going out with him."

Einara's whole face tightened in anger and her feather crest stood straight up. "Dariel doesn't own me. He has no right to judge my actions. If he tries to interfere with my private life he can find another dancer."

"You know what the Dancer's Guild thinks of mixed marriages," Negene said urgently. "It isn't just Dariel who'll object."

Einara stared at Negene, her crest relaxing. Then she laughed, a full-throated, musical trill that startled Negene as she had heard it so rarely. "Your romanticism runs away with you, child," Einara said finally. "We're not talking about marriage, just lunch."

"The one can sometimes lead to the other," Negene insisted.

"As a meal sometimes leads to food poisoning," Einara said, still laughing.

PERRIN'S CURRICLE WAS PAINTED DARK BLUE with bright yellow trim. The spokes of the wheels were also yellow. It was as handsome an equipage as Einara had seen in even the largest and most fashionable cities in Kandorra. She was impressed, as she was impressed by its owner.

Perrin Trevith was an attractive man. While he was probably considered short by human standards, he was much taller than any hailar male Einara had seen and nearly half a head taller than Einara. It was pleasant to rest her hand on the arm of a man and have to look up to meet his eyes. With Perrin as an escort, she felt delicate, feminine, instead of awkward and oversized, as she invariably felt when accompanied by one of her own people.

"Where are we going?" Einara asked as he helped her into the carriage. "I assumed we'd eat at the hotel."

Perrin frowned. "Would you prefer to? We can eat wherever you like, but I thought you'd enjoy seeing some of the countryside while you're here and there's a very fine restaurant only an hour's drive away."

Einara hesitated. She was tired of being cooped up inside hotels and closed carriages and theatres. A ride in the country sounded lovely. And, even if she was late getting back to the theatre, he could hardly penalize the troop when her tardiness would be his fault. "I'd love to see your countryside. I believe it's famous for its beauty."

He grinned. "Parts of it, at any rate. It's far too late to take you to Tiburra Falls today. They're the most spectacular site in the region, but maybe I can take you to see them another time, when you don't have to be back for a performance."

Einara smiled, surprised and a little excited by the admiration in his gray eyes. She was not used to being admired for anything except her dancing. "Perhaps."

They took the road north toward Tintinara. The low hills graduated from green velvet in the hollows to a soft gold on the crests as the grass died back in the heat of the summer. Puriri and marin trees dotted the slopes along with the occasional stand of eucalyptus. Small, red cattle grazed or lay chewing their cuds in the shade of the trees. A rich land, and a peaceful one, Einara thought, inhaling the clear sweet air.

The restaurant proved to be less than a full hour's drive. Situated on the bank of the Windona River, it was surrounded by feathery casuarinas, tall elandas and rough-barked kanuka trees. Fragrant ericala with white and golden flowers, ponga ferns with black, hairy trunks and silver-backed fronds, and red-leaved photinia grew beneath the trees and edged the green lawns.

Einara, with her passionate love for anything beautiful, smiled like a child, her eyes wide as they walked through the gardens to the entrance.

PERRIN, WATCHING HER, FELT STUNNED. The dance director of the theatre had told him before she arrived that Einara Hareel was as plain in person as she was beautiful on stage. But Perrin's first sight of her had nearly struck him dumb.

It was true that she lacked the small-featured, pretty face common to most of the hailarin of Kandorra. Einara's face was strong and angular with high cheekbones and a hooked nose. Her eyes and mouth were large and expressive. To Perrin, the whole of her face together was not simply pretty, but so vividly beautiful it was unforgettable.

He was still watching her when they were seated. Einara arched an eyebrow. "Do I have a spot on the end of my nose?"

Perrin smiled and shook his head. "Of course not. I was thinking how lovely you are. I didn't mean to stare."

Einara frowned. "I don't care for empty compliments. I know what I look like."

"What do you mean?"

"What I said." The bronze feathers rose with impatience. "I don't expect or desire pretty compliments. I'm plain. It's my dancing that's beautiful."

He laughed. "But your face is beautiful, strong and fine. I'm not mocking you. It's simply that I can't believe anyone with eyes could call your face plain."

Einara stared at him and the feathered crest settled into a tight cap that might be mistaken for bronze curls. "You mean that?"

"Of course I mean it." Perrin grinned. "Maybe it's the angle I see you from. I don't have to look up."

Einara laughed, a musical waterfall of sound.

EINARA ALMOST SHOOK HERSELF. Her own laughter had startled her. It was the first time in her life she had ever found anything about her height amusing.

On the way back to the theatre, Perrin said, "There's no performance scheduled for Jehansday. I'd like to take the whole day off and show you Tiburra Falls and the Birunan Valley. It's said to be one of the most beautiful places in Kandorra."

"That's a long way to go, isn't it?"

"You don't have to get back that night. There's no performance. We could go up in the morning, spend the whole day there, stay the night at the inn and drive back the following day." Unconsciously, his hands clenched on the reins.

Einara flushed. Perrin found her attractive. No, she thought, I must not fool myself, he desires me. But even that is more than I have known before. I cannot remember a male of my own race ever wanting me, ever finding me beautiful in any way. But Perrin does. What's more, when I'm with him I feel beautiful, admired, even delicate.

She smiled to herself. Nothing need come of it. And, if she were honest, he excited her as much as she seemed to excite him. She was no longer young. She had never felt this way before. Why shouldn't she enjoy his company for the short time she was here? Her answer mattered to him, she could see that in the tightening of his hands, in the stiffness of his body. She lowered her eyes and stilled her own hands that had been twisting in her lap. "All right," she said, "I've always wanted to see the falls."

V

4625, 463RD CYCLE OF THE YEAR OF THE DOLPHIN
MONTH OF DIRGA

> *"Owerra:* *'You were warned of the danger of this 'Wizards'*
> *Peace.' You chose to risk its poison rot.'*
>
> *Okene:* *'But we suffer so, and my children...'*
>
> *Owerra:* *'I feel no pity for you, but I will weep for your*
> *children, born crooked in this evil place. Your seed*
> *shall die here, your line end.'"*
>
> — FROM ACT III, SCENE 5, OF *SHAN JERCET: THE TWISTED TREES* BY BERTOUA
> MANJACAZE

MORRIEN WOKE JURA IN THE NIGHT. "Jura! Jura, I need your help. The baby's coming."

"What..." Jura rolled over sleepily. It was dark, but some light reached the slaves' dormitory from the oil lamp at the guard post in the hall. She could just make out Morrien leaning over her. "Your contractions have started?" she asked, sitting up.

"Sssh. No. They started last night, during dinner. But now I think the baby's ready to come," Morrien said, keeping her voice low. "I've already got the towels and I've had water heating on the stove with the basin next to it for hours. Just go down to the kitchen, fill the basin and bring it up," Morrien said, turning awkwardly and moving back to her own bed.

Jura nodded and ran down to the kitchen. She got the water and hurried back up the stairs, trying not to spill too much. When she reached the dormitory Morrien was lying on her bed with her legs spread apart and her knees bent, her feet braced against the bottom posts of her bed. And Jura could see the movement in her distended stomach.

The next minutes were a confused blur in Jura's mind, capped by the sight of the baby sliding out of Morrien's body in a rush of blood and slime. She screamed.

Then she was pushed out of the way as Magali, another of the slaves that shared the dormitory, bent over Morrien and started to do something to the baby.

"You trying to commit suicide?" Magali demanded.

"Having a baby is a natural process," Morrien gasped.

"Yeah. With only Jura to help and you nearly forty and this being your first," Magali said. Her hands were busy, but Jura couldn't see what she was doing.

"Is the baby all right?" Morrien asked.

"Yeah." Magali thrust the baby, now wrapped in a towel, at Jura. "Here, you can wash her." Then she bent back over Morrien.

Jura swallowed and looked at the small figure in her arms. There were still traces of mucous on the delicate skin, but they no longer looked like slime. The fine, black hair was wet, though, and stuck up in spikes. Jura laid the baby on her own bed and damped a cloth in the hot water. Then she unwrapped the tiny body and discovered that she was washing a baby girl.

A groan came from Morrien's bed. Then Magali said, "There, that's it. You're lucky. It really was an easy birth."

"Are you sure the baby's all right?" Morrien asked.

"Yeah. I told you. You've got a beautiful daughter."

"I mean, did you examine her? Make sure there were no deformities?"

"She's fine," Jura said, wrapping the child in the baby-sized wrappings Morrien had set out.

"You're positive? Let me see her."

Jura was surprised by the anxiety in Morrien's voice, but she carried the baby back to Morrien and handed the infant to her mother. "What's the matter?" She looked at Magali in bewilderment, but Magali only shrugged.

Morrien examined the tiny form almost frantically, feeling every one of the baby's fingers and toes, running her hand across the soft, faintly distorted head. Only when she had assured herself that every detail was normal did Morrien lie back in relief.

"What did you expect to find wrong?" Magali asked.

Morrien sighed. "My parents were among the first settlers to move back into Panjara near the Wizards' Peace," she said. "They were told it wasn't safe, that the land was still poisoned, but it had been so many hundreds of years since the bane they didn't believe the warnings. I was born there and so was my sister, but she died. She was born without a left arm and there was something wrong internally. There were lots of miscarriages among all the settlers, stillbirths and other babies deformed even worse than my sister. We moved to Candith when the Senangans retook the Nampalatam. That was the year after my sister died. I was seven. I never meant to have a child."

Magali nodded. "That's why you never married."

Jura bit her lip, quick tears of compassion filling her eyes. "She's all right, Morrien. She's beautiful."

Magali snorted. "You'll both be all right now, but you'll be better off if you keep to your bed today. I'll make it right with the supervisor."

"Thank you," Morrien said, "thank you very much."

"Forget it." She looked around the dormitory then nodded at the window through which a faint light was beginning to shine. "Sun's up. No point going back to bed. I'll go down to the kitchen, see if I can get us some hot tea." She turned and left.

Morrien looked down at her child. The baby's features were delicate but firmly formed. The eyes that looked back were a strange green-gold. And those eyes were not the blank, unfocused eyes of most new-born infants. They seemed peculiarly aware.

Jura said, "She's beautiful. Really beautiful."

Morrien shivered. "Yes, she is."

"What are you going to call her?"

"Saranith," she said, "for the passion that burnt in my blood when she was conceived and the hatred that's burnt in me since. She's a child of passion; I'll name her for it." She sensed some unusual strength in the child. That, more than the reason she gave, determined the child's name. "Saranith," she gazed into the bright eyes of her infant daughter, "'blood-fire.' Your name and your destiny. Miune grant that I'm dead before you attain that destiny." She felt tears flowing down her cheeks and didn't know whether they were from relief at having given birth to a healthy child, or from fear for the fate of that child.

Yet Saranith was strong and healthy. She rarely cried. But, when she was two weeks old, she started to lose the soft, black down that had covered her head at birth. By the time she was three weeks, new hair started to grow, striped hair, but not striped with the black and tawny cream normal to linlarin. Saranith's hair grew with bands of black and a copper red as bright as her mother's. Morrien stole dye from a store-room and dyed the baby's hair black so that not even Jura would know.

VI

4625, 463RD CYCLE OF THE YEAR OF THE DOLPHIN
MONTH OF INGVASH

Malikin ba pithsarin gulon. Malik deka puat sorem
acadend harin balpard:
1. Val ma brane malik.
2. Val ma fat ob malik dakar, amne fatin a gulon loku.
Sen, e amne sen, malik deka sorem harin, ea pon behedal
acad ambin, dekin, lahen, e va quen endya a papail.

*"Maliks are dangerous predators. The malik handler must
always remember the following rules:*
1. *There is no such thing as a tame malik.*
2. *There is no safe way to handle a malik, only ways of
reducing the risk.*
*If, and only if, the malik handler keeps these rules in mind, he
may keep all his fingers, hands, eyes and his life for the term of
his duty."*

— EXCERPT FROM *MALIK DEKASE TALATHAN* "THE MALIK HANDLER'S SURVIVAL
GUIDE"

N ATHAN EASED THROUGH A CLUMP OF UNDERBRUSH on
the edge of the clearing, then crouched down naked in the cover
of an ericala bush beneath a baobab tree. He had left his clothes in the
pack on his horse. The leaves stirred again and Antra Wallen and the
Wizard Jaith sank down beside him. Jaith, with her golden skin and
hair, managed to look cool even in the steamy, late summer heat of the
Senangan jungle. She had a knack for looking at ease, and for making
everyone else around her uncomfortable, Nathan thought, but she
could be counted on to jump the right way in a crisis.

Nathan was fifteen now and excited about being a full participant in
the mission. He evaluated the scene before him. It was close to noon.
The sun was searingly hot at the top of the arch of the sky, minimizing
shadows. The cleared area around the stockade was stripped of vegetation and the soil had baked to a hard brightness. A sentry post was
located roughly twenty meters away above the small rear gate on the
walkway that circled the inside of the compound. Nathan examined

the guard, relieved to note that he looked bored and sleepy. No danger of his spotting them yet.

The fort was an isolated outpost in the heart of the rain forest, one of the least settled areas of Senanga.

"We're opposite the gate," he thought, concentrating on a mental image of Balek. *"No sign of the patrol."*

Antra, Jaith's apprentice and two years younger than Nathan, shifted uneasily. She was sweating and strands of her long, brown hair stuck to her forehead and neck. *"Aren't you scared?"* she thought.

Nathan ignored the question, affronted.

Balek, Jaith and the Wizard Lyan had spent months locating this place some fifty kilometers north of Lake Owe, deep in the heart of Senanga. They were certain that at least one, and probably more, of the human wizards captured in Nemali had been brought here. The raid had been planned since before Derwen arrived from Ilwheirlane. Far from being frightened, Nathan was thrilled to be actually entering the compound with Balek. He had been afraid that, like Antra, he would be left with Jaith as a rear guard.

"Coming. Looks clear." Balek's thought was concise in Nathan's mind. He had finished his survey of the area and found nothing suspicious.

"Everything's quiet here." Derwen's thought. He was to warn them if the patrol returned by the front gate today. The Senangan military's basic unit was called a kam, or claw, and consisted of ten fighters. The patrol was made up of a dekam of malik riders, a unit of fifty, literally a hand claw. In the three days they had been studying the stockade, the patrol had not once duplicated its timing or route. If there was any pattern, they had not had time to learn it.

There was a stir in the undergrowth and his master crouched down beside Nathan. *"Ready?"*

Nathan nodded. Concentrating on the skin of his hand, he matched the color of it to the color of the baked, brown earth, then let the effect spread out until it covered his whole body. *I am the ground,* he thought, *the color of soil, the texture of it.* Only when the process was complete did he crawl out from under the shelter of the baobab onto the bare ground. The sentry moved and Nathan froze.

There was no outcry. Balek came up beside him. Even aware of his master's presence, Nathan could hardly see him. "Two are easier to miss than an army," Balek had said when the raid had been planned.

Nathan eased himself across the bare stretch of ground. Move one arm. Wait. Move a leg. Wait. The other arm. Wait. The other leg. Wait. Again. He could feel the sun burning into the bare flesh of his back.

He had asked Balek when they made their plans, "Why the middle of the day? Wouldn't we have a better chance at night?"

Balek had laughed. "You're thinking like a man. Think like a wizard. How does the sentry see you?"

"He's Senangan. He has were-sight. He'll see right through my disguise."

"He might, if you gave him reason to. But he won't. If the surface of your skin has the look and feel of soil, he's not going to look deeper. And he won't sense your body heat in the glare of the noon sun, or see your shadow. At night, you'd stand out like a beacon. It will be years before you're strong enough to change your body temperature to feel as cold as the ground at night."

Nathan shifted forward again, suppressing his body's instinct to sweat. "The guards will notice moisture," Balek had warned.

"*Very good, Nathan.*" Balek started to unlock the gate.

Nathan watched, awed, as the bolts slid back. Then, through the gaps in wooden palings, he saw the heavy wooden bars slide out of their sockets and float to the ground on the other side of the wall. Nathan's will could move a weight of up to nearly three pounds but the effort left him weak and exhausted. He could barely imagine the power of will it took to raise one of those heavy wooden beams, yet Balek did it casually, hardly aware of the effort. He's had hundreds of years of practice, Nathan reminded himself. The will is like a muscle: exercise it and it gets stronger.

The gate was unlocked. Nathan started to open it, but Balek checked him. "*Not yet. Soldiers crossing the areaway.*"

Nathan tried to extend his vision, but he couldn't sense anything more than a few inches beyond the stockade wall; the wood was too thick for him. No matter how much he learned, he kept running head on into his limitations.

"*Now.*" Balek slipped through the gate.

Nathan followed. No one in sight. The inside of the stockade was an open parade ground stretching to the main gate a hundred meters away. There were two buildings on each side of the open area, but only the first building on the left had barred windows.

He dropped back down to the ground inside the compound, which was still hard but dusty from the pounding of hundreds of feet. Easing out from underneath the overhang, he began the slow process of crossing the open ground between the wall and the jail. He knew that Balek, behind him, was closing and resealing the gate, but he was too busy concentrating on being a part of the ground to worry about anything else.

The skin of Nathan's knees, chest and elbows was sore from the abrasion of the hard ground. Powdery dust clogged his nostrils and his head ached from the heat of the sun and the pressure of concentration.

Crawl. Freeze. Crawl. He was vaguely aware of Balek passing him, flowing across the compound like a flicker of shadow. Crawl.

The shade of the roof over him told him he had reached the building. *"Where?"*

"The back."

Nathan rose carefully, pressing his body against the wall in the shadow of the eave. At first his skin looked dark against the stucco. He concentrated until it paled and took on a granular texture. Only after it matched the wall did he slip around the corner to where Balek peered through a barred window into one of the cells.

"Lagura?"

Balek nodded, then thought, *"Plus Evran, Marion, and Rainal, all capped."*

Nathan's delight at Balek's first news turned to worry. Caps could cause permanent damage and, while they had been prepared to bring out Lagura, they were now faced with transporting two adult wizards and another child as well, and the wizards might be badly disabled. *How can we move them?*

"I'll have to camouflage three of them myself, but Rainal's small. You can conceal him." Balek used his will to bend the iron bars out of the way.

A face appeared in the barred window, hairy and unkempt. It took Nathan a moment to recognize the Wizard Evran. "Balek? Thank Jehan!" he whispered. "Marion's breaking down."

Nathan thought that Evran didn't look far from the breaking point himself. There were dark circles under his hazel eyes, his flesh looked loose over the angular bones of his face, and his normally bronze skin appeared sallow. The top of his head was covered with a round, shiny cap of a silvery metal Nathan couldn't identify. He stared at it. He had heard of caps, but had never seen one before.

"Lagura and Rainal?" Balek asked, also in a whisper.

"They're all right. I don't suppose you can take this thing off now?" Evran asked, tapping the metal cap with a finger. Nathan noticed with horror that what he had taken to be the edge of the cap was only the point where it became embedded in Evran's skull.

Balek turned away from the window, as though unwilling to meet Evran's eyes. "Removing it will cause unconsciousness. We need you to cooperate, if we're going to get you out of here."

Evran nodded. "I can carry Marion."

"She can't manage herself?" Balek frowned.

Evran shook his head. "Doubt it. Been delirious on and off the past week. Her sane periods are getting shorter."

Voices came from around the side of the building. Nathan flattened himself against the wall, aware that Balek had done the same. The bars in the window looked straight again.

Twenty Senangan soldiers, two kams, in a straggling formation emerged from the space between the jail and the next building and marched across the open area toward the watch tower at the corner of the stockade.

"Changing the guard." Balek's thought.

Nathan was careful not to stare at the tall, nearly naked figures with their tawny and black striped hair. He only allowed himself brief glances out of the corner of his eye. They all had were-sight and might sense his presence if he looked at them too directly. He waited until they had disappeared into the tower before he spoke, "The others will be coming back."

"Hotter than Nithlane today. They won't dally in the open," Evran said.

"Aren't they used to it?" Nathan asked.

Evran shook his head. "Whole travkam's just been reassigned. Last billet was in the mountains."

Nathan looked around and thought that a travkam probably represented the entire fighting force at such an isolated location, a hundred claws was a thousand soldiers,.

Balek snorted. "I wondered why there was no one around. We'll wait til the last shift's gone back inside, then."

The returning soldiers marched out of the tower in an even more irregular formation than the guards who had relieved them, their dark skins glossy with sweat. Nathan held his breath when one linlar stared right at him, but his gaze was not motivated by interest or suspicion, only the fixed stare of exhaustion. The kams marched straight to the next building, apparently a dormitory, and filed inside.

When they had all disappeared and the bars were bent open again, Evran lifted out the body of a tall woman with glazed green eyes. She was tossing her capped head and muttering incoherently.

Balek placed a hand over the silver cap and she fell silent, as though she had suddenly dropped into a deep sleep. "I'll carry her."

Evran, climbing through the window on his own, looked as though he wanted to protest, but sighed and nodded instead. He was followed by a dark-skinned girl with a short fringe of kinky black hair around her cap, Lagura Atrano, Marion's apprentice, and by a small, pale-skinned boy with a fringe of straighter black hair, Rainal Sartori, Evran's apprentice.

At least, Nathan noted, the two wizards still had their crystals hanging from the chains around their necks. His eyes were drawn back to the silver caps. Called *laborin*, sense takers, they blinded a wizard's inner eye. Some wizards died if the cap was left on too long, others went mad. All suffered from an atrophy of will, a loss of strength that could become permanent depending on the time spent wearing the cap and the level of resistance of the wizard.

"*Patrol coming,*" Derwen's thought intruded, "*a kilometer and a half, two kilometers away.*"

"*We're leaving. Hold illusion,*" Balek thought in reply.

Nathan saw the picture that Balek sent to Derwen in his own mind, the interior of the cell with its four prisoners still present, but sleeping.

Balek gestured to Nathan. "You go first with Rainal." He nodded at Lagura and Evran. "Then you two. I'll cover and bring Marion."

Nathan nodded. "Come on," he said, taking Rainal's hand. He led the boy around to the side of the building closest to the back gate. "We're going to crawl across the open area to that gate," he said, pointing out the route he and Balek had taken coming in. "You'll have to stay under me as much as possible. When I stop, you stop. Do you understand?"

The boy looked up at him and Nathan was startled. Rainal's eyes were the same bright blue as the sky. "I understand," he said. "You're going to hold an illusion over me."

"Over myself. I'm not strong enough yet to cover you as well, so you'll have to stay under me as much as possible."

Rainal went down on his stomach and Nathan went down on all fours over him. Again, he matched his skin to the appearance of the ground as they crossed the open area. Crawl. Freeze. It was awkward straddling the smaller boy. When they paused to rest, he could hear Rainal's breath and that of Lagura behind him, panting with strain and fear. Farther back and louder, he heard the irregular rasp of Evran's breathing. Crawl. Freeze. His muscles ached and he could no longer control his sweat. It stung his eyes. He shut them and extended his senses with his inner eye. The sun was burning hot and his head throbbed. He couldn't find the gate. He opened his eyes, despite the sting. Crawl. Freeze. Almost there now, but noises were coming from the far end of the field. The main gate was opening. The patrolling malik riders were back.

Nathan crossed the last distance to the wall next to the gate without pausing and flattened himself into the thin width of shade under the overhanging walkway, dimly aware of the others doing the same behind him.

The mounted dekam came in fast and in precise formation. Malik riders were always the most disciplined troops in any force. Sloppy malik handlers did not live long.

Nathan stared in fascination at the huge lizard-birds through the clouds of dust stirred up by their clawed, three-toed feet. He had never been this close to one malik before, much less fifty. He was surprised at how graceful they looked with their long, slender necks and whip-like tails, but the narrow avian heads, more than half vicious beak, reminded him of their nature. Wild maliks were among the most deadly predators on Tamar.

The parade ground that had been so empty filled with ranked rows of mounted soldiery. An officer spoke briefly in the Senangan tongue; then the serried rows broke into a confusion of movement and shouting as the troopers dismounted and maneuvered their fierce mounts toward the building opposite the dormitory, a stable-aviary combination typical of posts used by malik troops.

Balek, with Marion tied in a sling on his back, reached the gate as the riders dismounted. Again, the bolts drew back and the bars floated to the ground.

Nathan looked nervously at the Senangans prodding their maliks but none of the soldiers looked toward the gate, even when it swung open wide enough for Nathan to crawl through it. On the far side, with the solid wall of the stockade between him and the Senangan forces, Nathan dared to stand up while Rainal, Lagura, Evran and Balek carrying Marion, slipped through.

Nathan breathed a sigh of relief. Then there was an outcry from inside the stockade.

"One of the guards saw through Derwen's illusion," Balek thought. *"We'll have to run for it."* He gestured to Evran, Rainal and Lagura. *"Run. They know you've escaped. The whole dekam's heading this way."*

Nathan grabbed Rainal's hand and ran for the trees, ignoring the cry from the guard as he broke into the open. No illusion could hide them when the Senangans were actually looking for them.

"This way!" Jaith thought.

Nathan veered toward another section of the jungle, away from the baobab toward which he had unconsciously been heading. Jaith was right, no point in retracing their steps. They needed to take the fastest route to the horses. Rainal was keeping up with him, but the distance to the trees seemed to have increased.

He felt something swish through the air near him and an arrow struck the ground just ahead of where his foot had come down. He veered, running in a zigzag pattern until Rainal fell, pulling him to a stop.

"Are you hurt?" he asked, falling across the top of the boy to shield him.

"No," Rainal gasped. "I slipped." His chest was heaving in his effort to catch his breath.

Evran paused to help them. Nathan jumped up and pulled on Rainal. Evran grabbed the boy's other arm and they started running. They had nearly reached the trees when Evran cried out and fell, bringing Rainal down as well.

There was an arrow in Evran's shoulder. Nathan helped him up while Rainal scrambled to his feet. Balek and Lagura caught up to them, Marion still supported by the sling on Balek's back, just as the gate behind them opened and malik riders poured through.

Nathan half-dragged, half-carried Evran toward the jungle as Jaith, Derwen, Antra and the Wizard Lyan broke through the trees on horseback leading Nathan and Balek's horses and the two extra horses they had brought for Lagura and whoever might be with her.

Jaith pulled up in front of Nathan and handed him the reins of the horse she led. Then she leaned over to help Rainal climb into the saddle behind Antra, who had already handed the horse she had been leading to Balek.

"Hang on," Antra said, turning her horse for the jungle.

"You and Antra get the prisoners out of here and run for the bridge," Jaith thought at Nathan. *"We'll give you time."*

Nathan pulled himself into the saddle, gripping with his knees as his feet couldn't reach the stirrups. He hauled the horse's head around and kicked it toward Lagura.

Derwen and Lyan delivered their spare horses to Balek and Evran and, with Jaith, turned to face the oncoming malik riders rapidly closing the gap between the gate and the escaping wizards. A line of fire sprang up in front of the malik cavalry.

The leading malik swerved sideways, knocking down another malik and its rider. Several more collided with the fallen and the one that had turned. The cavalry charge was halted as malik riders were forced to fight with their mounts who had no desire to approach the flames.

Evran pulled himself up on one of the spare horses as Balek, mounted, finished tying Marion across the saddle of the other spare horse. Nathan helped Lagura to mount behind him and guided his horse over to where he could grab the reins of Marion's horse. Then he turned both animals toward the jungle. Lagura gripped his waist and he urged the horses into a gallop, heading in the direction Antra and Rainal had disappeared, aware of Evran just in front of him.

As he made it through the first line of trees, he slowed to a trot to avoid being unseated by the low branches. Looking back he saw that Balek had joined the other three wizards. Even as he watched, two malik riders broke through the line of flames. Then the foliage closed in around him and he lost sight of the fighting behind him. Evran had stopped his horse, waiting for Nathan to pass, and Nathan realized that he and Antra were the only ones who knew the way. He also realized that Evran might not even make the rendezvous with the arrow still in his shoulder.

He pulled up his horse next to Evran and said, "Let me put a patch on your shoulder. We don't have time for me to heal you properly, but I'm ranked as a First Class Healer. I can remove the arrow and stop the bleeding long enough for us to reach the rendezvous point."

Evran frowned but nodded.

It only took Nathan a few moments to apply temporary first aid to Evran's shoulder. Then he was back to navigating the way through the dense underbrush, mostly ferns and broad leafed bushes between the trees. The heat and the humidity were almost suffocating. While Nathan knew it had only been minutes, it felt as though ages passed before they broke through onto the rough trail they had followed to reach the fort. After that the going was smoother, but it still took hours of steady riding before they reached the place where the wizards had arranged to meet: a clearing off the trail just beyond a high, rope-suspended bridge over the gorge of the Okoloka River. Antra and Rainal were waiting.

Nathan dismounted and was helping Evran lower Marion to the ground when Balek, Derwen and Jaith appeared on the other side of the gorge and crossed the bridge.

"*Lyan?*" Nathan questioned Balek.

"*Dead.*" Balek's mind felt hot with anger and pain. Nathan saw himself as Balek standing in the line of wizards, holding the flames that kept off the malik riders. When individual Senangans had broken through the barrier, the wizards had taken turns killing the riders, either stopping their hearts or shocking them with bolts of energy, while at the same time steadily retreating into the jungle. When they were deep amid the trees, they had moved the wall of flames to the jungle's edge and he set fire to the entire circle of trees around the stockade. But before the new, genuine fire had taken hold, three Senangans had broken through at once. Derwen had stopped two of them, but one had got past his guard and had struck down Lyan before the other wizards had realized the danger.

Balek and the others dismounted, giving the reins of the sweating horses to Antra and Rainal. Jaith then turned her attention to the bridge they had just crossed. Nathan watched as the heavy cables snapped and the whole length of the wood and rope structure fell into the gorge below. "They won't follow us by that route, anyway," she said.

"Can you take the caps off now?" Evran asked.

"You need healing as well." Balek knelt down next to the wounded man

"The cap first. I can finish healing myself when that's off," Evran said. His tanned skin had turned a shade of gray and he was shivering despite the intense heat.

Balek sighed. "Very well, Evran, but you've worn that thing for over a year. You know as well as I do, you won't be doing much of anything for a while."

Evran swallowed. "Just take it off."

"Give me your crystal, then," Balek said.

Evran took the crystal that hung from a gold chain around his neck and handed it to Balek. The wizard then looked at Nathan. *"Hold his head and link with me. You may need to know how this is done some day."*

As soon as Nathan had a grip under Evran's chin and the back of his neck, Balek thought, *"Sleep now."*

Evran sighed and his consciousness blanked out.

Then Balek looked into Evran's crystal and put his hands up and held them over Evran's head. The solid metal cap shimmered and detached itself from Evran. Nathan gasped. There was no skull where the cap had been, only a complex network of blood vessels on the surface of the soft, pulsing convolutions of Evran's brain.

Slowly, an incredibly intricate picture appeared in Nathan's mind, a complete cellular diagram of the top of Evran's head. Even glimpsing the image of it in his head gave Nathan a curious sense of distortion, and he knew that he was seeing only a small part of the reality of the image Balek was drawing from Evran's crystal. Much of it would be in the high sight, which Nathan was not yet able to see.

Balek held the crystal to his forehead and lowered his other hand until it was only centimeters above Evran's exposed brain. Then, cell by cell, he began to rebuild Evran's skull. Nathan stared as, slowly, the edges of bone grew out over the brain and knit together, the skin following, until, finally, the top of his head was complete and only a circular bald area was left to show where the cap had been.

"You can let go of him now," Balek said. "Make him comfortable."

"Will he be all right?" Lagura asked.

"Eventually," Balek said, but his expression was grim and he was looking at Marion where she lay as still as death on the ground.

Jaith said, "I'll take Marion, Balek. You need to rest. You've done more than enough for now."

Balek turned back to Jaith. *"Thanks,"* he thought tightly, so that only she and Nathan, still partially linked to him, sensed the thought. *"I'll take care of Marion; I know her best. But I'd appreciate it if you tended the others."*

Jaith's eyes met his, her face open in her concern and for once free of mockery. "Of course. If you give me Evran's crystal, I'll do Rainal right away."

Balek nodded. "I'll give you Marion's crystal for Lagura as soon as I've finished with her."

"Jehan and Maera guide you," Jaith said quietly.

VII

4625, 463RD CYCLE OF THE YEAR OF THE DOLPHIN
MONTH OF CERDANA

*"The ability to communicate mind to mind is more
difficult than it might seem. Almost anyone can perceive
another being's emotions. Even those without sight often
pick up such powerful emanations, but an emotion is not a
complete thought..."*

*"The transference of visual images can be taught in the
early stages of a wizard's training, but a visual image may
have more than one meaning..."*

*"The most common form of telepathic communication is
really only an extension of speech. This is the transfer of
agreed upon word images..."*

— EXCERPTS FROM *PROBLEMS WITH TELEPATHY* BY THE WIZARD AGNITH

N ATHAN PUSHED OPEN THE DOOR to Marion's room with his
leg, angled the serving tray through the gap, slid himself through
after it, and used one end of the tray to shove the door shut behind him.
Crossing the room, he set the tray down on the table next to Marion's
bed and walked over to the window to pull up the wooden blind.

Marion groaned and her arm came up to shield her face from the
light. Nathan crossed quickly to her side.

She looked thin and as pale as wax, with dark hollows below her
eyes, but those eyes were open. *"Balek,"* he thought, *"Marion's awake."*

She stared up at him blankly.

"Hungry?" he asked.

Her head moved on the pillow as though she meant to shake it but
lacked the strength. "Who are you?"

"Balek's apprentice, Nathan Ouakoro." He sat down on the stool
next to the bed. "You need to eat, rai, to regain your strength."

"Balek?" she said. "I remember Balek. Where am I?"

"In Candith, in Balek's quarters in the Palace. Balek, Derwen and
Jaith rescued you and the others from Senanga. You've been unconscious ever since. We've been concerned."

"My head feels funny." Her hand went up to feel her scalp where a short growth of black hair had sprung up over the circle of skin where the cap had been. "I can't seem to focus on anything."

"That's because of the cap the linlarin put on you. You had it on for nearly a year. There's bound to be a residual effect."

Her face convulsed. "I'm brain damaged, aren't I?" The tears welled from her eyes and slid down her thin cheeks. "I can't see except with my eyes. I've lost it all. Oh, Jehan, why didn't they just kill me?" She rolled over and buried her face into the pillow, bursting into tears.

Balek strode into the room and sat on the edge of the bed, putting his arms around Marion and stroking her back to sooth her. "What happened?" he demanded of Nathan.

"She was conscious when I came in, but disoriented. She asked where she was. I told her and then she said her head felt funny. When I said she was suffering from the residual effect of the cap, she got upset and started crying."

Balek nodded. "It's not your fault. This was bound to happen when she regained consciousness. She's lost a great deal of her mental capacity."

"But she said she couldn't see at all, except with her eyes."

Balek frowned and turned to the weeping woman. "Marion, you're going to be all right. Listen to me. You remember me, don't you?" He lifted her in his arms, pulling her face away from the cushion. "Look at me, Marion."

"Go away," she cried. "I should have died."

"Stop it!" Balek hauled her into a sitting position, pulling her hands away when she tried to cover her face. "Look at me, Marion. I'm not going away until you do."

"I can't see you. I can't see anything." She tried to pull away from him and burst into another flood of tears.

Balek held her face turned toward him and Nathan could feel the force of his will as he concentrated on Marion. "Look at me. Look at me now!"

"I can't!" she cried.

"You hear me!" he thought. "Answer me!"

"I don't...," she said, "I can't..."

"Answer me!"

"No. I can't," the thought came. It was only a faint trace, but Nathan sensed it.

Balek released her and she collapsed like a puppet with its strings cut. "Yes, you can, Marion. You just did." He rested his hand on her shoulder for a moment and then rose. Nathan was shocked by how tired he looked.

Marion lay still on the bed, her skin as pale as uncooked bread dough, but she had stopped crying and her eyes were open, staring at Balek. "I did hear you," she said.

"Yes, Marion. And your head will clear, and you will recover."

She bit her lip. "How long?"

Balek shook his head. "I can't tell you that. It depends on you, on how hard you work to get back what you've lost."

"Months? Years?"

He sighed. "Years, Marion, I'm afraid. No matter how hard you work, it's going to take years."

She nodded and pulled herself up into a sitting position. "How are Evran and the others?"

"Better than you. Rainal was too young for it to have much of an effect on him at all, and Lagura should be back where she was in another month or so. She's at about the same level of development as Nathan here," he nodded toward Nathan, "so I've taken over her training for the time being, unless you have another arrangement you'd prefer now you're conscious."

Marion closed her eyes and Nathan felt her anguish. "I won't be well enough to continue her training for a long time, will I?"

"No."

She swallowed and nodded her head. "Then that's the best arrangement I can hope for. Selene's current apprentice is much farther along and would resent Lagura. They've never gotten along." She hesitated, then said, "You didn't tell me about Evran? He was so strong while we were imprisoned. He can't have been as badly injured as I am?"

Balek shook his head "No. He's working through his problems. He closed down as much as he could while he was under the cap, so he didn't do as much damage to himself as you did, but he lost a lot and it's bothering him."

With Marion again conscious, Balek announced that the Council of the Varfarin in Cibata would meet the following week. Derwen could not remain in Cibata much longer and there were decisions that had to be made regarding the future.

THE COUNCIL WAS CALLED to order in the main room of Balek's quarters in the east wing of the Rabenate Palace. This was a high-ceilinged room with three arched windows facing north. The furniture was sparse: a desk and chair, a worktable with more chairs around it, two couches and a pair of side tables. Thick, hand-woven carpets covered strategic areas of the tiled floor, but no knickknacks or bric-a-brac decorated the whitewashed walls. Nathan watched from the corner, sitting cross-legged on the floor, as all the wizards who could or would attend filed in and found themselves places to sit.

As Derwen came in Balek said, "As Esalfar, do you wish to chair this meeting?"

Derwen shook his head. "No. This is your territory, Balek. My ignorance of the situation here would only interfere."

Balek inclined his head in a gesture of acknowledgment and Derwen sat down on one of the couches next to the Wizards Kaoda and Selene, who had arrived in Candith earlier that day from the Nyali Coast.

Nathan had seen Selene coming out of Marion's room earlier, obviously disturbed by the condition of her former apprentice. She still looked upset, her full mouth pinched together and her usually neat, brown hair tousled. Kaoda had his arm around her. Nathan sensed that the action was as much motivated by Kaoda's possessive instincts as it was designed to comfort Selene.

When Evran came in he asked immediately, "How's Marion doing? I heard she regained consciousness." He looked much better. His skin was still sallow, but he was clean shaven and his hazel eyes were no longer bloodshot. Also, his hair had been cut short all over to minimize the contrast in length with the area where the cap had been. He sat down on the other couch next to the Wizard Kindric, who had arrived earlier in the week from Mankoya.

Balek shrugged. "She can still receive mind speech, at least to some extent. I hope she'll recover, but it's going to take a long time."

Evran nodded. "I was afraid of that. Jehan knows, I've lost a lot. It's going to take me five, maybe ten years before I'm back where I was, and I didn't have anything like the reaction to the cap she had."

"Another few weeks and she'd have died," Balek said. He shook his head. "But we're not here to talk about Marion. Derwen has to return to Ilwheirlane soon, and we need to discuss what steps the Varfarin can take to check Senanga's aggression before he leaves."

Jaith, just entering the room, smiled and said, "At least we needn't worry about having to coordinate our efforts with those of the government of Cassinga." Then she sat down, positioning herself between Evran and Kindric.

Kaoda laughed, but the Wizard Marala, who had come with Kindric from Mankoya, frowned. "Can't anyone rouse Njombe to action?" A tall woman, taller than most men, she was sitting astride one of the straight chairs, her arms resting on its back.

"It's not Njombe that's the problem," Kaoda said. He was a lean man, but broad-shouldered. "I remember Njombe as a child. He showed promise of becoming a decent ruler. His problem was that he was both intelligent enough to realize the scope of Cassinga's problems, and sensitive enough to regret his inability to solve those problems. It's his recognition of his own inadequacy that led him to drugs, that and a belief that the situation is hopeless."

Balek sighed. "True, but recognizing the cause of a problem doesn't make it easier to cure."

"Look at his latest gubernatorial appointment," Evran said, "if you want proof of how disastrous that situation is getting."

Nathan grimaced, realizing that Evran was referring to Njombe's appointment of a new governor to the Gatoomatam, the southernmost district of Cassinga, and the one now most threatened by Senanga.

"Yes," the Wizard Marala said, pursing her full-lipped mouth, "Njombe should have appointed someone with a military background who'd stand a chance of holding the territory when Senanga attacks."

"Who has he chosen?" Derwen asked.

"Pasquale Ulein, the Lord Chamberlain's youngest brother," Evran said, shaking his head in disgust, "and we all know that his only action will be to siphon off money meant for military reinforcement into the Uleins' personal treasury."

Kaoda shrugged. "These are hard times. Njombe and his court have given up hope. Deep down, they think there's nothing they can do that will have any long term effect. Therefore, with their responsibility gone, they feel entitled to play their little games and cream off what they can in the way of pleasure or money."

"Hard times should bring out the best in people, not the worst," Lagura said, speaking up from her position with Nathan, Rainal and Antra on the floor. "We should rise to meet adversity, strive to overcome it."

Balek exhaled sharply making a sound that was half laugh, half snort. "Child, you're too young to know what you're talking about. Yes, there are many who may rise in a brief moment of crisis to heroism. But find me someone who can stand years of adversity and not bow beneath it, and I'll show you a great man, not an ordinary one. No, the bulk of humanity collapses on its face when confronted with real hardship."

"As true as that remark undoubtedly is," Jaith said, "it doesn't bring us any closer to plotting a course of action."

"Well then, does anyone have a suggestion?" Balek asked.

"The Gatoomatam is the key," Kaoda said, making a fist and bringing it down to slap his other hand. His hands were big and bony, the skin the color of polished walnut. "That's bound to be Dekese's next target. This time we have to be prepared to meet force with force, even if the civil forces aren't. This time we have to make a victory cost him something."

Jaith eyed Kaoda ironically. "You, a priest of Jehan, advocating a military solution?"

Nathan remembered with a start that Jaith was Kaoda's granddaughter and had been his apprentice as well.

Kaoda frowned. "Jehan teaches us to bend, to take the crooked path. There's no straight line to peace in the situation we face today. Even Cormor supported war when it came to preserving Cassinga. Can we do less?"

Nathan watched as a murmur of agreement spread among the wizards.

"So," Balek said, as the sounds of approval died down, "we actually agree on something. Now we have to figure out how to accomplish it."

"The ahars of Kingi, Tambura and Chirfa would supply both ships and men," Selene said, leaning forward on the couch as though to stress her words. "The pirates of the Nyali Coast don't like the idea of Senanga taking more territory," she continued. "Nor do they want Cassinga to fall."

"A niggling suspicion they might be next?" Jaith asked, smoothing back her golden hair.

"Their motivations are irrelevant," Kaoda said. "What matters is that they serve our purpose."

"But will they?" Kindric asked. "A military force located on the Nyali Coast isn't going to be able to reach Cassinga in time to stop Dekese."

"That might be true," Kaoda said, "if Dekese could strike without warning, but he can't. Half the pirates on the Nyali Coast knew when the Senangan fleet was due to attack the Mocubatam. Murgos, the Ahar of Chirfa, even sent a warning to Njombe. I know, because I helped him compose it. Balek tells me it arrived four days ahead of the invasion."

Jaith laughed. "What did Njombe do with it? Use it to wipe his hind end?"

Balek snorted. "He might just as well. He passed it on to Graff Ulein who canceled all shipping to Nemali."

"The point Kaoda is making," Selene said, "is that a fleet from Chirfa could arrive as quickly as the message."

"I don't think we should depend on the intelligence gathering of the rulers of the Nyali Coast," Marala said, frowning. "They may be the best informed people on Tamar, but they're also notorious for shifting loyalties at the last moment."

"We should also do something," Kindric said, "about supplying arms and military training directly to the people of the Gatoomatam, especially the population of the outlying plantations. They're the ones whose lives are at stake."

"I can help there," Derwen said. "I may not be able to get Vanda to send an army, but even Bray won't object to sending arms and Vordal won't object to shipping them. I might even manage to wangle a small number of troops experienced in combat training."

"That would help," Balek said, "but we have several issues before us still unresolved." He shifted his attention to the two wizards sitting beside Derwen. "First of all, Kaoda and Selene, as it's your idea and you both live on the Nyali Coast, I presume you're volunteering to raise the fleet you've suggested."

Selene nodded and Kaoda said, "Yes. Of course."

Balek looked around the room. "Then we all agree that such a fleet is a good idea, granted the reservations that we need back up intelligence of our own, and that the fleet not be our only approach."

There was a general nodding of heads.

"Does anyone disagree?"

The room was silent.

"Well then," Balek said, and turned to Marala. "Marala, you're the one who feels we need our own intelligence. How do you suggest we arrange that?"

She grinned. "I don't want to trespass on Wafar or Choma's territory, but he roams all around the borders and she spends most of her time in Azraq, Senanga's capitol, and the wizards they've trained and their apprentices do pretty much the same. We need to keep track of the fleet. I can pass as a linlar with a few stripes in my hair. I've done it before. So I could go to Feshi, the fleet headquarters, and get myself a job. Then I'll be able to give warning before any major action, whether it's against Cassinga or anyplace else."

Balek nodded. "Very well, that leaves Kindric's suggestion of training the civilian population of the Gatoomatam. I don't believe any of us have military experience, so, if Derwen doesn't manage to arrange for personnel proficient in such training, how shall we go about it?"

Marala straightened in her seat. "I've had military experience. If there's someone else willing to go to Feshi, I'd be happy to get the program started in the Gatoomatam, and to show whoever else volunteers what to do."

Jaith stretched, rotating her shoulders so that she rubbed up against both Evran and Kindric on either side of her on the couch. "I'd never make it in the military, but I'm excellent at undercover work," she looked up at Evran who stiffened at the contact, "all kinds of it."

Balek ignored the by-play and nodded. "Very well. That leaves Marala, Kindric and myself to go to the Gatoomatam. Opale and Emin can take care of the rest of Cassinga for the time being. And Evran can take Marion back to Mankoya and work with Morant there as Kindric and Marala will both have other duties." He looked back to Derwen. "We could do with more wizards, if the Varfarin can spare them."

Derwen frowned. "I'll put out a call for volunteers when I get back. I assume there will be some free to leave their present duties, but I can't guarantee how many."

"No. Of course not." Balek looked around the room. "Then we're all agreed on a two prong defense. One prong, a fleet from the Nyali Coast trained and ready to reinforce the Cassingan forces whenever they hear of an invasion from their own sources or our newest spy in Senanga." He nodded toward Jaith. "The second prong, a trained local militia ready to contest every foot of ground, supplied with arms from Ilwheirlane and the best training we can manage."

Nathan grinned as the wizards all agreed. Dekese was in for a surprise.

MONTH OF ANOR

"SHE WON'T BE ABLE TO NURSE the child." The linlar healer looked down at the unconscious form of Jura and then back at the infant in his arms. "You can try feeding him with goat's milk, but he looks sickly. Without his mother's milk, I doubt he'll live."

Morrien stiffened as she finished clearing away the bloody towels. Jura had hemorrhaged after the birth and would certainly have died without the healer's assistance, but Morrien didn't like the man's attitude. "The baby's father was a linlar officer. There's a chance he has the sight and can be a citizen; doesn't that matter?"

The healer shrugged. "I wouldn't have attended the birth if it weren't for that, but only the strong survive here in Senanga and both the baby and his mother are weak."

"I have enough milk to feed him as well as my own," Morrien said. "Jura's my friend. I won't let her baby die."

"Suit yourself," the man said. "I've done all I can. She'll have to stay off her feet and avoid strenuous exercise for at least two weeks, or she'll start bleeding again and that will certainly be the end of her."

"I can handle her chores as well as my own for a while."

The man's eyebrows rose. "She's lucky to have a friend like you, but you're only putting off the inevitable. She's too frail for this life."

Morrien shrugged. "She's my friend. I'll help her while I can. The boy will be a companion for my own child."

"For a time," he said. "Your child's what? Three months?"

Morrien nodded.

"Then she won't remember the companionship. The boy's not likely to live past nine months."

Morrien stiffened and her chin rose. "I'm aware of that too."

The man frowned at her sharp tone and drew out his notebook. "Very well, what does she want the boy named?"

"Luri. It was her brother's name."

He wrote it down, then eyed Morrien shrewdly. "If the boy does live past nine months, he'll be Luri Abandu and she'll lose him anyway when he's old enough to start his schooling."

"She knows that."

"Just don't let her forget it, and become too attached."

"Don't worry." Morrien's mouth twisted into a mockery of a smile. "I won't let her forget."

VIII

4626, 463RD CYCLE OF THE YEAR OF THE MALIK MONTH OF CERDANA

> *"Contrary to popular belief, the degree of vision and the nature of that vision varies greatly between the races of the larin. Where a hailar can read a newspaper spread out on a mountain slope ten miles away, a fallar cannot see even as far as a human being in the open air. Inside his tunnel, however, the fallar can see through the rock itself and detect pockets of minerals many body lengths away, whereas the hailar could not see more than a finger length through rock, or even dirt.*
>
> *"With such a diversity of vision, one might ask: How did the larin devise a simple test that would pass children with any degree of larin sight and still eliminate those who see only as men do? The answer is simple. All larin see into matter to one degree or another. No human being can see beyond the surface of any object without training..."*
>
> — EXCERPT FROM *KAGRESOD GRESACAD: UNDERSTANDING DISCRIMINATION* BY ENKAR HAKIST, ILWHEIRLANE, 3207

T HE KITCHEN OF THE KULHAR'S MANSION in Nemali was a huge, bright room. High, arched windows supplied light by day and an abundance of oil lamps illuminated it by night. At almost any hour, the huge room buzzed with activity. The bread cooks started the mornings only hours after the cleaning up from the evening meal was done.

Onions, garlic, sylvith pods and bright colored peppers hung in braided knots from the overhead beams, and bunches of spices such as saffron and cuna, rosemary, thyme, argerium, and sage hung in baskets to dry. Other spices such as nutmeg, lomida and cloves sat in bowls ready to be ground for use. They all lent their aromas to the hot, moist air, steamy with the vapors from the copper pots that hung over the open hearth or bubbled on top of one of the wood-burning iron stoves.

Morrien and Jura kept their babies in an old cage Morrien found in the attic. With a blanket in the bottom it made a satisfactory playpen and, when placed in a corner of the huge kitchen, they could keep an eye on the children while they worked. While Luri appeared small and frail, he never cried or fretted when Saranith was with him.

"If he doesn't pass their test, they'll kill him. And if he does pass, they'll take him away from me. You're right to hate them, Morrien. They're cruel," Jura said one day while they were peeling lorsks on the big chopping block at one end of the huge room.

"Has Zezere spoken to you since that day in the orchard?" Morrien asked.

Jura flushed and shook her head. "You were right about that, too."

In the middle of Luri's ninth month Kulhar Saroti and one of his aides arrived in the kitchen in the early afternoon. A tall, dark man with skin the color of a cocoa bean, he had eyes the same brilliant amber as the linlarin commander's had been. Morrien looked away from him quickly, afraid he might read her thoughts.

"Can I help you, your grace?" Keta Mar, the head chef, asked, bowing.

"Where is the child my son tells me I must test?" The Kulhar looked around impatiently.

"Over there, your grace." The chef pointed toward the corner where Morrien had placed the cage.

Morrien and Jura hurried over and opened the impromptu playpen. Saranith had been walking for three months. She stood looking through the bars, while Luri, who had not yet learned to stand, lay on his back and played with his toes.

"Which child was fathered by Zezere?" Saroti asked.

"This one, your grace," Jura said, picking up Luri and cradling him in her arms. He looked up at her and gurgled, happy to receive the unusual attention.

Saroti studied the child intently for some moments. Then he gestured to the aide who handed him a bag. From this he took what looked to Morrien to be two identical boxes. He put the baby's hands against one of the boxes, making sure that hand and box were right in front of the baby's face. Luri cooed with pleasure. Then Saroti took the second box and did the same thing. This time, however, Luri cried out with pain. The Kulhar repeated the process, making sure to mix the boxes up enough to confuse the baby as to which was which, and the same thing happened again.

Morrien couldn't see any difference between the boxes so she was surprised when Luri cried out and tried to pull his hand away from the first box before it could touch him on the third repetition of the process. Saroti nodded, however, and said, "Well, he's not blind, but I doubt he'll amount to anything. Still, he's Zezere's first. I suppose he'll want to keep him." He looked up at Jura. "Feed the babe up a bit. He won't survive long as he is."

"You mean he's passed? He's going to live?"

Saroti's shrewd eyes focused on Jura for the first time, and his expression was almost kind, "For a time, woman. He'll live for a time. He earned that much by being able to see inside the boxes. But if he's still undersized when he joins the other children," he sighed, "they'll tear him apart."

"If he's a linlar, won't you protect him?"

Saroti shook his head and Morrien thought she saw a trace of regret. "That's not our way. Only the strong have a right to survive."

After Luri passed his test a crib was sent to the dormitory. When Jura put him in it to sleep, however, he cried fretfully. Jura then asked if Saranith could sleep with him as she had done when they were tiny. After that the children were never separated. While Luri did grow healthier, he remained small and thin. He had wispy black hair with no trace of striping and skin the color of pale cocoa, where Saranith's was a glossy bronze. His soft brown eyes followed Saranith as though she, rather than his mother, were the center of his world.

MONTH OF ANOR

"THE ABILITY TO SHAPE-CHANGE is a part of you, Nathan. You must learn to face it," Balek said.

"I don't want it to be a part of me," Nathan said, shaking his head in denial.

Balek smiled wryly. "Since when has what we want had any effect on reality. Even the great wizards, although they could change many things, couldn't guarantee that what they'd changed would come out the way they wanted. I don't believe even the gods have that power."

Nathan glared at his master. At sixteen he was as tall as Balek, though leaner. His jaw set stubbornly, "Maybe not. But when I'm a full wizard I'll be able to change that part of me, so it's just like the rest of my brain. And, until then, I don't ever have to use it."

Balek sighed. "It's true that I can't force you to use the ability to shape-shift. But nor can I, in good conscience, ever advance you past the level of journeyman to apprentice wizard until you prove to me that you understand and have dealt with every part of yourself. So, if you ever hope to be classified as a wizard, you'll have to face the fact that you were born with the ability to change your shape. Why do you think I haven't given you a crystal of your own?"

"I've never thought about it."

Balek snorted and shook his head. "You should have. Most apprentices receive their crystals when they first become apprentice journeymen. I myself don't agree with that. I think it's more important for you to train your own mind to remember. Too many wizards use their crystals as a crutch, but I would have given you a crystal when you became a journeyman, if I'd thought you were ready in other ways. But you weren't then and, unfortunately, you still aren't ready now."

Nathan's eyes widened with hurt. The hot, humid air of the jungle pressed on his chest, suffocating him. The air was full of the scents of the jungle: damp earth and growing things, the fetid smell of rotting vegetation, the exotic perfume of some jungle flowers. Would those scents be even more intense if he became a beast? He had always done what Balek asked of him. But this was personal, a part of himself he hated. How could Balek expose him in this way?

"*Because I must,*" Balek thought, and Nathan realized that he had been so disturbed that he had lost control over his mental barricades and broadcast his feelings to anyone in the area. He looked around quickly, but he and Balek were alone in a small clearing and he could sense no one in the jungle nearby.

"We're alone," Balek reassured him. "*I made sure we were a long way from any of the others before I brought up the subject. I knew you'd be upset. I should have forced you to face the fact that you're a shape-changer long ago, but I kept hoping you'd deal with it on your own. In many ways you're the strongest apprentice I've ever had; I haven't wanted to see how badly you've warped yourself around this issue.*"

"If I accept that I'm a shape-changer, I accept that I was born a linlar, one of the people we're fighting," Nathan said, "one of the people who put caps on Marion and Lagura."

Balek frowned and shook his head. "*I didn't think my teaching had failed so badly.*"

"*It hasn't failed, rai,*" Nathan thought, shocked by the depth of sorrow in Balek's thought.

"*Then tell me, Nathan, what is the Varfarin's purpose here?*"

"*We're here to fight the Senangans, defeat them so badly they won't ever attack Cassinga again,*" Nathan thought.

Again Balek shook his head in sorrow. "*Don't you find it strange then that Jehan, whom we worship as a generous and caring deity, would turn against his own children?*"

Nathan hesitated. Jehan was the father of the were-folk. Somehow he had always simply thought of Jehan as the god who had inspired Cormor to create the Varfarin. He thought, "*Only the children who choose war over peace?*"

"*I beg Jehan's pardon for my failure to teach you properly,*" Balek thought regretfully. "*Cormor, my own master, was right when he warned me that I was too easily carried away by the moment, that I should always focus on the end result.*"

"*I don't understand, rai. If we're not here to defeat Senanga, then what is our purpose?*"

"Jehan's ultimate purpose in inspiring Cormor to create the Varfarin was to achieve peace and equality for all the sentient races of Tamar. And his definition of sentience included humanity."

"So we fight the Senangans because they're dedicated to war?"

"Partially, Nathan, but not to see them defeated," Balek thought. *"To make them lose a battle, yes. But defeat them absolutely, no. If that happens, then we of the Varfarin, we who are priests of Jehan, are also defeated, for we will have brought harm instead of enlightenment to his children."*

"Then why do we fight at all?"

"Because Cassinga must survive long enough for the minds and hearts of the Senangans, the Mankoyans, and eventually all the linlarin of Cibata to recognize that humans are people, entitled to all the rights of larin, even if they are born without sight."

"Do you really believe that will ever happen?"

Balek smiled wryly. *"Yes, Nathan. Otherwise I'd not be involved in this struggle, I'd not have devoted my life to it. I count it a terrible failure that I didn't made this plain to you a long time ago. I know I've explained it to you before, and thought it implicit in everything we've tried to accomplish."*

"But I hate the Senangans for what they've done," Nathan thought. *"I don't care if someday they change their minds. They've already hurt people."*

Balek scowled angrily. *"No, Nathan. The Senangans haven't hurt anyone. Some particular Senangan ordered that caps be placed on Marion and the others. You cannot blame an entire nationality, much less an entire race, for the acts of individuals. Do I hold you responsible for Njombe's failings?"*

Nathan swallowed. *"No, rai."*

"Then you must learn to give up your hatred. For as long as you hold on to hatred, you cannot advance further in your training. And, if you can't learn to give it up in a reasonable period of time, you'll cease to be my apprentice altogether."

Nathan felt stricken. Balek had never been so severe with him before. But how could he stop feeling what he felt?

"I suggest that your first step be to accept the fact that you yourself have linlarin blood and change your form," Balek thought. *"When you have walked the world as a tiger perhaps you'll understand the linlarin better. Understanding is the enemy of hatred."* He turned and walked out of the clearing.

Nathan stared after him. How could Balek demand that of him? And threatening to end his apprenticeship! What else would he do? All his life he had expected to become a wizard. What would Lagura think, though, if she knew he had linlarin blood? It was all very well for Balek to talk about not hating the Senangans, but Lagura had been imprisoned and tortured by them.

That evening he managed to get Lagura alone in the terraced garden of the plantation house overlooking the Gatooma River. The house was long and low, built in a natural clearing of the jungle on the crest of a hill overlooking the river. It had thick, cream-colored tiles on its roof to reflect the sun and thick adobe walls with wide porches. The garden was fragrant with exotic tropical blossoms, the warm air heavy with their sweet, spicy scents.

"All right, Nathan," Lagura said. "What do you want? I wanted to wash my hair tonight."

"Balek said I have to stop hating the Senangans, all the linlarin."

Lagura gaped at him. "That's it? That's what you brought me out here for?"

"How can I help but hate them, after what they did to you and Marion...?"

Lagura frowned. "But I don't hate all Senangans for that." She tossed her head. "Oh, I'd like to see the Senangan commander who captured us and had us capped hoisted on a pike, and some of the guards..." she broke off and shook her head, her eyes closed. Then she visibly pulled herself together and said, "But I don't blame all Senangans for what they did. And, as Evran and Marion pointed out endlessly while we were prisoners, the commander and the guards were only acting within the guidelines set by their culture at this particular point in history. The purpose of the Varfarin is to change the cultures of the were-folk until such acts are no longer permitted." Lagura pursed her lips. "Let's see if I can remember Marion's exact words, 'It is unrealistic to blame individuals for acting within the constraints of the cultures they were raised in. Only the truly exceptional mind can transcend its own culture's conditioning.'"

Nathan stared at her. "And you can accept that?"

Lagura sighed. "Yes, most of the time. I understand what Marion was teaching. Hating people is easy. People do horrible things all the time, humans as well as larin. Learning to understand is harder. But you can't change what you don't understand. The whole purpose of the Varfarin is to change the cultural mind set of all the people of Tamar."

Nathan looked at the ground and scuffed a line in the dirt with the toe of his sandal. "If you accept that, after being a prisoner, I guess I'll have to work on it."

Lagura tapped his shoulder and he turned, looking down to meet her eyes. "You take everything too seriously, Nathan. You can't dwell on the bad things or they'll eat you alive. You have to push them out of your mind and live in the moment. Like now." She gestured around at the garden and the river glinting in Ranth's light below them.

"Smell the flowers? Hear the river?"

Nathan sniffed and smelt a delicate sweetness perfuming the warm, moist air and heard the soft sound of the water flowing by.

"This moment is beautiful," Lagura said.

Nathan stared at her, noting the fine bones of her face highlighted by moonlight, her slender grace and the budding breasts of her womanhood, and his heart turned over in his chest.

Later that week he went into the jungle alone far from the house. Then he carefully removed all his clothing and moved the thing in his brain that meant that he was a shape-shifter.

He changed. The scents around him were suddenly a hundred times richer, stronger and more complex. He could separate them and follow their tracks in the air. Then he realized that he was seeing naturally with the were-sight built in to his tiger form. He did not have to strain to see through the underbrush.

He stretched. He felt strong. He smelt a sturik, one of the small rodents of the area, and the scent stimulated a rush of saliva in his mouth. His body tensed and he started through the brush without thought, tracing the scent and looking for the heat track of its body. He saw it some twenty meters away in the middle of a clump of dense foliage where he could never have seen it in his human form, not even with his inner sight fully extended. He leapt forward, claws extended.

The sturik heard him and started to run, dodging through the densest areas of undergrowth. He followed.

Only after the sturik found its burrow was he able to stop himself and change back to human form. Then he sank to the ground, shaking with reaction. The tiger form had been so strong, its urges so powerful. He felt sickened by his lack of control, but how could he control himself in that shape? His jaw clenched. However overwhelming the task might seem to him now, he would have to learn. A wizard must have self mastery under all conditions. The great wizards could change their forms to any creature they could imagine. A tiger could be no worse than some of the other shapes described in the tales. He would learn.

But not today. He breathed in and out, concentrating on relaxing. He had done enough for now. He had changed. Maybe, with time, it would grow easier.

IX

4626, 463RD CYCLE OF THE YEAR OF THE MALIK
MONTH OF TORIN

Valt ab celod al end illorincen,
Nan a rhesal end e lith,
Ean lot acad tamarin
Ful eanse remin a garth;
Ean lot acad illarin
Ful cer e sar a nith.
Ilad acad larin ba nan a lorin
E jastwe wa sarin.

"In the beginning the Five Gods,
Children of another time and place,
Created all the worlds
With their thoughts of power;
Created all the races
With seed and blood of fire.
Thus all the races are children of the gods
And joined by blood."

— FROM THE SONG OF CREATION, ONE OF THE TEACHING SONGS OF JEHAN THE
PLAYER

NATHAN PEERED THROUGH ONE of the large windows in the
plantation house's parlor at the deluge outside. This side of the
building faced the Gatooma River and he watched water cascade down
the terraces of the garden, overflowing them until they looked like a
stepped waterfall, pouring down into the dun colored torrent of the
river. He pitied the troops housed in tents in the compound on the
other side of the house. In the heat outside, even under cover, the air
was so humid he felt he might drown breathing it. At least it was cooler
in the house with its thick adobe walls.

"Any let up?" Lagura asked from behind him.

He shook his head. "No. If anything, it looks worse."

His eyes went back to the swollen river, discolored by its burden of
stolen topsoil. Rivers and storms always fascinated him. "You know,"
he said, "I was found in a storm like this. Some villager spotted me on

the bank of the Ouakoro on the day of a sudden, freak storm. The river was in flood, just like the Gatooma now. He took me to a nearby Sanctuary of Maera. Otherwise I 'd have drowned."

"Wow. How old were you?"

"Balek said I was about six or seven months old. I was just wrapped in a blanket, lying in a reed basket attached to a board of balsa. I washed up on the shore like a piece of debris."

"So you don't know who your parents were?"

"No. The kindred never found any trace of them, and there was no identifying mark on the blanket or the basket. They looked, but after such a flood there was no way to tell how far I could have been carried. As a small child I used to wonder if the river swallowed them, or if they consigned me to it, just sent me off to an unknown fate because my birth was inconvenient." He broke off.

He still didn't want Lagura to know he was a linlar shape-changer. He hadn't wanted to know that about himself, but after he had found that place in his brain, he had stopped wondering why his parents had abandoned him.

Balek had known, of course. Balek frequently pointed out that his parents could have allowed him to be put to death, that it had been love that entrusted him to the waters, not a desire to be rid of him. Nathan still felt betrayed, but he was old enough now to understand how that feeling of betrayal colored his emotions toward the linlarin.

The kindred named him for the river: Nathan Ouakoro, child of the Ouakoro. He had for the most part come to think of himself that way, as a child of the moving waters, and blotted out of his mind the linlar mother who actually gave birth to him.

"Any sign of the boats?" Lagura asked.

"No," Nathan said, turning away from the window. "They won't try coming upriver in this weather. Too dangerous. Whole trees are getting carried downstream. A boat could be torn open before the steersman had time to see what hit him."

Lagura sighed. She was stretched full length on the sofa and he could see the round firmness of her breasts through the thin material of her blouse. He swallowed.

"Even doing military drills is more fun than lounging around here watching the rain," she complained. Her body twisted as she spoke and her blouse tightened across her bosom. Nathan forced his eyes up to her face.

There were no traces left of her imprisonment. Even her hair was an even length, except where it had been cut short to shape it so that it bushed out around her head like a fuzzy black cap. She was fourteen, two years younger, and she was driving him crazy.

He squeezed his face into a grin. "You could practice your mental exercises."

She stuck out her tongue at him. "I've practiced until I'm surprised I still have a brain cell left." She sobered. "I've made up all the time I lost in Senanga." She tilted her face and made her big, golden eyes look wide and wistful. "Can't you think of something fun to do?"

Nathan could easily think of something fun to do, but it wouldn't be right and Balek would certainly object. Lagura was in their care, and she was too young. "Well, let me think," he said, looking up at the ceiling as though searching for inspiration. He nodded, and said, "We could find all those lists of personnel Balek has and sort them by home location and distance from the various mustering areas. He wants that done before the Wizard Rand gets here with the supplies from Ilwheirlane."

Lagura threw a cushion at him. "I meant something entertaining, not dreary. And you said yourself, the boats won't be coming up river in this weather. We have plenty of time."

Nathan fielded the cushion and walked over to drop it on her. "You know better. The rain will have stopped by tomorrow and we'll all have to be out drilling troops again."

Lagura sighed and held out a hand for him to pull her up. "All right, I'll help," she said, attaining her feet right in front of him so her breasts actually brushed his chest. Then she stretched and shook out her skirt. "Jehan, but you and Balek are slave drivers," she said, eyeing him sideways from under her lashes.

Nathan frowned. "If it's any consolation, my life was easier too, before we came down here and started to try and make soldiers out of a bunch of farmers and field hands."

Lagura pulled away and walked over to the window, her hips swaying. "What do you think the Wizard Rand will be like?"

Nathan sighed. "I don't know. Balek says he must have delusions of destiny because of the way he named himself 'tide.'"

Lagura turned back to face him. "I don't think there's anything wrong with taking a name that means something. I'm going to call myself 'Kwaneth,' the Orange Moth, when I qualify, like my grandmother."

"I agree, but you know Balek. He doesn't think much of the wizards from up north, anyway."

Lagura's chin rose. "He respected my grandmother, and she was from the north."

Nathan grinned. "Yeah. But she chose to stay and take a mate here. And she's dead, so he's no longer being reminded of all the times they disagreed."

Lagura turned back to the window. "Do you think Rand will have other wizards with him?"

"I don't know any more than you," Nathan said, "just the message from the relay saying that the Wizard Rand would be bringing the agreed on supplies and advisory staff."

"That doesn't sound like he's bringing more wizards," she sighed, "but it could mean the trained military personnel Derwen promised. At least we may get relieved from doing drills."

"Don't count on it. Balek thinks they're good exercise; that all of this, even the self-healing we have to do after being eaten alive by the insects, is great experience."

Lagura snorted. "Then we're lucky we're not outside now, drilling troops and being expected to breathe water."

Nathan laughed. "The troops don't have our skills. They'd drown. And anyway, we have paperwork to do. Remember?"

She grimaced.

THE WIZARD RAND ARRIVED with his supplies three days later. The river was still swollen and angry, and Nathan admired the skill it must have taken to guide the laden barges up the stream against such a current, at the same time warding off the debris churning amid the angry waters.

Nathan went down with Balek to the floating dock when the barges appeared around a bend in the river. He helped to secure the first of the heavily laden scows so it would not be swept away by the torrent, and to position the ramp that enabled the crew and passengers to disembark.

Rand stepped ashore first. He was not what Nathan had expected. The other wizards Nathan had met from the Northern Hemisphere were blond or, at least, light-skinned. Rand was swarthy, his skin tanned even darker by long exposure to sun, and his hair was as black as Nathan's. He looked tired but there was a sureness to his step, a brightness in his aura that bespoke a degree of power that Nathan had rarely seen except in Balek, the Wizard Opale, and, perhaps, Kaoda.

"Greetings, Balek," Rand said, then added, *"and Nathan, I believe."*

"You're the only wizard we're getting?" Balek asked.

Rand had yellow-gold eyes and a wide, thin mouth that twisted in a half-smile. "No. I brought two other fully qualified wizards, and my apprentices." He gestured toward a shed-like structure on the front of the barge just as two women stepped out of it.

Nathan blinked. He had seen many beautiful women, but none more beautiful than these two, and never before two who were identical. Were these the wizards or the apprentices? Nathan stole a glance at his master, noting that for once Balek looked as stunned as Nathan felt.

"May I present the Wizards Jaoda and Majaoda," Rand said, his smile widening to a grin, "Harmony and Discord."

"A pleasure to meet you," one of the women said. Nathan had no idea which was which, or how he could tell them apart even if Rand had identified them more precisely.

Nathan examined them as deeply as his sight would allow, but could detect no difference between them. They both had the same fine, straight black hair, eyes as green as budding elanda leaves and fair skin tanned to a light bronze by the southern sun. They both had high foreheads, straight noses and pointed chins. Looking internally, even their organs and the patterns of their capillaries were identical.

"Were you born like that, or did you have to work at it," Balek asked, recovering

The woman on the right, who had spoken first, laughed. "We were born identical twins, but you're right, we also work at it. It gave us an edge playing tricks on the other apprentices during our training years. Even Rand had to use the high sight to tell us apart. I'm Majaoda."

"And I'm Jaoda," the second woman said, speaking for the first time.

Nathan reached out to examine their mental shields and found the first difference between them. Majaoda's mind felt as though it were encased in a smooth, hard shell. Jaoda's shield was softer, lacking some of the hard reflectiveness of Majaoda's. Then, even as he sighed with relief at having found a difference, Majaoda's hard shell softened and began to match her sister's.

Nathan's eyes narrowed and she burst out laughing.

"Sorry," she said, "but I couldn't resist it. You found the way we usually allow ourselves to be identified, but that's only because we permit it, for convenience. Otherwise, there's no way you can tell us apart without the high sight."

"I can tell that one of you talks a lot, and the other's smart enough to keep her mouth shut," Balek said. "That's an easy method, but there are also differences on the cellular level in your brains. And you two refugees from a carnival side show, along with your barker," Balek nodded at Rand, "are the only wizards that Derwen could spare?"

"Not exactly," Rand said. "We're the only wizards who felt that our current projects were less urgent than your need. Derwen doesn't presume to command us, Balek." He turned back to the shed and called, "Bella, Renge, finish up in there. We're going ashore."

A young man and a young woman stepped out of the shed. They had straight, black hair like Rand and the twins, and amber eyes. Their skin was lighter than Rand's, but not the pale shade of most of the northerners Nathan knew. They looked as though they might be related, but they were in no way identical. The man was taller than the girl and more muscular. They both had straight noses, strong chins and full lips. The man's were fuller than the woman's, however, and he had dimples where she did not.

Rand said, "Bella and Renge Clarant, my newest apprentices." He stepped down onto the dock. Jaoda, Majaoda and his apprentices followed him.

"And what momentous happenings are occurring on the shores of the human sea?" Balek asked, when they had all reached the shore and were watching a number of the partially trained troops helping to tie up the rest of the barges.

Rand took a deep breath. "The eslarin and ingvalarin might object to that description of the Thallassean, but, even if you don't count their presence, the designation would no longer be accurate."

"What do you mean?"

"Gandahar is rebuilding the Road of Masters down the Valley of the Gwatar," Majaoda said. She was no longer smiling.

Balek scowled. "When did that begin?"

"In Cerdana," Rand said. "The Wizard Delanan watched part of the construction. He thinks it will take them close to twenty years to finish, but just the fact that they've dared to start is sufficient to upset a lot of us."

Balek snorted. "Well, what supplies did you bring?"

"Twenty thousand muskets, plus powder and shot, in the barges," Jaoda said. "We've also brought fifteen commanders experienced in training men in the type of strike and run techniques Ilwheirlane's navy has found most useful against the linlarin."

"Strike and run?"

Rand nodded, ignoring the disgust in Balek's voice. "I think, when you've had time to study the strategy, you'll agree it's the most practical for the type of jungle warfare you're facing here."

"At least the number of guns is adequate."

X

4628, 463RD CYCLE OF THE YEAR OF THE MOLE MONTH OF INGVASH

"Any lar born in Ilwheirlane or in the territories of Kandorra, Rawi or Fingoe shall enjoy all the rights and responsibilities of citizenship in those lands. Larin and humans shall enjoy equal rights and protection under the laws of Ilwheirlane..."

— EXCERPT FROM THE *ACT OF TOLERATION* ENACTED BY VYDARGA V OF ILWHEIRLANE, IN THE 405TH CYCLE OF THE YEAR OF THE DOLPHIN

EINARA HAREEL OPENED THE DOOR for Perrin Trevith and stood back to let him enter. Her face was an expressionless mask; her feathered crest, a tight cap flat against her skull. She spoke quietly, without a hint of emotion. "I'm glad you could come so quickly."

He caught his breath and strove for an equal calm, despite the fear her sudden summons had inspired. "I always come quickly when you call, Einara. I always will."

She shut the door. "That presumes I'll continue to call you."

He felt a pain in his chest as though his heart had actually missed a beat, and his eyes followed her as she crossed the room to the window. Something was wrong; her movements were almost jerky. What terrible stress could make Einara, the epitome of grace, lose even a fraction of it? "What's the matter? You weren't due back from your tour until next week."

For a moment she didn't answer, just stood at her window looking out. Then she turned to face him. "I was too ill to complete the tour. At least, that's the story I gave out publicly. As I only missed the last three performances, and Naradee is a long way off the beaten track, I doubt that anyone will question it."

"If you weren't ill, why did you miss them?" Perrin asked. "I've never known you to miss a performance, even when you were ill and shouldn't have gone on."

She stared at him, her eyes ablaze with pain and anger, and her tight feather cap rippled. "I'm pregnant."

Perrin shut his eyes, trying to conceal his own joy, knowing that his happiness would only anger her more, but her eyes were sharp and she knew him well. "That pleases you, doesn't it," she said bitterly, "but it may mean the end of my career."

"Then you can marry me and raise our child." Perrin refused to be ashamed of the joy he felt. He loved her and he wanted her as his wife. Sometimes it seemed to him that he had always loved her, always wanted her.

"And give up dancing?"

Perrin looked away from the naked pain in her eyes. "You're nearly thirty-seven, Einara. Even you can't go on dancing forever. You're already the oldest dancer in the Guild."

She stiffened and her feathered crest flared. "My jumps are still the highest."

He nodded. "Yes, but not quite as high as they were last year, and certainly not as high as the year we met. How long can you continue at the top, even without the baby? Another year or two? Three at the very most, and by then you'll be visibly failing. Wouldn't it be better to quit while you're still unquestionably the best?"

She sat down on the couch, collapsing into it as though her knees had given way underneath her. "I never meant to live past the end of my career. All my life, I've lived only to dance."

Perrin shut his eyes. "And the time we've spent together? It's meant nothing to you?"

She looked away from him, shaking her head, where the feathered crest had again become a tight cap, and bit her lower lip. "I didn't mean that."

He sighed. "No, but it's the truth. I've always known you were obsessed by your career, that you looked on the time we spent together as a fantasy, an escape, but never a part of your real life. But our baby changes that, Einara. We've created a life together, and that's real, as real as you can get."

EINARA SIGHED. Was Perrin right? Had she always looked on their affair as something to be kept separated from the true concerns of her life? She called up the memory of their last time together, a trip to Tiburra. It had been a celebration for them, commemorating the third anniversary of their first meeting.

The countryside at the start of the drive had been rolling green hills. As the morning progressed, the road climbed higher to where the grass covered slopes dotted with occasional trees gave way to stretches of real forest, puriri, elanda and eucalyptus mingling with hatha pines. Cattle were replaced by seralin lying in family groupings in the shelter of the trees. The soil where it was exposed was a bright red-orange and every few kilometers outcroppings of rock thrust through the soil crust. Einara thought of them as the bones of Tamar showing through its skin.

When they reached Tiburra, the lake below the falls had been the bluest blue she had ever seen, the falls a thunder of sound that shook the ground and yet held a fleeting trace of music, so that she had felt like dancing along the bank.

She shook off the memory. That had been the trip when her precautions had failed. She had conceived, but she still could not regret the trip itself, only its aftermath. Yes, Perrin was right in a way. Her memories of the time she spent with him did have a dreamlike cast to them. They always met in such beautiful places. And even after three years, Perrin never forgot to bring her flowers or some little present, never treated her in any way but tenderly. But could she live with him for the rest of her life? Could she live with anyone for even a day when she could no longer dance?

"I've thought of going to a wizard," she said, looking up at him from the chair, her face set.

"No!"

She had heard of people paling physically under the impact of strong emotion, but she had never witnessed the phenomenon, yet Perrin's skin did change color, turning almost gray.

"I wouldn't ask you to pay for it," she said.

Perrin's jaw clenched. "It's not a matter of money, Einara, and you know it. If you go to a wizard, I'll see that the whole affair is made public. You won't be able to get a booking anywhere in Kandorra when I'm done. You know the Guild will ostracize you for your affair with a human, if it becomes public."

She rose to face him, furious with him, feeling her feathers flare out to their fullest extent. "So my career will be destroyed in either event."

He shut his eyes in the face of her anger and shook his head. "All things end, Einara, one way or another."

MONTH OF ANOR

"YOU WANTED TO SEE ME, rai?" Nathan asked, entering the office Balek had created for himself in the plantation house's library.

"Yes, Nathan," Balek said, rising and taking something out of his pocket. "I believe it's time I gave you this." He rounded the desk and handed Nathan a brilliant yellow gem roughly the size of a large acorn.

Nathan stared at it, bewildered. He had hoped that it would be the crystal he had been waiting for, seemingly for years now. He was more than ready to graduate from journeyman to apprentice wizard, but Balek always signified that step by the presentation of a crystal and the clear yellow jewel was like no crystal he had ever seen before. "What is it?"

"Your own personal crystal. Your parents gave it to you."

"My parents?"

"Yes. The linlarin couple that gave you birth. I've been holding it for you since I took you from the Sanctuary. You should find it easy to use. You already had a slight linkage with it when I took you as my apprentice."

"My parents gave it to me?" Nathan frowned. He might have managed to get over most of his outright hatred of the linlarin, but he still didn't like to be reminded of his origins. And he hadn't known that his parents had left him anything, much less a focus crystal.

"Yes. You know, you seem to harbor a number of misconceptions about the way your parents abandoned you."

"What do you mean? Abandonment is abandonment."

"I'm sorry, but I overheard your description of the event when you told Lagura about being found by the river as a child. You were not 'cast adrift in a storm.' There was a storm on the day the villagers found you, but it didn't start until after they had picked you up off the riverbank. You were never in any danger from it. In fact, you were quite dry and very well fed. The couple who found you said you showed no signs of hunger until late that evening."

"What difference does that make?"

"I believe it indicates that at least one of your parents actually guided you to shore and watched over you until the villagers found you. You were not abandoned. You may have been given over to fosterage, but taking into account the present laws of Senanga that is a very different thing."

"Why are you telling me this now?" Nathan asked.

Balek shook his head. "Because I hadn't realized until I heard you talking with Lagura how the story of how you came to the kindred had affected you. I blame myself for being blind to that. I investigated the facts when I first discovered you. I should have informed you of the details then, or at least as soon as you were old enough to understand, but I thought you knew all that was necessary.

"I told Lagura the truth. My parents stuck me in a basket and floated me down the river."

"Your parents traveled hundreds of kilometers through some very rugged mountains into a land hostile to their kind to deliver you to a place where you could grow up in safety." Balek sighed. "I can imagine how they felt. One of them, at least, was a trained wizard of some power. He left his mark on the jewel. You'll feel it there if you look for it. He knew you would be a wizard. He had even started your training."

"He started my training..."

"Oh, yes. I knew you'd received some training prior to my discovery of you, but I always thought it was from one of the kindred. When I got that jewel out to give to you, I examined it more closely and noticed the mark. The stone bears the imprint of two people's pain, but only one of them was a trained wizard.

"You had that jewel in your hand when you were found. If the peasants had sold it, it would have more than paid for the cost of raising a child. It's a yellow diamond. The largest I've ever seen. It's not flawless, but it was shaped by a wizard of some skill. It's a more beautiful focus crystal than the quartz ones most wizards use. Of course, the crystal lattice is much finer than that of most crystals. If you had only average potential, you might find it difficult to use. But you are destined to be a very powerful wizard, Nathan, if you keep up your training. You should have no problem."

"No, rai," Nathan said, dazed. "Thank you, rai." He looked up at Balek. "I can graduate then?"

Balek smiled. "In good time, Nathan. But first you need to feel the imprint on that diamond and think about your parents again. Then come and tell me if that has made any change in your feelings toward linlarin."

As Nathan's face fell, he added, "Read what is on the crystal, then record your own cellular pattern to it. Once you have done that you will have completed all the prerequisites for advancement. Then I'll show you the high sight. You'll be an apprentice wizard the day you achieve that sight for yourself."

Nathan's face cleared and he nodded solemnly. "Yes, rai. I will, rai."

Later, alone in his own room, Nathan did examine the small yellow crystal. Small, he thought, for a crystal, but huge for a gemstone of such quality. He explored the tight lattice with his mind and found it vast, more than adequate to any need he could imagine.

He had always thought of his parents as something in the past, over and done with. But wizards didn't die easily. He touched the mark on the diamond again. Yes. His father had the high sight and was therefore a true wizard. That meant his father's natural were-sight had been blocked in his youth, so that his inner sight could develop. Only the highest levels of nobility in Senanga and Mankoya did that to their children. Nathan swallowed. That threw an entirely different light on his parents' actions.

He had resented them for not simply taking him to a Temple of Jehan and having him smuggled out of Senanga by the Varfarin. That was one of the Wizard Choma's chief duties, overseeing the rescue of children. But with nobility went responsibility, and the Varfarin was a criminal organization according to Senangan law.

He probed the crystal. His father, he hesitated at the thought, had left two marks recording memories. One seemed to be his own, another a recording of his mother. He opened his father's memories first:

Altira Kamrasi lay on the bed with her newborn baby clutched in her arms and stared at her husband, Timaru. "No," she said.

"I'm sorry, Altira," he said, feeling her pain along with his own, "but he lacks were-sight. We won't be able to keep him. You know Senangan law as well as I do. If we try, he'll be put to death."

"But Nyunze's so perfect, so beautiful," she protested, looking down at the baby's nut brown face, fuzzy black hair and great golden eyes.

"Yes," Timaru said, "But I can't teach him enough to enable him to pass the test of vision at nine months. And even if I could, my brother Bashan would know and betray us."

"Bashan," she said, grimacing as though she had tasted something rotten.

"I know," Timaru said, agreeing with her assessment of his brother. "But he'll want to see the baby as soon as he gets back from his training maneuvers. We'll have to get Nyunze out of Kobala quickly."

"It means giving up my baby."

"It means preserving his life."

Altira's eyes closed, but she nodded slowly. "All right." Then her eyes came open and she glared at him. "I hate the laws, the way this world is made, but I should be able to travel by tomorrow."

Timaru breathed a sigh of relief. "He'll be able to have a good life in Cassinga."

"But I'll never see him again," Altira said bleakly.

"No," Timaru agreed with deep sorrow. "Neither of us will ever see him again."

Nathan felt his father's pain and tried to imagine what he could have done in his father's place. Suddenly, his parents no longer seemed the unfeeling monsters he had thought them through most of his life, when he had thought of them at all. They became thinking, feeling beings trapped by unjust laws into an impossible situation.

He had seen his mother's pain through his father's eyes. Now he suddenly needed to feel what she had felt for himself. He probed the second recording:

Atira Kamrasi looked down at her seven-month-old son, Nyunze. He was so beautiful. How could she let him go?

"You must. You know we have no choice," Timaru said gently.

She had not spoken aloud, but he was a powerful empath as well as a wizard and they were linked. He could feel whatever she felt.

It was hot, the air around them close and still. Altira turned to him, her face wet with tears. "There's going to be a storm soon, a bad one. I can feel it . We can't let him go in a storm."

"The storm won't break for hours," Timaru said. "The family I found have a place on the shore only a hundred meters past the bend in the stream."

"We should never have left Azraq," she said, her voice sharpened with anguish. "There were Jehanites there. I know several at the University of Kobala. They could have found a way to get Nyunze out of Senanga safely without setting him afloat on a stream in the wilds of Cassinga."

"We've been over this before." He sighed, shaking his head. "We're too well known, Altira. If I were caught dealing with Jehanites, as a member of the royal family I could be accused of treason."

"We could have disguised ourselves."

"My brother Bashan was having us watched."

"Why?" Her voice rose.

"There's a lot of human blood in the Kamrasi family. We've been breeding for wizard talent for generations. At least half the children born to us are born without were-sight. Bashan's opposed to change. He wants the members of the family to set an example."

"He's never liked me."

"No," Timaru agreed. "Your hair isn't striped, an outward sign of your human blood. But more to the point, he knows you're a liberal and want change. He may be my brother, but he isn't fond of me either."

She clutched the baby closer to her chest. "He still needs me to feed him. He isn't even weaned yet."

"He's starting to eat soft foods and he's learned to take milk from a bottle." Timaru closed his eyes and his face wore an expression of anguish. "Do you think this doesn't hurt me as much as you?"

Altira sighed and wiped her wet face with her hand. He spoke the truth. A part of the pain she felt was his. She was not as powerful an empath and her wizard talent was untrained, but the link between them enabled her to feel part of his emotions and what they had to do this day was as painful for him as it was for her.

She looked down again at Nyunze, knowing it was for the last time. He was snugly wrapped in blankets, blankets that bore no identifiable markings, and tightly strapped into the basket. The basket was firmly attached to a board of balsa wood and weighted so it would not tip easily. She had just finished feeding him and changing him and he was full and sleepy. She took out the great yellow diamond her brother had given her and folded his tiny fingers around it.

"What's that?"

"A diamond from the mines at Eseka. It can't be traced to us. It will more than pay for the cost of raising a child. It's one of the largest ever found."

Timaru nodded and reached into the basket to touch the jewel in his son's hand. "I'll put recordings of our memories on it. That way, if the people who raise him don't sell it, but keep it for him, and if his talent develops as I believe it will, he'll know some day that we didn't abandon him lightly. That we love him."

"He'll know how I feel?"

"He'll know how we both feel."

She stroked Nyunze's hair. "The people you saw..."

"They'll take Nyunze to a Sanctuary of Maera. They're worshippers. I heard them praying. At a Sanctuary one of the healers will be sure to recognize his potential for developing the inner sight of a wizard and will see that he gets trained."

Timaru was right. Giving their baby up was their only choice. Other hands would raise him, but he would be safe. She had prayed to Jehan, and Jehan loved all children, even malarin children, those without sight.

Fortunately, Timaru had known from the day their son was born. They hadn't had to wait for the formal testing, when it would have been too late to save him. That testing was not due for another two months. By then they'd be back in Senanga. They'd tell the monitors that their son had died; that there'd been some internal defect too severe for Timaru to correct. Some might wonder. The monitors might even think that they'd killed the boy themselves, not wanting the shame of having birthed a non-sentient child. But Timaru was related to the estahar. They wouldn't dare question too closely.

Bashan was another matter. Timaru's older brother would guess what they had done and disapprove, but he'd have no proof and there was nothing he could do now to stop them.

Altira understood why Bashan had been so pleased when Timaru asked permission from his cousin Kaya to use the royal estate at Lake Moriki as a place for her to rest after having the baby. Bashan had thought them well away from their Jehanite friends.

Altira clenched her fists. Some of the teachers and students at the University talked of changing the laws, but those were kufi smoke dreams of some far away future. Her son was a malar and would be raised by malarin. Jehan, let his life be a happy one, she prayed. Let him someday understand that his parents loved him, but could not keep him safe. The world we live in is twisted and needs reshaping.

Timaru hugged her against his body and she felt his pain along with her own. "I heard your prayer," he said. "The world is twisted, but I have a vision. Perhaps one day our son will help to change the world. At least, let us have that hope."

Altira tried to smile through her tears. "Then we'll pray that it be so."

Nathan felt the tears running down his own cheeks. How could she have felt such pain and still gone on living. His mother had beyond all doubt loved him. "The laws and the culture that formulated such laws are what we must change," he said aloud. "The linlarin are just people like us."

He sighed and wiped his face. That was what Cormor had taught. Always before something in him had chafed at that teaching, but now he could understand and accept the goals of the Varfarin in their entirety. He gave thanks and prayed to Jehan.

MONTH OF TORIN

BY THE TIME THEY WERE THREE, Saranith and Luri had long since graduated from the cage. They played in the courtyard or silently in a corner of the kitchen. Sometimes they helped with small tasks like shelling nuts and peeling vegetables. Luri was awkward at such things but Saranith had quick, clever fingers and her eyes took in everything around her. She never needed to be told anything twice.

"She's so quiet." Morrien sighed. She was chopping caulis stalks and carrots for a stew and watching Saranith and Luri play a complicated game with a handful of straws that had been used to cushion the fruit in a crate of lomcans. Luri chattered constantly but Saranith rarely answered him.

"You know, I've never seen her smile. It's unnatural for a child to be so solemn," Magali said, coming over to collect some of the chopped vegetables into a bowl.

"She's reflecting our moods," Jura said. "I've noticed she always does that. She's sensitive."

"No!" Morrien said. "It's just her nature to be quiet."

Jura looked surprised at Morrien's vehemence but later, when Magali had left them, she said, "I upset you earlier, but Saranith does reflect our emotions. Do you think she has were-sight after all?"

Morrien felt her face crumple and she started to cry. "I don't know, Jura. How can I know?"

Saranith was watching them with dark, troubled eyes, the straws she had been playing with now ignored. "Think of something happy, Morrien," Jura said. "Think of the happiest time you can ever remember."

Morrien sighed and lowered her head in acknowledgment. She thought back to the day when she had been eighteen and received her first proposal. It had been in Ilfarnar and the hills above Candith had been strewn with wild flowers.

Jura's hand gripped her wrist, bringing her back to the present. "Look, Morrien! Look at her face!"

Saranith's face was transfigured with wonder, the strange green-gold eyes rapt.

"Oh, Maera, what have I done?" Morrien cried, and watched the smiling face of her tiny daughter change to an image of anguish. "What have I done?"

"You thought it was for the best. Can't you just tell them the truth now?" Jura asked.

"She's three. Too old for their test. They'll say she's learned somehow. Even if they acknowledge that she was born with were-sight, what's to say that her father wasn't a human half-breed unless I tell them the truth? And, if I do that, they're bound to find out how her father died." Morrien's shoulders slumped. "I'll have to try and teach her to hide it. I don't know what else to do."

XI

*"Children with wizard talent may be taught the correct 'image'
of each word as soon as they are capable of transferring any
image at all...*

*"The advantage of 'speaking' mind to mind is its range and its
privacy..."*

— EXCERPTS FROM *PROBLEMS WITH TELEPATHY* BY THE WIZARD AGNITH

N ATHAN WATCHED AS MAMFE ISIRO, now Mamfe II, waddled
back down the center aisle of the great hall of the Rabenate Palace
in Candith with the crown of Cassinga on his head. Although Mamfe
was only thirty-six, he was already fatter than his father had been, over
four hundred pounds. While not a kufi addict, there were few other
vices he had not thoroughly explored.

"Like an overdressed hippopotamus," Lagura thought in the intimate
mode so that only Nathan could hear her.

Nathan choked with laughter. Then he looked around to see if anyone had noticed his inappropriate response to the procession.

"You shouldn't do that to me when we're in public," he thought at
Lagura. *"And, anyway, you shouldn't be rude to the hippos. They're graceful
compared to Mamfe."* He risked a quick glance at her, but she seemed to
be concentrating solemnly on the members of the court taking up their
positions behind the new ahar and his family.

Nathan noted Rainal standing next to twelve-year-old Juba,
Mamfe's daughter and heir. The boy's stance and attitude appeared
protective. Balek had examined Juba when she was born and determined that she had wizard potential. He had persuaded Njombe to allow
the Wizard Emin to train her, despite Mamfe's objections. From the
time of the rescue until last year, Rainal had also been studying with
Emin here in Candith while Evran stayed with Marion in Mankoya.
Rainal was only a few months older than Juba, and it seemed the children
had grown close.

Nathan's eyes circled the hall, taking in the high, arched ceiling and
the brightly painted murals on the stucco walls. This was the place

where the ahars of Cassinga had been crowned since Gormal Raben had first taken the throne in the 288th Cycle of the Year of the Griffin, 2879, one thousand seven hundred and fifty years before, but Nathan wondered if it had ever witnessed the ascent of a sorrier looking ruler.

Njombe had been weak, but his son was a self-indulgent monstrosity. The walk down the aisle had to be the most exercise Mamfe had taken in years. In fact, Nathan could hear him puffing from his position halfway up the stands. Njombe had, in his better moments, tried to rule Cassinga as well as he was able, but Mamfe had no thought for anything except the gratification of his senses.

"How about a lorsk with legs?" Lagura thought.

Nathan looked sideways at her and stifled a grin as she rolled her eyes at him and then resumed her pose of solemn attention. At seventeen he thought she was absolutely gorgeous. She was tall, almost as tall as he was, but slender and graceful, with full breasts and well rounded hips. Her face was narrow and her jawline angular, yet the severity of the shape of her face was counteracted by her full lips and the huge golden eyes slanting up above her high cheekbones. Sometimes just looking at her took his breath away.

He looked back at the procession. Mamfe had almost reached the door. At least that meant the coronation was nearly over. Balek had felt it vital that the Varfarin be well represented during the ceremonies, both public and private, that accompanied Mamfe's assumption of the throne, but Nathan knew that his master would not feel at ease until they were back in the Gatoomatam. He had hated leaving the twins there on their own. But Balek's presence at the coronation had been absolutely essential. Mamfe was going to be difficult enough to deal with as it was. If Balek had slighted him by missing his coronation, he would have been impossible.

As Mamfe exited the palace to enter his carriage for the formal procession through the city, and the other nobility of Cassinga traipsed after in poorly-rehearsed order, Nathan and Lagura followed Balek as he slipped out a side door and headed for his private quarters in the east wing.

JUBA ISIRO EYED the less than enthusiastic crowd lining the route of her father's coronation procession from her position in the second carriage next to her mother. As Mamfe rarely left the palace, this might be the only time most of the population got to see him, so the number of people lining the route was as great as any monarch could have hoped. Their reaction to this rare sight of their new monarch was another matter. She did not have to extend her weak were-sight to hear their displeasure.

"That's the new king? Looks like a pig fattened for slaughter," a bystander shouted.

She wished fervently that she had been able to get out of being in the procession.

She would have much preferred to have gone to the wizards' meeting with Rainal. She had not seen him for nearly a year, since Evran had returned from Mankoya and taken his apprenticeship back from Emin. And now her grandfather was dead, her father might stop her wizard training. Then she would have no way of seeing Rainal at all.

THE COUNCIL OF THE VARFARIN in Cibata assembled in Balek's main sitting room less than an hour after Mamfe left the palace for his tour of Candith. As he and Lagura sat down on the floor against the side wall next to Rainal and Antra, Nathan thought about the changes that had occurred since the last council meeting he had attended four years earlier. They had managed to create a fighting force in the Gatoomatam. Chirfa had a fleet of ships ready to sail at a moment's notice, a fleet being financially supported by all the cities along the Nyali Coast. Those things were on the good side.

On the other hand, while Marion had physically recovered from her ordeal in Senanga, she had made little progress in recovering her will and mental skills. She had left for the Northern Hemisphere the year before, traveling with Kindric, whom Derwen had wanted for some particular task. Evran thought she stood a better chance of recovering in new surroundings where she wouldn't be constantly reminded of her loss.

He swallowed, disturbed by the track his thoughts were taking, and fingered his crystal. The clear yellow crystal had drawn a great deal of attention from the other journeymen when he had first started carrying it, but everyone was used to it now. He thought his change in attitude toward the linlarin had surprised them more. That change also made it easier for him to shapeshift, but he still found being in tiger form less than enjoyable.

Having his own crystal, he had quickly completed the skills necessary to becoming an apprentice wizard. It had taken him only two months to attain the high sight after Balek had shown it to him. It was an honor for him to have achieved such a ranking when he had still been, by Balek's reckoning, only eighteen.

He knew his advancement meant that Balek felt he had the ability to become a great wizard. That disturbed him. It had been fun studying wizardry while he'd been a child. But great wizards had the power to change the world, and the Council of Wizards had made terrible mistakes in their use of that power. He could barely control the urges of his own body when he changed his shape. If he achieved such power, might not he do an even worse job wielding it?

"Hey, stone-face! What are you brooding about?" Lagura jabbed him with her elbow to ensure she had his attention.

"Just thinking." She was sitting with him today, but Bella had replaced him as her closest confidant. He wasn't sure whether or not she was still having an on-again, off-again, affair with Bella's brother Renge, but he knew she wasn't anywhere close to thinking of him in the way he thought of her. He was jealous, but after talking to Balek about it, he figured it might be many years before she was ready to settle down after what had been done to her in Senanga. He would just have to keep hoping that she'd turn to him in the end.

"That fancy crystal make you too important to communicate with a mere journeyman?"

Nathan pulled himself together. *"Sorry!"* Lagura was sensitive to the fact that Nathan had received his crystal two years ago, and she still didn't have one. She felt she should have received hers when her training reached the level his had when he received his. Nathan sympathized, but knew Balek was withholding her crystal not because of lack of will or training, but because of what Balek thought of as emotional instability. He had much stricter rules regarding the crystals than most of the other wizards.

"It's just that this meeting is reminding me too much of the last big meeting we had, when Marion..."

Lagura wrinkled her nose at him. *"Dwell not upon sorrow, or it shall multiply,"* she thought, citing an old eslarin saying. Then she looked around and added. *"Anyway it's more crowded. And Jaith looks weird as a linlar."*

Nathan followed Lagura's eyes. Jaith's height and sleek appearance hadn't changed, but her golden skin was now a glossy bronze and her hair was black with tawny stripes. She sauntered in, pulled out a chair and sat down with her usual air of cool self-possession.

The Wizard Morant sat next to Balek in front of Balek's desk. "With your permission, Chairman," he said, "I'd like to make a suggestion. While neither I, nor any of my students were consulted when you made your plans for the defense of the Gatoomatam, I feel it my duty to point out a certain gap in your preparations."

Nathan gathered from the tension and positioning that Morant was trying to make it appear as though he were co-chairing the meeting with Balek.

Jaith had told Nathan that Morant resented Balek's authority. Nathan had gathered that Jaith disliked the older wizard, but had withheld judgment as he hadn't seen Morant since he'd been a child. He studied him now. There were frown lines around the close set hazel eyes, but no sign that he spent any time smiling.

Balek frowned. "By all means, Morant. If you have a suggestion, let's hear it."

"I'll let my former apprentice, who is more familiar than I with Senangan politics, explain the problem," Morant said, nodding to Wafar.

The Wizard Wafar, sitting next to Jaith, looked much better humored. He grimaced at the introduction, but said, "Basically, the problem is that all Cibata knows about the fleet assembled at Chirfa. Dekese may not be the shrewdest military commander Senanga's ever had, but he isn't a fool either. For every troop ship he takes when he invades the Gatoomatam, he'll have double the number of ships in a naval armada, all set to take on the Nyali Coast's fleet long before they can land any troops."

Nathan turned to the Wizard Choma who was also stationed in Senanga, but she was nodding. She said, "I was going to report virtually the same thing."

"But we've been careful to keep the goal of the fleet a secret," Selene protested. "None of the officers or sailors have been told the purpose for which they've been assembled."

Kaoda hugged Selene with the arm he had about her shoulders. Although she was senior to him, Nathan knew that Kaoda was by far the stronger and was clearly the dominant wizard stationed on the Nyali Coast. He said, "Nevertheless, I'm sure Wafar's right. The Nyali Coast isn't a place where secrets are easily kept, and with the monetary backing for the venture coming from so many sources, we should have realized we had no hope of secrecy."

Balek nodded slowly. "True, but it doesn't help us decide what to do next."

"Can you get more ships out of the Nyali Coast, some of them designed for combat at sea?" Rand asked Kaoda from the opposite couch.

Kaoda shook his head. "Even if we could get the rulers of the Coast to risk more ships, their fleet isn't equal to combat with Senanga's. We're talking about merchant ships converted to troop carriers. Only Sussey and Ilwheirlane build equivalent ships."

Balek turned to Rand. "Could Derwen arrange for a fleet from Ilwheirlane to cruise the area? They do occasionally raid the Senangan coast."

Rand looked thoughtful. "Ilwheirlane always has ships in Cibatan waters, the question is where? And would they cooperate? It wouldn't hurt to ask Derwen to put the question before Vanda. The problem is that it would take over a year to arrange, even if Vanda and her naval commanders agree."

"We'll just have to hope Dekese delays his attack," Marala said from the couch next to Rand. "In the meantime, we should all be thinking of alternatives."

MONTH OF ILFARNAR

IN THE FALL OF THE YEAR of the Griffin when Saranith was four and a half, Kulhar Saroti was promoted to a position in the central administration at Azraq, the capitol of Senanga. Dekese III, the Estahar, named his cousin Mutesa Kamrasi as the new Kulhar of the Mocubatam. Though still young, Mutesa had a reputation for lack of tact and ruthless ambition. With her came her two children, Aketi and Jadne Kamrasi.

Zezere Abandu did not follow his father to the capitol. He had been appointed Harbormaster in Nemali before his father's transfer and he continued to hold that position. Thus, Luri continued as a resident of the children's dormitory where he had gone to live in the month of Anor when he turned four.

There were twelve other half-breed children living in the Kulhar's mansion when Aketi and Jadne arrived, their ages ranging from two and a half to eleven. Aketi was ten and already possessed a strong wizard talent, having spent three years, from the age of two to five, in Gandahar where he received special training to develop his inner eye. He was easily the strongest of the linlarin children and soon became their leader.

Saranith had cried when Luri was taken away and after that Morrien had seen less of her. By the time Mutesa Kamrasi became Kulhar, Saranith had taken to wandering beyond the courtyard into the fields and orchards that surrounded the mansion. Morrien feared that her daughter's ramblings took her even as far as the town, where slaves were not supposed to go. But Saranith had a knack for being almost invisible when she didn't want to be found and, while Morrien worried about her, she had little control over her daughter. The only thing she could be thankful for was that Saranith had learned to suppress all expression of emotion. Not even Morrien could tell what Saranith felt. She sometimes feared that her daughter had succeeded in suppressing the appearance of emotion by ceasing to have emotions at all.

4631, 464TH CYCLE OF THE YEAR OF THE DRAGON
MONTH OF REDRI

SARANITH SLIPPED AWAY from the Kulhar's mansion into the jungle in the early afternoon.

The best times of her life had been spent there, either alone or with Luri, where no adults could see them. Luri wasn't supposed to play with her since he'd moved into the dormitory, but they still found ways to be together. Still, she had come alone today because there was something in her head she wanted to explore, but she didn't know what would happen when she did. If something bad happened, it might upset Luri. She hated it when that happened.

When she had penetrated far enough into the jungle that she no longer had to worry about anyone seeing her, she settled herself under a huge, old baobab and prodded the place in her mind.

The sensation was like nothing she had ever felt before, a mixture of both pleasure and pain as she felt her entire body shift and change. Then she was a young tigress.

She stretched, tearing the clothes that had not been designed for shape-changing. She hardly noticed. The new form was more powerful, more flexible, than her human form had been. She wriggled out of the clothing and set out to explore. The rich new scents intoxicated her. She found she could follow paths of scent like trails through the jungle. She followed one and came to a small hole in the ground. She followed another, aware suddenly of other creatures all around her fleeing as she neared them.

A small sambar broke from the brush in front of her and started running. Instinctively, she gave chase, straining her legs as she ran beside it, then leapt for its neck. She felt it fall beneath her as her jaws closed on its throat. She tasted the warm, saltiness of its blood. She felt it die.

Saranith pulled herself back from the beast within her, feeling her body change back to human form. Horrified, she looked down at the dead body of the sambar beneath her. It was hardly older than a fawn. She could still taste its blood in her mouth. So that's what it means to be a shape-changer, she thought. I can become a beast. Aketi must enjoy this part of his heritage. He's never anything else but savage. She shook her head. She had enjoyed the feeling of power, but she didn't like the aftermath, the killing. If she was going to change her shape again, she would have to learn control.

She grimaced. What else was new? Her mother had been teaching her to control herself all her life, it seemed. Now she understood better why. She loved watching the sambar run through the fields and edges of the jungle. They were so graceful. She bit her lip and got to her feet.

She looked down at her naked body then looked around at the dense foliage all around her. No time like the present to practice learning control. She had to find her way back to where she'd left her clothes, and she had no way of doing that in human form. She shrugged and moved the lever in her brain once more. Then, carefully, she followed the trace of her own scent back through the jungle until she found her clothes. Back in human form, she gathered up her simple shift. It was torn, but not too badly. She would gather some flowers and ferns. They would hide the tears from her mother until she could get back to her room and put on another shift.

XII

4633, 464th Cycle of the Year of Lizard
Month of Cerdana

> *"Beware the young of the dragon! They are fierce beyond their
> size. They kill and eat and fly to kill again. They know
> nothing of weakness and attack their own siblings as readily
> as the staked seral left by the trapper. The young of the dragon
> are all hunger and hate. You cannot train them. Just feed them
> and wait for them to grow."*

— from Chapter 3, page 78, *An Informal Guide to Dragons* by the
Wizard Ilfarnar

THE SPRING OF THE YEAR OF THE LIZARD was unusually
wet in the Mocubatam. On the first clear day in Cerdana after
over a week of rain, Morrien and Jura joined the other house slaves
washing the huge backlog of linens in the courtyard.

The linlarin children were also glad to be out of doors. They had
set up a target on the other side of the service area against the adobe
wall of the building, and were holding an archery contest. As they
were all of mixed blood, even the legitimate children of the Senangan
garrison, most of them had wizard talent. The strongest, like Aketi,
could guide their arrows into almost any target they could see, boost-
ing their range far beyond the strength of their young arms.

Luri, eight years old, but small and physically frail, lacked the
strength of will to compete in such a contest. The only bow he could
draw was smaller than that drawn by Jadne, Aketi's six-year-old sister.
Worse, even with the tiny bow and standing less than three meters
from the target, he still couldn't hit it.

"Come on, Luri, you can do better than that," Aketi jibed. "The
target's in front of your nose, not down by your feet."

Luri pulled back on his bow again and Morrien could see his forehead ridge with his effort to concentrate. The arrow started out fairly
well but fell short of the wall and to the right.

Aketi slipped the string from one end of his bow and twirled it. "I
don't think Luri has enough incentive, do you?" He turned to his
companions.

"Naw, anyone could do better than that, even a human," Natira, the daughter of the commander of the garrison, said.

"That's right, even a human, and our little Luri's a linlar, isn't he, even if his mother is nothing but a stinking human slave?" Aketi twirled the string in front of Luri's face.

Luri flinched but didn't dare protest; he could hardly tear his eyes away from the spinning bowstring in Aketi's hands.

"Go on, linlar, put the arrow into the target or you'll feel this across your back." Aketi spun the cord closer for a moment, enjoying the way Luri shied away.

"Hit him anyway, Keti," crowed Jadne, excited by the prospect of a new sport.

"Naw, we'll give him one more chance to hit the target. Go on, Luri, guide it in and prove you're linlar. If you don't, then I'll beat you as though you were a slave like your mother. You hear me?"

Luri stared up at his tormentor and nodded. His hands trembled so much he could hardly hold the bow, much less raise it and aim the arrow.

Morrien felt Jura's hand grip her shoulder and she put her own hand up to cover it.

"I can't stand it, Morrien. I can't stand watching them torment him," Jura whispered.

"Can't you stop them, Mommy?"

Morrien saw that Saranith had come up beside her. She bit her lip. Saranith should not watch this; she picked up emotions and she had been the object of so much baiting herself. "No dear. There's nothing anyone can do for him unless his father sees fit to interfere."

"There's no chance of that," Jura said bitterly.

"Hurry it up, linlar," one of the other children taunted.

Luri raised the bow and tried to aim. It was obvious even from across the courtyard that his hands were shaking. The arrow flew out at a wild tangent narrowly missing Jadne, even though she was well clear of the target.

Jadne stared at the arrow as it hit the wall behind her and bounced off. "He shot at me," she said. "He tried to hit me. Kill him, Keti."

Aketi had frozen when the arrow hit so close to his sister, but at her words he reacted violently. "So you'd hurt my sister, would you, you little human muloplen." He reached out and grabbed Luri by the shoulder and whipped the knotted bowstring down hard across his shoulders. Luri's shirt offered some protection but the cord left a red welt on his arm. Aketi drew back and hit Luri again.

"It would hurt him more if you took off his shirt," observed one of the other boys.

"I can't watch this," cried Jura, "I can't." She pulled away from Morrien and ran for the areaway that led back to their quarters. The slaves working at the wash tubs glanced up as she left but then diverted their eyes. Morrien understood that they didn't want to draw the attention of the children to themselves.

Saranith stared after Jura and said, "Doesn't she love Luri anymore?"

Morrien bit her lip. "She loves him, but she can't be close to him now. She's better off not seeing what they do to him, poor thing. There's nothing she can do and watching can only make it worse for her. We'd be better off not watching it, too." She took Saranith's hand and started to lead her back to the kitchen.

Saranith resisted. "You think they'll really hurt him? They tease him all the time 'cause he's not strong, but they won't really hurt him, will they?" Her eyes were solemn as she turned back to watch the confrontation across the courtyard.

Morrien looked over to where two of the bigger boys, Panyam and another, were trying to hold on to Luri and drag his shirt off. Aketi was standing by running the knotted cord of his bowstring through his fingers. Something about his expression gave Morrien the chills. "Of course not, Sara," she said, but the thought in her mind was that this time they might. She shook her head and looked down at her daughter curiously. "But he's a linlar now, Sara, why should you care?"

"He's my friend."

"But you haven't been close to him or talked to him for years."

Saranith looked up at her mother with her blankest face, the face that Morrien knew concealed her deepest emotions. "Of course I've talked to him. We still play together whenever we can get away from the others. I don't want him hurt."

"There's nothing we can do," Morrien said, thinking how little she knew of her daughter now. It was her own fault, of course. She had taught Saranith to suppress all outward emotion. But it still shocked her that she hadn't even known that Saranith's friendship with Luri had continued after he'd gone to live in the linlarin dormitory.

"Perhaps there's nothing you can do," Saranith said, sudden anger showing through her usual implacable calm, "but I have to try. He's my friend. We've only got each other." She pulled away from Morrien and ran across the courtyard.

Morrien started after her then paused. There really was nothing she could do, and her interference might escalate the incident to the point where it received official attention, which could cause both their deaths. She watched anxiously as Saranith reached the others.

Luri was down on his knees. "Please stop! I'll do anything, but please don't hurt me anymore."

Saranith put herself between Aketi and Luri. "That's right, don't hurt him anymore. Just because you're bigger than he is and stronger, it's no reason to pick on him."

"Aw, look at this. Another human muloplen come to plead for him," Aketi taunted. "You want to get beaten too, human?"

"No," Saranith said. "I want you to stop picking on Luri. He hasn't done anything to you. Why are you always picking on him?"

Aketi stared at her, obviously stunned by her lack of fear. All of the human children went in terror of him. "Grab her." He gestured to Panyam and the other boy who had helped remove Luri's shirt. "We'll beat her too, for insolence."

"No! Sara run," Luri cried, trying to rise.

Saranith stood still as the two boys each grabbed one of her arms. She seemed hardly aware of them, concentrating on Aketi in front of her. Although she was younger, almost a foot shorter and her arms were being held, she still faced him without any sign of fear. "If you hurt Luri again, I'll hurt you."

Aketi could not have looked more shocked if a stone had got up and talked. "You'll hurt me?"

"Yes."

Morrien felt a chill go down her back.

"Do you hear that?" Aketi turned to Natira. "The little human slave is going to hurt me." He gestured to the boys holding Saranith. "Get her out of the way. I'll deal with her after I've taken care of Luri."

The two boys pulled Saranith to one side. She went jerkily, managing to keep from being turned away from Aketi, her eyes still fixed on him.

Aketi stepped up and raised his arm to bring the cord down on Luri's bared back. His hand went down and the cord whipped out, but instead of following through to lash across Luri's back the cord twisted in mid air and wrapped itself around Aketi's neck.

Aketi screamed and dropped the bow and cord, both hands going up to try and pull the knotted bowstring from around his throat. The two boys holding Saranith's arms let go of her and ran to help him.

"Run Luri," Saranith said. Morrien could see her daughter's body trembling, but Saranith's eyes stayed fixed on Aketi.

Luri scrambled shakily to his feet and started toward Saranith. "What are you doing, Sara?"

Aketi's face turned red as the bowstring bit deeper into his throat. The attempts of the other children to help him only seemed to pull the cord tighter. He dropped down to his knees, gargling noises coming from his mouth.

When Luri reached her, Saranith grabbed his hand and ran, dragging him after her.

The moment she looked away from Aketi the cord went limp. He gasped and fell over, unconscious. The other children paid no attention to Saranith and Luri, as they ran through the gate to Nemali. They were too busy examining Aketi.

Morrien turned and went into the kitchen. She felt cold and shaken. Maybe it would be all right. Maybe no one would figure out who had manipulated the bowstring. But she didn't believe it. Her mind went back to the night Saranith had been conceived. The linlar commander had told her that she had great genetic potential and that potential had evidently been realized in Saranith. Her daughter might grow to be a wizard, if she survived. Suddenly Morrien hoped intensely that Saranith would live through this.

WHEN SARANITH CAME BACK from wherever she had gone with Luri and joined them in the kitchen, Morrien took her aside. "You know they'll come looking for you?"

Saranith looked up defiantly. "I had to stop them. They might have killed him."

Morrien nodded, wanting to cry. "I know that Sara, but this time they might kill you. I don't want that to happen. You're strong, Sara. When you grow up, you can make a difference. But now, while you're so young, you have to keep on hiding how you feel. Do you understand?"

"I know you're scared. I didn't mean to make you scared. I just wanted them to stop hurting Luri."

Morrien took a deep breath and let it out, trying to calm her fear. "The Kulhar will find out what happened in the courtyard. She'll come to examine you. I'm sure she has the high sight, so she'll know you were born with vision. I don't know what she'll do when she finds that out, but whatever happens, you mustn't interfere. You mustn't let them see how you feel. Promise me, Sara."

"Will she hurt you?"

MORRIEN NODDED. "Yes, Sara, they probably will hurt me, but not because of anything you did. They'll hurt me because of what I did long ago, before you were even born. Promise me you won't try to interfere."

Saranith stared at her for a long time, but finally she said, "I so promise."

Morrien, Jura and Saranith were all in the kitchen that afternoon when Kulhar Kamrasi entered with a squad of her troops.

"Where is the child Saranith?" Mutesa demanded. She was a tall, handsome woman with a disturbing resemblance to the linlarin officer who had been Saranith's father. She had the same high forehead and aquiline nose, even the same thin-lipped mouth. Morrien had been shocked when she'd first seen Mutesa but she'd grown accustomed to the Kulhar's appearance over the past two years.

Saranith got up from the table where she was shelling peas and stood before the Kulhar. "I'm here."

Mutesa stared at Saranith intently for some time and then looked around and demanded, "Where's this child's mother?"

Keta Mar grabbed Morrien's shoulder and pushed her in front of Mutesa before she could say a word. "This one's the brat's mother."

Mutesa examined Morrien. "You knew the child was linlar, didn't you?"

Morrien drew herself up and stared at the Kulhar. "How could I have known who the father was? I was a whore. I was used by lots of men."

"Who was the child's father?"

"How should I know?"

Mutesa slapped Morrien across the face hard enough to leave a red mark on Morrien's cheek. "Tell me the truth, whore." The Kulhar's eyes burned into Morrien's and Morrien shivered at the expression in them. "Who was he?"

"I don't know," Morrien gasped, but she was breathing hard and her eyes were fixed on Mutesa's in the way a pica watches a malik until the moment it's swallowed.

"Tell me."

"The commander," Morrien said, her defiance collapsing, "the commander of the troops the night they took Nemali. I don't remember his name. I wanted to forget all about him." She fell to the floor, her legs no longer able to support her. Her eyes went to where Saranith stood watching them. For just a moment the child's eyes were bright with a terrible understanding but even as Morrien watched her face went blank.

Mutesa stared at Morrien, her face twisting with shock and anger. "You killed him! Senrec Kamrasi. You killed my brother! I see it in your mind. I see it, but I can hardly believe it. A thing like you?" Shaking her head in disbelief, she exclaimed, "A knife in the back after he pleasured you. Your death won't be as swift." Then, as though she couldn't bear to look at Morrien any longer, she turned to Saranith. "Do you understand now, child, why you can do the things you do?"

Saranith looked up at the Kulhar with her most opaque expression. "Because my father was a linlar."

Mutesa shook her head. "No, child, because you're a linlar. Your mother has tried to keep you from your heritage. If I didn't have the high sight and weren't able to see your nature, you'd have been condemned to death for what you did. Your mother was willing to risk that."

"I'm a linlar," Saranith said quietly, watching the Kulhar as intently as Morrien had done, her face expressionless.

"Your father was my brother, Senrec Kamrasi." Mutesa put her hands on Saranith's shoulders. "You're a strong child. His marriage didn't give him a child, so you're his only heir. He'd have been proud of you if he'd lived. I'll take you into my household."

"What will happen to my mother?"

Mutesa frowned. "That no longer concerns you. She murdered your father and tried to keep you a slave. You owe no loyalty to her."

Saranith looked down and met Morrien's eyes where Morrien lay on the floor at her feet. Morrien saw her eyes shut for a moment but no other sign of emotion was visible on her daughter's face. Good, she thought, hoping Saranith received her emotions. When her daughter's eyes were on her again she focused her mind as best she could. I am doomed, but you will survive. Never show weakness.

"Take the woman out of here and put her in the punishment cell," Mutesa said, motioning to two of the soldiers. "Tomorrow she'll be flailed to death. I hope it takes a long time."

"Come, child," she said then, taking Saranith's hand. "I'll show you to your new quarters."

THE NEXT MORNING LURI and all of the Kulhar's household watched Saranith stand rigidly at the side of Kulhar Kamrasi in the courtyard when Morrien was brought out to be whipped.

Morrien stopped in front of Saranith as the guards were leading her to the whipping post. She stared at her daughter. "You were conceived in violence. Now you will be your father's heir after all, not mine. May Jehan guide you."

Luri was surprised to feel no emotion coming from Morrien. Then he remembered Saranith telling him that her mother had a still, quiet place inside.

Saranith made no sound, not then and not during the flailing. She never flinched as the cruel leather tore red lines in her mother's back. Luri watched Saranith anxiously. He was sure that most of the humans would blame Sara. Even the fact that Saranith had been protecting Luri wouldn't make Jura think better of her.

Of course Saranith's face was without expression, Luri thought. Of course it was impossible for humans to tell what she thought from how she looked. Morrien herself had taught Sara to suppress all signs of emotion. Luri understood that his mother knew that, but he also sensed that Jura felt that no normal child could hide emotion so well. And, of course, Jura was right about that.

Luri knew Sara as no one else did. He knew how hard it was for her. Saranith had learned to shut out pain, her own pain and the pain of those around her, but it required a terrible concentration. Luri noticed how grey Sara's complexion grew; the color drained away, and her green-gold eyes wide and fixed. Luri saw how the muscles of her hands wanted to clench into fists and how she kept them still.

Luri wanted to cry. There was nothing Sara could do for her mother. At least Morrien had spared her daughter some of her pain. But Sara felt not only her mother's pain, but all the other emotions around her: Mutesa's vengeful anger, Jadne and Aketi's blood thirsty glee, the resentment and anger of the slaves. It was her nature to feel the emotions of those around her, if she didn't shut them out. She always had. So she shut out feelings, or tried to. But she couldn't quite stop them all, Luri knew. At least, not yet. He wished she could.

Morrien lasted a long time before she started to scream. She lost the quiet place inside after that and even Luri felt her agony. The leather whip with its wire tips turned her entire back to a red pulp before she died from pain and shock. Saranith stood beside Mutesa and watched it all. Her face was blank.

XIII

4634, 464TH CYCLE OF THE YEAR OF THE TIGER
MONTHS OF TORIN AND AGNITH

"Of were-folk there are races six;
Be careful now, don't get them mixed...

"A linlar, when his temper's hot,
Is much more dangerous than not.
A tiger's stripy skin he wears,
With fangs and claws with which to tear..."

— EXCERPTS FROM "THE WEREFOLK" PUBLISHED IN *A CHILD'S GUIDE TO THE LARIN
AND OTHER BEASTLY TAILS* BY ENOGEN VARASH OF ELEVTHERAI, 4557

THE WIZARD JAITH STOOD amid a crowd of cheering onlookers and watched as twenty thousand soldiers of the Estaharial Army of Senanga marched into Feshi. Jaith eyed the banners at the front of the column again. She hadn't counted wrong. And Dekese III himself rode at the head of his troops.

Four lesdekin. Each lesdek, or great hand, consisted of five thousand soldiers, the largest military unit in any linlarin force, and ten percent of each lesdek was made up of malik-mounted troops. Jaith shuddered. Dekese was taking a force of twenty thousand against Cassinga, two thousand of them malik cavalry, the most deadly forces known on Tamar.

The entire Cassingan army stationed in the Gatoomatam numbered less than three thousand troops. The militia Balek and the others had raised might make up another five or six thousand, but those troops were completely inexperienced and could never face maliks. No matter how many troops Kaoda had assembled at Chirfa, even if they arrived in time, they could never match this force.

She had sent notice by telepathic relay two days before saying that the invasion was coming, but she hadn't known then its size. Now she knew. Over a hundred naval ships crammed the harbor, including fifty troop carriers, with more ships rendezvousing off the Point of Tagur. Her eyes followed the seemingly endless ranks of linlarin soldiers as they marched past. Four lesdekin, the largest invasion force Senanga had ever sent against Cassinga. They'd have to pack men in the regular naval ships as well as in the troop carriers.

Jehan protect Cassinga, she prayed, as she sent a new warning giving the number of troops involved to Balek in the Gatoomatam, to Evran in Candith, and to Selene, Kaoda and Imasa on the Nyali Coast. Hopefully, if he were in range, it would also go to Kindric, who had returned from Ilwheirlane the year before and was now the liaison between the Council of the Varfarin in Cibata and the naval fleet that Ilwheirlane kept in Cibatan waters. That fleet now constituted their only hope of saving not just the Gatoomatam but all of Cassinga.

May Jehan, the god of the bending path, find a way to navigate us through this crisis, she prayed again. And may Maera ease the pain of those who will be injured or die.

KAODA RECEIVED JAITH'S FIRST MESSAGE the morning of the day before the Senangan army marched into Feshi. The fleet from the Nyali Coast sailed the evening after that march with Kaoda aboard, having just received Jaith's second message. He counted the ships as they sailed, all thirty-eight of them, but they were converted merchantmen and the largest held no more than two hundred troops. He estimated that they would add a force of close to six thousand, and, while half that force was made up of newly trained recruits, the other half were experienced mercenaries. Some of those had even had experience facing maliks. Still, he knew that he might well be leading all these troops to their death and he too prayed to Jehan that their lives would be well spent.

KINDRIC RECEIVED BOTH OF JAITH'S MESSAGES and another from Evran in Candith on the second day of Agnith, when the *Papail*, the Responsible, the flagship of Ilwheirlane's fleet in Cibatan waters came in range of the relay. He took the news immediately to Admiral Irram Farrell whom he had come to admire immensely during the past year he had sailed with him.

"So you see, Admiral, it's imperative that the Senangan fleet be engaged before it can land Dekese's entire army in Cassinga," he finished, his thin face intent with anxiety.

Farrell nodded. "You say the army marched into Feshi two days ago?"

"Yes, sir, on Theosday."

"Take 'em at least a day to load an army that size, particularly with maliks, and the relay had no news that they've actually sailed. Still, that doesn't leave much time. I don't have enough ships to challenge half the Senangan fleet." Farrell frowned and turned to his first mate, "Talmon, set a course for Candith. Raise all sail. I want to be there as early tomorrow as possible."

Farrell turned back to Kindric, a mocking smile on his face. "Ilwheirlane supplied Cassinga with most of its ships. As this battle's on Cassinga's behalf, the least the Cassingan navy can do is participate. Gannet Wazzuli's a competent commander when Mamfe and his leeches aren't interfering with him. Send a message back to whoever the Varfarin has in Candith to notify Wazzuli to get the entire Cassingan fleet, every ship he has in port, ready to sail by tomorrow night. And have your agent get hold of Almon Jessell, Ilwheirlane's Ambassador. Tell them I'll be there by early tomorrow afternoon. I'll meet with Mamfe myself. Tell them to prepare him for my arrival.

JAITH GAVE NOTICE again when the Senangan fleet sailed out of Feshi. Evran gave Mamfe's court notice of that sailing before Admiral Farrell arrived and demanded an audience.

The audience chamber of the Royal Palace had changed since Njombe's time. The white-washed adobe walls and mosaic floors remained, but Njombe's throne had been replaced by a wide divan where Mamfe could recline, and he had supplied divans for his chief ministers as well, although Evran had declined the honor, as had Balek before him. Mamfe also liked an audience and to have servants about him to wait on him. As he supplied the same to his ministers, the chamber was often quite full of people.

It was even more crowded than usual when Admiral Farrell marched in with Ilwheirlane's Ambassador and the Admiral of Cassinga's navy trailing behind him. He strode up to the dais where Mamfe reclined and demanded, "Your majesty, I've ordered the ships currently under my command to assemble off the coast of the Gatoomatam. Admiral Wazzuli has thirty-eight ships currently in port and ready to sail. I demand that you order Wazzuli and his fleet to the Gatoomatam to resist the Senangan fleet. They must be ordered to sail today if they are to make the rendezvous in time."

Mamfe frowned. "All of them?"

"The Wizard Jaith estimates that the Senangan fleet will number approximately two hundred ships," Farrell said. "We'll need every ship Cassinga has to make any difference in the outcome of this invasion."

"That would leave Candith unprotected. What if they come here instead of to the Gatoomatam?" Mamfe demanded.

"Whatever their destination," Farrell said, "they have to round the Cape of Dirkou to reach any part of Cassinga. Attacking them at that point is your country's best hope of reducing the size of the army Dekese can land. As it stands now, if Dekese lands his entire force in the Gatoomatam or anywhere else along the coast, he can march straight to Candith and you won't stand a hope of stopping him.

What's more, your fleet could do nothing to protect you and would stand idle, having never been engaged. Is that what you want?"

Mamfe's dark skin took on a tinge of gray. "No. No," he spluttered, "but all of them?"

"Unless you commit your whole fleet right now, and order Wazzuli here," he nodded over his shoulder at the Admiral, "to sail immediately, I'll walk out of here and I'll order my entire fleet out of Cassingan waters. Then Dekese can sail or march on Candith with my blessing."

The gray tinge to Mamfe's skin increased and his eyes went to Ilwheirlane's Ambassador. "Master Jessell, can he do that?"

Jessell nodded soberly. "He commands the fleet, your majesty. It's within his authority. The decision might be questioned when he returned to Ilwheirlane, but that would be too late to do us any good."

"And the questions would cease, your majesty, when I explain that I withdrew from a combat that Cassinga's own navy was unwilling to fight. Ilwheirlane keeps a fleet in these waters primarily to retaliate for Senangan raids on Ilwheirlane, and only secondarily to support Cassinga. Engaging in a battle against the entire Senangan navy can only be justified if I do it in support of Cassingan naval forces."

Mamfe's eyes went to Graff Ulein on his divan to the Ahar's right, but the Lord Chamberlain, looking as distressed as his monarch, only asked, "But what can Wazzuli's fleet do against an armada of two hundred?"

"At least a quarter of that force will be troop ships, clumsy in the water and without much armament," Farrell said. "Our plan will be to sink as many of those ships as we can."

"That's all?" Ulein demanded. "You have no better plan than that?"

"Whatever more detailed plans I may have," Farrell stated, "this is not the place to discuss them." He turned back to Mamfe. "Now, your majesty, I need your decision. Does Wazzuli here sail, with my fleet to support him, or do I leave Cassinga to its fate."

Mamfe's eyes went to the Cassingan Admiral. "What do you think, Wazzuli?"

"The fleet is ready to sail, your majesty. I agree with Admiral Farrell that we have no choice but to attack at a point of our choosing."

Mamfe's form seemed to deflate as he sighed. "Then go. Take the navy. The Court will take refuge in the fortress at Dabbar."

THE FLEET FROM THE NYALI COAST reached Bamuli in the morning of Kyrasday. Nathan watched the troops debark and assisted Balek in deploying the various units to the military camps Balek had commanded be set up along the coast both north and south of Bamuli.

Bamuli was situated on the south shore of the mouth of the Gatooma River. The camps to the north were, therefore, located in the

Kipembawetam. The Governor of that district, on hearing of the size of the invasion force, had dispatched a third of the military forces stationed in his district to reinforce the militia camps in his territory. The remainder he put on alert to guard the rest of his own section of coast in case the Senangans should choose to land farther north than expected.

Pasquale Ulein, the Governor of the Gatoomatam, was intercepted by Balek attempting to flee with one hundred of his personal guard and the only armed ship of the Cassingan navy in Bamuli's harbor. Nathan and Lagura watched the encounter with glee. It was the only light moment in what had become a nightmare of last minute preparations for a seemingly hopeless conflict.

"It's not that I object to your departure, your excellency," Balek informed the Governor when he met him on the pier, "but the Gatoomatam, and all Cassinga, needs every soldier it can muster right now, and every ship."

"Let me pass," Pasquale demanded. "My brother is expecting me in Candith."

"Your brother, and the rest of Mamfe's Court, are no longer in Candith, but holed up in the Fortress of Dabbar," Balek said.

"All the more reason for me to join them," the Governor said. Nathan detected a slight tremor in his voice.

"I'd be delighted to assist you in joining them, but your bodyguard and this ship are needed here."

"I'm the Governor of the Gatoomatam. I'm entitled to the use of both the guard and the ship."

"A position you're relinquishing by your departure," Balek said, "which removes your entitlement to either." He paused and looked Pasquale up and down. "However, I really don't want to detain you against your will. There's an unarmed merchantman in port as anxious to leave as you are. He'd be delighted to take you on as a passenger, if I then authorize his departure."

Pasquale's face lightened. "He could leave soon?"

"Within the hour, if you wish," Balek said. "I'll escort you myself." He turned to the commander of the guard. "Return to your previous duty station."

The commander saluted. "Yes, my lord wizard."

Nathan chuckled at Balek's grimace.

JAODA, ACTING AS LOOKOUT, gave warning of the approach of the Senangan fleet to the narrow strait between the offshore islands and the Cape of Dirkou just before noon on Miunesday. She was in a small fishing boat just at the edge of Kindric's range of sight. He looked through her eyes to watch as the first ships neared the coast.

They waited tensely, their shields raised to their maximum extent, as were the shields of all the human wizards in the area. All their hopes depended on whether Dekese would choose the short route through the strait, or sense a trap and choose the much longer route around the offshore islands.

The battle plan Farrell had worked out with Wazzuli relied on Dekese choosing speed over caution, and the contingency plans, if Dekese did the unexpected, stood little chance of doing major damage to the Senangan fleet. Kindric and Jaoda sighed with relief when the Senangan fleet chose the course toward the channel between the Isles of Chirga, Morgai and Elak and the rocky cliffs along the south coast of the Cape. Kindric reported the arrival of the fleet to Farrell and the course it was taking.

"The advantage of dealing with Dekese," Farrell said, "is that Senrec would have taken the longer route just to be safe when he failed to hear from his spies. We were lucky there, that Evran had spotted the spies in Mamfe's Court and was able to eliminate them before they could send off a warning. But the lack of information would have put Senrec on the alert. Dekese assumes that the size of his force will overwhelm anything in his path."

"He may well be right, despite our efforts. He has more than double the ships we do," Kindric said.

"The emplacements along the cliff should even the odds a bit, and our purpose is not so much to defeat his fleet, as to destroy as many of the troop carriers as possible."

"I'm still amazed that Rand and Majaoda managed to get sixty-two cannon up there."

"One every hundred meters along the length of the cliffs," Farrell agreed, "but it leaves my ships short of cannon."

"But, as you pointed out, they'll only be firing one broadside at a time," Kindric said wryly.

"Until the Senangans break through my line," Farrell said grimly, "which they're bound to do eventually. Then we'll have to flee. Are the guns ready?" Farrell asked.

"Yes. Jaoda's and Majaoda's apprentices will relay your orders to men with signal flags as I send them.

"Tell them to hold their fire until I give the signal. We may have to let a few Senangan ships through the strait, but I want as many as possible of the troop carriers in the trap before I spring it," Farrell said. "They'll have soldiers on most of the ships, but the maliks will be on the carriers. Is Wazzuli in position?"

"His fleet's in Elak's south bay, where you told him to wait. Majaoda is with him. Shall I tell her to have him raise sail now?"

"Can you sense the end of the Senangan fleet?"

"Not yet. The farthest ships are still out of Jaoda's range."

"Then tell him to wait another ten minutes."

Kindric took a deep breath of the sea breeze coming from the southwest out of the Gulf of Mekkai and let it go. Tension was the enemy of concentration. He could see the red sails of the first ships approaching with his own sight now.

Jaoda was counting. She reached two hundred and fourteen. *That's the last of them,* she thought. *The troop carriers are in a bunch about two thirds of the way back.*

Kindric reported to Farrell.

"Signal Wazzuli to move," Farrell ordered.

"It's been over ten minutes. His sails are up. He's already moving south out of the bay," Kindric reported.

Farrell turned to his first mate, "Battle stations. Signal the fleet. Ready the guns and start heating the shot."

"Aye, aye, sir," Talmon said.

The Senangan ships sailed into the strait. Kindric watched them with his mind's eye. They moved majestically before the wind, their scarlet sails partially reefed for the passage. They were beautiful, Kindric thought with surprise, the red sails bold splashes of color against the deep aquamarine of the sea and the pale azure of the sky.

The battle plan devised by Farrell and Wazzuli divided their forces into three parts. Wazzuli, with all the Cassingan navy, would attack the rear of the Senangan fleet as soon as the major part of that force, including the troop carriers, entered the channel. At that point, also, the cannon on the cliff would begin firing down on the fleet.

The forty-three ships of Ilwheirlane's fleet that made Dirkou in time were divided into two units, twenty-one under the command of Vice Admiral Rolan Veddar, and twenty two under Farrell.

The Vice Admiral was to attack the front of the fleet at the same time Wazzuli attacked the rear. His fleet also included a number of the converted merchantmen from the Nyali Coast, which would be used as fireships and sailed in to ram Senangan ships and block the mouth of the strait as soon as the signal was given.

Farrell's force was to block the only other exit from the channel, a narrow deep-water passage between the islands of Morgai and Chirga. The *Papail* and the rest of Farrell's small force was currently at anchor in a cove on the southeast side of Morgai, out of sight of the channel. There was no passage between the islands of Morgai and Elak deep enough for a ship to pass through.

Farrell turned to Kindric. "Notify Veddar when the lead ships reach the mid point of the channel."

Kindric nodded and reached out with his mind to Rand, who was aboard the Vice Admiral's ship. Coordinating the timing of the attack of each unit was critical to the success of the operation.

Time passed. Finally, Jaoda reached the lead ship in Wazzuli's fleet and was picked up, joining her sister. Then the lead ships of the Senangan fleet began to emerge from the strait.

"Are the troop carriers in the channel?" Farrell asked.

"All but the last ten," Kindric told him.

"Where's Wazzuli?"

"He'll clear Elak's northwest point and be in view of the Senangan fleet in two minutes."

"Then that's the best we can do," Farrell said. "Tell Veddar and the shore crews to be ready in two minutes."

To Kindric the following hours became a blur of cannon fire, the sound of splintering wood and the cries and shouts of injured men. He spent his time alternately forwarding Farrell's commands and requests for status, healing the wounded, and warding off cannon fire from the Senangan ships when it was *Papail*'s turn to sail across the channel between Morgai and Chirga.

Farrell arranged his ships in a long line which twisted back on itself so that their course resembled a figure eight, with one of the ships of Ilwheirlane's fleet always broadside across the channel. The period when each ship was not exposed to Senangan fire was spent repairing damage and lugging cannon from one side to the other, so that, despite the cannon mounted at the top of the cliff, each ship always had a full broadside to send against the Senangans.

But, inevitably, as many of the Senangan officers had at least some wizard talent and could ward off cannon shot themselves, some Senangan ships survived the passage and were able to pump their own broadsides at the ships of Farrell's line. Then other ships farther from the gap would have to leave the line and take on the Senangan ship.

In between Kindric's own experiences of the battle, he felt the other wizards' and apprentices' experiences as he linked with them to relay information. In glimpses, he saw Wazzuli's fleet as it drove a wedge through the Senangan fleet to the troop carriers; he saw the fireships successfully ram five ships of the Senangan fleet and he watched the sea battle that followed as Veddar's ships closed the mouth of the channel for nearly an hour. And in between the other images, and his own mind's eye view of the battle, he saw the view from the cliff as the cannon there hammered at the exposed ships.

But all Senangan officers had at least a little wizard talent, and the Senangan fleet outnumbered its attackers by more than two to one. The moment came when Farrell had Kindric relay the order to retreat in the best order they could and flee southwest, so that, if any Senangan ships followed, they'd be drawn away from Cassinga.

Only twelve ships of Cassinga's navy escaped the Battle of Dirkou, all of them badly damaged. Admiral Wazzuli himself was killed when Jaoda failed to block the cannon shot that took the mast of his flagship and a splinter drove through his heart moments before the signal came for retreat. Twenty-one of the ships from Ilwheirlane survived. Vice Admiral Veddar was injured, but the Wizard Rand saved his arm, almost severed by heated shrapnel, and healed him.

One hundred and eight Senangan ships sank, including thirty of the fifty troop carriers. Yet Dekese III, Estahar of Senanga, despite the loss of half his fleet and over half of his land forces, chose to continue with the invasion.

XIV

4634, 464TH CYCLE OF THE YEAR OF THE TIGER
MONTH OF AGNITH

> *"The malik is a fearsome beast*
> *With taloned claws and horny beak.*
> *He's ready to make you his feast,*
> *If him you're fool enough to seek...*
>
> *"Now larin folk are said to mount*
> *Upon the backs of malik kind,*
> *When they go out upon a hunt.*
> *If you try this, you've lost your mind."*

> — EXCERPTS FROM "THE MALIK" PUBLISHED IN *A CHILD'S GUIDE TO THE LARIN AND OTHER BEASTLY TAILS* BY ENOGEN VARASH OF ELEVTHERAI, 4557

A S MOST OF THE SURVIVING SHIPS of the Senangan fleet had sustained at least minor damage, Dekese ordered his troops put ashore in the first suitable cove on the southern coast of the Gatoomatam. Balek had failed to foresee a landing so far south. With all the militia camps farther north, Cassinga could only field a small unit of scouts that had been patrolling the coast to locate and give warning of the approach of Dekese's forces. They were far too few in number to stop an army from coming ashore and those who did not flee to give warning were quickly overwhelmed.

When mustered on land, the remaining Senangan army consisted of approximately nine thousand foot soldiers and nine hundred and fifty malik cavalry. Dekese then marched them north along the coast toward Bamuli.

Unprepared as the Varfarin forces had been for such a southerly landing, they still managed to field a greater level of resistance than previous Senangan invasions had encountered. At first it was only scattered snipers, firing from the jungle and fleeing, but as Dekese's forces reached farther north into the areas where he had been expected to land, the resistance stiffened. While the main force of the Cassingan militia gave way before his malik troops, they maintained a constant barrage of small attacks against his army's rear and flanks.

Word of the naval battle had given hope to the Cassingan troops. And the time it took Dekese's forces to march to Bamuli gave the forces from the Nyali Coast time to integrate to some extent with the newly trained militia and the small number of experienced troops of the Gatoomatam.

When the Senangan army reached the cleared farmland south of Bamuli, it faced a Cassingan force of fourteen thousand. Moreover, a quarter of the two thousand halberdiers at the forefront of the Cassingan forces had faced malik cavalry in the past and survived.

"According to the books," Nathan said, watching the maliks emerging from the edge of the jungle to the south, "each malik rider is equal to five foot soldiers."

"Which makes our forces now evenly matched," Balek said with satisfaction.

They were standing on the flat roof of the building they planned to use as a field hospital. It was constructed of adobe and painted what Nathan considered a garish shade of pink.

"I still think we were doing better at harassing his forces from the sides and rear than we will with this frontal attack," Nathan said. "The Senangans lost more troops than we did with every encounter."

"Mosquito bites won't send Dekese back to Senanga with his tail between his legs," Balek said. "We have a chance of doing that now, thanks to Admiral Farrell and Admiral Wazzuli. We can't let that chance go to waste."

"You worry too much, Nathan," Lagura said. "After what the naval forces did to Dekese at Dirkou, I'd think you'd be anxious to see us do the same here."

"Farrell and Wazzuli didn't line their forces up against the entire Senangan fleet. They took advantage of terrain and laid a trap," Nathan said.

"So now you've become a military expert, have you?" Lagura said, eyeing him with asperity.

Nathan shook his head. "Marala agreed with me," he said. He still loved Lagura, but he'd begun to realize that she was never going to return his feelings for her. Moreover, these days she criticized everything he did. It was bad enough that Balek never listened to him, even though he was twenty-five and almost a journeyman wizard. Lagura was his junior.

"And you were both outvoted," Lagura said with satisfaction and turned back to watch the field of battle.

Nathan's jaw clenched, though he turned to watch as the claws of malik cavalry advanced across the fields toward the ranks of halberdiers. He realized that he was holding his breath and forced himself to breathe evenly again. But, he thought, if the mere sight of the maliks affects me that much, what does it do to those men on the ground with only thin, pointed stakes in their hands to ward off the most feared predators on all Tamar?

Then the maliks hit the line of halberdiers. And broke through. Nathan gasped. Some of the halberdiers held. A few maliks went down, but the points of the line that held were so widely separated they did not stand a chance against the next line of maliks.

Nathan watched in horror as the maliks then charged into the lines of foot soldiers, who stood even less chance against them than the halberdiers had done. Even their new guns had little effect against the combination of steel armor and the maliks' own bony chest plates. To bring a malik down, a halberdier had to bring his halberd up at the last minute, so the point went under the armor into the gap in the malik's bony plates between its front legs. Killing the rider only made the malik more dangerous and unpredictable.

"Call the retreat," Nathan said. "Save our forces for another day. We can go back to small raids and pick the maliks off one by one. Dekese may take Bamuli, but that's a long way from taking the whole Gatoomatam."

"It's too late," Balek said grimly. "If I call for retreat now, the maliks will just bring them down as they flee. We still outnumber them. And maliks are going down. I'm going to help fight. Are you coming?"

"I'm ready," Lagura said, her eyes lighting up at the challenge, her smile savage.

Nathan swallowed, but nodded. Maybe he could help to muster some of their forces and get them away so that they could at least harry Dekese and slow his takeover of the whole of the Gatoomatam.

The rest of the day became a blur to Nathan, as he used his wizard talent in ways he had never wanted to use it. He killed three maliks as they charged him, their vicious beaks extended. He stopped their hearts. One got so close to him before he could kill it that it fell across his foot and he could smell its fetid breath. He also slew countless linlarin.

The battle for him had come down to individual conflicts. He wished desperately for a way to oversee what was going on across the entire battlefield, but except for the obvious fact that the human forces around him were fleeing, he could get no larger view. He was not yet a strong enough wizard to send part of his mind out of body to get an overview and manage to do anything else at the same time.

By the end of the day he and Marala, with the eventual assistance of Balek and the others, managed to bring over four thousand of the Gatoomatam's defenders away from Bamuli. Others, he knew, had fled into the jungle. But over seven thousand of the human forces had died.

It gave him no satisfaction to know that nearly five thousand linlarin had also been killed, including nearly five hundred of Dekese's malik cavalry, which brought Dekese's losses to over three quarters of the force he'd started out with. Dekese had won. No Senangan invasion had been turned back in recent history, and Dekese's would not be the first.

"I owe you an apology," Lagura said, coming over to his tent that evening, her expression haunted by exhaustion and pain. They were camped in a clearing in the jungle some miles northwest of Bamuli and on the opposite side of the Gatooma River.

She pressed her lips together and looked at the ground. "You were right. We might have even managed to save the Gatoomatam, if we'd followed your advice."

Nathan remembered his resentment of her attitude that morning, but shook his head. "It was Balek's decision and he still thinks of me as a child. I love him, but his mind isn't flexible. He has no concept of subtlety, and he's certainly not a tactician."

"He's lived so long..." Lagura said.

"It's more than that," Nathan said. "I don't think Balek was ever capable of anything but the most direct approach. In some ways that's a virtue. You always know where he stands on any issue. But it isn't a virtue in combat. It's like a duelist telling his opponent every thrust he's going to make in advance. What Cassinga needs is a real tactician, someone from the Northern Hemisphere with Derwen's authority to take control of military matters."

"You're dreaming," Lagura said frowning.

"No," Nathan said. "I've talked to Marala and she's going to talk to the others on the Council. We're going to see that a petition is sent to Derwen. Even though we've lost the Gatoomatam, we've bought time. The Senangan losses were terrible. And we can use the force we have here to continue raiding them. It will be several years, maybe even a decade, if we harry them hard enough, before they'll be ready to launch another attack, and I'm willing to bet that the Senangan military won't trust Dekese again. So they'll be looking for a new military commander as well. We have to find someone better."

Lagura shook her head. "Won't Balek be mad a you?"

Nathan shrugged and shook his head. "Give him his due, Lagura. Balek respects anyone who stands up for what he believes. And, I think, after today, even Balek will admit he isn't a good field commander."

She sighed. "I'm sorry for more than what I said this morning."

Nathan looked at her. Even tired, dirty and disheveled with her clothes in rags she was beautiful. He felt a surge of hope as she turned her golden eyes up to him.

"I've treated you badly," she said. "I've been doing it for years, I guess. I know you think you're in love with me."

"I do love you, Lagura."

She cocked her head and her mouth twisted in a wry smile. "Actually, I don't think you love me as much as the idea of loving me. You don't really know me at all. You have an image you've built up in your mind. I look like that image, but I'm not her."

"I've known you since we were both children," he protested.

"But that's just it, Nathan," she said, her expression intent. "I lost my childhood in Senanga, before we ever met. And, while you may be a man now in most respects, in others you're still a child."

"I'm..."

"No, Nathan, hear me out," she said, cutting him off. "I'm fond of you, but despite your being the older in years, I think of you like a younger brother. That's not going to change. I'll never love you the way you want me to. So start looking for someone else, someone who's capable of loving you back. I'm not."

"You're tired," Nathan said, "and upset. I know you don't love me now, but..."

"You're not listening to me Nathan," she said sharply, and he saw anger in her eyes. "I will never love you. A part of me has enjoyed teasing you for years. A part of me enjoys hurting men." She sighed.

Nathan felt frozen. After all the rest of this day, he felt like he was living through a nightmare. But this was Lagura; he tried to imagine why she would say such a thing.

She was studying him. She said, "Bella says I've been getting even, but getting even with the wrong people. I suppose she's right. At least I know that I don't want to tease you or hurt you any more. Goodbye, Nathan." She turned and walked away, crossing the clearing and dodging the campfires until she reached her own tent. Nathan watched her all the way.

XV

4635, 464TH CYCLE OF THE YEAR OF THE DOLPHIN
MONTH OF REDRI

Halda less puat reba less.

"Great success requires great risk."

— ESLARIN PROVERB

IT WAS SPRING IN CIBATA. The palasarin trees drooped with the heavy weight of their scarlet blooms all around the palace grounds in Candith. And on Jehansday, the fourth day of Redri, while rain swept across the Bay of Dagana and added the weight of water to make the brilliant blooms sag almost to the ground, Nathan stood next to Balek in a crowded audience chamber of the palace as Juba Isiro gave birth to her child by Rainal Sartori.

Juba was eighteen. Nathan could hardly remember seeing her since her father had stopped her wizard training. But Rainal had found a way. He looked across the room at the soon-to-be father, who stood by the birthing platform clutching Juba's hand. There were beads of sweat on Rainal's forehead, as though the exertion were as much his as Juba's. But they were in rapport, so maybe he did feel her pain as much as she did.

Nathan shook his head. This should have been a private moment for them, but Mamfe had turned the proceedings into a circus, saying that the whole Court should witness his daughter give birth to a wizard.

Nathan hoped Mamfe would not be disappointed, but he knew enough of the complexity of the genetics involved in wizard talent to know that there was no way at this point to be certain of the child's potential. Further, Mamfe had boasted of a grandson, but Nathan's sight told him that the baby was a girl. Why had no one told Mamfe? Rainal, while still only an apprentice wizard, would have been able to determine the sex of the child months ago. Perhaps Juba hadn't wanted her father to know?

JUBA RELAXED from yet another contraction, knowing that her daughter would be born soon. The daughter that would buy her freedom from her father's authority. She might be feeling the pain of birth now, but it was worth any pain to escape from her father and his friends.

Rainal couldn't marry her. Wizards married by the linking of minds, and she would never be a strong enough wizard to link with him, even if her father hadn't stopped her training. But having a child by a wizard meant that both she and the child would be the wizard's responsibility. Her father couldn't now force her to marry one of his cronies. He could no longer force her to do anything at all. She was free.

She would call her daughter Palesla, Pala for short, for the heavy scarlet blossoms blooming on the day of her birth, and for the weight of Mamfe's control that her birth had lifted from Juba's back. Rainal had said that he couldn't tell before the child's birth what kind of wizard talent she might have, but Juba felt in her heart that her daughter would be a good wizard, perhaps even a great one, and her training could not be interfered with by Mamfe.

4637, 464TH CYCLE OF THE YEAR OF THE BEAR
MONTH OF TORIN

"IF I HAVE THE POTENTIAL, why can't I become a great wizard like the human wizards of old?" Saranith demanded of Rethen, their teacher. Four years had passed since her mother had died and her will had developed rapidly with the tutoring she received from her linlarin kin. Without the dye her mother had used on her hair, the copper striping had emerged. She stood out from the other linlarin children like a flaming brand. She had made no friends among them. Luri remained her only confidant and companion.

"You're a linlar, my child. You have no need to use the inner eye of the wizard to see. You have two perfectly good eyes already." The old teacher looked patient, Luri thought, as though he'd been asked such questions by many talented children.

"The Estahar is a linlar and he has the high sight. The Kulhar has it. Aketi says his mother is going to teach it to him when he's older. If he can learn it, why can't I?" Saranith demanded.

"You're related to the royal family, that's true," Rethan said, "but your relationship was only discovered when you were too old for the treatment the others were given. All of the children of the royal family were blindfolded through much of their early youth, forcing them to use their inner eye. It was a great cruelty. Dekese, Mutesa and even Aketi suffered to gain their sight. Power such as the great wizards wield demands a price."

"If I were blindfolded now, wouldn't my inner eye develop?" she demanded.

"It is less likely, and it would be a much greater hardship for you. A baby that can barely walk doesn't need to see as well as a girl with chores and duties to perform. Also, a baby's vision is weak. A few layers of cloth with a strip of lead between them will serve as a blindfold. You could see right through anything short of thick lead shielding, and you could hardly carry that on your head. No, child, it's too late for you to be concerned with such things," he chided her.

"But if I wanted to try, even if it was a hardship?" she asked.

"I hardly think that your aunt would permit such a thing," Rethan said. "You're too young to understand, but there are prices too high for any sane person to pay."

Saranith stared at him with her blank, expressionless face and said, "Some people fear to risk the least coin even if it might gain them a fortune. I'll not be bound by your fears or my aunt's dictates."

Luri expected Rethan to reprimand her, then remembered that Rethan was little better than a slave, a houseless linlar whose wizard talent was too weak to gain him a position in the army. He had no right to punish them. Nevertheless, Luri would never have dared to speak to anyone the way Saranith had. He sighed and felt uneasy at the glint in her eyes.

Later, after the class, Luri said, "You already have the strongest will of us all, Sara. Why do you work so hard and why are you so concerned about the high sight?" They were sitting in the orchard outside the Kulhar's palace.

Saranith looked at him with the expressionless face in which even Luri had trouble reading emotion, although they were alone now and she usually let her guard down more when they were alone. Finally, she said, "Power is safety, Luri. The other children leave you alone now because I'm strong. If I'd been strong enough, like the great wizards were, I might have been able to save my mother."

"That's crazy," Luri said. It was true that, since she'd been accepted as a linlar, none of the other children had dared to tease him, but sometimes Luri wished she weren't so aggressive, didn't take quite so much responsibility on her shoulders. "There was nothing you could have done once Mutesa found out you were a linlar and who your father was."

"Only because I'm weak," Saranith answered. There was an expression on her face that frightened Luri. "I have to learn to be strong, strong enough to protect everyone I care about. My mother knew Mutesa would kill her, and she made me promise not to interfere. She thought I could make a difference. So I have to learn how to be strong. If I don't, Aketi will have us at his mercy when we're older. You know he and Jadne hate us."

Luri licked his lips nervously. He was afraid of both Aketi and Jadne but sometimes Saranith's single-mindedness frightened him more. Once she had an idea in her head, he knew from experience that nothing could sway her. "Rethen said that what you want is impossible," he said.

"No! He didn't say it was impossible, Luri. He said it would be a much greater hardship; that the blindfold that would work on a baby wouldn't work on me." She sighed and for a moment she looked as uncertain as he had ever seen her. "He said that power demanded a price. Wouldn't achieving such power be worth any price?" she continued, her strange, green-yellow eyes suddenly aflame.

THAT NIGHT SARANITH CREPT SOUNDLESSLY down the long hall from the children's dormitory to the main hall of the mansion, and from there down the stone staircase to the corridor near the kitchen, hugging the shadows and avoiding the flickering light cast by the oil lamps. Her long striped hair was spread across her back like a silken curtain and her thin nightgown was of a dark material.

The halls and corridors were empty, however, and no one saw her as she slipped into the kitchen where she had once spent so much of her time. Her bare feet were soundless on the worn carpet. She paused at the entry, her bright green-amber eyes searching the shadows, but she had chosen the time carefully. All the evening kitchen staff had gone to bed and the bakers wouldn't be up to start on the next day's bread for another hour. She tip-toed across the room to the great, open fireplace where a whole seral could be roasted, turning on the spit. She had feared the fire might have died down too far, but the embers were still hot enough for her purpose.

In front of the fire she hesitated, gazing entranced at the complex of forces in the glowing embers. There was beauty in the fire and in the swirling of the air currents above it, the beauty of motion and heat, the everlasting dance of the elements. She would lose all this.

But not for long! So she'd be blind for a few months, maybe even a year, but she'd regain her sight and with it the potential for greater vision. Vision and power! Angry with herself for her momentary lapse, she turned her face from the fire and lifted a poker from the rack beside the hearth, driving its point deeply into the bed of glowing embers.

"Everything has a price," she whispered, "and the greater the goal, the greater the price." She was young and the bones of her face were still padded with the soft flesh of youth, but her chin was set and in that moment of resolution she looked much older than her twelve years.

There was a sound from the back of the room and she sank into the shadows beside the fireplace, but it was only Sather, the old iskrail, stirring in his sleep.

"Stupid," she whispered to herself, upset that she had missed seeing him when she entered.

The poker was hot. Saranith licked her finger and touched a point near the end. It hissed with the heat. Satisfied, she wrapped part of the cooler end of the poker with her nightgown so that she could lift it without burning her hands. Then she pressed the hot end of the poker into her right eye. Although she had some control over the nerve endings and attempted to block the pain, she wasn't totally successful and she couldn't prevent a gasp of agony. She had to struggle to retain consciousness and the poker fell down on the hearth. Her face convulsed in a rictus of pain and overriding will. She overcame the dizziness and blotted out all feeling. She could not falter now. She lifted the poker again and put out her left eye.

This time all her skill and self control could not block the agony. Blinded and in torment, Saranith fought for enough control to enable her to shove the poker back into the fire before she gave way and passed out.

Book II

THE WINDS OF CHANGE

Amne tan marheod a amvalod ba acad ren rhe.

*"The universe's only unchanging truth
is that all things change."*

— ESLARIN PROVERB

XVI

4641, 465TH CYCLE OF THE YEAR OF THE DRAGON
MONTH OF ILFARNAR

> *"No person of mixed blood shall be permitted to dance
> on any stage regularly used by any group sponsored by this
> organization. If this rule is broken, the offending theatre
> shall be declared off limits to all groups so sponsored.
> Furthermore, there can be no rehearing of the theatre's status
> for a period of ten years following the stage's last use by the
> non-sponsored dancer or dancers..."*

— EXCERPT FROM THE CHARTER OF THE HAILARIN DANCER'S GUILD

LEAP AND SPIN. Her head and her lungs ached and she jerked coming out of the spin, dizzy, and only barely able to maintain her balance. Too much to drink last night, she acknowledged, but the oblivion the alcohol granted her was too tempting to resist. She dragged her mind back to concentrate on the precision needed for the steps crossing the stage. A gesture then, so hard to reach up when her arms felt like lead. Bend and rise and leap again, but her leap had no height. The heat was oppressive. The air was too thick; she could not breathe and the pain in her head was beginning to blur her vision. A series of pirouettes, another bend and another leap. Her daughter Cyrene, only twelve, could get better height on her jumps than she was managing tonight.

Yet landing hurt. Her feet were in agony, but there would be no blood. She could no longer reach high enough, or hold the point long enough to cause blood, yet strangely the pain was greater now than it had been when she did bleed. Thank Jehan the dance was nearly over. Only one more leap, the highest she could reach, but her vision blurred. Her balance failed on the landing and her foot slipped. She fell.

There was a moment of startled silence. Then the audience laughed. Einara lay on the hard, rough surface of the carnival stage gasping for breath. It felt like a moment out of her worst nightmares. But it was real. The pain was too great for it not to be real. Her hip hurt where she had fallen on it. Her whole body ached. But the agony of her humiliation was worse.

The audience's laughter shifted to boos.

Someone cried, "Get her off the stage."

Another added, "We paid to see a dancer, not a clown."

Still Einara could not force herself to move. The shame was too overwhelming. Then she felt a tug on her arm and her daughter's voice said, "Come on. Get up. You can't just lie here. Josie needs to send another act on."

She rose then, staring at Cyrene, the cause of her exile from the Dancer's Guild, the beginning of all her failures. She looked around her at the carnival tent and at the audience booing her. Where was she? Had not Josie told her they would be performing in Dandaburra today? Dandaburra was the place where she had first met Perrin. But she could not dance in his theatre now. She could not dance anywhere anymore. She could no longer dance at all. "When I can no longer dance, I will die," she thought. How many times have I said that? She sighed, but what she felt was almost relief.

Cyrene offered her arm, but Einara shook her head, took a deep breath and walked from the stage. "You can tell Josie that I won't be dancing tomorrow," she said. "He'll probably be relieved. You could have done a better job than I did this evening."

Cyrene's eyes widened. "You really think I'm ready?"

Einara smiled wryly. "You're quite good enough to dance for the chorus here. Not for the Dancer's Guild. They won't take you no matter how good you get to be, but Josie's already said he'd be happy to have you in the chorus."

"But what will you be doing?"

Einara rubbed a hand across her forehead, wishing she could wipe away her pounding headache. A drink would help, but then she would be drunk again tomorrow. No. She would face tomorrow sober, die with some dignity. "I'll complete the cycle," she said, meeting her daughter's eyes. "I'll return to Tiburra. You were conceived there. Have I told you that before?"

Cyrene shook her head. "No. But I'd like to see the place. Can I go with you?"

Einara looked down at the floor and sighed, but Cyrene would have to face her death either way. And the falls were very beautiful. "If you wish to come, you may."

CYRENE HAREEL STARED DOWN at the twisted, dead body of her mother. Einara lay on the rocks at the base of the cliffs next to Tiburra Falls. The water in the pool below the rocks was pink with her blood, although even as Cyrene watched the spray from the falls was washing the color away.

Cyrene closed her eyes, but the image didn't disappear. She screamed.

Later, when her mother's body had been taken away, she walked the path she had walked with her mother that morning and stared for a long time at the little, grassy glen where she had been conceived. So her mother had felt her death completed a cycle, a cycle begun with Cyrene's conception?

Cyrene shook her head. Einara had always said that, when she could no longer dance, she would die. But her mother had chosen the oblivion of alcohol that had accelerated the destruction of her talent. Others may have decreed her ejection from the Dancer's Guild, but she had selected her own path to self-destruction. Cyrene had watched her choose that route night after night for half the years of her life.

Cyrene turned and walked back to the hotel, her hands clenching into fists. Maybe she'd never be acceptable to the Dancer's Guild, but that was their loss. She'd be as great a dancer as her mother some day. Greater. Dancing in a half-breed troop on carnival stages might not offer the prestige of dancing in a theatre, but she'd be so good people would flock to see her anyway.

XVII

4643, 465TH CYCLE OF THE YEAR OF THE LIZARD MONTH OF ANOR

"Now that sailor I met said he loved only me,
But he lied, like all sailors will do,
For the love of his life is the sea, not me,
And to it he will always be true."

— VERSE FROM "THE SAILOR AND THE SEA" COLLECTED IN *SONGS OF THE SEA AND SHORE*, EDITED BY BAR PANYARA

S IX YEARS AFTER SARANITH put out her eyes she graduated with honors from the Senangan Naval Academy at Feshi. Luri Abandu graduated with her, although without honors. Soon after, they took their first posting.

The sky was cloudless as the boat pulled away from the shore. A brisk wind whipped strands of Luri's dark hair across his eyes and snapped the pennant mounted on the stern. Whitecaps marched across the Gulf of Mekkai and the water heaved with a choppy surge even in the sheltered lee of the Point of Tagur. As the boat danced on the uneven waves Luri huddled as low as he could on his seat, clenching his teeth and praying he could control his nausea until they reached the schooner *Kanakar* at anchor beyond the naval docks.

Two seamen belonging to the Port Authority were rowing them out to their ship. The little boat rose and fell, dipping its bow into the waves and sending spray over passengers and crew alike. Luri was soon wet and cold as well as sick. Occasionally he glanced wistfully at Saranith sitting erect beside him. She looked excited and eager with her head raised to sniff the salt scent of the sea. Her face was wet with spray. Even the faceted rubies that filled her eye sockets were wet, the salt water dripping from them like sparkling tears.

"How near are we?" she asked in the intimate mode so that only he could sense her question.

He diverted his eyes and squinted against the wind and spray until he saw the sleek lines of the schooner at anchor. *"Soon,"* he thought back, knowing she didn't want the oarsmen to hear.

"Warn me when we're about to pull alongside," she commanded.

"*Of course.*" Luri felt a moment's hurt that she hadn't trusted him to warn her without being asked. He always warned her of the times when she would need to start using her inner vision. Watching the distance narrow between the small boat and the anchored schooner, he couldn't remember a time when he hadn't served her, even before she had put out her eyes.

"*It's time,*" he warned as the boat drew up along the starboard side of *Kanakar*.

Saranith didn't answer in words, but her hand reached out and squeezed his arm. She wouldn't need his help again; she was watching now for herself, seeing with the inner eye of a powerful wizard. Her vision was keener than his, but that vision was tiring for her to maintain for long periods of time, although her strength grew steadily. She refused to restore her natural eyes. She felt that using her native were-sight would slow the development of her inner sight, and nothing must interfere with that. Instead, he was her eyes whenever she needed rest, as he had been her eyes during the two and a half months when she had truly been blind. He was the only one to whom she exposed her weakness.

A crewman from the schooner lowered a rope ladder. It hung down the side of the ship, its end alternately buried in the surging waves or exposed, dripping against the planks of the ship. The boat bobbed in the water near it like a cork. Luri suddenly realized that, to reach the ladder, he'd have to jump the gap between the boat and the side of the ship, a gap that constantly shifted as both the schooner and the boat rode the waves. As he hesitated, Saranith rose, balanced for a moment and leapt across the seething stretch of blue-green water. Then she scrambled up the side of *Kanakar* with the natural agility of a monkey.

Luri swallowed nervously and looked down again at the boiling surge between him and the frail security of the rope ladder. Fear intensified the knotting of his stomach caused by the motion of the boat. How had Saranith managed to leap so far across that swirling maelstrom? He saw himself miss the ladder and get dragged down into the dark, turbulent water, and suddenly his stomach revolted and he sank to his knees and was thoroughly sick over the side. He hardly heard the jeers of the oarsmen; he was too miserable to care what they thought of him.

"Come on, Luri. It's only a short jump," Saranith called from the deck.

The sound of her voice woke him out of his dazed misery. He looked up and saw her standing above him outlined against the bright sapphire sky, her ruby eyes flashing in the sunlight, her black and red hair blowing about her like a silken banner. She was so strong. It shamed him for her to see him as he was, cowardly and weak, but he couldn't help himself. He felt too weak to even stand and there was no way he was going to be able to jump across the abyss of seething water that separated him from the ship. "I can't, Sara," he cried up to her. "I can't do it."

He saw her frown and turn away and in that moment he realized that he might be better off dead. What would it matter if the cold green water swallowed him? Surely it wouldn't hurt for long and then he'd be dead. That would be better than living if Saranith lost her faith in him. The memory of her frown sent a jolt of fear through him. He struggled awkwardly to his feet and his arms flailed in the air as he tried to balance in the heaving boat.

"It's all right!" Saranith called down to him. "They can lower a chair for you."

He looked up again and saw her waving from the deck. The meaning of her words had barely penetrated when the boat beneath him twisted in a new direction as one of the oarsmen stroked his oar. Luri's feet went out from under him and the cool, salty water closed over his head. His sandals slipped off his feet as he kicked desperately for the surface. He was not a strong swimmer and the choppy waves kept slapping him in the face, blinding him and making breathing difficult even when he managed to regain the surface. It was not until he felt the rope ladder rub against him that he realized he had fallen between the boat and the ship and was now right next to the ladder he had thought never to be able to reach. He grabbed it convulsively and hauled himself up to the deck.

The officer of the watch grinned, his white teeth startling against the coal black of his skin, as Luri pulled himself over the side. "Glad to have you aboard," he said when Luri gave his name. "I'm Tazo Kenge, first farail. The arrai's ashore."

Luri had to bend his neck back to meet the officer's eyes. They were dark eyes, almost as dark as his skin, but they were bright with mirth. Luri looked around and saw the officer's grin reflected on most of the other faces around the deck. Only Saranith looked concerned for him. "I'm glad to have made it," he said lightly, mocking himself. It was the only way he'd ever managed to deal with his own ineptitude.

The deck was a hive of activity as stores that had been brought from shore were taken below. He and Saranith were the lowest ranked of the officers aboard, having just graduated from the Academy. Saranith, of course, was superior to him. Her grade had been the highest in their class, while he had been near the bottom. In fact, Luri knew that he wouldn't have been posted to a ship if Saranith had not interceded for him. Her relationship to the Estahar did allow her certain privileges, for which he was very grateful.

"Arrai's coming aboard, rai," reported the watch.

Luri looked down to where another shore boat was pulling along side. Arrai Harar Mazilek came aboard much more gracefully than Luri had done. He was a tall, rangy man with thin lips and a nose like a raptor's beak.

Saranith presented herself and reported her assignment and Luri followed her lead.

"Don't usually carry a fifth officer," the Arrai commented, eyeing Luri curiously. "No separate quarters available."

"He's to be quartered with me, rai," Sara said quickly. "He's my consort."

Mazilek eyed Saranith up and down and Luri could sense his hostility. "You're here to work, Farail Kamrasi. When you're on my ship you're under my command, no matter what your connections are. Do you understand?"

Sara saluted gravely. "I wouldn't want it any other way, rai. I asked for this posting because you're known for your discipline."

The arrai nodded but with less apparent hostility. "Very well. You're dismissed. Kenge, show them their quarters."

Mazilek was a well known commander. Many of his crews had grown rich off the prizes he had taken. He preferred an independent command and *Kanakar* rarely sailed as part of one of Senanga's pirate fleets.

On this voyage, the schooner was headed for the southern waters of the Lessar Jevac, the waters that carried human shipping to and from Kandorra. Over the following days the ship clawed east under reduced sails, the southwesterly wind laying her over so that the deck was constantly sloped.

Mazilek drilled the crew constantly. They practiced sailing maneuvers and gunnery until both the officers and men responded with almost mechanical efficiency.

By the third day, Luri, who had been seasick since the ship weighed anchor, wished only for an end to his misery. The wind sang in the rigging over his head. The day was cloudless and beautiful, but he huddled on the port side of the main deck after the last drill aware of nothing but the constant motion that intensified his nausea.

The schooner climbed the great rolling swells of the sea one by one. First the port bow nosed into a wave and rose, tipping the ship sideways and back until the bowsprit heaved up toward the sky. As the wave passed under the bow, the bowsprit climbed more steeply. Then, while the ship was still rolling, the port bow shook free of the crest of the wave and started the slide down the far side, foam creaming around it. The ship leveled on the crest and, finally, as the bow descended, the stern rose as the last of the wave passed under it. For each wave the ship completed this corkscrew roll. Pitch, roll, heave, roll. And each movement made Luri sicker.

"Luri, you can't go on like this," Saranith said, coming up behind him.

He shuddered. He'd tried to keep out of her sight as much as possible so she wouldn't notice how sick he was, but she always discovered his weaknesses. "I can't help it, Sara."

"No, I understand that," Saranith said wryly, "but you should have told me sooner. I can help. It's a matter of adjustment of the inner ear. Now, hold still."

She put her hand on his shoulder and he felt a strange feeling in his head. His ears tingled. Moments later, the intense nausea began to fade. He swallowed.

"Isn't that better?"

He nodded ruefully. "Much better."

"Mazilek has his eye on us. We have to perform better."

"I'll try."

She smiled and hugged him. "I know you will, Luri. I've always depended on that."

That night, feeling strong enough to make love to Sara for the first time since they'd sailed, he thought that a career at sea might not be so bad. At least his duties were clearly defined and, so far, within his capabilities. And he could be with Sara.

XVIII

4646, 465TH CYCLE OF THE YEAR OF THE MALIK
MONTH OF MINNETH

*"Where possible, the element of surprise is extremely
valuable to a plan of attack. It can enable lesser forces to
overcome much greater ones. Even when the numbers are
equal, or in the attacker's favor, it reduces bloodshed."*

— FROM *THE COLLECTED WRITINGS OF VYDARGA THE RED*

P ALA ISIRO WOKE TO PAIN AND THE IMAGE of a lance being
driven into her chest. Then her mind was bombarded with a host
of sensations: the copper scent of blood, the rank musk of angry
maliks, more pain and terror. She carefully built up the mind shield
her father had taught her, but she still felt the agony. She had to
breathe. She had to get up. The man whose death she'd felt had been a
gate guard.

She sat up slowly, fighting off the nausea that the intense fear and
pain had brought. It was not her pain, not her fear. She was eleven,
too old to panic like a baby.

But it was all right to be afraid. Nathan had told her that everyone
felt fear. It was how you dealt with it that mattered. Pala concentrated
on controlling her breathing as she threw off her covers and her night-
dress, grabbed the pants and shirt made from the camouflage material the militia used and scrambled into them. Her regular clothes
wouldn't be suitable for the jungle if the fortress fell and she had to
escape.

The fort was being invaded by Senangan forces. She could hear the
screams, and even her mind shield couldn't entirely block the flaring
images of maliks. They were in the outer courtyard. She extended her
own vision through the window as she stuffed extra clothes in her
emergency pack and saw that the outer gate was down on the ground
with Senangan infantry troops pouring in over it.

Her brother Niolan! He was in the room across the hall. He wasn't
as sensitive as she was, but no one with any mind sense could have
slept through the death cries, and Nio hadn't yet learned to shield
himself properly. She gave her room a last look to see if she'd forgotten something, then crossed the hall.

Niolan was standing in his crib, his eyes wide and frightened, but he wasn't crying. She reached out to him with her mind, *"It's all right, Nio. I'll help you shield it all out."*

But his mind was shielded. He must have reacted instinctively.

She heard a sound in the hall and ducked behind the door as her mother rushed in.

"Nio, Nio. It scared you, too, didn't it. But we'll be all right. Really we will. We've just got to escape," Juba cried.

"Will we, Mother?" Pala said, stepping out from behind the door and eyeing her mother's nightgown with disgust. "And how are you going to escape through the jungle dressed like that?"

Juba turned around quickly at the sound of Pala's voice. "Thank Maera you're all right. When I saw you weren't in your bed I was terrified."

"You expected me to sleep through that?" Pala said, referring to the screaming coming from the courtyard. She picked up a pile of clean cloths for Nio's bottom and stuffed them into his emergency pack, then turned back to her mother who was cradling Nio in her arms and crooning to him. "Come on," she said, grabbing her mother's arm and pulling her back into the hall. "We'll get your clothes on our way to the escape passage. You can dress in the tunnel."

Pala knew all the escape routes for wherever she and her mother stayed. Her father, Rainal, had seen to it that emergency procedures were drilled into Pala from the time she took her first step.

The fort that guarded the pass at Tibati had been built into the mountainside. The commander's private quarters, which Pala, Niolan and Juba shared with Juba's lover, Commander Rovan Millet, were built into the mountain. The builders had also included a means of escape for the commander and his family, should the fortress fall. There was a hidden door which only a wizard with the high sight, an eslar or a fallar could see. The tunnel behind it ran through the mountain to a ravine more than two kilometers to the northeast.

Pala got her mother and Nio to the room her mother shared with Rovan and found her mother's emergency pack in her closet. When she turned round, however, she found Juba getting into a dress. She sighed, but it was too late to try and change her mother's clothes. She grabbed the camouflage and added it to her mother's pack. Whatever else her mother had forgotten would have to be left as well.

She heard a crash from somewhere below. It sounded as if the gate to the inner compound had been forced. That meant they had only minutes left. She picked up Nio, who was silent and pale with shock. A quick mind touch showed that he was still shielded.

"I'll get the panel open in Rovan's study," she told her mother, picking up Nio's and her packs. She couldn't carry her mother's as well so she said, "Don't forget to bring the pack with you."

"What about Rovan?" Juba said.

"He must be with his troops, trying to hold the Senangans back," Pala said. "He knows where the panel is. He'll come if he can get free."

She took a deep breath and said, "Be sure to put on sturdy shoes. You'll need them in the tunnel and in the jungle afterward. And hurry up."

She couldn't run while carrying Nio and the packs, but she made her way to Rovan's study as quickly as she could. She had to put Nio and the packs down to open the panel. It had a tricky catch hidden in the carving on the paneling. Once she had it open, she grabbed up Nio and the packs and carried them through into the tunnel.

Her mother still hadn't come. The sounds of fighting from below were getting louder. She guessed from their location and the occasional images still breaking through her mind shield that the Senangan troops had forced the back door into the kitchen. They hadn't yet reached the stairs.

She put Nio and the packs down and ran back into the hall. She saw her mother heading for the staircase. She ran and caught her mother's arm. "You can't go that way. You have to come to the tunnel with me now."

"But Rovan..."

"He'll come if he can. If you go down there now you'll just endanger him further."

Her mother gave a convulsive sigh and allowed herself to be led back to the den and into the tunnel. Once she had Juba inside, Pala closed the panel carefully, making sure it was completely sealed. Then she picked up Nio and the two packs she'd carried in and grasped her mother's hand to lead her farther inside.

"Can't we wait here for Rovan?" Juba asked.

Pala grimaced at the irony of her mother asking her permission, but Juba always needed support.

"No, Mother," Pala said. "We have to get as far into the tunnel as possible so the Senangans can't sense our presence."

"I thought the tunnel was shielded?"

"It's supposed to be. But I don't want to risk our lives relying on that. It was built over a thousand years ago. The shielding could have worn down."

"Anyway," she added, "we need to get to the other end and out into the jungle as soon as possible. Hopefully we'll be able to find some of the militia and warn them that the Senangans have taken the Pass."

Pala could see quite well in the dark tunnel with her wizard sight, but there was a lantern hanging from a metal rod driven into the wall and she lit it for her mother's benefit. Even with the light, Pala couldn't get her mother very far before Juba insisted on stopping to wait for Rovan. After several minutes, however, she got her mother moving again by telling her that the lantern wouldn't last forever and they could wait at the other end of the tunnel. It took hours to reach the tunnel's exit.

By that time she was exhausted and ready for a rest herself, even though she knew that was unwise. Her relief was almost overwhelming when she felt Nathan's mind touch, *"Pala? You got away then. We were almost afraid to hope."*

"I've got Nio and my mother with me," she answered. *"Juba wanted to wait for Rovan, but I don't think he got to the panel. Do you know if he's dead?"*

"No. We know the Senangans took the fort. We don't know if they took prisoners. I was about to go in and see what the situation was, and if it might be possible to rescue you. I should have known you'd take care of that for yourself."

"Dad taught me how to get away," she thought. *"But someday maybe I'll be able to do better than that."*

"You've a strong will, Pala, but you're only eleven. Believe me, getting away and bringing Nio and Juba with you was a great accomplishment."

She smiled. *"Then you can take care of them now."* She turned to her mother. "Mother, Nathan's here. He'll look after you and Nio now."

Nathan was Pala's favorite of all the wizards she knew except for Rainal, her father. She knew she and her family would be safe now. She sat down and let herself fall into sleep.

XIX

4646, 465TH CYCLE OF THE YEAR OF THE MALIK
MONTH OF MINNETH

Ulmla ba ceanle acadend qua atla.

"Hindsight is always clearer than foresight."

— ESLARIN PROVERB

A WEEK LATER and safely back in Candith, Pala was excited by the prospect of her first Council meeting. As Rainal was Evran's apprentice, she was also counted as Evran's apprentice and so should have attended many such meetings.

Juba hadn't been willing to live in Candith, however. Too close to her father for comfort, she said. So Pala hadn't ever attended a meeting before today. Evran and her other teachers, like Balek and Nathan, had come to wherever she was living, which in recent years had been wherever Rovan was posted.

Pala brushed a fly away from her face. Juba was distraught. She loved Rovan, Pala acknowledged. And Rovan's fate was still unknown. The Senangans had taken some prisoners, but no one had yet managed to identify them. Most of the soldiers defending the fort had died.

Pala looked around the large room in Balek's quarters where the meeting was being held. Sunlight flooded in from three arched windows facing north. The midsummer heat was enervating. But she was safe with the wizards now. Rainal had told her that she would be living with him from now on and that her training would intensify. She hugged herself and her mouth widened in a smile of pure happiness.

NATHAN NOTICED THE JOY on Pala's face, and couldn't help smiling himself. She had done well, and he agreed with Rainal that her future growth and education could no longer be left in Juba's hands. Juba meant well, but the only assertive thing she had ever done in her life was to persuade Rainal to get her pregnant.

Pala was a sword forged of much finer metal. If she lived to become the wizard she gave promise of being then Cassinga might have a future, after all. If, that is, we can keep enough of the country intact for her to inherit.

Nathan surveyed the room, his attention lingering, as it always did, on Lagura. She was sitting next to Bella on one of the couches. Their hands were linked together. Lagura had been true to what she had told him after Bamuli. She never flirted with him now, hardly spoke to him at all. He had come to understand that her relationship with Bella might be permanent But even after twelve years he hadn't found anyone else that made him feel the way she had. Perhaps he never would.

He tore his eyes away and noted that everyone present seemed to have settled down.

"Does anyone have any comments to make?" Balek asked.

"Choma warned us that something was going on," Evran said from his seat next to Kaoda and Selene. "We should have known it meant another invasion."

"Jaith reported no unusual activity in the fleet. The Senangans have always come by sea before. How could we have known?" Balek asked.

"We should have been prepared for a land assault this time round. After all, Dekese's worst losses were at sea, at Dirkou," Kaoda said. "But none of us," he looked pointedly at Balek, "have any insight into the military mind. It's not what we've trained for. Our instincts are all wrong. We need someone who understands tactics like the new Senangan commander, this Bashan Kamrasi. He's another of Dekese's cousins, and this one seems to be the equal of Senrec. We have to find someone who can out think him."

"We asked Derwen to find someone with military training years ago, after the last invasion," Balek protested.

"So we ask again," Marala said, from her backward perch on one of the straight chairs by the worktable, "and this time we attach some urgency to the request. With the success of this most recent invasion, Senanga won't wait long before trying to take the Kunguatam or an even larger chunk. Cassinga isn't going to last long if they succeed with their next attack as well as they did with this one."

"Our scouts hadn't even noticed the buildup in the Gatoomatum," Nathan said quietly. "They came across the river in five places and swept across the Kipembatam. They'd have succeeded even without taking the fort." He was glad that Marala had spoken before he could say the same thing. Balek still had a tendency to brush off anything he said because of his youth. Yet in a few years he would qualify as a full wizard and, in some ways, he felt that he was already wiser than Balek. Balek was strong, straightforward and honest, but he was also rigid and, Nathan had come to realize, unimaginative. He still loved Balek, but the hero worship he had felt in his youth was long gone.

Balek snorted. "Given the scope of their victory, the only surprise is that they stopped at the Kungu River and didn't try for more."

Jaith smiled wryly. "I talked with Choma in Azraq before leaving Senanga. She says Bashan has political aspirations. Dekese's unpopular. Everyone in Senanga remembers the bloodbaths of Dirkou and Bamuli. She thinks Bashan wants to draw out his victories to get as much political advantage from them as possible, with an eye to being Senanga's next estahar."

MONTH OF ILFARNAR

CYRENE HAREEL LOOKED INTO THE MIRROR of the carnival's dressing tent, fanning out the bronze feather crest around her face, the face that was so like her mother's, except softer, prettier. Cyrene's feather crest contracted to a tight cap at the thought of her mother, but she forced herself to fan it out again. That had been over five years ago. But today was Taratsday, the thirtieth day of Ilfarnar, and she was eighteen.

This was the day she'd been waiting for all her life, the day she would dance her first solo. She would prove that she could be as great a dancer as her mother. She would show the audience and Roche Laris as well! He was too clumsy to be a soloist, even if he was half-hailar, and danced in the chorus.

She had been meeting with him away from the carnival. She liked him. He could be sweet and funny. He wanted to marry her, but he thought she was too proud. Well, she'd show him. She could leap even higher than her mother had done.

The music started. Her cue came. She took a deep breath and danced onto the portable, wooden stage set up in the carnival tent.

A series of fluid pirouettes, then leap and spin. She was floating across the stage. The thick, humid air seemed to hold her up. She could feel the audience, gained even more height for her leaps from the energy of their approval.

A slow sequence, freezing on point, extending, breaking free with the music. Another leap, the highest yet, with full extension at the peak. The gasps from the audience made nothing of the pain of landing. She felt no strain. She could hardly believe it when the music came to the finale. She bowed as the audience applauded, elated by her triumph.

Roche was waiting for her in the wings. "You looked beautiful, Cy."

The words sounded right. She smiled, breathless with joy. "I did it, Roche."

"You sure did."

His eyes weren't right. He wasn't happy for her. He was angry. Her happiness dimmed. "What's the matter? Aren't you glad? I was better than my mother. I know I was."

He smiled, the anger gone. "Sure I'm happy for you, Cy. Let's celebrate. Just you and me."

She agreed, euphoric from her own performance and the audience's applause. She didn't listen to the itchy little mental warning that there was something wrong with Roche's response, something wrong about their whole relationship. He was very handsome. The other girls in the chorus were jealous of her.

She was eighteen, and that night her relationship with Roche was consummated and they conceived a child.

XX

"Yes, I took my first ship when I was but a lad.
We set sail at the dawn with the wind at a roar,
But the crew was unsure I could lead them to prey.
So we took twenty ships ere we reached the far shore.

For my nose is unmatched when it comes to the scent
Of a fat merchant ship with a hold full of gold.
Yes, a trail of destruction I left behind me
When I first took my ship out on the deep sea.

Chorus: Oh, I took me a ship for to sail on the sea,
And a heigh, nonny heigh, I did sail on the sea."

— VERSES FROM "THE PIRATE'S BOASTING SONG"
FROM *SONGS OF THE SEA AND SHORE*, COLLECTED BY BAR PANYARA, 4592

IT WAS JUST AFTER DAWN when the lookout in the crow's nest cried out in Senangan, "Hakir. Omiran."

Prey, Saranith thought, to the northeast. She had the duty watch. She ordered the helmsman to change course to the new setting.

"*Hakir, rai.*" She sent to Mazilek in the intimate mode. He was asleep, but she had orders to wake him if a prize were spotted.

She sent warning of the change of course to Kenge and Gaten, the captains of the following ships. She was the second farail of *Kanakar* now, and Mazilek, in turn, had risen from arrai to arhan, commander, with three ships following his lead. They were sailing in the southern reaches of Lessar Jevac after delivering cargo to Gatukai in Macosia and taking on cargo destined for Senanga.

"Sakan," the lookout cried.

"*So, a convoy,*" Mazilek thought to all his crew, emerging from his cabin. "*Riches, indeed. But how many?*"

There was a wait. Mazilek joined Saranith on the bridge. She could just make out the first ship the lookout had seen, a speck on the horizon almost lost in the mist as the heat of the morning sun hit the cold waters.

"Seven ships. Four prey. Three warships," the lookout cried.

"Three warships," Mazilek said to Saranith. "Should we go for it, or let them go?"

Saranith grinned. "If there had been four warships and only three merchants, you might have let them go, rai. But those ships will fill our holds and supply prizes."

Mazilek nodded. "Ah, yes. The prizes." He eyed her closely.

Saranith almost held her breath. Did he think she was ready?

Then he smiled. "We'll be careful not to sink any of the warships. If we get them all, I'll give you your pick, young Kamrasi. You've earned it."

"Thank you, rai."

His smile grew wider. "Then see that more sail gets put up. We don't want to keep our prizes waiting."

After being promised her own command, the actual battle was almost an anticlimax to Saranith. Instead of waiting for the faster Senangan warships to come to them, two of the guard ships turned back to attack. Saranith deflected the cannon shot aimed at *Kanakar* with her will. When they were close enough for grappling hooks, she led the boarding crew and took the first ship. Kenge, who had been *Kanakar*'s first farail the year she had come aboard, did the same with his own ship.

Ancil Gaten had a little more trouble with the guard ship that stayed with the convoy. One of the merchant ships got lucky and put a ball through one of his masts, taking it down. And one of his own cannon shots went too low, damaging the prize. But he, too, eventually grappled with the enemy ship and took it.

Mazilek then left Gaten to guard the enemy warships and went after the cargo vessels. Having watched *Kanakar* take out the warships, the merchants weren't anxious to fight and soon surrendered. Especially as Mazilek offered them their freedom and two of their ships: the damaged warship and one of the cargo ships.

"There's no use being greedy," he told Saranith. "Gaten's prize won't make it back to Senanga without refitting, but she can be patched to make a human port."

"The merchant ships are undamaged."

"But not all their cargo is useful. We have no need for lumber or wool. We'll take the cotton, the metal ore, and most of whatever else they have. It'll take us about a day to sort, but then we can send the humans off with two of their ships. We're still ahead two warships, three cargo hulls plus all the valuable cargo. What's more, the next time we hit a human convoy, they'll be more likely to surrender, knowing we won't take everything and won't kill them."

Saranith nodded. "Just good business sense."

"That's right," Mazilek said. "I may as well tell you, now you'll be having your own command, that I didn't want you for *Kanakar*. If you hadn't placed first in your class at Feshi, I'd have managed to refuse you. But that gave you the choice."

He paused and Saranith waited. She had known from the beginning that he hadn't wanted her initially.

"I'm glad now to have had you under me. You're a good officer and I think you've learned the things I've been trying to teach. In fact, I think you understood a lot of it on your own. That surprised me." He hesitated, then added, "You see, Arrai Garrunda is a friend of mine. He got your cousin Aketi just out of Feshi."

Saranith stiffened.

Mazilek nodded. "I thought you might be like your cousin, and those jewels in your eye sockets don't help."

"They may not help me with others," Saranith said carefully, "but they do help to protect me from Aketi. They make him nervous and remind him that I don't always follow the rules."

Mazilek grimaced. "That explains a lot. I knew you were raised together."

Saranith faced him. "I was a slave until I was eight, when I defended Luri from Aketi. My defense indicated wizard talent. When Mutesa examined by mother she took my father's identity and how he died from my mother's mind." She paused and her head sank. "Which brought about my mother's death."

"I'm sorry," Mazilek said.

Saranith shook her head. "It happened long ago. But Aketi was not pleased that Mutesa then fostered me. Nor was Jadne, his sister."

"Still, I'm glad to know there are some healthy branches in the Kamrasi family tree. I don't think much of Bashan either, and he's gained a lot of popularity with his victory in Cassinga, especially after Dekese's bloodbath."

"Kaya is the best of my cousins. He deserves your support. I understand Timaru is decent also, but I've never met him. He rarely leaves the University at Kobala."

"You think Kaya deserves support even though it's been announced that he'll be marrying Jadne Kamrasi next spring?"

Saranith's head jerked. She felt as though she had received a physical blow. "Are you sure of that?"

"*Lysofe* carried the news. The announcement of a royal wedding is no small thing."

Saranith remembered the messenger ship they'd passed two days earlier. "Bashan's victory must have changed things more than I thought."

"Would you still have me support Kaya?"

Saranith cocked her head and eyed her commander. "I don't know." She paused, then added, "The *Gemek* will need refitting, so I should be present for my cousin's wedding. I'll know more after I talk to him again. He was one of my professors at Feshi. Was he not respected there?"

Mazilek shrugged. "I believe his mind is well respected. There may be some question with regard to his resistance to certain types of pressure. But I don't know him personally." He chuckled. "I thought *Gemek* would be your choice. A good ship."

"Badly commanded," she said.

They both smiled, and Saranith knew that in Mazilek she had found a long term friend and ally. And *Gemek*, Endeavor in the human tongue, would be her first command. She would rename the ship *Moalo*, Frightener.

XXI

4648, 465th Cycle of the Year of the Mole
Month of Redri

> _"The worst mistake made by the Council of Wizards in dealing with Cibata and the linlarin, other than even attempting the partitioning, was to give Senanga, the site of Cinkarrak, to mankind. To the linlarin the Red Tower was the symbol of their race. Having it in human hands was intolerable."_

— EXCERPT FROM _KAGRESOD GRESACAD: UNDERSTANDING DISCRIMINATION_ BY ENKAR HAKIST, ILWHEIRLANE, 3207

AZRAQ, THE CAPITOL OF SENANGA, was located on a high ridge of land along the southwest bank of the Zamfara River at its confluence with the Oweta. At the highest point of that ridge, and at the heart of the city, stood Cinkarrak, the Red Tower, one of the six towers supposedly built by the gods, the Cenlorin, when the werefolk were first brought to Tamar.

Like Ninkarrak, the Black Tower in Ilwheirlane, it rose straight and unadorned to over one hundred meters in height. It also extended more than fifty meters down into the bedrock of the headland. From the outside it appeared to be constructed of featureless red granite. Yet from the inside, large sections of that stone appeared as clear as glass. Only a very powerful wizard could duplicate that material.

Saranith and Luri had hired a carriage to bring them to the Tower. As Kaya had chosen a traditional linlarin wedding, the ceremony itself would be performed outside, in the park, and the grounds were already crowded when they arrived.

"Stay close to me, Luri, and for Jehan's sake, don't leave me alone if Jadne deigns to speak to me," Saranith said, taking hold of Luri's arm as they started across the grass toward the reception line. "I still don't understand what Kaya was thinking when he chose her."

"Maybe he's changed," Luri said. "There's a lot of pressure on him. You've heard the whispering. They say that Dekese's line is decadent, that Kaya will prove as incompetent as his father."

Saranith shook her head. "Dekese isn't a bad ruler. A bad military commander, yes, but not a bad Estahar. Senanga's done well under him. Trade and industry have prospered."

Luri shrugged. "It's all a matter of perception, isn't it? People like to think of their rulers as victorious."

Saranith sighed, but smiled as they approached the parents of the soon-to-be bride and groom. She thought that Dekese looked much older than he should at seventy-nine. He was a wizard, after all, even if humans would only classify his talent as that of a journeyman.

He greeted her absently, "Good day."

Saranith suspected that he didn't even remember who she was.

Mutesa's greeting was warmer. "I hear you achieved the rank of arrai this past year," she said. "Congratulations." She had always tried to be impartial in the many disagreements that had arisen between Saranith and her own children.

"Yes, Aunt Mutesa, I've risen in rank, but not nearly so far as your daughter," Saranith acknowledged.

Mutesa laughed. "Jadne has done well for herself, hasn't she. It's quite disconcerted Aketi, who was all set to support Bashan. Now, of course, we'll all support Kaya."

She said this without thought to the fact that she was standing next to Dekese. Saranith noted his shocked disapproval.

Having negotiated the receiving line, she and Luri headed across the wide swath of lawn fronting the Tower toward the refreshment tables.

"I don't know about you," she said to Luri, "but I need a drink after that. It's a wonder Dekese hasn't murdered her."

"She never thinks before she speaks, Sara. Dekese must know that."

"Even if she had thought, she wouldn't have considered there to be anything wrong with what she said. 'But it's the truth, isn't it,'" Saranith said, mimicking Mutesa's voice and mannerism.

"You shouldn't do that in public." said a voice from behind her.

Saranith turned abruptly. "Who..."

She saw a tall, dark man with solid chestnut brown hair and green eyes. She recognized one of her professors at Feshi, Matel Zandezi.

"Not everyone will realize that, as a foster daughter, you have family privilege to support your criticism of a new member of the royal family," he continued wryly.

"Professor Zandezi," said said. "You gave me a start. I hadn't realized anyone but Luri could hear me."

"Matel, please. You're not a student anymore. In fact, I heard you made arrai. Congratulations." He grinned. "But that's the hazard of speaking frankly at public occasions. There's always the risk of being overheard. Mutesa's an impossible woman but Kaya gains much needed support from the old line families by marrying her daughter."

"Luri and I have been at sea. I hadn't realized how much Bashan's victory would change the political situation."

Matel made a point of scanning the lawn around them, but there was no one else close. "Bashan's ambitious. He's plucked every last scrap of down from the sulcath of that victory."

"Then I'm glad Kaya has found a way of gaining back support."

Matel grimaced. "Even this marriage won't help if Bashan's next attack on Cassinga is as successful as his last. If that happens, I don't think Dekese will hold his throne for long."

Saranith stiffened. "Why are you speaking of this to me?"

"Because I'm fairly certain where your sympathies lie." He paused and one side of his mouth tilted lopsidedly. "Kaya and I, and other professors at Feshi, have discussed you fairly frequently, Saranith."

"In what regard?" Her chin rose. "I take it you're not simply referring to my grades."

"No," Matel said soberly. "My colleagues and I thought that you agreed with us as to the need for basic changes in Senangan society."

Saranith drew a deep breath and let it out. "If you mean, do I believe Senanga has to move away from a total war economy, then you're right. I do believe that. But I can't see it happening until after Cassinga has fallen. The people's hatred of Cassinga and humanity seems too firmly fixed."

Matel nodded. "You're probably right about that. But Bashan won't be satisfied with conquering Cassinga. He'll want to move on to the Nyali Coast, and then to the nations of the pure-blooded linlarin."

"Not even Bashan would consider that. The pure-blooded never fight wars."

"Then I suggest you talk to Bashan. Find out for yourself," Matel said. "I trust our conversation will go no farther?"

"Of course it won't. You've given me a lot to think about."

He smiled and nodded. "Yes. I forgot you've been at sea. Shall we continue to the refreshment tables and fortify ourselves for the ceremony?"

"Yes," said Luri, speaking up for the first time. "I think it's definitely time to fortify ourselves with food and drink."

Saranith laughed lightly and took his arm as they set off again across the grass.

The actual ceremony marking the union of Kaya Kamrasi, heir to the Estaharion of Senanga, and Jadne Kamrasi, his second cousin, twice removed, took place in the wilder park to the south of the formal gardens surrounding the Tower compound. Saranith had been surprised to learn that Kaya, not generally known for his adherence to tradition, had chosen to celebrate the conclusion of the ceremony in the most ancient way of the linlarin.

This required that Kaya and Jadne take their tiger forms and hunt together. He, being larger and faster, flushed the herds. Jadne sprang from cover and brought down a jidron, one of the small, swift antelope of the plains. She did not kill it, however, but waited until he joined her and let him give the killing stroke, symbolizing that he would be master in their union. He tore the beast open then and gave her the heart while he ate the liver, sealing their union in blood.

There was a break in the festivities after that while Kaya and Jadne changed back, cleaned off the traces of the hunt and dressed for the final reception. When the receiving line was ready Saranith approached her cousins with some trepidation.

Kaya greeted her affectionately, however. To her congratulations, he replied, "Congratulations back to you. You made arrai in nearly record time."

Jadne was also apparently on her best behavior, saying only, "Hello, Sara. I see you still have Luri glued to your side."

Saranith smiled and nodded and passed on.

Later, Tasan Wukari, the High Chancellor himself, singled her out. "Kaya would like to speak with you privately, Saranith."

Saranith looked at Luri.

"Your companion, of course, is welcome also," Wukari said.

"What does he want to talk about?"

"I really have no idea," Wukari said. "He only told me that he would like to see you. You are one of his cousins."

"Very well," she said.

"Then I'll take you to him." Wukari led the way to a small pavillion that had been set up in the park to enable the royal couple to change and dress without returning to the Tower.

Saranith was surprised to note that there were guards at the entrance.

"A traditional ceremony, cousin?" she said when she found him.

"Sometimes the old ways have their value, Sara," Kaya said, arching his left eyebrow and giving her his usual crooked smile. While he was tall and well built, his face could not be called handsome being made up of parts that never seemed to quite fit together. His ability to mock himself, however, had always appealed to Saranith.

"With this ceremony Jadne had to agree formally to my being the master in our relationship," Kaya added. "Can you imagine her doing so otherwise?"

Saranith laughed, relaxing. He still seemed to be the same Kaya she had known. "Nor can I imagine her not still testing your authority at every opportunity."

Kaya shrugged. "But, apart from you, she has the strongest talent of any eligible female. And you have Luri."

"Your wife had to be one of your cousins?"

"My father's unpopular. Bashan's victory in Cassinga is causing many to question my position as heir. I respect Bashan's military expertise. However, I don't think he would make a good Estahar." His face stretched wryly. "So, completely aside from the effect on my future, I feel it would be bad for Senanga. Destablizing. So I had to act to strengthen my claim. Marrying Jadne or a daughter of one of the noble houses closely allied with Kamrasi serves that purpose, but I couldn't find anyone but Jadne with a strong enough talent to ensure that my children will also be eligible to succeed me."

"That's why you stopped your father from discontinuing the captured wizard breeding program, despite the problems it causes?" Saranith asked, voicing a long time grievance.

"Ethical problems or the fact that they usually escape?"

"Both."

"I'm not sure it would ever be wise to allow ethics to rule in this case," Kaya said.

"You condone breeding sentient beings like animals?"

Kaya shook his head. "It's unethical, I know. But the offspring, either first or second generation, are often powerful wizards."

"If we don't have to put them to death for lack of sight," Saranith said.

"True," Kaya said, "those born without sight must be destroyed, but the survivors do well. Most of our noble houses were founded in such blood. I've no desire to see that change. Nor should you, as you were such a child. If our laws didn't recognize your right to inherit, you'd still be a slave. If I were to seek to change the law to eliminate such breeding practices, the repercussions might endanger your status, and the status of those like you."

"I'm willing to take that risk."

Kaya shook his head. "But I'm not."

"I met Matel just before the ceremony," Saranith said, changing the subject.

Kaya head came up sharply and he looked both startled and wary. "What did he have to say?"

"He expressed some unorthodox views regarding Senangan society. He seemed to imply that you shared those views."

Kaya sighed. "And so I did at one time. But his views are philosophical and I need to be practical."

"I remarked to Luri as we arrived here that Dekese may not be a good military commander, but he's been an excellent Estahar. Senanga has prospered under him."

"But the common people don't think about trade and industry when they think about rulers," Kaya said. "They think about conflict and victory."

"Luri said the same thing, but that makes the people fools," Saranith said. "Bashan will raise taxes to support a larger army and will curb trade and industry. The whole country will be poorer."

"Thank you, cousin. That is what I needed to know."

XXII

4649, 465TH CYCLE OF THE YEAR OF THE GRIFFIN
MONTH OF DIRGA

*"Candith is a city of contrasts. The walls of splendid
palaces often abut acres of hovels. Great wealth has been
generated by the plantations of the interior. Great poverty
has ensued from the dislocation of people during Cassinga's
constant war with Senanga."*

— FROM *A TOUR GUIDE TO CASSINGA* BY SEGAL LAFITT, ILWHEIRLANE, 4638

D EL MARAN STOOD IN THE BOW of *Meldeth*, the ship that had
carried the Wizard Ashe and himself from the shores of the
Thallassean Sea to the coast of Cibata. Despite the oppressive heat, he
watched eagerly as they approached the brightly painted adobe walls
of Candith, the capitol of Cassinga.

"Clever of you to find a bit of breeze," Ashe said, joining him.

"Yes, hard to believe it's still winter in Ilwheirlane."

Ashe studied the shoreline for a moment. "Colorful, isn't it. Can't
imagine anyone in Ilwheirlane or Duragan painting a house pink or
pale blue, but they look natural in this setting. Must be something to do
with the quality of light. It's so much brighter here."

Meldeth had slowed and was coming about, heading for one of the
long wooden piers extending into the water at the southern end of the
town, farthest away from the mouth of the Ouakoro River. Then the
slight breeze shifted. For weeks Del had smelled nothing but fresh sea
air. Now he was suddenly overwhelmed by a rich melange of odors
dominated by the reek of rotting vegetation, dead fish and other scents
he couldn't even name.

"Ah, the perfume of the tropics," Ashe said wryly. "I'd been
warned."

Del grinned. He was glad of Ashe's company. He had heard that
Balek could be difficult.

His vision went to the tall figure in white robes at the end of the pier
Meldeth was approaching. Another, younger man equally as tall was at
his side. "They're both powerful," Del said. "Even if the older, darker
one isn't Balek, our arrival is being honored."

There was more activity on the deck as the remaining sails were lowered and *Meldeth* came to a stop in the slip next to the pier.

"I'll notify the purser to have our bags brought ashore," Ashe said, turning away.

Del sighed. So he would face Balek on his own. Well, begin as you mean to go on, he thought, and headed for the ramp and confrontation.

He walked up to the tall, black-skinned wizard with the simple, white muslin robes. "Greetings, the Wizard Balek, I presume? I'm Del Maran, the military expert the Council of Cibata requested."

"It took Derwen long enough to find you, and you're not even a full wizard," Balek said.

"Military tactics aren't a usual field of study for members of the Varfarin," Del said, deliberately mild.

"Then why did you study the subject?"

"I had personal reasons," Del said. "And once I'd started, I found the subject fascinating, with many applications beyond that of war."

"Well, let's see if you can stop Senanga from taking the Kunguatam."

"You're sure that's where they'll attack next?"

Balek shrugged. " Bashan didn't attack from the sea in this last attack, as the Senangans have done in the past. Who knows what he'll try next time?"

"What do you know about Bashan and the situation in Senanga?"

"We have spies, at least in Azraq and Feshi, the capitol and the naval headquarters. We don't know much about Bashan personally except that he's related to the royal family. But we try to keep track of what's going on."

"I'll need all of that information and more about Bashan's personal life, plus available manpower and detailed maps of the entire country."

"We sent maps. Didn't you receive them?"

"I've studied the maps you sent, but they weren't adequate. I need detailed elevation maps, giving contours. I need them for the entire border with Senanga and particularly for every meter of the Kipembatam, the Kunguatam, the Mekambatam and the territory on the Cassingan and Senangan sides of the Pass of Fadiat."

Balek nodded and, for the first time, Del sensed approval. "Information about Bashan will take time, but I should be able to supply the maps within a week. You'll be staying with me tonight, at my quarters in the Palace. You're welcome to stay longer until you decide where to set up your headquarters."

"I won't be able to make such a decision until I've seen the detailed maps."

"Then for the time being you'll be my guest," Balek said. "Let me introduce my assistant, Nathan." He turned toward the younger man. "Like you, he's a journeyman wizard."

"*Congratulations*," Nathan sent in the intimate mode. "*I've never seen Balek handled better at a first meeting.*"

NATHAN ENTERED THE DOONA EWAN, the Setting Sun, a bar in the waterfront district, in a state of suppressed excitement. All the other journeyman wizards presently in Candith were gathered there waiting for him: Lagura and Bella, Renge, Marrak, visiting from the Nyali Coast, and, of course, Rainal with Pala. She was still just a journeyman, not even a wizard, as she hadn't yet achieved the high sight, but they let her join them most of the time as there were no other apprentices in her age group in Candith.

They were all sitting around two tables pushed together in a corner of the back room. The light was dim, coming from lanterns located on only a few of the tables. The bar was moderately full, but other customers avoided the area where the wizards usually sat.

He pulled up a chair and a barmaid came and took his order for a mug of the local beer.

"Well," Lagura said, when the waitress had gone. "What was he like?"

Nathan noted that she was sitting next to Bella as had become her custom. He wished he could break himself of the habit of always seeking her out first. But his eyes looked for her, just as his tongue always sought out sore spots in his mouth.

"More to the point," Bella said, "did Balek manage to intimidate him right off?"

Nathan looked around at the anxious faces and recalled his excitement. "I didn't have much hope before I saw Del in action, but he handled Balek like a master."

"Balek didn't do his classic put-down number?" Bella asked.

"Oh, he tried," Nathan said, "but Del just brushed aside the attack and went straight for Balek's own weak points. 'You didn't give me enough information about this,'" he mimicked. "'Tell me about that? Why don't you know about the other?' It was beautiful. I've never seen Balek handled better. Even Kaoda doesn't have this journeyman wizard's touch."

"So what's he like otherwise?" Lagura said.

"He's about my height, pale skin, rangy build, chestnut hair. I didn't notice anything particularly remarkable about him physically. But I have a feeling now that he may be a superb tactician."

"What about the master? We didn't even get his name." Rainal asked.

"His name is Ashe," Nathan said. "He looks pale, nondescript and his mind shield's so smooth he's almost not there. Balek said Ashe qualified at the age of forty-three. He was impressed by that. He was looking forward to meeting Ashe." Nathan turned to Marrak. "His reaction was the same as yours, but after meeting Del, he hardly noticed Ashe, and I think that was deliberate on Ashe's part."

"So what do you think of their chances of changing the situation for Cassinga?" Renge asked.

"I think that we should give thanks to Jehan," Nathan said. "I think we've got just what we asked for this time, and that there are two new human wizards in Cibata, both of them with the potential to be great wizards. Whether that will be enough to save Cassinga, I don't know."

BARELY A WEEK AFTER THEIR ARRIVAL the Wizard Ashe was watching young children playing in Vyrlit Kameticin, the Park of the Red Kamet, when he noticed Balek crossing the grass toward him in a deliberate manner. He sighed, but he had known Balek would seek him out at some point.

"*Ashe, I want to know more about your protege. What led him to study military tactics?*" Balek demanded, coming to a stop right in front of Ashe.

"*Good afternoon, Balek. It's a beautiful day, isn't it?*" Ashe responded mildly.

Balek frowned, glancing around at the sunlit park. "*I suppose it is, but that doesn't answer my question.*"

"*Have you asked Del?*"

"*He only said that events in his childhood led him to develop techniques by which a weaker force could manipulate a greater one. He wouldn't tell me any more. Said the memories were painful and he'd rather not dwell on them.*"

"*Why do you need to know? Isn't he doing the job for which you requested him?*"

Balek frowned. "*He's certainly got a vast repertoire of tricks. Whether they'll work against Senangans is something else again. I need to know more about him.*"

Ashe shrugged. "*He's a descendent of Agnith and Ilfarnar, so he was tested at birth. He was Derwen's apprentice until you summoned Derwen to Cibata after the fall of Nemali. After that he became mine, but he's long past needing me to guide him. He'll qualify as a wizard in the next few years, and after that he'll go on to be a great wizard, one of the greatest. You don't need to know more than that.*"

"*You're so sure of his power?*"

"*You have sight, Balek. You can feel it yourself.*"

"*It twists in ways I've never seen.*"

"His ability with animals," Ashe thought. "A rare talent. It was strange to me, too, at first. Ilfarnar's gift."

"Ilfarnar cared more for beasts than men."

Ashe's eyebrows rose. "You may be some centuries older than I am, Balek, but you're not old enough to remember Ilfarnar."

"The histories give clear accounts."

Ashe shook his head. "Of superficial things, not the contents of a man's heart. And Del inherited his talent, not his nature."

"So I should accept him because of your judgment? But what do I know of you, save that you make yourself invisible?"

"I'm merely a tourist here to see the sights. Accept Del by what he does or does not achieve. That's the only valid basis for judgment."

"You don't deny that you conceal yourself? Your barriers are formidable. They make me wonder what you're hiding behind them."

"Secrets, of course," Ashe thought, and turned and walked away.

XXIII

> *"Leading an enemy to a battle site of one's own
> choosing can, if one has chosen well, lead to
> great advantage."*
>
> — FROM *THE COLLECTED WRITINGS OF VYDARGA THE RED*

"**B**REEDING PIKAS AND DOVES," Balek exclaimed, charging into Del's new office. "What does that have to do with combat, may I ask?"

"Actually, a great deal," Del said calmly, looking up from his chair behind a desk covered with paperwork. "An army of any kind depends on regular supplies."

After completing his preliminary survey of Cassinga, Del had decided that, as Candith was the center of supply, it was the logical center of command as well. Then, when the Varfarin had insisted on his being named Commander-in-Chief of the Armed Forces of Cassinga, Balek had arranged for him to be granted his own quarters and office in the Rabenate Palace.

The only problem with the arrangement was that it made it easy for Balek to learn what Del was doing and to criticize.

"Our troops eat hunical and seral meat," Balek said, leaning forward across the desk aggressively. "I see no reason for pikas or doves."

"But you had no warning of Bashan's last invasion," Del said, smiling wryly. "Nathan told me that you weren't even aware of the troop buildup in the Gatoomatum."

"We've had wizards or apprentices along the border since then, and I don't see..."

"But wizards could be better used for other purposes," Del said, "as can fully trained apprentices. And out-of-body viewing, which is what you need to really judge enemy movements from a distance in the jungle, is taxing."

"So pikas and doves are going to do our scouting for us?" Balek said angrily.

"No," Del said calmly, "but eagles will, and they eat pikas and doves."

"Eagles?" Balek said, startled.

"The kaja eagles of the Kuta Lafuno will be laying extra eggs this spring. Their offspring will need to be fed. The need will be greater than native populations of rodents can provide, so I need the breeding program for the pikas and doves to begin now."

Del paused, watching the confounded expression on Balek's face with well concealed glee.

"You communicate with animals," Balek said finally.

"It's a valuable talent," Del said. "I'll also need to visit more schools, not only in Candith, but all over Cassinga. Nathan took me to one here in the city last week and I found six potential apprentices and Ashe has found over a dozen in other nearby schools, but I'll need at least a hundred, if not more."

"A hundred apprentices. You and Ashe can't possible train that many in wizardry. You aren't even a full wizard yourself."

"We don't need to train them to be full wizards," Del said, with obvious patience. "We only need to teach them how to mind link with a specific animal. Any child able to attain basic were-vision can learn that. Each child will have his or her own kaja eagle. They'll see what the eagle sees, and be able to guide the birds to the areas we want to view."

Del watched the changing expressions on Balek's face. He had deliberately broached the subject backwards, because he had wanted Balek to protest, and then be shown to be wrong.

The following week, instead of charging into Del's office, Balek walked. "I understand that you've had Nathan searching for a suitable site for the raising of rats?"

"Yes," Del said, continuing to study the supply lists on his desk.

Balek drew a deep breath. "May I ask what rats have to do with fighting Senangans. I could understand eliminating them, as they destroy food stocks, but breeding them?"

Del looked up and smiled. "Maliks hate them."

"That's it? We're to breed rats because maliks hate them."

"Precisely," Del said.

Balek took another deep breath. "You've demonstrated over the past several weeks that you do have a keen intelligence and an unusual way of looking at problems, but that's the most ridiculous..."

"Look," Del said, deliberately interrupting as Balek began to build momentum, "what is the single worst problem with facing linlarin or isklarin forces?"

"Maliks," Balek said, "but..."

"No," Del said, "no buts, maliks are the worst problem, so I've been studying everything that's known about them. They hate rats, because in the wild rats eat their eggs. It's an instinctive hatred. If a malik sees a rat, even in the middle of a battle charge, the malik forgets everything else and chases the rat. There are many instances of this noted in the histories of the Dragon Wars. It was considered a curiosity, but no one seems to have thought about using the knowledge in combat. I plan to."

"They've actually been known to break off in the middle of a battle charge?"

"Yes," Del said grinning. "And given a few hundred rats that I've trained myself, I believe I can make the Senangans' maliks more hindrance than help in the next battle."

Balek sighed and nodded. "I should have learned." He looked down at Del gravely, "I'll leave you to your work."

"YOU SEEM TO HAVE ESTABLISHED yourself satisfactorily," Ashe said, leaning against the wall in Del's office.

Del eyed his ex-master warily. He'd known from the beginning of this journey that Ashe wouldn't stay with him for long but, if this was Ashe's farewell, it had come more quickly than he'd expected. Much more quickly than he'd hoped. "Yes. If the Senangans hold off for a year, we stand a good chance of defeating them."

"Then I think I'll be moving on. I have a fancy to see the rest of Cibata while I'm here in the Southern Hemisphere. Cassinga reminds me too much of Kailane."

"The seige mentality, it can be depressing. You'll see the rest of Cibata as a linlar?"

Ashe smiled. "Of course."

"I remember Derwen telling me long ago that wizards rarely change their natural form. He hadn't met you then, of course."

Ashe laughed. "No. He hadn't, but meeting me didn't change his mind."

"He never noticed," Del said, shaking his head. "I don't suppose you'll tell me before you leave. Elise and I spent many hours trying to guess."

Ashe laughed. "I know. But a little mystery in your lives is good for you."

4650, 466TH CYCLE OF THE YEAR OF THE OX
MONTH OF ILFARNAR

NATHAN SAW CHILDREN GATHERED around the giant aviary Del Maran had ordered. They were watching the young eaglets with awe. Soon many of them would be assigned one of those eaglets. While usually, since the Bane, children and their parents were wary of attempts to recruit young wizards, the idea of being linked to an eagle and scouting for the army was actually drawing volunteers.

Then he noticed Pala, standing slightly to one side, but watching with an intensity equal to that of any of the younger children.

She turned to him. "They're so beautiful," she said wistfully. "I want one for myself."

Nathan grinned. He'd already talked to Del and picked out his own when Del first got back from the mountains with the eaglets roosting on an entire train of carts filled with cages full of pikas and doves. "I'm sure Del will let you have one. I hear you've been studying tactics with him."

Pala looked up at him defensively. "He takes my interest seriously. He says I have a natural talent for the subject."

Nathan spread out his hands. "I wasn't criticizing, Pala. I think it's a good idea for you to learn as much about military tactics as you can while we have Del here."

"My father thinks it's a waste of time, that I should concentrate on my wizard training. But I can do both."

Nathan frowned. "Rainal hasn't forbidden you to study tactics with Del has he?"

She sighed. "No. He didn't go quite that far. He just said he was disappointed in my choice. But it's my choice. Del may not be here forever. And the fate of Cassinga will rest on my shoulders, not my father's."

"Even though Rainal's still young," Nathan said cautiously, "he's a conservative. He doesn't believe the Varfarin should be involved in warfare. A lot of wizards feel that way."

Pala kicked at a clump of grass. "I know. Maybe that way of thinking works when you live in Ilwheirlane or Mahran. But it won't work in Cassinga, and I live here and now, with my country under siege."

Nathan put a hand on her shoulder. "Come on. We'll get Del to issue you an eaglet. I'm here to pick up mine. I understand their minds are fierce. Maybe linking with them will help us deal with our own aggressions."

Pala laughed and her hand went up to grip his. "Thanks, Nathan. You have a great way of putting things in perspective."

4651, 466TH CYCLE OF THE YEAR OF THE DRAGON
MONTH OF ILFARNAR

WHEN ERRIN YAR POMORRY ANIFI arrived in Candith he did not immediately make himself known to Balek. He did, however, seek out Del.

Del sat up in his chair in shock when Errin entered. *"I didn't know that any of the living crystals other than Belkarion had a full linkage with a wizard. I'm honored to meet the bearer of Lyskarion,"* he thought, rising and bowing.

"Will you still accord me such honor when I tell you that my name is Errin Yar Anifi?"

Del's mouth opened, then snapped shut, but he recovered his self-possession quickly. "Elise was usually a little better at describing people. I'd never have imagined that the Errin Yar she spoke of could become the bearer of Lyskarion."

Errin laughed, impressed by Del's reaction time. "I believe emotion usually colors her image of me."

"You've seen her recently then?"

Errin opened his mind. *"I had nearly persuaded her to form a permanent linkage with me, but then my cousin tricked me into accepting this,"* he held up an opalescent crystal the size of a goose egg. *"Needless to say,"* he added ruefully, *"Elise decided I'd deliberately changed the rules on her yet again and sent me away. But she is my life mate and someday we shall make it work between us."*

Del's face relaxed slightly. *"You do care for her then?"*

"Always," Errin thought simply.

"Then welcome to Cassinga. Although I can't imagine what the heir to the Isle of Sussey could be doing in Cibata."

"I arrived on the *Golden Rose*. I may not be a member of the Varfarin, but I was taught by the Wizard Delanan and recently I've been working with the Wizard Rand to try and keep Darenje from being taken by Gandahar. It was my thought, as I needed to be away from Sussey for a time, that the Varfarin here in Cassinga must keep track of any large movements of the Senangan navy."

"Oh, yes, there's an agent of the Varfarin on permanent duty in Feshi."

"Then would the Varfarin here be willing to notify Ilwheirlane if a fleet of empty troop carriers sails for the North?"

"I'm sure the Varfarin here would be willing," Del said. "The question is, how would they get the news to Ilwheirlane before the fleet arrived. The Varfarin owns no ships. The best they could do would be to put a message on a merchant ship."

Errin grimaced. "But you think they'd send the information if I could get a ship assigned here to carry it?"

Del grinned. "I suggest you put the question to Nathan. Balek may head the Varfarin down here, but Nathan pretty much runs the day to day operations and he'll undoubtedly be willing to help. Balek might object just on general principles, but if Nathan agrees, he'll accept a fait accompli."

"Thank you. Will you introduce me?"

"How long are you going to be here?"

Errin hesitated. "That depends on how quickly I learn to use and control Lyskarion, but probably a year or two."

"Are you willing to help the Varfarin while you're here, or will you just observe."

Errin hesitated. "As I'll someday be the head of a nation of larin, I've no desire to make an enemy of Senanga. Sussey depends on its ability to trade with the world. The actions I've already planned will undoubtedly jeopardize Sussey's ability to trade with Gandahar. I don't want to add another country to that list. Unless my participation is vital to the survival of Cassinga, which I doubt, I'd prefer to be merely an observer."

"Then I think I'll put off the introductions until after we've defeated the Senangans. Otherwise, Balek might think to make our help contingent. He has a narrowly focused mind."

"I understand."

4652, 466TH CYCLE OF THE YEAR OF THE EAGLE MONTH OF REDRI

NATHAN WAS ON RELAY DUTY when the Wizard Choma gave the first warning of the next Senangan invasion over the telepathic relay. *"Bashan's boasting that this next invasion will be the end of Cassinga. I haven't been able to get many details, but I know he'll be attacking from more than one direction. He's planning to involve almost as many troops as Dekese did."*

Jaith gave the next report the following day. *"The Senangans are only loading one lesdek of infantry aboard the troop carriers. There'll be a thousand malik cavalry with them, however. Bashan himself is not in command here in Feshi. I don't know where he is, but he isn't here."*

Nathan accompanied Balek when he took the second report to Del's office. When Del heard the update he smiled. "Bashan's splitting his forces. He's overconfident."

"He thinks he can take out Cassinga once and for all," Balek said. "Can he?"

Del shook his head. "He might have done just that if he'd launched a major attack through the Pass of Fadiat two years ago. Now, no. Especially not if he's dividing his forces. He'll be spread too thin at each of his points of attack."

Del paused, angling back his head as though looking at the ceiling. Nathan could almost see the calculations going through his head. "He'll try to come through Fadiat. That leads straight into the heartland of Cassinga. He'll also have troops crossing the Kungu from the

Kipembatam. Those forces will actually pose the greatest threat because we won't be able to be prepared for every possible crossing. Still, if he's overconfident in one respect, he'll probably underestimate us in every way. We'll prepare for the most obvious points and just have observers at the others in case he surprises us."

Del brought his focus back to his desk and shuffled through a pile of maps. Then he got a tape measure and measured distances from Fadiat to the coast. Finally, he studied detail maps of several areas of coast. Then he said, "Bashan's troop carriers will try to land on the beaches just north of the mouth of the Kama. The only other possibilities are just south of the village of Majoh or north of Venga, but neither of those locations would give him a direct path to meet with the troops he hopes to bring through Fadiat. We'll make some preparations for all three sites, but concentrate on the beaches at Kama."

Nathan said, "You sound so sure."

Del grinned. "Oh, I am sure. If he's split his forces the way it sounds like he has, then we have him. Either his intelligence information isn't as good as ours, or he completely discounts any effect I've had on Cassinga's forces."

"Could this be a feint? Could he be planning to attack from some other direction entirely? Perhaps through the Kuta Lafuno up near the headwaters of the Ouakoro? We have very few defenses in that direction."

"No, but we have eagles on watch," Del said, "and no broad trails to make it easy to move an army. We'd have plenty of warning if he tried to attack through those hills. But he won't. He'll come through Fadiat and I'll see that Fadiat breaks him."

XXIV

*"While the mixed-blood populations of Gandahar, Senanga
and Mankoya tend to forget the fact today, lack of sight was not
the only reason the were-folk originally labeled mankind
malarin, non-sentients. The other reason was mankind's
propensity toward organized violence...*

*"War was unknown on Tamar until the coming of mankind.
While an individual lar might engage in violent behavior,
it would have been unthinkable for a group of larin to organize
themselves for the sole purpose of facilitating such aggression..."*

— EXCERPT FROM *KAGRESOD GRESACAD* "UNDERSTANDING DISCRIMINATION" BY
ENKAR HAKIST, ILWHEIRLANE, 3207

S PRING HAD COME ONCE AGAIN to the Kuta Lafuno, the
Mountains of the Moon. The elakan trees were in full bloom, brilliant sprays of purple and blue amid the dense forest growth of thorn
and karee trees on the steep slopes leading up to the Pass of Fadiat. Del
noted them idly when scanning with his distance vision. Once he found
what he was looking for he switched to the eyes of a scout's eagle. His
attention was on the front line of the army of Senanga. The maliks were
four abreast on a broad sloping switchback of cleared trail.

Bashan must have learned of the eagles, Del thought, for there was
no attempt at surprise in this attack. Two thousand malik cavalry and
two lesdekin of infantry, ten thousand soldiers, were marching directly
up the steeply graded slope heading for the narrow crest of the pass
and the fort that guarded it.

He hoped that his predictions of Bashan's plans were correct. He
hadn't dared show uncertainty in front of Balek, but the fate of
Cassinga depended on his guess that Bashan would land his troop
ships just north of the mouth of the Kama River. If they landed at one
of the other possible sites, then Cassinga was in dire jeopardy. Del had
based his entire defense on the premise that Bashan would plan for the

easiest and most direct routes of attack without even considering what the Cassingans could do to defend against such attacks.

He shifted his view to his own distance vision and scanned Bashan's main army. Those forces weren't going to get through the Pass of Fadiat if he and a major part of the Cassingan army could help it. He had used his position as Commander-in-Chief of all Cassinga's armed forces to reorganize the entire Cassingan army. He had supervised the training and chosen the officers that would serve him this day. He reached with his mind and gave the signal to his trained rats.

Suddenly the jungle to either side of Bashan's forces swarmed with rodents. Del saw the maliks breaking ranks to chase them through the eagle's eyes. The rats did not run back into the jungle, however. They ran right down the steep slopes between the switchbacks and through the feet of the second rank of malik cavalry. Most of the malik riders fell off as their mounts plunged down the rocky scree, but even those who managed to hang on had no control. The rats, a moving sea of them, ran straight down the slope through all the lines of cavalry and into the columns of Bashan's infantry. The maliks followed.

"Time for the archers," Del said, watching the ordered ranks of the Senangan army break up into chaos.

NATHAN WATCHED THROUGH THE EYES of his eagle, Ketan, as the Senangan troops started across the river in one of the places Del had predicted. The telepathic relays told him that the two other crossings Del had chosen were also correct. There were lookouts at four other places that Del had labeled possibilities, but the bulk of their preparations had been at the three locations Del had marked as almost certainties.

"Archers may begin firing," he sent to the commander of the forces with him. *"Tell the rat handlers to get ready"*

Nathan watched as the arrows struck the first line of malik riders. Arrows wouldn't hurt the maliks unless they hit an eye, but a riderless malik was as dangerous to the troops around it as it was to an enemy. And maliks hated water. Getting them across the river was a test of their training even without interference.

As predicted, the orderly line of malik riders broke up as several of the riders went down. The now uncontrolled maliks turned immediately to go back to the far shore, attacking anything in their way.

The archers were well concealed high in the trees overlooking the ford. When the Senangan infantry troops finally did make it across, they would shift back farther into the jungle and continue sniping. There were ropes linking a network of trees that stretched for miles along the path the Senangans were expected to take.

Nathan grinned. *"Rat handlers, now it's your turn."*

The rats appeared on the rocks at the edge of the river up stream from the shallow crossing point. Several of the maliks not trying to return to the far shore spotted them and charged toward them, floundering as they hit pools of deeper water. Enraged, many actually attacked their riders. Then those maliks, too, were heading for the far shore, back the way they had come, charging any Senangan troops in their way. In the end only a handful of malik riders actually reached the near shore, and those were met by intensely trained pikemen camouflaged so that they had been invisible until the maliks were almost on top of them.

Nathan, remembering the charge at Bamuli, watched, awed, as this time the few remaining maliks, already in ragged disarray, went down before the pikes.

However, the Senangan infantry was reforming and starting across the stream. Their numbers were reduced and they were somewhat demoralized, but they were still a formidable force that outnumbered the Cassingans. Nathan noted with approval that the lieutenant in charge was signaling the pikemen to retreat. It was time to begin the second stage of the defense.

He checked with Marala and Balek, the Varfarin liaisons at the other two crossing points, but their actions had gone as smoothly as his.

SARANITH ORDERED the helmsman to bring *Moalo* another notch into the wind. Saranith had removed all the old cast iron cannon and replaced them with bronze. She had stripped most of the upper deck as well. Since being refitted, the ship was lighter in the water and had a longer reach.

She would need it today. *Moalo* and the other ships in Mazilek's command, two full pods now, eighteen ships, would be challenging an entire fleet. Granted most of the fleet was a disorderly rabble put forth by the Nyali Coast, but there were still a great number of them, and all with guns. Mazilek had been elevated to the rank of arhan, full commander, and chosen to command the advance guard. Their assignment was to clear the way for the troop carriers and the main Senangan fleet behind them.

Saranith suspected that Mazilek's success over the years had generated jealousy among the high command of the Senangan navy. There was a little too much honor involved in this current posting for her peace of mind. However, if any commander could succeed under such conditions, it would be Mazilek, and she would back him to her final breath.

Bashan had boasted that, after this coming battle, Cassinga would be no more. Saranith was not sure how she felt about that.

Still, there was nothing she could do but follow her orders and disperse any sea borne opposition to the Senangan forces. She brought *Moalo* about with the rest of Mazilek's force, sailing north northwest into the Bay of Dagana. Then she saw the mass of ships emerge over the horizon.

BY THE SECOND DAY of the battle, Bashan had given up on massed attack by the malik cavalry. Instead, what maliks had been recaptured he had ranging through the jungle, trying to pick off Cassingan archers. Del ordered them to withdraw.

Bashan's infantry troops were again climbing the switchback trail up to the pass. Del gave the signal to begin firing the outlying cannon. He had built emplacements on the cliffs overlooking the approach to the pass. Supplied by dropping ropes down from above, they were almost impossible to reach from below. He had reinforced the rock under them himself, so that it wouldn't give way under the constant pounding. Bashan's forces had not yet reached a point where they could even see the Fortress of Fadiat, yet already they had been reduced by over ten percent, not counting the loss of more than half the maliks. And loose maliks were still causing problems farther back in Bashan's supply lines.

SARANITH WATCHED AS THE LUMBERING troop ships started to land on the beach below the mouth of the Kama River. *Moalo* had taken damage, but nothing serious, and she had sunk five of the ships in the fleet defending Cassinga. Seven of Mazilek's fleet had gone down, reducing them to eleven ships. She had managed to pick up most of the crew from one of the sunken ships and other members of Mazilek's fleet had taken on survivors too, but many lives had been lost, some of them friends.

Still, they had done what they had been commanded to do: they had broken a way through the Cassingan naval forces before the main Senangan fleet arrived. Every one of Mazilek's ships that had gone down had taken three or more Cassingan ships down with it. The Cassingan fleet had already been in disarray when the main Senangan fleet arrived with the troop carriers. While the main fleet had taken damage getting the troop ships through, that damage would have been much worse if Mazilek's pods had not prepared the way.

New enemy ships were still sailing in from the Nyali Coast, but the main goal had been accomplished. The ten troop carriers had made it to shore intact. Not a single shot had touched their sides. The

Senangan navy had performed well this day, and Mazilek's force had performed almost miraculously.

Then cannon fire came from the shore and the stuttering roar of several great explosions. Saranith looked back and saw that eight of the troop carriers were suddenly aflame. There had been no time for them to have unloaded. The cannon firing from land emplacements could not have set them afire so quickly. The beach itself must have been mined. The two carriers that had not already landed were trying to back off from the shore, but the cannon fire was cutting in to them. She didn't think they would get out of range before they took enough damage to sink them. Someone in Cassinga had anticipated Bashan's landing site. But the fate of the troop ships once ashore was not the responsibility of the Senangan navy.

NATHAN BROKE OFF FROM THE TELEPATHIC relay with Del. Everything was going more or less as planned. Lagura would take over for him as liaison with the four remaining companies dedicated to breaking down this branch of the Senangan forces invading Cassinga. It was already reduced by a third of its original numbers, and its morale was fading rapidly. The snipers, the flank attacks and the myriad of traps were all taking their toll. And the best thing about the entire operation so far was how light their own losses had been. He remembered Bamuli and gave thanks to Jehan that this time they had Del directing their forces.

But now it was time for him to accompany the hand-picked troops under Colonel Edron Menkor, the son of the commander of the Cassingan forces during the fall of Nemali. They were assigned to cross the Kungu River and retake the Pass of Tibati. Menkor would lead four companies, two hundred fighters. Nathan hoped they would have surprise on their side, but success would also depend on whether or not the linlarin had discovered the secret passageway. If they had missed the passage, then Nathan could lead the General and his troops into the very heart of the fortress. Given that advantage, the Cassingan forces should be able to take it.

He called to Ketan to land and to ride the padded perch on his shoulder. The troops set off quietly. Stealth was their ally. That, and the fact that the last thing the Senangan forces at Tibati would be expecting right now was an attack from Cassinga.

DEL WATCHED THROUGH THE EYES of still another eagle as Bashan reformed his forces on the now flattened meadow at the foot of the slope leading to the pass of Fadiat. This time, however, he did not attempt to march them back up that slope. This time they marched away to the southwest.

"He's heading for Tibati," Del said.

"How long will it take him?" asked Rainal. He had been acting as Del's aide thoughout most of the battle.

"His forces are exhausted and demoralized. He won't be able to push them. Say four and a half days," Del said, doing the figures in his head. He knew all the mountain trails now on both the east and west slopes of Kuta Lafuno. "He doesn't know yet what happened to his landing party, or the forces from the Kipembatam. He's still hoping to join a successful invasion force."

"When's Nathan due to reach Tibati?"

"Tomorrow night. Attack's due the next day before dawn," Del said. "If the passage is clear."

"Then Nathan should have a least a day to prepare for Bashan," Rainal said.

"It won't be enough," Del said frowning, "not without more help. I expected Bashan to hang on longer here. And he's bound to get warning that Tibati's been taken before he gets there. I want four companies: Goat's Foot, High Points, Aeriemen, and Keriarin ready to leave with me in an hour. We won't beat Bashan to Tibati; the eastern route is longer than the western. But we may get there in time to make a difference. Also, tell the relays to move most of the mop up crew away from the coast to help with the rest of the invasion forces that came over the Kungu. If any of the troops dealing with those forces can be spared, send them after Nathan."

THE TELEPATHIC RELAYS Del had set up all over Cassinga worked overtime that evening. By the time Del with his four picked companies specializing in mountain combat reached their camp roughly thirty kilometers south of Lake Kama, he had heard from most of his field commanders. Virtually all of the Senangan forces attempting to land on the beach south of the mouth of the Kama River had been destroyed.

The three pronged attack from the Kipembatam across the Kungu River had also been stopped. All those forces were in retreat. None were being allowed to turn west toward Tibati. Instead, they were being herded toward the coast.

Nathan and Colonel Menkor's forces were already in the foothills below Tibati. They would have to be careful in their movements the next day, however. The attack on Tibati would have to be a complete surprise to succeed. Fortunately, as Del remembered from the maps, the entrance to the tunnel into the fortress was on the opposite side of a steep mountain slope and could not be seen from Tibati, not even by someone with high sight.

NATHAN WAS TIRED AND SWEATY when he and the troops with him reached the opening of the tunnel where he had found Pala. He grinned at the memory. She had been so brave, bringing her family out. She had been excited to learn of this expedition and glad to help him with images of the fort as it had been.

He eyed the opening. The tunnel didn't look as though it had been disturbed since the last time he'd seen it, except, perhaps, by some predator. There were small animal bones strewn about near the opening, which meant that the Senangans had not found the tunnel. If they had, they would surely have closed it up. He put a hood on Ketan, so the close walls wouldn't bother the eagle. Then he nodded to Colonel Menkor and started up the tunnel, knowing that the troops would follow.

They camped in the tunnel. There was less chance of being observed. An hour before dawn Nathan extended his senses through the panel into the fortress. It took full use of his high sight to penetrate the barrier. No one was in the room on the other side. He opened the panel gently and slipped through. The room was being used as an office. Most of the shelving was still as Pala remembered it, but held files and ledgers now. Nathan moved out into the hall. He sensed that several rooms were occupied. He signaled the all clear, but use caution, to Menkor.

The Colonel divided his first company into small bands that went from room to room. They killed quickly, taking no prisoners. Surprise was their ally. A prisoner could make noise. When the top floor was clear, the Colonel brought the rest of his troops out of the tunnel. The first company then cleared the next floor. There were two dormitories off the lower level of the main compound and another two on either side of the gate in the outer compound. Each had been designed to bed one hundred soldiers. Menkor had drilled all his men on the map of the fort.

Unfortunately, all the dormitories had more than one entrance.

Menkor's men had no trouble taking out the sentries around the inner compound. They didn't expect to be killed by figures in their own uniforms coming from the area they were protecting.

When everything else in the inner compound had been secured, Menkor set his four companies to take the inner dormitories. One company at each door. They entered as silently as possible. They used knives to slit throats until someone woke. Then they used muskets point blank. Most of the Senangans never woke up. Those that did died quickly.

Unfortunately, there was no way to secure the dormitories in the inner compound without alerting the forces in the outer compound that something was wrong.

If nothing else, most of the Senangan troops were of mixed blood. They felt the violent deaths of their fellow soldiers, at least those awake and fighting.

Menkor ordered two companies to man the walls of the inner compound and took the remainder of his troops out into the outer compound just as the Senangan troops began to emerge from their dormitories. The first few stragglers, still confused as to the source of the danger, were easy to pick off. The fighting in the actual dormitories took longer and was much bloodier.

The retaking of the Fort of Tibati was completed by noon. The Cassingan casualties were close to twenty-five percent. Nathan reported to Del by the telepathic relay, surprised to find Del in the foothills above the source of the Mekambo River, half way to Tibati from Fadiat.

"Is the outer structure of the fortress and the wall across the pass still intact?" Del asked.

"There's no damage to the outer structure or the wall, but we've lost nearly a quarter of our manpower. Tibati usually holds a force of four hundred. Menkor has less than half of that, if Bashan is going to attack."

"There should be reinforcements coming from the Kunguatam. Some of those forces should reach you by this evening. Get the lookouts set up on the western slopes. Don't let Bashan take you by surprise. Even if no one made it out, the lookouts in the emplacements above the fort will have sensed that something's wrong. Some may head for their base in the Kipembatam, but someone is bound to head west and meet the main army. Bashan still has the bulk of the Senangan forces with him. He may even have managed to retrieve more of his malik cavalry by now."

"Understood," Nathan responded. "What were your casualties at Fadiat?"

"We lost thirty-eight of the archers on extended patrol beyond the pass and Bashan managed to knock out one of the cannon emplacements. Five dead. There were over two hundred and thirty lost among the mountaineers. We lost over four hundred rats and three eagles. As for the beach action, we've lost over a hundred, and the count on the losses from the forces crossing the Kungu is at one hundred seventy-nine and still rising. But the Senangan losses have been much heavier and they haven't yet gained anything for their deaths. In fact, with your action at Tibati, they may lose the whole Kipembatam. All we have to do now is stop Bashan one more time. When his troops realize that they've lost Tibati as well as failing to take Fadiat, I don't think they'll follow him any longer."

"How soon can you get here?"

"I expect to arrive within an hour or so of when Bashan does. I have another two hundred of the best mountain fighters we have with me. Just hold on until I get there."

"Yes, rai, we'll do our best."

Nathan wiped a hand blackened with gunpowder across his face, pressing against the pressure points above his eyes to ease an incipient headache. He was exhausted, and he knew all the Cassingan forces were just as tired as he was. But preparations still had to be made. He went to find Menkor and report.

XXV

4652, 466TH CYCLE OF THE YEAR OF THE EAGLE
MONTH OF ILFARNAR

"Morale is always a key factor in any conflict."

— FROM *THE COLLECTED WRITINGS OF VYDARGA THE RED*

N ATHAN WATCHED AS COLONEL MENKOR, exhausted from a forced march and heavy fighting, rose to the new challenge of preparing Fadiat for attack from the west. The first problem Menkor faced in preparing for Bashan's arrival was that the guns were all facing the wrong way. Since the Senangan takeover, all the cannon emplacements had been shifted to face east into Cassinga. But they couldn't all be moved, because there was still a large armed force of Senangans based in the Kipembatam. It was a matter of balance.

Already tired soldiers worked late into the night turning the majority of the heavy guns. Some even had to be dragged from one side of the fortress to the other.

Armed and watchful crews went out to turn the guns in the emplacements on the slopes above. The Senangans who had manned those emplacements were not yet accounted for. Most of them would undoubtedly have fled to the Kipembatam or west into Senanga to warn Bashan, but a few might have stayed around, waiting for a chance to cause damage. The Cassingans had been lucky that those guns were not designed to fire at the fortress, but away from it in its defense.

The arrival of three companies of soldiers from the Kunguatam late that evening helped. Although they had been traveling rapidly to reach Tibati, they had seen no other action and were able to relieve troops who had been both fighting and laboring since the previous night.

At midnight Menkor ordered all the troops who had seen combat to rest in the dormitories in the inner compound, which had been emptied of bodies and thoroughly cleaned. The wounded were bedded down on the upper floor, which had been officers' quarters and offices under the Senangans. Menkor took a room for himself there as well.

"Let me sleep for two hours," he told Nathan. "For the rest of what I need, you can simply clean the fatigue toxins out of my system."

Nathan grimaced. "It's not customary for us..."

"To supply that service for laymen and non-wizards," Menkor finished. "Yes, I know that. But for Jehan's sake, man, this is an emergency. I have to have a clear head and I don't have time to rest."

Nathan nodded. "You're right. But do get your two hours of natural sleep first. Clearing the toxins out won't guarantee a clear head if you don't do that."

Menkor grunted. "Are you going to do the same?"

Nathan shook his head. "It's different for..."

"Wizards," Menkor supplied.

Another company arrived from the Kunguatam just after dawn and Nathan heard again from Del.

"How soon before you reach us?"

"We should be approaching Tibati by early afternoon. I'll send one company to reinforce you in the fortress and use the rest to cause some damage to his rear. I expect that Bashan will be at your gates by then."

"The lookouts have seen no sign of Senangan forces."

"Keep them alert," Del warned.

Nathan made the round of lookout points himself, insisting that they sound the alert for any sign of movement coming up the pass. He also flew Ketan.

Then he surveyed the Cassingan forces as a whole and noted that, despite the stress of recent combat and hard labor, the mood was one of suppressed excitement. The Cassingan soldiers were almost looking forward to the coming action. Their side was winning for once, and they knew it.

The eagle, ranging far down the slopes into Senanga, was the first to spot Bashan's forces just before noon. The infantry which led the way marched in squares of one hundred. There were a great many squares and behind them Bashan had assembled almost a thousand malik cavalry. The total number had been reduced by half.

Menkor ordered the cannon on the fortress walls and the slopes above to begin firing as soon as the Senangans came within range. Then the Senangan army charged, the front ranks carrying scaling ladders.

DEL SENT AERIEMEN COMPANY straight to Tibati to reinforce the walls. He took his other three companies over Mount Karim, northeast to southwest. Tibati blocked the pass on the south slope of the mountain. Del used his soldiers to attack Bashan's flank and reserve forces.

They started with sniper attacks from the high slopes above the trail leading up to Tibati. When the Senangan forces attempted to charge up the slopes to reach them, they melted back to higher ground while their fellows picked the Senangans off from the side.

In some places, falling boulders caused minor avalanches, always at points where the Senangan forces were tightly packed on the trail.

Del had not had time to bring his rats with him, but he had his own native ability to affect the minds of living things. He could only affect two or three maliks at a time, driving them into a killing frenzy, but that was enough to disrupt the ranks of cavalry and make the infantry distrust having cavalry anywhere close.

NATHAN CURSED AS HE CLEARED the sweat off his face with a tattered sleeve blackened with streaks of gunpowder. His skin itched and he had no time to deal with the discomfort as he surveyed the fortress from an observation point high on the inner wall. There were wounded manning some of the walls now, but they had held through two waves of attack. Bashan was regrouping his forces yet again just beyond the range of the cannon.

Fortunately, the Aerieman and two more companies from the Kunguatam had arrived during the morning, and the telepathic relay told him that another two would arrive within the hour. The wounded were already being evacuated to make room for the new troops.

Menkor came up beside him on the wall. "You think they're losing some of their enthusiasm?"

"They should be," Nathan said. "Their losses have been heavier than ours, and I haven't seen any sign of their seige engines. They must have left them behind on the trail, thinking they still held Tibati and wouldn't need them."

Menkor angled his head, "One of many miscalculations on Bashan's part." He waved a hand at the Senangan forces. "That army out there is beaten. Del Maran has not only stopped an invasion from Senanga, he's taken back territory from them. That hasn't been done for generations."

"Del says that Bashan was overconfident, that he left himself wide open to a counter attack."

"That may be," Menkor said, "but I don't know of any other Cassingan commander with the vision to have seen the opportunity, or the nerve to have taken it. I myself would never have dared to even suggest such a thing. We've been beaten too often."

Nathan gripped his shoulder. "Now you'll have to get used to accepting victory."

As though Nathan's words had given them a cue, the Senangan forces suddenly started to form up, but this time they were facing away from Tibati and back into Senanga.

Menkor and Nathan stood side by side and watched as Bashan's army marched away.

DEL MARAN SAT ON A BOULDER high on a slope above the retreating Senangan forces. He was almost light-headed with exhaustion but also buoyed up by a deep sense of satisfaction. His plans had worked.

A bee flew by his face and landed on a wild iris growing in a pocket of earth amid the scree. The sight reminded him of the first linlar he had ever seen, the first he had killed. The reason he was sitting on this hillside.

He'd been eleven when the Senangans had raided Bria, his home village. They'd killed his mother and, after finding her body, in a rage of grief he'd charged down the hill into the village, not caring that all of the linlarin hadn't left. Elise and Entanu, his best friends, had followed him. It had been his fault that Entanu had died, his throat slit by a linlar knife. He and Elise might have died as well, if he hadn't used bees from the beekeeper's hives to kill. Hundreds of bees had died in the process, but so had the last of the Senangan pirates. The following week he had carefully restored the hives, restocking them from wild bees when they'd been too depopulated to survive. It had been painstaking work, altering each individual bee to fit into its new hive, but he'd welcomed the concentration necessary as it had kept him from thinking of his guilt and pain. And he'd never again manipulated a bee.

Yet that event had led to this moment. He sighed and got back to his feet. There was still a lot to do. He wouldn't shadow this moment with any more thoughts of the past.

"BASHAN'S FINISHED. His loses may not have been quite as heavy as Dekese's, but they were close, and Bashan lost territory where Dekese at least gained the Gatoomatam," Balek said. He was pacing back and forth in front of the arched northern windows of the main room of his quarters. He looked as though he were too charged with energy to be able to keep still.

Nearly two weeks had passed since Bashan's defeat. The Kipembatam had been secured and the Council of the Varfarin was again in session. This time to review a victory.

Neither Choma or Jaith had been able to make it back from Senanga, but all of the other regulars were present.

Nathan looked around at the familiar room. It seemed somehow lighter today. Then he realized that it was not the room, but the auras of the people in the room.

"The navy of the Nyali Coast suffered heavy losses," Kaoda said from his usual position next to Selene on one of the couches, "but they count them well spent. This was a great victory for all the humans in Cibata."

"It will take the Senangans years to recover from their losses," Evran said.

"No," Del responded. "I agree with Balek that Bashan's career is finished. But the Senangans won't accept this defeat. They'll try again for Tibati. It may take them a year or two. They lost a large percentage of their forces. They'll need to reform their dekamin. Most of all, they'll need to decide on a new commander, but they'll be back in force within two years. We can't rest on this victory. We need to start now to prepare for the next."

Marala nodded soberly from one of the chairs in front of Balek's desk. "Del's right. The Senangan populace simply won't accept that their troops were out planned and out fought. They'll blame the defeat entirely on Bashan and demand Cassinga's destruction. Dekese will have to appoint another commander and authorize a new offensive or lose everything he gained by Bashan's loss of face."

"Why Tibati?" Pala asked. Nathan felt the defiance in her attitude. She was sitting next to him in one of the chairs by the worktable and she was almost broadcasting, *"I'm an apprentice wizard now. I have the right to speak up."* She was still angry about being shut up during the fighting. "Why won't they try for Fadiat again?"

"Tibati's easier to take," Del said. "It lacks the protection of the cliffs that Fadiat has. Moreover, Tibati's what they lost."

"I think the more pertinent question is how they may adjust their tactics to deal with Del's methods of thwarting their old ones," Marala said.

"They'll never again be able to use large blocks of malik troops in combat against us," Del said. "It depends on who they get to replace Bashan. I'll need information on the new commander as soon as he takes charge."

"I'll get word to both Choma and Jaith so you have as much information as soon as possible," Balek said. "In the meantime, even the Uleins are agreeing to enlarge the military budget and get us more troops in training."

Evran laughed. "Now they're willing to expand the military. When we were desperate, they wouldn't spend another rik."

"Ah," Nathan said, "but then they didn't see the chance for profit off distributing newly reconquered lands. They're planning to make a fortune off the Kipembatam."

Pala frowned. "Can't something be done about that?"

Nathan shook his head. "Not unless Mamfe himself objects."

"That's as likely as having a hippo get up on its hind feet and dance," Pala said bitterly. "At least his health is failing. Cassinga shouldn't have to suffer under his misadministration much longer."

Nathan grimaced. Perhaps Pala shouldn't speak of her grandfather in such a way, but at least she was being honest. She wasn't saying anything the rest of them hadn't thought.

XXVI

4652, 466th Cycle of the Year of the Eagle
Month of Minneth

> *"We set sail when the sun had scarce sunk 'neath the sea,*
> *Then we sailed for four days with the wind shifting tack.*
> *And we failed to sight prey, not a ship could we see,*
> *But we wouldn't give up, no we wouldn't sail back.*
>
> *With our food nearly gone and the water all foul,*
> *We caught sight of a merchanter, fat with his greed,*
> *And we loaded the cargo hold tight as you please*
> *And we ate and we drank up our fill, yes indeed.*
>
> *Chorus: Oh, I took me a ship for to sail on the sea,*
> *And a heigh, nonny heigh, I did sail on the sea."*
>
> — VERSES FROM "THE PIRATE'S BOASTING SONG" FROM *SONGS OF THE SEA AND SHORE*, EDITED BY BAR PANYARA, 4592

SARANITH'S POSTURE BESPOKE HER OUTRAGE as she strode across the chamber where the inquiry was being held. She took her oath flatly, as though the words offended her tongue.

The room was in the east wing of the naval headquarters at Feshi. Instead of being greeted with honor when they sailed into the port for repair of their damaged ships, Mazilek and all his officers had been arrested, as had the officers of all the ships sailing under his command.

While they were later released on the condition that they present themselves at the Court of Inquiry, Saranith was still seething from the insult.

"We have heard from Mazilek and his other officers," said the officer conducting the Inquiry. "None of them have given a proper explanation as to how the troop carriers came to be destroyed while under your fleet's protection. Perhaps you can give a better answer to this Court."

Saranith stiffened at the question, but then spoke firmly in response. "No, rai. Your information is incorrect. None of the troop carriers were damaged prior to their landing on the beach. Not a single shot hit even one of them while they were under our protection."

"Then how do you explain the complete destruction of the landing force?"

Her chin rose even higher. "It is not my responsibility to explain the destruction of the landing force. However, it was obvious to anyone observing that the Cassingans had expected a landing at that site and mined the beach. They also had cannon emplacements all along the shore that had not been present when earlier surveys of the site were made."

"Is it not true that the Cassingan fleet was larger than you expected when you first sailed into the Bay of Dagana?"

"The number of ships in the Cassingan fleet were within the range predicted."

"But they kept on coming. It didn't bother you, an inexperienced arrai, that however many ships you sank, more kept on coming?"

"The additional ships arriving from the Nyali Coast were not a factor in the combat. We achieved our objective of clearing the route to the landing site designated."

He kept on at her for nearly an hour, but he couldn't shake her testimony.

"That will be all we require for today. You're dismissed."

Later, in a bar on the Feshi waterfront she and Luri joined Mazilek and several other of the arrain and officers from his pods. There was a magnum of a robust red wine from Mokoko on the table and Mazilek indicated that they should help themselves.

"Why are they trying to blame us for that debacle?" she asked when she had filled her glass and taken a drink. "Surely they must have realized that was a sail that wouldn't hold wind. There were too many witnesses."

Mazilek shrugged. "I think Bashan simply assumed the navy would be vulnerable after what happened off the Cape of Dirkou. He's been thrashing around to find somewhere else to lay any part of the blame. It's the first time Senanga's lost territory to Cassinga in over a century."

"Well, I'm sorry about the loss of territory," Saranith said, "but I can't say I'm sorry Bashan's lost face."

"No," Mazilek said. "And this little attack of his has backfired badly. If he hadn't made it a formal inquiry, he might have simply implied that much of the blame lay with the navy. Now it's on record exactly who is responsible for the loss of those ships and men. I wouldn't be surprised if Bashan himself faces charges after this"

Later, when a third magnum was nearly empty and several of the officers had taken themselves off to their quarters, Saranith was startled to see Matel Zandezi make his way across the barroom to their table.

"What are you doing here, Matel?" she asked.

"Arrai Kamrasi, Ilarhan Mazilek, I'm pleased to report to you that all the charges against you have been dropped."

One of Mazilek's eyebrows arched. "One of my officers was due to report the outcome as soon as it was known."

Matel smiled wryly. "I imagine he's fighting his way through the crush. I was seated at the rear of the hall, just so I might be able to make a quick escape."

Even as he spoke a somewhat disheveled officer pushed through the entry and hurried across the barroom to their table.

"All charges were dismissed, rai," he said.

Mazilek nodded. "So we've just been informed."

Matel turned to Mazilek. " I must say I'm honored to meet you."

"Must you, indeed. And why would that be?"

Matel looked flustered for a moment, but said, "Because I feel that your acts and your stated position on a number of subjects have had a positive influence on Senangan society."

Mazilek snorted. "And exposed myself and my subordinates to the type of nonsense we've had to undergo during the past three days."

"The Court of Inquiry was certainly an unfortunate occurrence, but I'm fairly certain from the outcome that it caused more harm to your enemies' reputations than to your own."

Mazilek's mouth twisted. "So am I. That doesn't make up for the irritation factor."

The arrain and other officers discussed the finer points of the Court of Inquiry for a time. Saranith noted that Matel had not left, but taken a seat at a neighboring table. When Mazilek's party began to break up, Matel came back over to their table.

"Ilarhan Mazilek, Arrai Kamrasi, I wonder if I could speak with you alone for a moment?"

"What about?" Mazilek asked.

Matel hesitated, then said, "The interesting question of who will replace Bashan?"

Both of Mazilek's eyebrows arched. "An interesting question, indeed." He looked at Saranith. *"Shall we?"* he asked in the intimate mode.

She wanted to refuse but was also curious. *"I've met him before. He has radical opinions, but I don't know anything else about this."*

"Then we'll learn what he wants together," Mazilek thought wryly. "Very well," he said to Matel, "we'll join you. But it's late. Be brief."

"Thank you, Ilarhan. I appreciate that your time is valuable."

Mazilek, Saranith and Luri joined Matel at his table.

"So what is this about?" Mazilek asked bluntly.

Matel said, "You and Saranith are in a position to affect the final decision of who replaces Bashan." His eyes darted back and forth between them. "You could speak to Kaya directly. Saranith has access to him as his cousin, but he might dismiss her opinion." He turned to Mazilek. "She has only recently been raised to the rank of arrai. However, if you were to accompany her, he wouldn't dismiss you."

"The final decision is Dekese's, not Kaya's," Mazilek said.

"But I believe Dekese listens to Kaya more than his other advisors these days."

Saranith watched as Mazilek considered Matel. She knew he was thinking rapidly. There were few people who could weigh issues as quickly as Mazilek. The question was, which way did she hope he would go on this one?

Despite her relationship to the royal family or, perhaps, because of it, she'd never wanted to play politics. But if Bashan had succeeded, his success would have been a disaster for Senanga. If she could use her influence to get someone better selected to replace him, shouldn't she do just that?

The problem with that, she realized, was that she had no idea who might be better to succeed Bashan. Even when she was in port she'd deliberately ignored the give and take between the various political factions.

As though echoing her thoughts, Mazilek asked, "And what name should we be putting forth to replace Bashan's?"

Matel didn't hesitate. "Timaru Kamrasi. He may have no field experience, but he's a brilliant tactician. Ask anyone who's played war games against him at Kobala. I believe he's deliberately avoided field experience because of his brother."

"You want us to recommend Bashan's brother?" Mazilek sounded honestly amazed.

"Timaru's politics are the exact opposite of his brother's. His mate is now openly a worshiper of Jehan."

Mazilek looked thoughtful, then said, "I'm sorry to disappoint you, but whatever Sara's decision may be, I'll have no part in such an appeal. I've never interfered in politics in the past and, if I were ever going to do so, this is not the time I'd choose to begin."

Saranith released her breath. She was both greatly relieved and slightly troubled. She smiled at Matel and said, "As you admitted yourself, my opinion would mean nothing to Kaya or Dekese."

"Then I'm sorry to have interrupted your evening," Matel said, rising abruptly. Saranith felt his acute disappointment.

"Perhaps another time," she said.

He nodded and left.

She turned to Mazilek. "I'm sorry..."

"No," he thought, *"don't appologize. As I tried to tell your friend, it wasn't so much the request I refused, but the timing. Whoever gets appointed to succeed Bashan is bound to fail. Bashan was a good military commander. He made one bad assumption."*

Saranith scanned the room. The bar was less thickly populated now. That would make it easier for listening ears to overhear them. Mazilek was probably wise to use the intimate mode for this conversation. *"I've been hearing strange stories all week about rats and eagles."*

"And archery and avalanches. Cassinga has found someone truly brilliant to guide their defense. To beat the humans now we'll have to find a whole new method of offense. Even if the new commander sees the problem and tries to initiate a new form of tactical offense, he'll be accused of being weak and delaying the Senangan retaliation."

Saranith inclined her head. "You're right."

"I usually am," Mazilek said, a wicked glint in his eye. "But tell your friend that, given better timing, I might well be willing to help his cause the next time the issue comes up. In the meantime I'll find out what I can about your cousin Timaru."

4653, 466TH CYCLE OF THE YEAR OF THE LIZARD
MONTH OF ANOR

SARANITH STARED AT THE INVITATION in her hand, wishing she had not made port that morning, that she had stayed at sea for another month. But she and Luri had disembarked from *Moalo* an hour earlier. They had come home to the house they shared, and she'd picked up the envelope off the tray and opened it.

"From the way you're staring at that piece of paper," Luri said, "I might mistake it for a poisonous snake."

Saranith smiled ruefully. "It might as well be," she said. "It's an invitation to the naming ceremony for Kaya and Jadne's baby."

"At least that won't bite you. Bore you to death, perhaps," Luri said.

"But that's just it, it may bite. Bashan will be there."

"He managed to keep his position as Commander. He should be smiling and keeping a low profile."

"Bashan?"

Luri inclined his head. "You're right. His ego's too big for him to back down, even under these circumstances."

"He wouldn't have kept his position, if Dekese hadn't proposed completely reorganizing the military. Just as Mazilek predicted, none of them are ready to admit that they were honestly beaten, outmaneuvered and out-thought."

The naming ceremony for Nema Kamrasi was held in the audience hall of the royal apartment in Cinkarrak, the Red Tower. The room was shaped like a piece of a pie cut into quarters. The interior walls were paneled with nekatim, a tan colored wood with reddish streaks, and hung with vivid tapestries showing scenes of tigers hunting in the central plains.

"It's good to see you again, cousin," Kaya greeted Saranith at the door.

"I'm glad to attend so happy an occasion," she said, relieved to note that Jadne was with her new baby on the other side of the room.

"Yes, Jadne and I are lucky," Kaya agreed. "Our first is both sighted and gifted with some talent. Perhaps, not as much as I'd hoped. But we'll have others."

Saranith and Luri took seats and waited through the ceremony, which was mercifully brief. A priest of Kyra spoke a few words and drew the baby's name in blood across her forehead. Among the common people of Senanga the naming ceremony was not usually held until after a baby had passed the test for sight, but, as both Kaya and Jadne had the high sight, they'd known the child was sighted from its birth and felt no need to wait.

After the ceremony refreshments were served on tables set against one wall. Saranith and Luri were helping themselves when Jadne came up to them.

"I understand that you testified against Bashan," she said abruptly to Saranith.

"I described honestly my own performance and the performance of Ilarhan Mazilek's fleet in regard to the landing at Kama," Saranith replied carefully.

"Nevertheless, I'm grateful." Jadne smiled crookedly. "Politics makes strange allies at times and I appreciate your support of my mate."

"Kaya will do a better job of guiding Senanga than Bashan would have done."

"I'm glad you see that," Jadne said and departed.

"Whoo," Saranith thought to Luri, *"I never expected that."*

Saranith was carefully keeping most of the room between herself and Bashan and waiting until she could gracefully leave, when a tall, handsome linlar she didn't recognize approached her.

"Good afternoon, cousin. I'm Timaru Kamrasi. I've been told that we share certain interests."

"And what would those be?" she asked.

"A dislike of my brother's politics and beliefs," Timaru said wryly.

"I've tried hard not to take part in politics," Saranith said. "I see no reason to change that policy."

Timaru looked around, checking on who could overhear them and kept his voice low. "Nevertheless, cousin, as a member of the House of Kamrasi, you'll be drawn in. I've supported Kaya in the past because of his moderate leanings, but Jadne is not a moderate, no more than my brother is."

"Kaya killed the jidron"

"But Jadne ate the heart."

XXVII

4654, 466TH CYCLE OF THE YEAR OF THE TIGER
MONTH OF INGVASH

"An ingvalar is lord of the sea,
When he takes the form of a dolphin free.
He loves to play with anything,
But best of all, he loves to sing."

— EXCERPT FROM "THE WEREFOLK" PUBLISHED IN *A CHILD'S GUIDE TO THE LARIN*
AND *OTHER BEASTLY TAILS* BY ENOGEN VARASH OF ELEVTHERAI, 4557

"THE INGVALARIN, THE DOLPHIN FOLK, never come to the shores of Cibata," Nathan said wistfully.

He, Pala and Del were sharing a table at the Doona Ewan. It was only late morning, however, and none of the other regulars were present.

"Well, that's not quite true," Del said. "I've seen ships from Sussey in your port here. But, you're right about the free-living seafolk. They prefer islands as a rule. Although I believe there are colonies around the coast of Kandorra."

"What's he like, this ingvalar friend of your's?" Pala asked Del. She had insisted on joining them when she heard that Errin Anifi might stop by this morning. His presence in Cassinga was frequently discussed, as was his linkage to Lyskarion.

"You'll meet him for yourself in a few minutes," Del said. "I asked him to stop by because Nathan wanted to meet him. But you must remember that Errin's not a typical ingvalar. For one thing, he's a full wizard, a very powerful one."

"But he's not willing to help us against Senanga," Pala said.

"He's not human. This isn't his fight," Del said. "As it is, I understand that he's agreed to help humans in the Thallassean region against the isklarin, the lizard folk. That, by itself, is an almost epic change of policy for one of his race."

"But he bears one of the living crystals," Nathan said. "Doesn't that obligate him?"

"No."

Nathan turned and saw that a tall, broad-shouldered man had come up behind him. The man had straight black hair and blue-green eyes and the jewel that hung around his neck blazed.

"I did not volunteer to bear Lyskarion," the newcomer continued. "I have no obligation toward it and, despite its ability to act on its own, it has no control over me."

"Good morning, Errin," Del said. "May I introduce Nathan Ouakoro and Pala Isiro. Nathan, Pala, this is Errin Yar Anifi, the bearer of Lyskarion and the next Ahar of Sussey."

Errin snorted and sat down in the chair beside Nathan. "Sorry, but I'm touchy on the subject." His hand tapped the gem. "I'm glad to meet you." He looked at Nathan and then at Pala and smiled.

Pala gaped. Nathan could think of no other term for her expression as she looked at the ingvalar. Then she licked her lips and said, "It's good to meet you, too."

Nathan told himself that the lip-licking was a nervous gesture, but it looked sexual, and she was still gazing at Errin as though he were something delicious to eat. Surely she was too young to look that way at a male?

Nathan forced himself to nod politely and say, "I'm also glad to meet you. Sorry if I offended."

"You said that Lyskarion could act on its own," Del said. "There was nothing in our history texts that indicated that the living crystals were capable of that."

"No," Errin said. "But it's true. Lyskarion wanted me to be its bearer and took action to achieve that end."

"Do you think all the karionin have such volition?" Del asked.

"I don't know for sure, but I suspect they do," Errin said. "They're alive, after all. When they were originally made, that aspect may not have been apparent, as their wills would have matched those of their creators."

"But now many of them have been left without guidance for centuries," Del said. "Put that way it does sound inevitable."

Errin shrugged "But that's enough about Lyskarion." He studied Nathan for a moment. "Has Del told you why I wanted to meet you?"

Nathan stiffened. "I thought I'd requested to meet you." He looked at Del whose face looked singularly blank. "I had no idea you'd made a similar request."

"I asked Del to introduce us some time ago, just after I arrived in Cassinga," Errin said, also glancing at Del, "so I suppose it's possible the mighty strategist simply forgot."

"Not forgot," Del said. "I simply thought you might each be more open with the other if you each thought the meeting your own idea."

Nathan chuckled and glanced at Errin. "Manipulating people is what Del does. He doesn't have to have a reason. For him it's just a habit."

Errin nodded. "Yes, Elise told me the same thing about him, illustrated with a number of colorful episodes from their joint childhood."

"Who's Elise?" Pala asked.

"She was my fellow student under the Wizard Ashe," Del said.

"And she's the woman who will someday link with me through Lyskarion," Errin said.

Pala blinked, her attention still on Errin, but Nathan noted that some of the blatant admiration in her eyes abated.

"So," she said, "Why did you want to meet Nathan?"

"Because I'd like to ask for the help of the Varfarin here in Cibata."

"And how could we help you?" Nathan asked.

"The Wizard Rand and I believe that Gandahar has been negotiating with Senanga for the use of a fleet of troop ships for the purpose of invading Darenje," Errin said. "We've already asked Vanda if Ilwheirlane could block the Strait of Belarrai to prevent the fleet from entering the Thallassean. She's willing for Ilwheirlane to attempt to do that, but her advisors indicate that there's no way it can be done without a precise estimate of when the fleet will attempt to pass through."

Errin paused and looked at Del. "When I first arrived, I asked Del if the Varfarin here kept track of Senangan fleet movements. He told me they did. He also said that I'd be better off approaching you rather than the Wizard Balek. The defence of Darenje is Varfarin business, but I was already committed to the cause before I came to bear Lyskarion, or knew that I would succeed my cousin as Ahar of Sussey."

"The problem, as I see it," Del said, "is that at present we have no way of getting a message to Ilwheirlane ahead of the Senangan fleet."

"I'll be returning to the Thallassean within a year. I'm certain, when I tell Vanda of the situation, she'll be willing to station a courier ship here in Candith," Errin said. "If you can get notice of when such a fleet leaves Feshi by your telepathic relay, such a ship leaving from here should arrive in Ilwheirlane well ahead of the Senangans."

"Then, as what you're requesting is Varfarin business," Nathan said, "I see no problem with agreeing to it." He made a face. "I'd better be the one to inform Balek, however."

Pala chuckled.

MONTH OF ANOR

NATHAN STOOD AT THE TOP OF THE WESTERN wall of the Fortress of Tibati and surveyed the activity as the troops manning the walls prepared, once again, to defend them from Senanga. Then he turned to Errin, beside him, and asked, "What made you change your mind?"

"I didn't exactly change my mind," Errin said. "I'm only going to be helping with healing the wounded, unless it looks like the fortress might actually fall. Then I'd be a neutral caught in the cross-fire and entitled to defend myself. As the Senangans will be attacking Tibati, I can't be accused of being an aggressor here."

Nathan angled his head and looked at Errin wryly. "Cutting a few fine hairs."

Errin shrugged. "I've never seen actual combat. I was present when Gandahar took Nadrum, but there was no resistance there. My people, the ingvalarin, have never fought in any war. It goes against our basic nature. I thought I ought to see what it's like." He hesitated, then added, "I suppose I want to see if I'm capable of doing what I must do."

Nathan felt both envy and sympathy. "War is a very ugly business. As I understand it, none of the pure-blooded races of Tamar were familiar with the concept before humans came here, and only the half-breeds have ever taken to it."

He felt a twitch in the link he had with his eagle Ketan and switched his sight to see through the eagle's eyes. The Senangan army had reached the base of the trail leading to the pass. He gazed in awe at the force Bashan had assembled for this offence: five lesdekin, twenty-five thousand soldiers and three thousand malik cavalry.

Nathan relayed the information to Del who commanded seven thousand troops on the slopes of Mount Karim and Mount Esaja on either side of the pass.

Nathan brought his attention back to Errin and said, "It's starting."

"Then I'll leave you to concentrate on your eagle and relays," Errin said. "I do understand what you were saying. My blood is mixed." He turned and departed down the inner steps.

Nathan watched him go, trying to imagine what it would be like to have never experienced war. Then he returned his mind to the link with Ketan and watched as the battle began to unfold.

PALA ENTERED WHAT HAD ONCE BEEN her bedroom, conscious that this was the first time she had been in Tibati since the attack seven and a half years ago. There was nothing familiar in the room, however. It was just another temporary hospital ward with three beds holding two of the injured. A steady stream of them were coming in now from the mountain slopes.

Pala sat down on the edge of the bed next to one, a man younger than she was with a concussion and a bullet wound in his thigh. She made sure their was no brain damage and repaired a few capillaries around the head wound then turned her attention to his leg. The bullet had passed clear through, but left debris in its path. She used her sight and concentrated, cleaning out the wound, relinking torn capillaries, reknitting the flesh.

Part of her training had been healing in the clinics in Candith, but she had rarely had to deal with open wounds. She sighed when she was done and the injury was closed. He had lost blood and was not fully healed. He would be weak for days, but she could do no more for him under these conditions, not with so many more to treat.

She moved to the other bed. It held a woman some years older than Pala with a bullet wound in her shoulder. Unlike the boy, she was awake and said, "The bullet's lodged. You look real young to be a healer. You any good at this?"

"I'm not just a healer," Pala said, suppressing her indignation. The patient had a right to ask. "I'm an apprentice wizard. I assure you I know what to do."

"All right," the woman nodded. "Get on with it then."

DEL WATCHED AS A DEKAM of Bashan's malik cavalry set out after a unit of archers. The archers retreated quickly, keeping to the preset route. When they were all clear, Del applied the force of his mind to the rocky cliff above where they had been. The maliks and their riders, halfway up the slope, had no chance to escape the resulting avalanche.

He sighed, feeling the deaths as sharp pains. He could have shut them out, but feared to do so. What might he become if he did not feel the pain of every death he caused?

He took a deep breath and let it out. He had passed all of the qualifications to be a full wizard. This would be his last battle for a long time. He would go back to the Northern Hemisphere and let his family watch him be elevated. He would take the name, Arrun, which was what Elise had called him when they were young. Arrun, the Jester.

But death was not a jest and he was tired of it. Sick to his soul of it, if truth were told. He would hold together for this last battle, because he believed that what he was doing had to be done. But then he needed a break. He would come back. Cibata was in his blood now. But first, he needed time to heal himself.

A call came in from the relay and Del returned his attention to the battle.

PALA WALKED OUT INTO THE COURTYARD. Her head ached from overuse of her talent, the stretching of her mind to heal just one more, and then another. Errin, who had taken charge of the hospital as the most powerful healer present, had finally ordered her to rest.

She rubbed a hand over her face. She knew she needed to rest, but she was too tense. She looked up and saw Nathan on the western wall. She climbed the inner stairs and stood next to him on the parapet. "How's it going?" she asked, when he registered her presence.

"About as we expected it to go. Bashan hasn't brought any surprises. He hasn't even managed to train the maliks."

"Can maliks be trained?" Pala asked, surprised.

"Del says they can be, with a little work on the part of the handlers. If they're accustomed to seeing rats on a regular basis, they'll eventually get over the chase and destroy instinct."

"It seems so strange," she said. "I remember how terrified I was that Cassinga would fall the last time I knew Bashan was coming. This time, I'm worried about what our losses will be, of course, but I'm not afraid of losing."

"No," Nathan said and their eyes met, more, their inner awareness met, the linkage almost forming itself. They both pulled back almost as quickly, but Pala had felt his understanding and his admiration for her. Yet, he still thought of her as a child.

She would have to change that. For years she had sensed that he might be the one with whom she could link, now she was sure of it. Even that brief moment of contact had felt so right, so good.

Pala made herself smile at Nathan as though nothing had happened. "Errin sent me off to get some rest. I'd better get it now."

"Yes. You'd better," Nathan said, turning away to refocus on Ketan and the relays.

DEL WATCHED as his ten picked companies of horse-mounted cavalry charged into the Senangan infantry reserves at the foot of the trail up to the pass. He couldn't have used them if any of the Senangan malik cavalry had still been a factor, horses were terrified of maliks. However, they were highly effective against the Senangan infantry. The linlarin had never faced cavalry before and had no idea how to defend themselves from it. The human cavalry mowed through them like a scythe through a field of wheat.

When the cavalry had cleared the field at the foot of the trail, Del ordered them to take Bashan's supply train. Then he ordered them all to retreat and set fire to the train. Bashan's ammunition supplies made a satisfying explosion.

BASHAN KAMRASI HEARD THE NEWS that his reserves and his supply train had been destroyed with fatalistic calm. He had long ago accepted that he would either win Tibati back, or die in the attempt. It appeared now that he would die, but he would take as many of the human scum with him as he could.

He prayed to Kyra the Destroyer that whoever became commander after him would succeed where he had failed, and cleanse Cibata of the human taint. Then he ordered a final charge on the Fortress, leading it himself. He actually made it halfway up the wall before taking a musket shot in the chest, which stopped his heart instantly so he had no chance to heal himself.

NATHAN STOOD ON THE WALL and watched as the last of the Senangan forces fled down the trail to the west. He felt as though he'd been standing in that spot for a lifetime, but the entire battle had taken less than two days. Marala came up beside him. "So, it's done. We've turned them back again, and again they took losses of over fifty percent. Do you think that this time they'll give it up and let us have peace for a while?"

"Del says we'll have at least five years," said Nathan. "The Senangans will recognize this time that they need to completely remodel their army to deal with our new strategies. I hope he's right about how much time we have, because I don't know how we'll function if they attack while he's gone."

"He will come back won't he?" asked Marala.

"He says he will."

XXVIII

4655, 465TH CYCLE OF THE YEAR OF THE DOLPHIN
MONTH OF DIRGA

Dom ba nik et lomcaul
Cum taga am u dom.

*"Love is pain or pleasure
as wills the one who loves."*

— ESLARIN PROVERB

NATHAN WATCHED AS DEL MARAN, soon to be the Wizard Arrun, stood on the pier next to Errin, supervising the loading of their luggage onto the *Gallinule,* a two-masted ship somewhat broad in the beam for carrying cargo. It would be sailing for Ilwheirlane within the hour.

"There's nothing I can say to keep you here?" Nathan asked.

Del shook his head. "No, not now. I want my father to see the ceremony that elevates me to being a full wizard and, frankly, I need a break from heat and jungles."

"And death," Nathan said quietly.

"That, too," Del acknowledged.

"I've come to understand that you of the north aren't as accustomed to death as we've become in Cassinga. I envy you that."

Balek, Evran and the whole group from the Doona Ewan arrived then to say farewell, primarily to Del, but to Errin as well since in the past few months he, too, had become a regular at the dockside tavern.

Errin said his goodbyes then followed the luggage to the cabin he would share with Del.

Balek looked at Del. "I'd like a private word before you depart."

"Very well, rai," Del said politely.

Nathan watched as Balek bore Del off to a point where they could not be easily overheard. In such an exposed place as the port, Balek would also erect a privacy shield.

"What's that about?" Pala asked, turning to him.

"Balek being Balek," Nathan said ruefully. "Even after Errin helped us at Tibati, he's concerned about a non-human bearing one of the karionin. He's also worried about the fact that the crystal showed volition. He wants Del to find out if Errin has complete control or not."

"And what he'd really like to do is take Lyskarion away from Errin and give it to someone here," Pala said.

"You've got it."

PALA GRIMACED WHEN NATHAN went all wistful at the sight of Lagura and the Clarants heading back to town after the *Gallinule* sailed. It seemed as if, all her life, Nathan had been pining for Lagura.

Pala looked around the pier, but the others had all departed leaving her alone with Nathan. She swallowed, then blurted out, "You could never have had a long term relationship with Lagura, even if she hadn't found Bella."

Nathan stiffened and scowled at her. "What are you talking about?"

"The way you watch Lagura all the time," Pala said, knowing she should stop and let it go, but unable to now she had started. "You think you're in love with her, but you never see her, just the image you created long ago. You're too stubborn for your own good. You've carried a childhood crush into manhood and made it into an obsession. But it would never have worked."

"You're too young to know what you're talking about, Pala," Nathan said stiffly.

"Am I?" she said, her chin rising and thrusting forward with her anger. "Imagine touring the dockside bars and attending large, noisy parties. Imagine actually living with her the way she likes to live. You don't even like the same foods. I may be years younger than you, Nathan, but in some ways you've never grown up, and you need to start."

"What difference does it make to you?" he protested.

"Because I am a woman now. I care about you, but you've never even looked at me," Pala said. Then she turned and marched away up the pier. She knew she shouldn't have said what she had, but he made her so angry she hadn't been able to stop herself.

NATHAN STARED AFTER PALA, stunned. She was just a child, a voice in his mind protested. But had he considered himself a child at the age of nineteen? He remembered all the times recently when just the sight of her had brought him pleasure. Then he smiled ruefully. His heart hadn't lifted at the sight of Lagura since he had been even younger than Pala was now. That by itself was something he needed to think about. Pala might be right. Maybe what he thought about Lagura had simply become habit.

But before Pala had spoken, he had never had anyone else he cared about, or to whom he was attracted. That seemed to have changed without his even realizing it. He did care about Pala. He did find her attractive. Maera's mercy, he found her beautiful.

He took a deep breath and let it out. He would meditate and purge his mind of the old habit patterns. That should not be hard now that he knew the feeling was gone from them. He was a wizard, training his mind was part of what he was. Then he would see.

Book III

THE HEART OF FIRE

"There was a time when wizards ruled the world,
And in that Golden Age the wizards made
Eight living crystals to enhance their power
And guarantee their patterns never fade."

— EXCERPT FROM "ILKARIONIN: THE LIVING CRYSTALS" FROM *LEST WE FORGET: A BOOK OF TEACHING RHYMES* BY WILTON WIRRAMARETH OF ILWHEIRLANE, 4207

XXIX

"Then came the plague when millions died and all
Of human life was nearly swept away,
When Agnith and Ilfarnar did conceive
Cinkarion, the Heart of Fire, that they

"Might fight for others' lives and never mind
Their own. And Luth and Dirga in despair
Brought forth Lyskarion, the Song of Wind,
To heal the sick and cleanse the world of care."

— EXCERPT FROM "ILKARIONIN: THE LIVING CRYSTALS" FROM *LEST WE FORGET: A BOOK OF TEACHING RHYMES* BY WILTON WIRRAMARETH OF ILWHEIRLANE, 4207

I T BEGAN AS AN ITCH IN HER MIND. Saranith ignored it at first. The *Cinhai* was in dangerous and unfamiliar waters. She needed to focus her attention on the sea, or at least on the charts that plotted their location.

They were sailing southeast out of Nadrum, the newest port friendly to Senangans in the Thallassean. As a relative of Dekese Kamrasi, she had been sent from Cibala to continue the ongoing negotiations with Aavik of Gandahar for the use of Senangan ships in a planned invasion, date still uncertain. Gandahar had no fleet of ships or seagoing tradition, although, Saranith understood, ships were beginning to be built in Kavarna and part of the negtiations had included her taking isklarin aboard for training in seamanship.

As this was a political mission, and as she was due to rendezvous with Aketi before leaving the Thallassean, she had not brought the other two ships now under her command, her own old ship *Moalo* and a ship captured at the Bay of Dagana, *Salasar*.

With the political maneuvering behind her, Saranith planned to follow the shipping lanes from Lamath, Sardom, Anat and Mahran east across the south coast of the Thallassean to Ravaar. She felt sure of a rich prize to reward her crew for the long journey without, heretofore, any other bounty, not even a decent cargo load, as the markets in the Thallassean were unknown. Senangan pirates were rare in these waters and her ship was better built than those sailing from Ravaar. She'd see that her crew didn't suffer because of her political connections.

Still, despite her attempts to ignore the itch, it niggled at her mind. She couldn't close it out and it grew stronger as they sailed south. She shook her head.

"What's the matter, Sara?" Luri asked. "You've seemed distracted all afternoon." They were in the captain's cabin in the stern of *Cinhai*, Saranith at the chart table and Luri at the desk putting entries in the ship's log.

"It's nothing," Saranith said, turning and smiling at her mate. She hesitated, then added, "It's just that I feel like something's calling me." She never kept anything from Luri.

"From the west? That's where you keep looking. I thought the Bane disturbed you."

She rose and went to the porthole facing west and studied the ragged coast of what had once, before the Bane, been Arduin, one of the richest coastal regions on Tamar. "No, I hadn't even realized that's where we are."

"People don't live there anymore."

Saranith had a sudden image of something red and sparkling, lying in the westering sun. She remembered the history of the Bane, where most of the wizards on Tamar had died some eight hundred years before. "Cinkarion was never found. Cormor took most of the others, but he couldn't find the Heart of Fire."

"The living crystal that caused the Bane?"

"Agnith caused the Bane, not her crystal," she said sharply, feeling the denial in her mind and knowing it wasn't her own.

"Are you all right," Luri asked, sounding concerned. "You're pale. What's the matter?"

"I have to go ashore," Saranith said, feeling breathless, unsure whether the cause was shock or anticipation.

"What? We're off the coast of Arduin. There's nothing ashore and what happens if we're spotted by one of the naval vessels that patrol these waters? Without you we'd be a sitting duck."

"There's a cove to the southwest," she said, remembering the chart she'd been studying. "If we put in there, we'll be out of sight of any passing patrol. I don't think I'll be gone long. I don't have far to go."

"How do you know?"

"It told me." She shook her head. "I can't tell you how. It's not in words. It's images, feelings. But it's out there and it wants me. Me. No one else will do."

They took shelter in the cove and two crewmen rowed her ashore.

She set off along a path paralleling a small stream. The land was not a desert as she had half expected it to be. Grass and low bushes covered the ground inland, as they had on the shore. There were even insects, snakes, lizards and other creatures that might have been some kind of rodent. She noticed a lizard lying on a rock still warm from the setting sun, and directed her inner vision to it again because it had two tails.

It took her nearly three hours of steady walking to reach an area where the sparse grass dwindled and the ground seemed to have been glazed. The call inside her summoned her to the very center of the cracked and blasted field. There she found a blood red crystal the size and shape of a goose egg lying on the ground by itself. It wasn't buried in the earth or concealed in any way. There wasn't even any dust on it. She remembered her vision of it sparkling in the sunlight, but its core was dark.

She contemplated it for some time, knowing that picking it up would change her life forever. But there was never any doubt in her mind as to her final decision. She was merely savoring the moment. This was Cinkarion. She had felt it from *Cinhai*, but now she could sense it with her inner vision. It belonged to her. It had called her, and no one else.

She reached down and picked it up. A flame flared in the red heart of the crystal, then diminished, then flared again. She realized it was pulsing in the same rhythm as her heart. And then she felt the pain, the deep and terrible pain. It tried to tear her mind apart. She felt the flesh burning away from her bones, but they weren't just her bones. There were thousands of bodies and minds, all burning inside her. She felt the agony as each life was burned away.

She cried out, the immeasurable pain rushing through her mind like a great wave, trying to drown her. But the wave could only spread so far before it struck against the rocky center of her being. She was stone and slowly the wave retreated. A lifetime of control took over and she pushed the pain away, shut it down, stopped it. "Enough," she said.

It took some time to regulate her heart from pounding and reduce her adrenaline level. Only when she was again calm and barricaded did she concentrate on the crystal once again.

The light at its core still pulsed steadily with the beat of her heart. Would she have to endure that pain every time she wished to use it? She reached out carefully. No. She'd shut the pain away and it would stay that way in future. It would always be there in Cinkarion's memory, but she'd only needed to feel it once. The price of the linkage to Cinkarion was that her mind had to feel what Agnith felt when she died in fire, still linked to all the other wizards also dying in fire. She'd had to experience the Bane, and Cinkarion had chosen her because the crystal sensed that her mind would not break.

Many minds had come close enough for Cinkarion to call them over the centuries since the Bane, but hers was only one it had called. Saranith closed her inner eye and meditated in silence. She'd been tested, but she'd triumphed. She was now the bearer of Cinkarion. She would be a great wizard. And no one would threaten anyone she loved ever again.

XXX

4655, 466TH CYCLE OF THE YEAR OF THE DOLPHIN
MONTH OF ANOR

Ocala uthadin a sarcaul.
Dacabo ut less ba cum gulon at dabaod cum malacab.

*"Beware extremes of emotion.
Too great a happiness is as dangerous to well-being as
despair."*

— ESLARIN PROVERB

T HE JOURNEY BACK TO *CINHAI* SEEMED shorter to Saranith. Cinkarion felt warm in her hand. She thought that there must once have been a clasp attached to the narrower end of the crystal, but it would have melted away in the fires of the Bane. She would replace it when she got back to Senanga. She imagined a clasp in the form of an eagle's foot with the talons grasping the jewel. The eagle's foot would be gold, but the talons would be black enamel. She would wear Cinkarion on a gold chain around her neck. The image pleased her and she smiled.

Then it occurred to her that it might be wise to conceal her possession of the crystal, at least until she had learned how to use it fully. Cinkarion was a great prize. People had died for far less. She pressed the crystal against her forehead, relishing the sense of connection, then tucked it away in the pouch attached to her uniform harness.

Luri was examining her trail when she got back to the cove. "Sara," he greeted her. "We were worried. You said your errand wouldn't take long, but it's been over six hours since you went ashore. I was about to lead a search for you."

"No need, as you see," she said, too exhilarated to be bothered by his worry She ordered everyone back to *Cinhai*. Then she oversaw the raising of sails and tacking back out of the cove to the open sea. Only when they had resumed their previous course and were sailing southeast again toward Sardom did she turn command over to the Second Farail Enoch Kaltos, and return to her cabin where Luri was waiting.

"What did you find?" he asked as soon as she entered.

"What I hoped to find," she said, reaching into her pouch and holding out Cinkarion. "See, the Heart of Fire, just where I saw it last evening. I can't communicate with it very well yet. I need to learn the high sight. I'll be able to speak to it then. Now, it's just images and feelings." She sighed.

"You planned to learn the high sight anyway, when you find someone to teach you."

"But now the need is more urgent," Saranith said. "All my relations will want it, and none of them will think twice about killing me to get it."

"None of the males can use it," Luri said. "It's Jadne you have to worry about. She'll think it belongs with the Royal House."

"It's linked to me. It can only be unlinked by my death. Once I wouldn't have expected Kaya to support her. Now I'm not so sure."

Luri shook his head looking at her. " I've never seen you so excited. It frightens me. It's as though you're glowing."

Saranith crossed the room and hugged him. He was her support and her conscience. She sometimes forgot that he was also frailer than she. "Then we'll link and we'll both feel my joy," she said. "I'll give you my strength, and you can give me your worry."

"Not an even trade," he said weakly. She ignored the fear she saw in his face.

"But it is," she said, looking him straight in the eyes. "What you give me has always been equal to what I've given you. I need you, Luri. I need you close to me. I know you think I'm the stronger, but you're part of my strength. It wouldn't be there without you."

Saranith felt a burning sensation from Cinkarion, as though it were trying to get her attention, but her relationship with Luri was too important for her to heed the crystal at that moment. "Link with me, Luri," she said. "We've linked before, when making love. This time make it permanent through Cinkarion."

"Sara, I can't..."

She grabbed his shoulder with her free hand as he tried to turn away from her. "No, Luri. This time I won't let you say no. It's too important. The living crystals were designed to link two minds. I can never link with anyone but you. You must link with me."

His eyes were sad. Saranith wanted to shake him, make him see that everything would be all right now. "Don't you love me?" she demanded.

His eyes widened. "Of course I love you, Sara, but this..."

"You can do this," Saranith said, full of her own vision of their future.

"You said it wanted your strength. I'm not strong," Luri said desperately.

"But I'm strong enough for both of us," she said.

Luri swallowed and nodded, knowing that this time he couldn't sway her. This meant too much to her. He'd put himself in her hands, as he'd always done. Saranith knew best, and he loved her.

She brought the crystal up between them. "Link your hand with mine around the crystal."

His hand came up slowly and then linked with hers. As it closed around the crystal pain flared through them. They screamed and he drowned in the flames.

Saranith tried to shut it away, as she had before, but it was in Luri's mind now, as well in her's and in Cinkarion. She couldn't get it out of his mind. She screamed, but his mind was burning and she couldn't stop it. She felt him die, as she had felt Agnith die, and all those other minds. But this was Luri. He wasn't supposed to die. He was hers. She was going to link with him forever.

But Luri was dead. For a moment she wanted to let the pain swallow her, too, but her instinct for survival was too strong. She shut the pain away. She wanted to cry out, to scream, but could do neither. She could only stare at the dead body of the man she loved collapsed on the floor at her feet. Her jeweled eyes had no tear ducts. She could not even cry.

XXXI

"They fought upon a field in Arduin,
Where Agnith, mad with rage and bitter hate,
Called down the very power of the sun.
So did the Age of Wizards meet its fate.

There was a time when wizards ruled the world,
And in that Golden Age the wizards made
Eight living crystals. So, while wizards die,
The karionin live and never fade."

— EXCERPT FROM "ILKARIONIN: THE LIVING CRYSTALS," FROM *LEST WE FORGET: A BOOK OF TEACHING RHYMES* BY WILTON WIRRAMARETH OF ILWHEIRLANE, 4207

A T DAWN OF THE TENTH DAY AFTER LURI DIED, Saranith was summoned from her cabin. There were two ships to the west of them, in obvious pursuit.

"Why weren't they spotted before now?" she asked the lookout. "They must have been chasing us for a good part of the night to have gotten so close."

The lookout stared down at the deck. "Wasn't looking behind us so much as south an' east. Looking for prey."

"And forgot to check for predators," Saranith said. "Well, it can't be helped now, but let it be a lesson to you for the future. Check in all directions. And I'll deduct a half point from your share this trip."

Saranith turned and eyed the two naval barkentines from Sussey slowly closing on *Cinhai*, glad of the need for action, glad of anything that might help her forget, even for a moment, the horror of Luri's death.

The shipwrights of Sussey were the finest on Tamar, their hull designs superior. *Cinhai* had been built from designs copied from the ships of Sussey, but *Cinhai* was older, her hull design not quite as sleek as that of the predators that chased her. *She* had no hope of outrunning the pursuers on a straight course before the wind. Nor would she want to face two naval ships of Sussey in battle. The ingvalarin were uncanny sailors, sensing every nuance of wind and wave. Saranith nodded, pleased by the challenge.

She might not be able to outrun the pursuers before the wind, but her schooner rig could reach closer into the wind. The barkentines could outpoint any other square-rigged ship, but not a schooner.

She wondered why they were chasing her. She had not yet taken any prizes in these waters, and those were naval ships. Sussey was, moreover, a neutral country. Were they somehow aware of the Heart of Fire now locked in the desk in her cabin? If so, she wished she could just fling it overboard or present it to them, but she knew that would mean her death. In other hands it could be used to reach her, a direct conduit into her mind. She wasn't ready to die. Choosing death was not a part of her nature.

And, in any event, they couldn't know about Cinkarion. She'd have to watch out for paranoia. It would be ironic if mere possession of the jewel drove her to madness. She shook her head. Cinkarion hadn't driven Agnith mad, that was caused by the death of her life mate, Ilfarnar.

She reached out with her sight and read the names of the pursuing ships, *Cyring* and *Tolu*. The second name drew a wry smile. "Tolu," peace, the beautiful fruit, the sublime moment of the gods. But like all fruits, peace was evanescent. She ordered the hands to the rigging and turned *Cinhai* north northeast, almost into the wind.

She was fairly sure she could lose her pursuers if the wind held from the north and she kept this course, veering only slightly northwest to avoid the Dalossian Archipelago. However, she still had no prize for her crew. The ships behind her were warships. They would make an extraordinarily fine prize, even if she had to share them. Moreover, there would be no innocent passengers on a warship. She'd let them chase her straight to her rendevous point with Aketi and *Sukatta Bel*. Aketi, as an ilarhan, commanded three ships and usually kept them close, so there would probably be two, but at least one other ship with him. That would put the odds back in Senanga's favor.

She grimaced. She didn't like the idea of doing Aketi a favor.

"Hold this course," she said finally to Kaltos, her first farail now Luri was dead. He had the duty watch. She added, "If they get too far behind, nose us a little out of the wind."

Kaltos grinned. "Yes, rai."

Saranith wanted enough lead that, if the wind failed or shifted, she'd have time to correct without being caught, but she also didn't want to lose her pursuers. And she had a time factor to consider. Aketi wasn't due at the rendevous point for seven days. If she got there too early, she would have to flee in earnest.

All the way through the Dalossian Archipelago the chase had been tighter than she'd expected it to be. She thought her pursuers' uncanny awareness of depths was due to better charts and the natural werevision of the ingvalarin. She herself had spend hours with her vision extended, mapping the islands and plotting *Cinhai's* course. The drain on her strength had forced her to get Cinkarion out of her desk. She carried it now in a cloth purse tied to a loop of string so it hung between her breasts.

On the last afternoon she planned on spending amid the islands she let the pursuit get close enough for the wizards to try an attack.

She was still well out of cannon range. She hadn't known before then that the pursuing ships had wizards aboard. Fortunately, she was on deck with her vision extended and saw the force of the mind link closing in on *Cinhai*.

She had never taken part in a wizard duel. The other children, even Aketi, had been wary of her after she regained her sight so she had never practiced the techniques of wizard combat. All she could do was strike out at the force attacking her ship. She envisioned her will as a hammer and struck with all her force and all she could draw from Cinkarion.

She felt the blow from her will break up the linkage. She was suddenly so tired she could hardly stand. She turned to the nearest crewman. "Summon Farail Kaltos. Tell him he has command."

She turned to the helmsman. "Keep to the plotted course."

She waited until Kaltos arrived, running. "What happened?"

"They have wizards aboard. Powerful ones. I've defeated their first attack. But I need rest. Try not to let them get this close to us again. Use the chart I made and break for the open sea as soon as possible."

"Yes, Ilarhan."

She had barely three hours rest before Kaltos had her summoned.

"What's happened?" she asked, seeing the pursuing ships too close behind *Cinhai*, almost within cannon range.

"I haven't been able to lose them," Kaltos said. "I thought you needed to be warned with them so close."

She nodded. "I'll take the duty now. We've less than an hour's sail to open sea."

The rest, brief as it had been, had restored her somewhat and she was glad that she'd taken the duty when *Tolu* fired her forechasers full of grape shot. It took concentration to deflect the mass of tiny metal pieces, much more difficult than deflecting a single cannon ball. She realized that the wizards counted on that and were trying to wear her down. They fired four rounds before apparently deciding the effort was futile.

She was extremely relieved when they reached the open sea north of the Archipelago and *Cinhai* was again able to widen the gap, but just after midnight the wind suddenly shifted and nearly died.

It took all her skill to keep ahead of her pursuers and still keep the ship on course for the rendezvous. When, just before dawn, she spied *Sukatta Bel* and *Kanakar* she felt relieved.

She went to her cabin and put Cinkarion away in her desk. She'd have to warn Aketi about the wizards and, much as they hated each other, she and Aketi knew each other well. She didn't want him to feel any difference in her mind touch.

"*Aketi,*" she called out to him mentally, "*I bring prizes on my tail. Warships from Sussey. I thought you would have another ship with you.*"

"*My lookout has seen them,*" Aketi responded. "*We're preparing to come about and attack. I sent Karadnin to Ravaar to renew our supplies. I wasn't expecting you to bring such fine company.*"

"*They have wizards aboard.*"

"*What have you been doing to make you so popular?*"

"*I don't know.*" She put as much conviction into that thought as she could. She might suspect that, with wizards aboard, it had something to do with her finding Cinkarion, but she didn't know that.

She added, "*They may not have understood that this was a diplomatic mission. In fact, they may have mistaken me for a pirate.*" Aketi might be an evil-minded little fathik, but he wasn't totally lacking a sense of humor.

"*Very good, cousin,*" he responded, and she sensed his amusement. "*But I get the credit for any prizes taken. After all, I'm rescuing you.*"

"*I could have left them behind days ago, and you'd have had nothing,*" she protested.

"*And now I have a nasty battle with wizards,*" Aketi answered. "*I can't seem to muster much gratitude.*" He broke off the connection.

XXXII

4656, 466TH CYCLE OF THE YEAR OF THE MALIK
MONTH OF ILFARNAR

Amlar ba grel u mo garm a lorin.

"One is wise who fears the anger of the gods."

— ESLARIN PROVERB

AKETI BROKE OFF THE CONNECTION with Saranith. He sensed that she was trying to conceal something from him. The beikasar thought she was clever enough to fool him. But he would find out what she was hiding when the battle was over. In the meantime, he had prey to take.

He ordered all twelve cannon on the port side out and loaded. They would make a direct pass and catch both the ships from Sussey, then come about and rake them with the starboard cannon. He had Mobley Hamel, his first farail, relay the orders to Arrai Stalik of *Kanakar*.

He knew he need not bother to send orders to Saranith. Much as he resented her independence, he respected her skill in battle. She'd know what to do.

Even as he had the thought, he saw her ship come about to fall in line behind *Kanakar*. If only he could get her under his command long enough to tame her, what a mate she'd make.

"Tell the gunner crews to go for the masts. Don't hit below the water line," he ordered Gatek, his second farail. "We want prizes, not wreckage."

As *Sukatta Bel* drew abreast of *Tolu* he gave the order to fire. *Tolu* fired its cannon at the same moment. Aketi strained to deflect the shot, angered by the fact that most of it was aimed at or below the water line. In the end, he couldn't deflect it all. His ship took two hits, but he did manage to deflect them upward so that they only penetrated the lower deck.

At least his own gunners had crippled *Tolu*, bringing down the foremast. He told Mobley to order crews below to plug up the holes.

Then they were abreast of the second enemy ship. Again, he gave the order to fire. But this ship was as well protected with wizards as the first had been. All the cannon shot from his ship was deflected, and again he had to strain to deflect the shots aimed at *Sukatta Bel*. And these also were shots aimed to sink his ship, not disable it for capture. Aketi's jaw clenched as his ship took another hit.

He ordered his ship to come about and looked back to see what *Kanakar* had achieved. Then he cursed fluently. *Kanakar* had done no noticeable damage to *Tolu*, but had hit *Cyring* below the waterline. Stalik was an idiot. He'd see that the man received no further promotions. He'd see the man reduced to a garbage scow. Then he saw that *Kanakar* was also hit below the waterline.

Well, he thought, that takes care of Stalik. He can sink with his ship.

Then he saw that *Cinhai* had taken out *Tolu's* rudder. He might at least break even when this battle was over. He ordered the starboard guns primed as *Sukatta Bel* approached *Cyring* for the second pass. It might be sinking, but that didn't mean its teeth had been pulled, he thought savagely. This little adventure of Saranith's was costing him. But his dear brother-in-law, the wishy-washy Kaya, had ordered him to see to Saranith's safety on this mission.

He forced his attention back to the approaching enemy. *Cyring* was now obviously going down. He ordered half the starboard cannon loaded with grape shot. At least he could inflict a little pain on the wretched ingvalarin.

What were they doing chasing Saranith? And with wizards on board. It had to be something to do with the Varfarin. But what?

The Varfarin would undoubtedly disapprove of the negotiations with Gandahar, but to send warships after Saranith when the negotiations hadn't even been finalized?

The puzzle nagged at him as his ship pounded the already crippled *Cyring* and proceeded on toward *Tolu* which had been dead in the water.

Now, however, he saw that the ingvalarin crew had performed miracles. The rigging from the fallen mast had already been cut away and the rudder repaired. *Tolu*, which he had expected to be easy prey, was coming about to match him broadside for broadside.

Saranith, you'll pay for this, he swore, as he ordered the cannons readied and primed. Then he was too busy deflecting cannon shot to even think. This time he got them all. Unfortunately, he noted, so had the wizards aboard *Tolu*. No damage done, no damage inflicted. Well, maybe *Kanakar* would still manage to show some teeth. Or Saranith. He ordered Mobley to tell the helmsman to bring *Sukatta Bel* about for another pass.

"Yes, rai? But shouldn't we be preparing to take on the crew from *Kanakar*?" Mobley asked. "She's going to go down."

Aketi frowned at Mobley, angered that any member of his crew would dare to question his commands. Then he looked toward the second ship of his pod and saw that *Kanakar* had broken away from the combat.

"Then let her go down," he said sharply. "*Cinhai* can take on any survivors after the next pass. We have a prize to take."

Cyring was sinking. Rescuing the crew of *Cyring* would distract *Tolu*, make the surviving ship easier to take.

He noted that *Tolu* was already closing on the sinking ship, but *Cinhai* wasn't moving to attack. Instead, *Cinhai* was changing course toward *Kanakar*, now definitely listing and about to sink.

He cursed Saranith again. He ordered both the port and starboard cannon reloaded. He would take *Sukatta Bel* right between the two ships from Sussey and blast them both. He tried to reach Saranith by mind touch. There was no response.

"Signal *Cinhai* to have the Arhan report to me immediately," he ordered Mobley, his eyes daring the man to question his authority once again.

"Yes, rai," Mobley said, with dutiful humility.

"Tell Gatek to use grape shot in half the starboard cannon," he ordered. "We don't want to sink *Tolu*. We want to take her. The more of her crew we eliminate the better, but if any shot goes below the waterline, I'll hang the gunner crew. Do I make myself understood?"

"Yes, rai."

Just when Aketi had almost given up on any response from *Cinhai*, he received a tentative mind touch from Farail Kaltos. "*Reporting to the senior officer in charge, this is acting Arrai Kaltos.*"

"*Where's Saranith? Why did you break off from the attack?*" Aketi demanded.

"*Saranith's unconscious. She was injured in the last action. Without her Cinhai has no way to block cannon fire and Kanakar's sinking. I judged that saving the crew of Kanakar was our best course.*"

"*How badly is she hurt?*" Tarat's furies, Aketi cursed, was nothing going to go right this day?

"*She took a blow to the head, but she was already exhausted. She's hardly slept for days while we were coming through the Archepelago. I don't think she's badly hurt, but I can't wake her.*"

"*Then continue as you are. Save those you can from Kanakar, then get the hell out of the Thallassean and back to Senanga.*"

"*Yes, Arhan.*"

Aketi broke the connection and swore again. So much for his hopes of getting any more information out of Saranith. He hoped her wounds would be painful.

He forced his attention back to watch as *Sukatta Bel* closed once again with the two naval ships. They both had boats in the water, loaded with crew from the sinking *Cyring*. He grinned. The boats would be easy to sink. He wouldn't even be going out of his way to do so. And *Tolu* was turned in the water so she could hardly bring her guns to bear, while he could fire a full broadside over the stern and into the body of the ship.

Sukatta Bel sailed into the gap just as the Cyring actually sank, disappearing beneath the waters. Some of *Tolu*'s protection was down, too, he noted as at least two cannon shot scored solid hits on the enemy ship.

Then he noticed an unusal disturbance in the water. It was a man, no, a wizard, swimming, but the largest wizard he had ever seen. The creature was grotesquely fat. Aketi ordered a net thrown down to pick him up. He was curious.

So curious he missed noticing the cannon shot from *Tolu*'s stern chaser, which struck *Sukata Bel* just at the waterline.

Aketi swore once again, but this time he knew the fault had been his own. He ordered Mobley to get men to fetch a spare sail to use as an emergency patch. Then he ordered the helmsman to head the ship toward the Archepelago. The naval ships would not be able to pursue and he needed to effect repairs. If anyone questioned his loss of a ship, he would with absolute truth be able to blame the whole fiasco on Saranith.

"Get a cap on the wizard right away," he ordered Gemek, noticing that they had the swimmer in a net and were hauling him aboard. "At least I'll get some amusement out of this."

XXXIII

4655, 466TH CYCLE OF THE YEAR OF THE MALIK
MONTH OF ILFARNAR

Lomcaul, dem ac thel canod,
Theo pa aar kom, thev cancatod.

"Pleasure, leaf to light turning,
Sun on still water, sky reflecting."

— ESLARIN TAJAO

T HE WIZARD ELGAN HAD SEEN THE SMALL, black-haired girl
from a distance several times since he joined the carnival in
Dandara. He had never seen her up close before, though. She seemed
as shy as a bird with adults, but brave enough running with the other
carnival children.

He was doing the "see the way the wizard sees" routine. When it
was almost her turn, he looked at her again and was startled to note
that what he had taken for black hair was really a cap of fine black
feathers. She had hailarin blood!

He forced himself to remain calm and deal with the children ahead
of her. By her appearance he estimated that she was somewhere between eight and nine years old. She was wary of adults, which meant
she had probably been abused. It wouldn't do to startle her.

He felt fear radiating from her when she stepped up to take her
turn. The small, grubby hand that extended the sic as payment
trembled.

He took the coin carefully. "You've seen before, haven't you?" he
asked.

Her huge, green eyes widened even further and she shook her head
in denial. For a moment he was afraid she would run away but she
swallowed and stood her ground.

He held his hands out slowly to touch the fine, downy feathers on
her head. She flinched at the contact and he could feel tremors of fear
but she didn't break away. He extended his awareness to hers.

She had brought a marin leaf with her as the object of focus. He
looked at it with his wizard eye and passed the vision on to her. He saw
through the waxy outer cells of the upper epidermis into the mesophyll

where the chloroplasts carried out the process of photosynthesis, saw the stomata on the lower surface that allowed air to circulate through the mesophyll, and identified the complex network of the veins which circulated the xylem and the phloem, the nutrients and the food substances produced by the leaf to feed its tree. The leaf was still a living thing, fresh picked, and its complex organic processes had not yet ceased.

Elgan showed all this to the child and at the same time shifted part of his attention to her. He felt her flinch as his mind examined hers and knew immediately that she hadn't been examined before or she would have been among his students. No child without potential could have felt his mind-touch.

Her talent was strong, among the strongest he had ever felt. She could become his equal someday, if trained. Elgan felt the thrill of discovery greater even than that a miner might feel on striking a rich vein of ore. Cormor had ordered him out of the Varfarin, sent him to the wilds of Macosia and Kandorra to search for the children of his vision. And Elgan had searched and searched and found nothing but human talent, but here at last was one of the children his grandfather had sent him to find. All the hundreds of years were suddenly justified: here she was, a hailar with the power to become a great wizard.

Her fear had lessened somewhat with the pleasure the vision had given her. "Would you like to see something else?" he asked, keeping his voice at an even level.

"Don't have money," she said, eyeing him warily again.

"I'll give you another vision free any time you like."

When her face showed immediate suspicion, he added, "I've seen you around the carnival. We don't usually charge our own people. Ask the other kids, they'll tell you."

"I'll do that," she said and ran away.

He had told her the truth. He didn't usually charge the carnival children, but only the children who could still learn came to crave the visions. And his whole purpose touring with carnivals was to reach just those children. He would be happy to show them all visions for free, but, due to the perversity of human nature, he knew he would actually have fewer customers if he didn't charge for the privilege.

That evening when he spoke with Kytal Domeki, the manager of the Carnival of Amazing Splendors, he mentioned the part-hailarin child.

Kytal was a wiry, dark skinned man of medium height, one of the hereditary Larafarin, the People of the Road, and he spoke with their idiomatic dialect. When Elgan described the child, he nodded and said, "Magra Laris. Mother Cyrene Hareel, daughter great hailarin dancer."

"Why hasn't she been tested before now?"

"Not dance Larafarin carnival. Dance troop half-breeds."

"How long has she been with this carnival?"

"Two months. Came month before you."

Elgan was disappointed when Magra did not come the next day, but the following day he saw her in the line again. This time she had brought a beetle, still alive, and she was much less nervous of him. As he showed her the insect's life processes, he also scanned her.

Hailarin bones were fragile. Although Magra was not pure-blooded hailarin, and her bones were not completely hollow, they were still less sturdy than those of humans or the other were-folk. And several of those bones had been broken at one time or another. There were also ruptured capillaries and bruises visible even to a human eye. Seeing so much damage, Elgan was certain that his guess about her being abused was correct.

"If you come back after the crowd has gone, I'll be happy to take you deeper into the beetle," he said gently.

She stiffened and looked at him warily. "Why would you do that?"

"Haven't you talked to the other children?" Elgan asked. "Didn't they tell you that I'm always willing to show them whatever they want?"

"Yeah," she said. "But I figure you must get something out of it."

Elgan smiled. "Shrewd child. Of course I do. Every time I let you see with my eyes, it stimulates a part of your brain. If you have talent, that part of your brain will develop so that eventually you'll be able to see on your own."

Magra's eyes narrowed. "That might be good for me, but what does it do for you?"

"Maybe nothing, if you're not interested in learning more," Elgan said. "On the other hand, if at that point you are interested in learning more, I gain a new apprentice. And every wizard is always looking for new apprentices."

"Why?"

"Because there are so few of us, child. And there's so much that we need to do."

"So being an apprentice is hard work."

Elgan nodded. "Yes. It can be very hard work indeed."

"Were you an apprentice?"

"Yes. I was an apprentice of the Wizard Cormor himself, and he was not an easy man to please."

"Would you be easy to please?"

"Probably not."

"Then why would anyone want to be your apprentice?"

"Because you enjoyed seeing into the leaf and the little I was able to show you of the beetle. You like seeing how things work. Learning to be a wizard lets you see for yourself, not just a leaf or a beetle, but how everything works. Isn't that worth a little effort?"

Magra frowned. "I don't know."

Elgan laughed. "Then don't decide now. Learn what you can. Learn to see for yourself. Then decide whether you want to learn more, or not. The choice will always be yours. I only know of one man who has ever been forced to learn wizardry, and I had no part in that."

"What happened to the man who was forced?"

"No one knows yet. He's still an apprentice. But I wouldn't want to be the wizard who forced him when that man does become a wizard, would you?"

Magra grinned and shook her head.

The grin exposed a dimple in her right cheek, and Elgan realized that, with her fine bones and huge eyes, she would be strikingly beautiful when she grew up.

She came back that evening and Elgan showed her the inner workings of the beetle for almost an hour before she tired. She came almost every night after that for four weeks, until one evening Elgan felt she was ready to see on her own.

That night Magra held a cat in her arms. Elgan recognized the animal as the mottled orange tom belonging to one of the clowns.

"It won't hurt Miggs to look at him, will it?"

"No," Elgan said. "He won't feel us looking. Why don't we start with the blood vessels in his tail."

He focused his mind on Miggs' scruffy tail and showed Magra the vision, but instead of holding it he immediately withdrew.

Magra said, "It's blurry." Then she broke off and looked at him. "It was blurry and my head hurts. What happened?"

"I stopped looking, but you saw inside with your own vision for a moment. As you haven't used those mental pathways before, they're sensitive."

"I saw on my own?" Magra asked.

"Yes," Elgan said carefully, stroking the cat. The child had lost most of her fear of him, but she was still not inclined to trust any adult too much. He added, "You'll have to make your mind up soon now. Do you want to learn more? Or not? Remember there is a price for learning wizardry and you would have to swear to obey me until you reach the level of journeyman wizard."

"If I became your apprentice, would I have to live with you?"

"You could if you liked. Or you can stay with your parents for the time being. The choice is up to you."

"My mother wants me to dance, like she does. She won't want me to be your apprentice. My father won't want it either."

"The choice is yours, not theirs. If they object, I'll talk to them."

Magra eyed him up and down and he sensed she was weighing him against her mother and father, calculating who would come off best in such a confrontation. Finally, she nodded. "I'll have to see how I feel in the morning."

Elgan bowed slightly. "Then I'll await your decision, Magra. 'Til the morning."

He was no longer worried about losing her. She had seen on her own The strength of her talent would drive her to see more.

MAGRA LARIS LIFTED THE LOOSE CANVAS flap and peered into her parents' caravan. Her father was no longer able to dance. He'd never been particularly talented and over the years he had gained too much weight and lost his flexibility. Now he could only work as a roustabout, doing manual labor. Magra knew that at this time of the evening he should be out breaking down the tents after the last show. Still, it was always wise to check before going into the closed wagon. If he'd managed to sprain something and was unable to work, he'd be back in the caravan and in an even worse temper than usual.

Magra knew that her father resented that her mother earned more money than he did, that her mother had always been the more talented. He got angry when he caught Cyrene teaching Magra to dance, too.

Until Magra had started working with the wizard she had seen no way out of her life with her parents. She didn't mind learning the dance steps her mother taught her, but she hated it when her father got angry. She was afraid that some day he'd hit her so hard she wouldn't be able to dance any more. Her mother's solo career had ended after one of his beatings. Cyrene's right leg had never healed quite right.

She felt she ought to tell her mother that she'd be moving in with the wizard. She had been watching him now for four weeks and he'd shown no sign of violent behavior. To the contrary, he was the gentlest man she had ever met. That had worried Magra for a while, but then she'd asked some of the other carnival people about him, and they'd told her that he was a great wizard, which meant he could kill with a glance.

If they'd told her that in the beginning, she might have been too frightened even to ask him for a vision. But after working with him for four weeks, the information only reassured her that she need not be afraid that her father could hurt him.

Magra went round to the steps leading to the door and climbed up into the caravan.

"Where have you been?" Cyrene demanded.

"With the wizard. He wants me to be his apprentice. He's been showing me things and this evening I saw something by myself. He says I have wizard talent."

Cyrene frowned. "I asked Kytal about him when you first started visiting him. Kytal said he wouldn't hurt you, but why would he want to train you?"

"He says he's always looking for children with talent. The other children say he's strong enough to stand up to Daddy if I tell him I want to stay with him."

Cyrene's face took on an intent look and she met Magra's eyes. "If he truly intends to train you, I won't stand in your way. That promises a better future for you than the dancing, which is all I can offer."

Magra suddenly felt ashamed. "It's not that I don't like to dance..."

"No, don't apologize," Cyrene said. "It's my fault we've stayed with your father and if you really started to dance, he might hurt you out of jealousy, just as he hurts me. But I still want to speak with the wizard before you move in with him."

MAGRA STOOD BACK and let her mother knock on the door to the wizard's caravan some minutes later.

Elgan opened the door and smiled at them both. "So Magra decided she might like to be my apprentice. I'm glad to meet you Cyrene Laris. I believe I once saw your mother dance."

"My jumps were even higher than hers in my youth," Cyrene said, stepping inside.

Magra followed her in and her eyes widened. She had always met the wizard in one of the carnival tents or out on the grounds. She had never been in his caravan before and found its size and compact fittings impressive.

The wizard's smile widened. "I believe you. You have your mother's hollow bones, but less fragility and greater strength. I've never understood the strict rules of the Dancer's Guild here in Kandorra and in Macosia. Such discrimination is actually illegal in Ilwheirlane."

"Yes. I wished I could have afforded to emigrate when I was younger."

Elgan studied her for a moment. "Before you were injured?"

Cyrene stiffened. "Yes."

"I could repair the damage done to your leg."

"Why? And why would you want to train a hailar child in wizardry when the Council of Wizards demanded oaths that such training only be given to human children. Kytal told me you're descended from a member of that Council."

Elgan smiled wryly. "True, but my grandfather, the Wizard Cormor, demanded no such oath of me. He pursuaded the survivors of the Council to change that rule after the Bane. In fact, it's because of his vision that I've spent the last several hundred years here in Kandorra or in Macosia searching for half-blood hailarin, or half-blood fallarin, children to train. Your daughter is a treasure I've sought for a very long time."

Magra stiffened. "You never told me that my blood made a difference."

Elgan turned to her. "You have enough talent that I'd have trained you in any event, but your hailar blood is definitely a bonus to me. I'd have told you that soon enough, it just never came up."

"Why is her blood important?" Cyrene demanded.

"Because my grandfather had visions of possible futures. In one of those visions he saw the Council of Wizards restored, but with one major change. In that vision, which was the brightest of all the futures he ever glimpsed, every race on Tamar was represented on that Council."

"The isklarin and the linlarin have wizards," Cyrene said.

"So do the gamlarin and the ingvalarin," Elgan said. "Only the hailarin and the fallarin do not at this time. Therefore, my grandfather sent me out to find half-blood children of those races to be trained. That was almost four hundred years ago. Your daughter is the first such child with talent that I've found."

"So, if you train her, my daughter may one day sit on the Council of Wizards?"

"That is my greatest hope," Elgan agreed, meeting her eyes.

Cyrene's mouth twisted wryly. "Then any fears I had that you might abuse her were misplaced."

Elgan gaped at her for a moment, then said, "Very much so. I'll defend her with my life."

"Then you won't mind if I come with her. She is still young to be parted from her mother."

Elgan studied Cyrene for a moment, then said, "I take it that her father is not included in this arrangement."

"No," Cyrene said, "and you'll need to defend us both. I should have left him a long time ago, but saw no way to do so safely."

"Then I shall arrange with Kytal to have your caravan moved next to mine and another supplied to Magra's father. You might want to pack his things so that they can be delivered to him, and," he paused, then added, "you won't mind if I hurt him somewhat when he protests the changes?"

Cyrene pressed her lips together and shook her head, adding, "I don't think he'll accept any argument but pain."

Elgan turned back to Magra and she saw his concern. She said flatly, "He's my father, but when he drinks or gets angry he likes to hurt people, anyone weaker than he is. He deserves to feel some pain of his own." She hesitated, then added, "And I've watched you and you don't like giving pain, so I know you won't hurt him more than what's necessary."

Elgan nodded gravely. "No more pain than what is necessary, and no permanent injury."

It was early the next morning, while the carnival was setting up at its new location, when Magra heard her father shouting outside the caravan she now shared with her mother.

She heard Elgan responding more quietly. Then there were noises and her father was shouting again, but this time there was fear in his voice. The sounds dwindled and Magra smiled. She had found a protector who could and would stand up to her father.

NATHAN REINED IN HIS HORSE as they topped a small rise and he looked down at a pale, sand beach ringing a small cove south of Candith. Pala came up and reined in her horse beside him.

"Is this isolated enough for you?" she asked.

It was early fall and just after dawn. The beach was deserted except for seagulls. Three were flying overhead and there was at least one more on the rocks where the shore curved out to sea. Nathan knew, if he searched, he would find clams and other sea life in the wet sand and in the water, but such things would make no noise that could distract him. "Yes," he said reluctantly, "this will be fine."

Pala grinned at him. "You know, you'll do fine when you just do it. It's just that you've built it up in your mind as a big deal."

"Wizards have died in their first attempts," Nathan said.

"Careless ones, perhaps," Pala said. "The only one to die that I've heard of didn't even have a proper cell map of the creature he intended to change into. He took a dare that he was ready and tried to wing it."

Nathan dismounted and she followed, taking the reins of his horse from him.

Nathan walked down the beach. Just above the tide line he stripped off his clothes, folded them and placed them on the dry sand. Then he walked down to the water's edge. He put his foot in the water. It felt wonderfully cool. He took a deep breath and walked into the sea until it was up to his thighs.

While he was quite accustomed by now to changing his shape to that of a tiger, that was done by simply shifting something inside his head. He had never yet changed his shape in the traditional way of wizards: holding the cellular blueprint of another creature in his mind and deliberately shifting his body to match. And such a change was required before he could graduate to being a full wizard.

Nathan felt he was ready. He'd asked Errin Yar Anifi for the cellular map of a dolphin before the bearer of Lyskarion had left Cibata. With that image in his mind he moved deeper into the water until it lapped at his waist. There was almost no wind and the surface of the cove was calm.

Except where Pala's young, sleek body cut the water nearby. He watched her swim for a moment, caught up in the beauty of her motion through the water, the sheen of her wet skin in the sunlight.

"Hey, Nathan, if you aren't going to shift, you should at least swim," Pala called to him. "The water's wonderful."

He smiled and shook his head, yelling back "But I am going to shift. I just need to be allowed to concentrate."

Count on Pala not to take his fears seriously. But somehow her comment had eased his own fear and he was able to slip into the meditative state necessary. He levitated his body, holding it still in the water and concentrated on the image in his mind. Then he started to change.

He had known that shape-shifting was painful if one wasn't a natural shape-shifter, still it startled him. And it was a strange pain, almost pleasure as his body melted and flowed into the new pattern he commanded it to take.

Then he was a dolphin and receiving the full sensory input of a dolphin in water. The song of the sea was quiet here in the cove, but it was still infinitely complex and beautiful. He dove for deeper water so that he could hear more. The music changed as he swam deeper. He lost track of time, swimming ever deeper into the music, until he had a sudden thought of Pala on the beach.

He realized he was all the way out of the cove in the open sea. He turned back and swam to shore, wondering how far he would have gone if he'd brought anyone else but Pala with him.

Switching back to being a man again went smoothly and he walked up the beach to where Pala was now stretched on the sand.

"I wondered how long you'd be gone," she said cheerfully. "You're back before I expected you. I've heard the song of the sea can be addictive."

"I thought you might be worried," he said.

She focused on him and he felt her attention meeting his. "No. I have every confidence in your ability to withstand temptation."

Nathan realized that she did not mean the latter as a complement, and was ruefully aware that it wasn't really accurate either. With her he was having a great deal of trouble avoiding temptation and the temptation seemed to grow stronger with every hour he spent with her.

XXXIV

4656, 465TH CYCLE OF THE YEAR OF THE MALIK MONTH OF CERDANA

"Protocol and secrecy do not blend well."

— FROM *THE COLLECTED WRITINGS OF VYDARGA THE RED*

T HE *KERIAR NIN* SAILED into Candith in the late fall. She was one of Ilwheirlane's fastest courier ships and her captain requested a private interview with Balek and Mamfe immediately.

Balek took Nathan with him to the interview, which Mamfe insisted be in his throne room, despite the lack of privacy.

When the captain, in the blue and gold uniform of Ilwheirlane's navy, entered the room, he said, "Rolf Burns, captain of Her Majesty's ship *Keriar Nin* at your service, Your Majesty."

Nathan noted that the captain's eyes widened at the sight of Mamfe reclining like a bloated hippopotamus on his divan, but otherwise he concealed his shock well.

Mamfe demanded, "Well, what's this about? I'm told you carry an urgent message from the Varfarin. What's Vanda and Ilwheirlane got to do with the Varfarin?"

"The Varfarin requested the use of my ship from Vanda, and she was pleased to grant that request. *Keriar Nin* is to be posted here in Candith to carry word back to Ilwheirlane should a fleet of Senangan ships be seen to sail north toward the Thallassean Sea."

"Why would a Senangan fleet want to sail north?"

"The Varfarin suspects that Gandahar has been negotiating with the Senangans for the use of troop ships to transport an army to invade the human nation of Darenje."

Mamfe grunted. "Nothing to do with me or Cassinga. Be a relief to see a fleet of Senangan ships go somewhere else. Talk to Balek." He waved his hand, dismissing them all.

Later, when Balek ushered the captain into his own quarters, he said, "So much for secrecy. Couldn't you have spoken to me privately?"

Captain Burns frowned. "I did ask for a private interview, but I'm constrained by my position. As an officer in the Royal Navy I couldn't deal with you, or the Varfarin in Cibata, without notifying Mamfe."

"Politics," Balek said, his mouth twisting as though the word tasted foul.

"It can't be helped now," Nathan said. He glanced at the captain. "We'll just have to hope that, when the time comes, your ship really is fast."

"What's more," Balek said, "a fleet headed toward the Thallassean would sail past the Cape of Dirkou on the same route it would take to attack Cassinga."

"You do keep surveillance on Senangan fleet movements then?" Captain Burns asked.

"Of course we do," Balek said gruffly. "And we've already agreed to supply the information," he cast a jaundiced glare at Nathan, "if Ilwheirlane supplied the ship."

MONTH OF ANOR

SARANITH ENTERED MAZILEK'S OFFICE in the Amarraite, the Senangan Admiralty, with grave misgivings. She knew that Aketi had returned to Senanga with harsh words about her performance in the Thallassean, and she didn't know how to defend herself as she had been at fault. She should have determined the presence of the wizards much earlier and simply fled. She could have escaped easily at any time prior to entering the Archipelago.

The fact that she probably would have made such a determination and escaped without harm had she not still been distracted by Luri's death was not an acceptable excuse. She had welcomed any action because it gave her something else to think about, and that had been extremely stupid and she knew it.

Mazilek looked up from his desk and saw her standing in the doorway. "Come in, Sara," he said, "and shut the door. We don't want the whole Amarraite to hear me rake you down."

Saranith shut the door and sighed with relief because the emotion she felt coming from Mazilek wasn't anger but curiosity.

"I do deserve to be raked down," she said. "I behaved stupidly."

"But I understand Luri had just died?" Mazilek said.

Saranith's face was immobile. "Yes, rai."

He regarded her quietly for a time. Then he said, "You forget, Sara, that I've known you for many years. You always show the least emotion when you feel the most. How did Luri die?"

"I killed him."

His eyes widened with shock. Then he deliberately relaxed and sat back in his chair. "No, Sara. Nothing you say will convince me that you deliberately killed Luri, so how did it happen?"

Sara stood stiffly, still torn by indecision. But she had no choice but to tell Mazilek the truth. There was no one else in all Senanga she could trust with the knowledge of Cinkarion, and she believed she could trust him not to betray her. "I was called, rai, into the Bane."

"Called how? And into the Wizard's Bane in Arduin?"

"Yes, rai. I was called by Cinkarion."

Mazilek inhaled sharply. Then his thin lips twisted. "I should have known that any mystery surrounding you would be more complex than a simple accidental death." He shook his head. "So how did being called by Cinkarion kill Luri?"

Her immobile face spasmed. "I was so happy, rai. I thought access to such power would end all our problems. I asked him to link with me..."

She broke off and looked him straight in the eyes, her face pale. "No. I demanded that he link with me. When he tried to object I questioned his love of me." She stopped.

MAZILEK, WATCHING SARANITH, felt stunned. He had known her for thirteen years now. She usually suppressed all appearance of emotion. Even now a stranger would think her blank face meant she felt nothing, but to his eyes she looked very close to cracking. "Go on."

"So he linked with me to Cinkarion and the fire..."

"So the linkage killed him?" Mazilek prompted when it became apparent that she wasn't going to continue on her own.

She drew in a shuddering breath, then steadied again and said, "Cinkarion carries the death memories of all the wizards who died in the Bane. Agnith was linked to them. They burn you if you can't shield your mind. I thought I'd shut them away, but anyone linking with Cinkarion wakes them. I felt him die."

Mazilek studied her, amazed she was still functioning at all. But he had always respected her strength. Her love for Luri had been the only weakness he had ever seen in her.

And now she bore Cinkarion. That made her a major player in the politics of Senanga. Of course, she had always been that, even if she tried to ignore the fact. Now there would be no possibility of denying it.

But no one else had reported anything about Cinkarion. He had known that Luri died mysteriously after she made a previously unscheduled trip ashore. But nothing else. So she was trying to keep Cinkarion a secret. Wise of her, but doomed to failure without his help.

Should he help her? What would having a member of the royal family being the bearer of Cinkarion do to the balance of power in Senanga? He snorted. What balance? The scales would be upside down and backwards.

"You'll need to learn the high sight now," he said abruptly to break through the almost trance state into which she seemed to have lapsed.

Saranith straightened. "Yes, rai. That has been my intent for years, if I could find someone willing to teach me."

"Aketi's been raising waves," he added.

"I'm sure he has. This time I gave him a good reason to do so."

"He wants to know why the wizards were chasing you. I imagine I can figure that out for myself now."

"Yes, rai. But the ships were naval ships from Sussey. I don't know why they were bearing wizards. And if they were Varfain wizards, how did they know?"

"Good questions. Ones I suspect you won't get answers to until you gain the high sight and can communicate better with Cinkarion." He rose from his desk and walked over to a map on the wall. "I have a new assignment for you."

"Now, rai? I was afraid..."

"Of an inquiry?" Mazilek asked. "No. Aketi doesn't have that much influence here in the Amarraite. Your previous record has been exemplary, and most officers understand the effects of grief. You made a minor mistake in judgement while under stress. It will go on your record, but if it's not repeated it shouldn't seriously affect your career."

"Thank you, rai."

"I called it as I saw it, Arhan." He frowned at her. "Don't make me regret the decision."

"No, rai." She stiffened, but he noted there was a little more color back in her face.

"Now it just so happens that we've recently received word from Cassinga that they've got a new courier ship," Mazilek said, tapping the map over the dot that indicated Candith.

"A courier ship?"

"Not your normal prey," Mazilek said wryly, "but this is a special courier ship sent by Vanda personally at the request of the Varfarin. It's supposed to warn Ilwheirlane when a fleet from Senanga sails toward the Thallassean."

Saranith inhaled. "How did they learn?"

"I don't know, but, as the leak apparently came from the Thallassean end of the negotiations, I don't really care either."

"So the courier will need to be intercepted," Saranith said, "but we're still negotiating. The fleet won't sail for at least a couple of years."

"Nevertheless, I plan to station a pod of ships in the Petalwan Archipelago to be in a position to intercept the courier, *Keriar Nin*, when it does sail for Ilwheirlane."

"The Archipelago is a good place to intercept," Saranith agreed, studying the map. "There are only two routes through it that a courier ship, one not expecting ambush, would choose if it were in a hurry to get to Ilwheirlane."

"Precisely, although a third ship could watch this other route over here," Mazilek again tapped the map with his finger. "And someone on site may discover other routes that bear watching. The Varfarin must know that we would hear of the existence of such a ship. Mamfe interviewed the Captain in his throne room, of all places."

"One of the reasons you want the pod in place so early," Saranith said, "so their spies here won't associate its departure with intercepting the courier ship."

"That was my main reason originally," Mazilek said, "but now I think that the fact that the Isle of Elevtherai is said to lie in that Archipelago might outweigh it."

"Elevtherai? I thought that was a children's tale. My mother told me of it when I was very small."

"No. Elevtherai is no children's tale. If you had grown up among humans you would have learned more of it. Although I believe the tales are most common where Miune is worshipped, as that god alone gives men power over women."

"The Isle of Exile, the Woman's Refuge, but what can that possibly have to do with the interception of the courier ship?"

"There's no connection to the courier ship, but the Mistress of Elevtherai is Leilana, one of the oldest and most powerful wizards on Tamar. As you are a woman, she might aid you," Mazilek said.

Saranith's head came up. "You think she might train me?"

"I believe from what I've heard of her that she might," Mazilek said. "I don't know of any other place to suggest outside of the Thallassean region, unless you think you could appeal to the Varfarin."

That drew a rueful smile. "I know they'd love to get the opportunity to kill me and take it back."

Mazilek said, "May I see it? I've heard of them all my life, but I never thought to see one. I find that I would like to do so."

Saranith drew a small cloth sack closed with a drawstring from around her neck. She opened it and showed him a ruby crystal the size of a goose egg and the same color as the rubies in her eyes, except for the pulsing light in its core.

"It's beautiful," he said.

"Yes," she said flatly, and he realized it still hurt her even to look at it. She wore a very thin mask of calm, but underneath she was raw and bleeding.

"So, will you take the assignment?"

"An opportunity to get away from Aketi and Senangan politics for two to three years," she said, "how could I possibly refuse? Of course I'll take it." She hesitated, then added, "And I thank you very much. I won't ever forget how much I owe you."

"Putting you under obligation to me was not my motivation," he said carefully.

"I know," she said, "which is why the obligation is as great as it is."

4657, 465TH CYCLE OF THE YEAR OF THE BEAR
MONTH OF REDRI

"A FRIEND OF MINE WILL BE VISITING US," Elgan told Magra. They were walking along a path beside the sparse trees marking the course of a dry streambed in the northern plains of Kandorra. It was late summer, dry and hot. The trees were already losing their leaves. The air smelled of dust. The carnival and the village it was playing at were some distance behind them.

Magra eyed him curiously. She had been his apprentice for nearly two years and he had never before mentioned friends or even associates. Now she realized that he must have a vast net of acquaintances all over Tamar.

Elgan's mouth twisted wryly. "Most of my one-time associates have no idea where I am and many would not approve of my training you."

"Because of my hailar blood?"

"Yes. Cormor forced a change in the wording of the Oath of Council, but there were many wizards opposed to that change and many who have disregarded it. They claim that the change was invalid as not enough members remained alive to make a quorum."

Magra looked out over the dry, flat plains, golden brown under the noontime sun. The Hailarin Dancers' Guild wouldn't take her because of her human blood. Most wizards wouldn't want her trained because of her hailar blood. Both her halves rejected by someone, yet Elgan had sought her out because of the mix. The world was a funny place. "What's your friend's name?" she asked.

"The Wizard Valanta. She's been a very dear friend of mine for centuries now. We've even lived together at times, but she's a creature of cities and civilization. She had no desire to join me in the hinterlands, but she's coming now to bear witness to your first test of talent," Elgan said. "She and I are among those who believe that my grandfather's visions are our greatest hope in the years to come. They will welcome the news that I've found you. I sent for Valanta over a year ago, after you agreed to be my apprentice and I discovered the extent of your talent, but she was on the other side of the world and it's taken her some time to get here."

Valanta arrived that evening. She swept into the caravan and up to Elgan and hugged him. The air was suddenly scented with essences of orange and ginger. Then she turned and her gaze found Magra's unerringly. "So you're the child wonder I've been hearing so much about. Elgan didn't mention how beautiful you are."

Magra could not help liking Valanta. She was tall and full breasted with long, blond hair and golden skin, and she radiated a sense of warmth and kindness. Her smile came from her eyes as well as her lips, and Magra felt her sincerity. She smiled tentatively. "It's nice to meet you."

"You don't mean that yet, but I hope you soon will," Valanta said, "and you needn't worry, I won't be here long. I must take a report of you back to those concerned."

"What news do you have?" Elgan asked.

Valanta turned back to Elgan. "Only that time is growing short for all of us. There's evidence that Gandahar will soon attempt to invade Darenje. Rand, Delanan and the others are doing what they can but the war of Cormor's visions is coming."

Elgan nodded. "Then I think it's time that Magra take her test."

Magra walked over to the table and lit the row of candles with her will, then lifted a pile of small, thin-shelled balls that she knew weighed precisely eight ounces and made them dance over the table, changing their colors as they rose and fell.

"What is the first rule of wizardry?" she heard Elgan ask in her head.

"The first rule of wizardry: What you can truly see, you can alter," she said in mind speech.

"Very good," Elgan thought. *"Do you remember who discovered that rule?"*

"The Wizard Vydarga Cinnac, the founder of the Royal House of Ilwheirlane," Magra answered. *"He was born a slave of the isklarin, but his master gave him sight when he was still a boy and he then discovered that he could change things. He led the rebellion and started the Dragon Wars that freed humanity. All of the lands around the Thallassean were part of Gandahar back then."*

So began the long list of questions and tests.

"What is the greatest distance that two minds can communicate over if both of them are on the surface of the sea?" Elgan asked.

"One hundred thirty kilometers," Magra answered.

"Why might that vary on land?"

"Someone standing on a high place could reach farther."

Elgan took out his pocket knife and cut a shallow scratch on his palm. *"Can you heal this?"*

Magra took his hand in hers and focused on the cut. After a moment it began to close and heal. Two minutes later there was only a thin red line, already fading, but Magra was sweating, her head ached, and her hands were not quite steady.

"*I've been testing you for nearly a quarter of an hour now,*" Elgan said. "*Do you know what that means?*"

"*That I've nearly qualified as an Apprentice Journeyman,*" Magra guessed, sensing that the ordeal was almost over, and feeling a rush of pleasure as she realized what she had accomplished.

"*What else do you need to be able to do to qualify?*" Elgan asked.

"*I need to swear to the healer's oath and be able to record information on a crystal and retrieve such information.*"

"*And will you swear to me with your mind that you will strive always to heal and not harm with the knowledge you gain until other, more complex oaths may supercede this one?*"

"*I will,*" she thought.

"*Then all you need is a crystal.*" He held out a large quartz crystal, roughly shaped and faceted to about the size of a chicken egg.

Magra cradled it carefully in her hands. "Can I have it mounted on a chain so I can wear it?" she asked aloud, knowing the test was over.

"Of course, child. You've more than earned it," Elgan said. "You'll complete your qualification in the same number of years it took Cormor. Of course, he started when he was six and you were eight, so he was younger, but it's still the same number of years of training."

"Then you think I'll be a strong wizard?"

She felt his eyes studying her. "Very strong, Magra. One of the strongest." He turned and looked at Valanta, and Magra followed his gaze.

Valanta was smiling, too. She said, "I'll be happy to bear a piece of good news for a change."

XXXV

4658, 466TH CYCLE OF THE YEAR OF THE MOLE
MONTHS OF INGVASH TO TORIN

"Golden sunlight piercing bright,
Crimson flowers, verdant green,
Look you now behind the screen
At Leila's garden of delight.

"Life that riots, mutant, strange,
Trees with faces, plants that cry.
Have you never questioned why?
Never thought what caused their change?"

— EXCERPT FROM "THE GARDEN OF LEILA" FROM *A CHILD'S GUIDE TO THE LARIN AND OTHER BEASTLY TAILS* BY ENOGEN VARASH OF ELEVTHERAI, 4557

F INDING ELEVTHERAI had not been easy. There were hundreds of islands in the Petalwan Archipelago and the inhabitants of those islands had not been cooperative. At first, when Saranith had sent First Farail Kaltos ashore to ask if anyone had heard of Elevtherai, no one had. It occurred to her after several months that, as Elevtherai was a refuge for women, she should send a woman. She had then sent Third Farail Elas Harken ashore to do the questioning. Many of the women had still been wary, but she had been given a general direction in which to search. Finally, when a full year had passed, she'd gone ashore and done the questioning herself.

Which had brought her here. Saranith studied the shore of Elevtherai. The Wizard Leila who had named it was long dead, but her cloned daughter, Leilana, still ruled here: Leilana, who had to be well over a thousand years old herself.

Saranith had *Cinhai* anchored in deep water. Then she ordered a boat lowered and had herself rowed ashore.

A woman came to meet her as Saranith started to climb the slope, a woman wearing a white robe similar to those worn by the kindred of Maera, Saranith thought, except that the edging was purple instead of the red. *"You're not the sort of petitioner I'm accustomed to greeting,"* the woman thought in the intimate mode.

This had to be Leilana, Saranith realized, studying her. Leilana was not as tall as Saranith, nor as lean. Her smooth hair, cut short at the level of her chin, was the color of a raven's wing. Her skin looked like milk with a hint of pink rose petals on her cheeks and her eyes were warm, butter-amber. She might have been twenty, until Saranith looked more closely into those amber eyes and saw years and knowledge beyond her reckoning.

"*But I am a petitioner,*" Saranith thought, striving for humility, "*dependent upon your good will.*"

"*None of your own people would show you the high sight,*" Leilana thought. "*They feared your power too much.*"

Saranith frowned. "*You can tell that from just looking at me?*"

"*All I had to see was what you carry and that you lack the high sight,*" Leilana thought. "*What other reason would the bearer of Cinkarion have for coming here?*"

"*I don't know,*" Saranith thought. "*I've heard rumors about this place, but know nothing of the truth except that you and the bearers of Belkarion may be the last of the great wizards left alive. And I wish to become a great wizard.*"

Saranith felt Leilana examine her.

"*You have more than enough power for it.*" Leilana smiled. "*And I like your eyes. I admire a flair for the dramatic, but you won't be able to stay here long.*"

Saranith stiffened. "*Why not?*"

Leilana laughed, but the laugh was brittle. "*No, I'll not expel you. You'll expel yourself. But not before I've taught you what you need to learn. Tell your crew to return on the tenth day of each month to see if you're ready to depart.*"

"*I'd thought to stay a year or more,*" Saranith protested.

"*And so you may, if you wish,*" Leilana thought. "*I leave the date of your departure entirely up to you. But I warn you, your ship should come each month. You, of all the people on Tamar, will be least able to endure my hospitality for long.*"

"*What do you mean?*"

"*When you've learned what you wish to learn from me, you'll know the answer to that question yourself,*" Leilana thought, and Saranith detected a trace of regret.

So Saranith took up residence in the home of Leilana, in the Garden of Leila.

On her second day Leilana took her through the Garden, but it was no ordinary garden. Several acres in extent, it was surrounded by a tall, adobe brick wall, the only entrance through a wrought iron gate. Leilana opened the gate with a key that hung from a chain around her neck.

"You may enter and leave at your will," Leilana thought, "for the gate will answer to your will as easily as to my key, but the lock protects those without sight from coming here."

"Why should a garden be denied to those without sight?" Saranith asked, feeling a strange sense of unease that was almost pain, but not her own pain.

"Some of the plants and the beasts that roam here can be dangerous," Leilana thought, and led the way through the gate.

Planted between the elanda trees, the banks of flowering ericala, and the colorful flower beds were strange, twisted trees and vines with thick stumps and knarled tendrils. Saranith stared at them, feeling an ache inside her. They had once been men, those trees and vines, and many of them still had the awareness of men. Then she saw a small boar with a deformed head, rooting in the ground near a bank of anathallia, and the boar had also been a man. It looked up, saw them and ran away.

"Why?"

"To give back control to the women they hurt," Leilana thought, but Saranith felt a mixture of emotions from the ancient wizard. "All of these men hurt one of my women, either a woman who lives with me now, or one who came to me and has since passed on. And, after hurting the woman, he also pursued her here."

Leilana shook her head, and added, "If, during the woman's life, she forgives the man for what he did, I restore his humanity and send him home. If she does not, he dwells here until he dies."

"Isn't this a greater cruelty than any they visited upon your women?" Saranith demanded.

"There is little pain, and that only in the very beginning," Leilana thought. "They may live for years, centuries even, and they do no more harm."

"But some of them have gone mad," Saranith protested. "Of what value is life to a madman?"

"Only a few go mad, and those rot and die quickly. Others may even learn wisdom in time. Walk through the Garden and speak with them. The vine-man near the pool is a poet. My apprentices write down his words and send them to a publisher in the human lands. We show him the books and the magazines with his work in them, and we do what he requests with the money he earns." She smiled. "He wasn't only a woman beater, but a murderer; he'd killed more than a dozen people and would have killed more. He's very old now. He'd never have lived so long as a man, and he'd never have written a word."

In the days that followed Saranith thought about what Leilana had told her, but she didn't visit the Garden again. There were men she knew, like her cousin Aketi, whom she disliked, perhaps even hated. But could she imagine punishing even Aketi in such a way?

No. Leilana had said that the tree-men learned wisdom, but Saranith didn't think that was true. She thought that, as their blood turned to sap, it slowed and cooled, leaving them incapable of the anger that had driven them as men. That was not wisdom, merely a numbing of self.

Leilana showed Saranith the high sight each day of the first week she spent on Elevtherai, looking down with her into the fabric of matter where even a single atom became a large and complex arrangement of forces, constantly affected by other forces, that the will could influence. After that, Leilana demonstrated every other day, and after the first month, once a week.

Saranith grew frustrated that the vision hadn't come, but Leilana reassured her, *"Don't worry. It will come. Each time I demonstrate, I deepen the pathway in your mind, but you won't see by yourself until your mind forms its own connections to that pathway."*

"I know," Saranith thought. *"I should remember patience."* She pointed to the rubies where her eyes had been. *"It took me nearly three months before I learned to see after I put out my eyes."*

"Patience is the hardest lesson a wizard must learn," Leilana thought. *"Many never do learn it."*

In the third month after her arrival on Elevtherai Saranith attained the high sight on her own. She managed to hold it for only a second, but what she had done once she knew she could do again. She had achieved her purpose in coming to Elevtherai. The knowledge relieved her, and she realized that Leilana had been right, she wouldn't be able to stay the full year she had planned. Something about the place disturbed her too deeply.

XXXVI

4658, 466TH CYCLE OF THE YEAR OF THE MOLE
MONTH OF AGNITH

"Are those who live in Leila's lair
Blind or innocent of blame?
All who dwell there share the shame;
Merciless is Leila's care.

"See the new tree by the gate,
Trunk still split like human legs,
Listen when it weeps and begs.
Could you endure an equal fate?"

— EXCERPT FROM "THE GARDEN OF LEILA" FROM *A CHILD'S GUIDE TO THE LARIN
AND OTHER BEASTLY TAILS* BY ENOGEN VARASH OF ELEVTHERAI, 4557

L ESS THAN A WEEK AFTER ATTAINING the high sight, Saranith
entered the Garden for a second time, to see a man planted. The
next day she returned, despite herself, to stare at the man in numb
horror. She had thought him an ugly, hulking beast when Leilana's
attendants bound him and forced his feet into the ground. He had
screamed curses and sworn he would kill them all. But now, in the
morning light, he looked pathetic.

His feet were roots now, delving deep into the ground for nourishment. His flesh was starting to turn green.

His curses had changed to tears during the night. Saranith saw the
tracks amid the stubble of hair on his cheeks. She had thought him
unconscious, but his eyes opened suddenly. He flinched at sight of her,
but his eyes were desperate. "Help me," he begged.

"Too late," she said. "You've taken root."

The terror in his eyes was somehow frightening. She turned away.

"No! Don't go! What's happened to my feet? Why have you done
this?"

Saranith hesitated, studying him. He had brown eyes, full of anger
and pain. "What did you expect coming here? Leilana judged you."

"Judged me? By what right? I came here for my wife, the wife you
witches seduced away from me."

"The wife you abused." Saranith turned her back and walked away. His curses followed her, but they sounded hollow.

She left the Garden, taking the path toward the beach She felt restless and disturbed.

This man was the first she had watched Leilana plant. Why should seeing a man changed affect her so much more than the knowledge that such changes had been made in the past?

Saranith shook her head. Right or wrong? Justice or abomination? And what right did she have to decide, either way? The fate of this man wasn't her business. Whether planting the man had been just or not, she owed Leilana respect and loyalty while she was on Leilana's territory.

The man was brutal. He'd beaten his wife, or so she had told Leilana. But, some inner voice protested. They had lived together for six years. He must have given her something back, or surely she'd have left him long ago. He hadn't killed her, or done anyone a permanent injury. Saranith's mind churned with conflicting emotions.

An arm came suddenly out of a bush as she passed and grabbed her shoulder. She was swung around until her back impacted against a hard chest. A hand clamped over her mouth and her feet were knocked out from under her. She felt herself lowered to the ground.

A knife waved in front of her face, then sank until its point pricked her throat. A hoarse voice spoke in the human tongue her mother had spoken, "I'm going to uncover your mouth. Scream, it'll be the last sound you make. Understand?"

Saranith nodded. She could force the knife away from her. Her will was strong enough to overpower any ordinary man. But his attack had steadied the churning of her thoughts. She was curious.

The hand came away from her mouth. The voice said, "All right, where is he? Where's Rethen? What have you done with him?"

"Rethen is the man who came here yesterday?" she asked carefully, her tongue rusty in his language.

"The man you witches captured. Came to find his wife and you dragged him off somewhere. Where've you put him?"

"He's in the Garden. He's been planted."

"Planted?"

She didn't know how to explain so she remained silent.

"What have you done to him?" He pulled her to her feet and swung her around to face him. He was huge; as tall and as hairy as Rethen, but not so thick around the chest. "I'll kill you if you don't tell me. Rethen's my uncle and a good man, so don't think I'll hesitate," he said, then paused, his eyes widening in shock.

Saranith knew he was looking at her eyes, her eyes that were not eyes but faceted rubies.

"What are you?" he asked, drawing back from her.

"My name is Saranith. I'm a guest on Elevtherai."

"What happened to your eyes?"

"A childhood...indiscretion."

He grunted, but said, "Take me to my uncle."

"You'd risk the same fate for yourself to save him? You might be seen."

"Up to you to see I'm not. I'll make sure you die first." He reached for her, but she deflected his hands with her will.

"I'll take you to your uncle," she said. "But you mustn't threaten me again."

He stared at her, obviously frightened. "You plan on doing to me what was done to him?"

Saranith shook her head. "That's not within my power, any more than I can undo what was done to him. Come, and you'll see." She turned and walked back toward the garden.

"Alden," Rethen called from his plot by the wall as soon as they entered the Garden, "thank Miune. Get me out of here."

Alden ran to his uncle. "Are you all right? What have they done to you?" He hugged Rethen.

"They stuck my feet in the ground and I can't pull them out. You'll have to help me. There's a shovel in the shed by the gate."

Saranith blocked Alden's path to the shed. "He'll die if you dig him up."

"What do you mean?"

"His feet are roots now. If you uproot him, he'll die for lack of nourishment."

"Don't listen to her, boy. Just get me out of here."

Saranith turned to Rethen. "You know I'm telling the truth. You can feel the changes in yourself."

He stared back, eyes full of hate. "Mind your own business, witch." He twisted to face Alden. "The changes haven't gone far yet. If you get me out of here, I may be able to find a wizard on the mainland to fix me up."

Alden's face went slack with shock.

Rethen swallowed. "Just get me out of here before someone else comes." Alden looked around at the rest of the Garden. The vine-man near the pond shifted a branch and Saranith saw Alden's attention turn toward it. He crossed the grass until he stood near it, his eyes on the face that peered out of the bark. "Were you a man?"

"Trees with faces, plants that cry. Have you never wondered why?" the plant intoned. Its voice was thin and high, the sound of branches creaking in the wind.

Alden shut his eyes and turned away.

"I'd rather die than stay here," Rethen said.

Alden nodded. He headed for the shed, brushing Saranith aside.

He drove the shovel into the soil next to the point where Rethen's legs disappeared. Rethen winced, but said, "Hurry."

The soil was still loose from the planting. It didn't take long for Alden to expose his uncle's feet and the pale rootlets growing out of them. Rethen sat down and tried to raise one leg and then the other, but the toe roots and the smaller shoots growing from the bottom of his feet were too strong. Alden set the shovel in the hole next to one root-foot, then drove it in at an angle. Rethen screamed.

Saranith had watched, frozen by indecision, but the scream was too much for her. She ran up to Alden and grabbed his arm before he could lift his shovel to free the other foot. "Can't you see you're killing him. He could live for years here."

He shook her off, knocking her to the ground. Then he stared down at her, his eyes full of contempt. "What do you care whether he lives or dies?"

"I care. I don't want to see anyone die unnecessarily."

"Then change him back. You're a witch, aren't you?"

She looked away from the accusation in his eyes. "I'm only a student. Leilana cast the spell. Only Leilana or a stronger wizard can undo it."

"Then Rethen may die, but at least he won't have to go mad living as a specimen in this freak show." Alden pulled the shovel out and put it down next to the second root-foot.

"Wait," she said urgently. "At least dig down a little deeper so you get some of the roots. There's a planter in the shed. If you put soil in that and you keep his feet buried, you could manage to get him back to the mainland alive." Saranith bit her lip, but she couldn't stop the words. "There aren't many wizards who could change him back. Leilana's old. Give me twenty years and I'll be strong enough to change him."

Alden's eyes narrowed. "You're one of them. How can I trust you?"

She stared at him and swallowed. What could she tell him? What was the truth? She didn't know herself. "Because...," her voice faltered.

He grabbed her shoulders and shook her. "Why, damn you?"

"Because Leilana's wrong. This isn't justice and I cannot be a part of it, even by so much as refusing to act," she said, the answer welling up from deep inside her. His hands dropped from her shoulders and she backed away. "Dig up as many as you can of your uncle's roots and fill the planter with soil from the hole. It has special nutrients that will help to keep him alive until you reach Eylas. There's a wheelbarrow in the shed. You won't have to carry him and the planter. I'll see that you have at least another half hour before anyone comes this way."

"What about you? Won't Leilana know you helped us?"

"Yes. She may be angry, but she won't hurt me. I bear Cinkarion," she bared her breast so Aldan could see the pulsing jewel at her throat, the same color as her ruby eyes. "I'll be leaving here within a month. I'll come to Eylas. Rethen can sail with me until I find a wizard to restore him or can do so myself. It may take me twenty years, but I will be stronger than Leilana."

"Cinkarion? It died in the Bane," Alden said staring at the jewel.

"No." She sighed, understanding suddenly that she hadn't needed the high sight to communicate with the living crystal. It would help make communication clearer, but they were linked and she had felt, and been influenced by, the crystal's thoughts since the moment she had picked it up. That was why she had to help Rethen.

"Cinkarion waited to choose a bearer until it found someone strong enough to feel the deaths it was instrumental in causing, as it feels them even now, and not be destroyed. But though I am witness to the deaths of tens of thousands and have caused deaths of my own, I cannot watch any unnecessary death without trying to prevent it. That's why I'll help you, and your uncle, if I can."

Rethen said, "If you did take me aboard your ship, what could I do for the years it may take until you can free me? Be an ornamental plant for your cabin?"

Saranith turned to him. "You could be my helmsman."

Rethen stared at her for several moments, then turned to Alden. "Do as she says. Dig up the roots."

When Saranith returned to Leilana's home and was directed to Leilana's private chambers, she knew Leilana was aware of what she'd done. She entered defiantly.

"*So they're off, the man Rethen and his nephew?*" Leilana asked. She was reclining on a divan with cushions of lavender silk. Her personal chamber was carpeted with a deep pile carpet of white wool and hung with silken draperies in shades of violet and purple.

"*You knew about the nephew?*" Saranith exclaimed in surprise.

"*I know of every living thing on this island,*" Leilana thought. "*I told you when you came, that you wouldn't stay for long, and now you plan to leave when your ship comes back next week.*"

"*How did you know?*"

"*If you stop and think, you can answer that question yourself. The answer is the same as the one you found in the Garden.*"

"*Cinkarion?*"

Leilana nodded. "*Cinkarion belongs to Jehan. It's appalled by the games I play here on Elevtherai.*"

"*What god do you worship?*" Saranith asked. "*You wear robes like the kindred of Maera, but this is no Sanctuary.*"

"*But I do worship Maera. Her darker side,*" Leilana answered, smiling faintly. "*As Kyra the Destroyer is the darker side of Kyra the Chronicler.*"

"*I cannot worship any of the gods,*" Saranith thought. "*If they were worthy of worship, they would have produced a better world than this one.*"

Leilana's head came up in surprise. "*But the gods cannot control the world, Sara, they only influence it. You, as a wizard, should realize that instinctively. The universe was created in such a way that we would have free will. Free will and control are incompatible.*"

Saranith shook her head, as though to drive the thoughts that disturbed her away, then looked at Leilana. "*Will it hurt you when I break the spell on Rethen?*"

Leilana smiled. "*Not at all. The spell was designed for you to break.*"

"*If you knew I'd release him, why did you curse him?*"

"*So that you'd release him,*" Leilana thought. "*You've learned enough from me and I find Cinkarion's presence here disturbing.*" Leilana fingered the clear crystal that hung from a chain around her neck. "*Rethen isn't like most of the men here. He only abused his wife when he was drunk. But he's been getting drunk more frequently in recent years. A few years as a plant will cure him of his craving and teach him to think before he acts. There's no real evil in his nature.*"

"*And there is evil in the nature of all the others you've changed?*"

"*To one degree or another, yes. If there's no evil in them, I find some other way to deal with them. Some that have come here I've simply put back ashore. I reserve the Garden for the ones who are twisted to start with. I only make their outer form reflect their inner being.*"

"*It still feels wrong to me,*" Saranith thought.

Leilana nodded. "*I know. You may not worship Jehan yet, but you are his through Cinkarion. Go with my blessing, and know I wish you only good.*"

XXXVII

4659, 466TH CYCLE OF THE YEAR OF THE GRIFFIN
MONTH OF DIRGA

> *"I remember the day that my ship became prey.*
> *In the light of the dawn the tall sails were so red,*
> *Like the blood that ran freely across the plank deck,*
> *And the guns they were blazing out fire and hot lead."*
>
> *It was ambush it was, and the fighting so fierce,*
> *That a guardsman he put out my eye, so he did.*
> *But I put my good steel through his heart in return,*
> *And we fought 'til the decks were awash, and he slid*
>
> *O'er the side, and his buddies did too, for we won*
> *That fine day, and we took as our prize the good ship*
> *With the captain who thought he could win 'gainst the scourge*
> *Of the sea. And, in case ye ha doubts, that's still me."*
>
> *Chorus: Oh, I took me a ship for to sail on the sea,*
> *And a heigh, nonny heigh, I did sail on the sea."*
>
> — VERSES FROM "THE PIRATE'S BOASTING SONG" FROM *SONGS OF THE SEA AND*
> *SHORE* EDITED BY BAR PANYARA, 4592

NATHAN WAS CONCERNED when he received an order to report to Balek's quarters immediately. Balek was usually much more circumspect in issuing commands now that Nathan had qualified as a full wizard; but Balek was still head of the Varfarin in Cibata and, technically, his commander.

Nathan arrived at Balek's quarters. *"You summoned me, rai?"*

"Yes, Nathan, your message has arrived from Jaith."

"My message?" Nathan questioned.

"The one you agreed to forward to Ilwheirlane," Balek supplied testily.

"Jaith has reported a fleet of troop carriers leaving Feshi?" he asked.

"Yes, a fleet of empty troop carriers. Jaith reported forty ships."

"Then I'll notify the courier immediately," Nathan thought.

Balek merely turned back to his desk.

Nathan found Captain Burns on his ship, supervising the loading of some supplies.

"A fleet of forty empty troop carriers has just sailed from Feshi. You should depart as soon as possible to give the alert to Ilwheirlane."

"Aye. And I think, as our notice of intent was so public, I'd better avoid the main channels when I hit the islands."

"I was going to suggest that myself," Nathan said.

MONTH OF CERDANA

RETHEN WATCHED AS THE CREW of *Cinhai* raised more sail.

"Helm north northeast five more degrees."

Saranith always gave him his orders in the human tongue, he thought to himself as he turned the wheel, though he had picked up quite a bit of the linlarin language over the past six months. In fact, he had adapted to being a member of her crew amazingly well.

His roots were planted deep in a large planter box. It had wheels, so he could retire to a cabin she had assigned him, but he did not seem to need as much sleep as he once had. Saranith saw that he drank soup at least once a day and applied nutrients to the soil of his box. His life had fallen into a regular routine which wasn't at all uncomfortable.

He had expected hostility from the crew, but all he received was unfeigned curiosity. The crew had all examined him and his box at least once. Most had expressed a sort of good humored sympathy, but there had been no pity. The attitude had been more, "Tough luck, mate."

The reason for that had come to him gradually. Saranith had told the crew that his condition was temporary, until she was strong enough to heal him. Where he still doubted her, the crew never had. If she said his condition was temporary, then it was.

And that had reassured him more than anything else. Of course, Saranith had made one change in him before she brought him aboard. She had changed his eyes so that he saw now with were-sight. Otherwise, she told him, the crew would not have accepted him. With all the other changes, he had hardly taken that one in at first. But being able to see in the dark came in handy, and being able to see into things was useful too. It had taken him a while to learn to use the new sight, but now he wondered how he had managed without it.

Sometimes his old life was hard to remember. The blood-sap in his veins flowed more slowly than pure blood and time took on a hazy quality. Still, he knew that Saranith had been quartering the Archipelago waiting for something, and that something was about to happen.

SARANITH WAS IN HER CABIN when the lookout she had put ashore on Mandan gave warning of a ship entering the strait.

"What name?" she sent back.

"Courier ship out of Ilwheirlane. The name on the bow is Keriar Nin."

At last, she thought. She sent orders to Arrai Walen Thar, whom she had placed in command of the merchanter *Irriling*, the Talented Fish, telling him to up anchor and move out to block the direct line through the strait. Then she ordered *Cinhai* to come about.

AS SHE HAD PLANNED, the *Irriling* caused *Keriar Nin* to swerve and bring down sail.

Cinhai then emerged from behind the headland, her guns out, ready for a full broadside, blocking any escape toward the open sea.

"Lower your sails and drop anchor," she ordered the signals sent to the other ship, "and no one will be hurt." Human ships rarely had telepaths aboard to receive clearer signals, so she regularly carried human signal flags and someone skilled in their use.

Instead, *Keriar Nin* tried for the gap between *Cinhai* and *Irriling*.

"Fourth gun," Saranith commanded, estimating the angles, "take out the mainmast."

The cannon fired. The ball would have missed, but not by much. Saranith reached out with her mind and made the slight correction necessary. *Keriar Nin*'s mainmast came down in a seething mass of canvas and splinters. The ship jerked and lost way. Saranith ordered *Cinhai* to close and board the other ship.

Keriar Nin signaled for surrender.

"Now that there's no choice," Saranith said to her first farail, "but we'll honor it. And once we're past the Point of Sarayan we'll put the captain and crew ashore at one of the human settlements on the south coast of Noia. There'll be no chance of getting a message to Ilwheirlane in time for it to do any good."

SARANITH WOULD BE BRINGING a total of seven prize ships back with her, a notable achievement and one that would make her crews quite wealthy. That and stopping the courier ship should go some way toward restoring her reputation with the naval command. Aketi was a fairly effective commander, but he'd not brought in nearly as many prizes over the years and wasn't popular with his crews. If he continued to defame her after this success, he'd only damage his own reputation, not hers.

XXXVIII

> *"Yet in the end the wizards fought each other,*
> *For power unchecked will often madness cause;*
> *So Rav conspired and sought to reign supreme,*
> *Despite the Council's strict and binding laws."*

> — EXCERPT FROM "ILKARIONIN: THE LIVING CRYSTALS" FROM *LEST WE FORGET: A*
> *BOOK OF TEACHING RHYMES* BY WILTON WIRRAMARETH OF ILWHEIRLANE, 4207

SARANITH WAS ON THE DECK OF CINHAI as it lay in anchor off the port of Fethi when she felt a flash of song and an image of minds merging from Cinkarion. The shock of the image was so strong she nearly lost her footing. She opened her mind to the high sight and probed the crystal to find out what had happened, but already the image was fading. Still, she managed to understand that what she had felt had been Lyskarion finding completion. Its bearer had mated, apparently in the midst of some kind of struggle.

She shook her head and put her hand on the railing to steady herself as she reevaluated the image. There had been a battle in progress and the bearer of Lyskarion had linked with his mate to increase their power during the struggle. She wondered why they hadn't linked before, as the image she had was not of a new relationship, but a very old one finally coming to completion. The flash Lyskarion sent out had felt triumphant.

Such a flash, she suddenly knew, would have gone out from Cinkarion when she formed her linkage, and probably again when Luri died. She analyzed the directionality of the image she had just received and knew that what had happened had taken place on the southwest shore of the Thallassean Sea, just off the coast of Darenje.

The bearers of the other crystals would have known of her bonding. No, she suddenly understood. Only two of the other crystals currently had full bonds with their bearers. She probed Cinkarion further. Lyskarion and Belkarion were now fully active with two linked bearers. Vyrkarion was held by a wizard but he was the wrong sex to form a full bond with the crystal. He would have felt the flash of communication, however. All of the other crystals were currently without bearers or held by minds that could not be linked to at all. Those bearers would have felt nothing.

But the communication between the crystals had to be how the wizards had known to chase her in the Thallassean. The ship had come from Sussey. She examined again the image of Lyskarion's bearers. The heir to the crystal created by the Wizards Luth and Dirga was an ingvalarin. She remembered that Lyskarion was supposed to be held by the Ahar of Sussey, but she had thought him to be untalented. Obviously he was not the actual current bearer.

She would have to report this to Mazilek right away. She straightened and looked around her. The crew were staring and she realized the vision had made her break off in mid sentence on the instructions she'd been giving for loading supplies.

She signaled to her first farail, "Carry on. I must go ashore."

Less than an hour later she was in Mazilek's office.

"So the Karionin are all interconnected," Mazilek summarized her report.

"So it would seem. Also, forming a full linkage would have given Lyskarion's bearers a great deal of power. I'm concerned with what may be happening to the fleet we sent to aid Gandahar. The vision I had definitely took place off the coast of Darenje."

4660, 466TH CYCLE OF THE YEAR OF THE OX
MONTH OF DIRGA

"OVER HALF of the fleet was destroyed?" Mazilek demanded.

"Yes, Ammarai Mazilek. Only nineteen of the ships we sent to the Thallassean have returned. The others were destroyed by undersea sabotage just after the Gandaharan takeover of Darenje."

"Undersea sabotage? Just what does that mean?"

Arhan Komeki hesitated, intimidated by his commander's ill-concealed anger. Finally, he said, "As Arhan Jakala explained it to me, it means that teams of men with breathers swam under the ships and cut holes in the hulls into which they inserted explosive devices. According to Jakala there may even have been ingvalarin among the humans."

"Ingvalarin involved in war," Mazilek expostulated, "impossible!"

Komeki shook his head. "It might have been impossible in the past, but there are disturbing rumors among the fleet. The ship that rescued the prisoners Aavik took came from Sussey and there were powerful wizards aboard."

Mazilek remembered Saranith's report of the linkage formed with Lyskarion. She had also said that the lead bearer was an ingvalar. If the ingvalarin had chosen to fight with humanity, that would change the very nature of the war. He didn't like the implications at all.

MONTH OF TORIN

PALA TOOK HER NOW USUAL PLACE on one of the chairs in front of the worktable in Balek's living quarters in the east wing of the Rabenate Palace, where the Council of the Varfarin in Cibata had been meeting for centuries before she had been born. Nathan was sitting in the chair next to her. She was excited for him, for today he would retake his oath and become a full wizard at the age of only fifty-one.

A few wizards had risen to that rank at an earlier age, Ashe and Arrun among them, having been only forty-five, and the legendary Cormor, having made it at the age of forty. Most wizards were sixty or more before they achieved that level of skill. Some didn't make it until they were over a hundred years old. And Nathan had been ready for over a year; there just had been no opportunity before this to gather a large number of wizards together for the ceremony.

Pala no longer caught him watching Lagura, not since she had confronted him on the day Del, now the Wizard Arrun, left Cibata. But nor had he approached. Oh, he took her places quite frequently. But he had never kissed her. Their relationship was strictly platonic. She feared he still thought of her as a child, but she was twenty-five now and almost ready to advance to Journeyman Wizard. An age difference of twenty-five years might seem a lot to a normal human, but wizards could live for over a thousand years and she didn't think Nathan was any more mature than she was.

"So who will the new commander of the Senangan forces be, and what do we know of him?" asked Kaoda.

The Wizard Jaith, still in her disguise as a linlar, said, "The choice was a surprising one. Choma and I expected Dekese to simply appoint Kaya, his son. However, the surviving military officers apparently put forth another candidate. None of us can understand precisely why they chose him, as he has no more active military experience than Kaya, perhaps even less, but he's been a professor at the University of Kobala for many years and is well known for his brilliance in the kind of war games they play there. He's also a distant cousin of Dekese. His name is Timaru Kamrasi."

Pala saw Nathan flinch and noticed that Balek also turned to look at Nathan as soon as that name was mentioned.

"Why was the choice so surprising, if he's known for his brilliance?" Selene asked.

"Because he's also rumored to be a worshiper of Jehan," Jaith said, "and has been known to speak against the war. Most interestingly, he's also Bashan's brother."

"Does he have any children?" Nathan asked.

"One, a daughter," Jaith answered.

Nathan looked at Balek who was watching him.

Nathan nodded slowly and said, "Then I have a sister. Timaru and his mate are certainly worshippers of Jehan, and my parents. They identified themselves on the focus gem they left me." He held up the acorn-sized yellow diamond he used instead of a normal crystal.

"Still, that doesn't mean that he'll put any less effort into trying to wipe Cassinga off the map," Choma warned. She and Evran were sharing the couch opposite Kaoda and Selene. "The military wouldn't have supported his appointment if they didn't think he would do the job."

"Have you heard from the Wizard Arrun?" Jaith asked. "Does anyone know when he plans to return to Cibata?"

"We've heard from him," Nathan said, "but he's given no definite date for return. Apparently, he helped Errin rescue Jerevan Rayne from Ravaar, and then went on tour. We know he's visited Mahran and Kailane, but he's given us no definite date for return."

"Does anyone know anything yet about any specific changes Timaru plans to make in the Senangan military?" Kaoda asked.

"They're starting to build a munitions factory able to mass-produce longer range rifles," Choma said.

"Yes," said Jaith, "and they've started to condition the maliks to face rats."

"Is there any chance that the Uleins could be persuaded that a new munitions factory here in Cassinga could be profitable to them, as well as aiding in their country's defence," Nathan asked.

"Probably, if you don't have moral objections to making the Uleins even richer than they already are," Balek said.

"Moral objections aside, they have the money and the power," Nathan said, "and we need the weapons to match the Senangans "

"We'll need to import trained weapons makers from the Northern Hemisphere," Marala said.

"We're followers of Jehan," Balek said. "The production of arms is the promotion of war. That shouldn't be our goal here."

"No, rai," Nathan said, turning to his master. "It should not. But, as you've taught me, the survival of Cassinga is our goal, and Cassinga will not survive without modern weapons. We do what we must, and pray."

Balek glared at Nathan for several moments, but then his lips pressed together and he nodded. "Yes. You're ready for your elevation." He smiled wryly. "It's never been a requirement that a pupil agree with the master to rise in rank, only that he never oppose his master's interests." He looked around the room. "If agreement had been the criteria, many of you would never have become masters."

Pala watched as most of the wizards in the room at least smiled and many broke out in outright laughter. Jaith clapped.

"Then I think the business part of this meeting can be completed tomorrow. We should now join and witness the oath of my one-time student, Nathan, now my right hand in the work we do here in Cassinga on Jehan's behalf," Balek said.

Nathan stood and all the wizards in the room linked minds.

"Cosar ya ma pon cam redrem resalt a keremod yase ac gib remfarin a Corril a Nalorin, Varfarin, et yase rai," Nathan thought.

Pala translated in her head, "I swear I will not use the knowledge gained from my teaching to oppose the interests of the Council of Wizards, the Varfarin, or my master," except the words in Eskh, the language of telepaths, had many more subtle shadings of meaning. "Interests" for instance, was a very bland translation of *remfarin*, which literally meant "thought paths." That was why, Pala knew, starting students took the oath in their own language, but full wizards had to take the oath in Eskh. A complete fluency in that language was an unstated requirement for all wizards.

"Cosar ya ma pon cam he redrem resalt a keremod yase ac lar ilame gib remfarin a Corril a Nalorin, Varfarin, et yase rai," Nathan continued.

"I swear I will not pass on the knowledge gained from my training to any being opposed to the interests of the Council of Wizards, the Varfarin, or my master," Pala translated, remembering that this was the most controversial clause. In the original form of the oath drawn up by the Council of Wizards, the knowledge could not be passed on to any being not of human blood.

Still, if while taking the oath, a candidate was detected in falsehood, it was the job of those linked with him to destroy him the moment the falsehood was sensed. Pala shuddered at the thought, but with Nathan, of course, there was no question of his honesty.

"Cosar ya ma pon jer nalor rham ilame ken ilame remrion, big kunende, quen bohedal va sen nalor rham ba malate et ma acke kiret sive eava a bova," Nathan continued.

"I swear I shall not alter another wizard in any way for any reason, except temporarily, to sustain life, if the other wizard is unconscious, or not yet trained enough to save himself," Pala translated. Her mind immediately flashed to the most glaring breach of this law, performed by, of all people, the Wizard Derwen, when he had forced Jerevan Rayne, the Hetri of Leyburne, to study wizardry by cursing him.

She wondered if she'd ever meet the wizard Jerevan Rayne would eventually become. Having been forced to study wizardry, what respect could he have for the rules of the Varfarin?

Nathan's telepathic recital of the rules went on for some time, and while Pala attended to his intent dutifully, a part of her mind still considered how the older wizards could stand by when the rules were first rewritten and then breached so violently, justified only by the mention of a wizard centuries dead.

XXXIX

4660, 466TH CYCLE OF THE YEAR OF THE OX
MONTH OF REDRI

Benevad a am grelar ba dale
squa gaidom a trav shemin.

*"The friendship of one wise man is better
than the adoration of a hundred fools."*

— ESLARIN PROVERB

The Wizard Ashe extended his vision to examine the ridge across a narrow valley from where he stood. He found a level, clear spot near the crest and fixed it in his mind, registered it on his crystal, then willed himself to the new location. From there it was only a few steps before he could look across the next valley to the next ridge. The new valley was broader and the next ridge not so high. He was coming out of the foothills of the Myerly Mountains, Kandorra's spine. He could see a town on the bank of a stretch of river where the valley opened onto the Plains of Kerin to the west. The town would be Merrytan according to his map, and there were tents set up in a level field near the edge of it. He thought that, were he in the form of a dog, he'd wag his tail. He'd found the Wizard Elgan.

Finding Elgan, he reminded himself, wasn't his primary purpose here in Kandorra. Then he grinned and admitted to his conscience that it was a decided side benefit. He'd heard far too many conflicting things about Elgan. He wanted to meet the man.

He extended his vision to examine a field near the carnival, but not too close. He found a nice open place near a grove of trees, fixed it in his mind, registered it on his crystal, and willed himself there.

Once arrived in the field, he strolled through the grove of trees, across a meadow into the campsite. There he walked up to the first roustabout he met and asked, "Which caravan belongs to the Wizard Elgan?"

"Who you?" the roustabout asked in the typical Larafarin pidgin.

"The Wizard Ashe, at your service," Ashe said, bowing.

The man nodded and pointed to a caravan at the edge of the campsite, shaded by a large marin tree, obviously a preferred location.

"Thank you," Ashe said, and walked over to the caravan and knocked on the door.

He was startled when the door was opened by a young woman not out of her teens, a young hailar, he corrected himself, taking in her feathered head. He was even more startled when his delicate mind probe met a strong shield.

"Who are you? What do you want?" she demanded.

Ashe smiled wryly. "I am the Wizard Ashe and I would like very much to speak with your master. Now even more than before I arrived at your door."

The Wizard Elgan appeared behind the young hailar. As he had never met him before but had been told he resembled his grandfather and, indeed, the man before him looked as though he could have posed for any of the portraits Ashe had seen of the Wizard Cormor. The broad brow, the square chin, even the chestnut hair was the same, worn the same length and curling the same way over the forehead. Perhaps the green eyes held a trace more blue than Cormor's had, but that could be the light or an artist's failing.

"My eyes are bluer than my grandfather's. Also, I'm taller, broader in the shoulder and some pounds heavier than he was," Elgan said, sounding amused.

Ashe nodded. "You must be accustomed to the astonishment you elicit on first meeting. Of course, you could always change your hair-style, if you didn't like it."

Elgan laughed. "Touché. Why don't you come in and sit down. Magra has just finished her lesson."

Ashe saw Elgan's eyes go to Magra and her head lower slightly, and he knew some communication had just passed between them on the intimate mode.

She stepped back out of the doorway so he could enter and he stepped past her into the immaculate and beautifully appointed caravan.

Elgan touched his hand and gestured toward a chair. A quick evaluation of Elgan's shields told him that this wizard was his master. Even Kaaremin and Andamin, his own teachers and the last surviving great wizards of the Council, did not have Elgan's power.

Ashe blinked and controlled his astonishment. He pulled his mind back to examining his surroundings. This end of the caravan contained four padded chairs and a small, round table. There were fitted shelves against one wall and Ashe's mind felt a kind of displacement about them. He realized that Elgan had built a little pocket universe behind those shelves to contain his entire library.

"I'm a teacher," Elgan said, obviously taking in the focus of Ashe's attention, "and I've been stuck in Kandorra for centuries now. I couldn't go without my library, now could I?"

"Obviously not," Ashe said, sitting down in the chair Elgan had indicated. He wondered how many more surprises he was in for this day.

Magra eyed him carefully and he felt her probe of his shields. "It was nice meeting you, rai," she said politely.

"Yes," he said. "I hope we'll get to talk some more later."

"You'll be staying with the carnival then?" she asked eagerly.

"For a time at least."

She smiled then and left, shutting the door behind her.

Ashe turned back to his host. "You are not at all what I expected," he said frankly.

Elgan's head cocked. "What did you expect then?"

Ashe shook his head. "I'm not sure. My expectations were quite vague, but certainly not so much raw power."

"You've heard me compared to my grandfather. My power was much slower to develop than his, but even now I'm not his equal."

"Then I begin to understand better why all the wizards I've met and respected defer to his visions."

"Act as his puppets, you mean," Elgan said wryly, "even hundreds of years after his death."

"That, too," Ashe said with a grin. "I take it Kandorra was not your own choice of residence."

Elgan laughed. "No, I'm a great fan of large cities and urban amenities. The wilds of Kandorra would have been close to my last choice had I been given any."

"Then what was your assignment by the master?"

"Can't you guess? You saw my apprentice," Elgan paused and Ashe felt his examination, "and I know your nature."

Ashe stiffened. No one but Kaaremin and Andamin knew his true nature. He had been very careful to keep it that way.

Elgan shook his head. "Be easy. I can't break through your barricade of a mind. I won't even try. But I touched you as you came in, and I'm perfectly capable of doing a cellular analysis of your DNA. You've changed your appearance, but not your DNA, gamlar."

Ashe felt naked sitting in the padded chair. His mind reeled.

"As it happens," Elgan continued, ignoring his reaction, "I've been expecting you."

Ashe had thought himself incapable of feeling greater shock. "Expecting me..."

"You know my grandfather had visions of possible futures. Why should it surprise you that you were in such a vision?"

Ashe tried to gather his faculties back together. Too many shocks, too quickly. "I was in one of Cormor's visions?"

"Oh, not by name or detailed description. Cormor merely told me that he was sure Kaaremin and Andamin would find a gamlar to train, a gamlar with the power to be a great wizard which Minlis, their own daughter, lacked." Elgan hesitated, then asked with genuine curiousity, "How tall are you in your natural form?"

"Just under seven feet," Ashe said with a snap, recovering.

"Wow," Elgan said. "I can see why you chose nondescript."

Ashe felt the tension inside him relax a bit. "It's been a great relief to no longer be stared at. Eyes glance off me now. I'm never noticed in a crowd."

"You know that can't last, don't you?" There was sympathy in Elgan's tone.

Ashe frowned. "What do you mean?"

"Only that, when you take your place on the Council of Wizards, your face, whatever form you give it, will come to be known. There will be portraits of you all over Tamar and people will recognize you in the street."

"My place on the Council of Wizards?" Ashe repeated in astonishment.

"That was Cormor's vision, the only future he ever saw that gave a chance of a permanent peace for Tamar. He saw a new Council of Wizards, not a human council, but one representing all the races."

Ashe's mind jumped. "So that's why you're training a hailar. Is she that good?"

"You read her," Elgan said. "I saw you do it as you came in. Her shields are good for her level, but you went right around them. What do you think?"

Ashe set aside the repeated shocks he'd just received and retrieved the memory of the scan of the hailar girl he'd made as he came in. He evaluated it carefully, hardly surprised at all after the other, greater shocks, to discover that, if properly developed, she would be almost his equal in power. Much more powerful than most pure human wizards. He looked up and met Elgan's eyes. "Yes. She has the potential to become a great wizard."

"I hope that you'll be willing to stay long enough to hear her journeyman's oath. Valanta is due any day, but it will be good to have another witness. Wizards are rather scarce in these parts as a rule."

Ashe hesitated, studying Elgan. Finally, he said, "Yes. I'll be willing to hear her oath. You understand that I am currently, at least technically, sworn to the Varfarin."

"Are you now?" Elgan eyed him. "Then what are you doing in these parts? I doubt if Derwen has even thought about Kandorra in years."

"After completing the last assignment given me by Derwen, as he seemed to have forgotten about me, I went back to completing a quest of my own, which seems to be the usual modus operandi for members of the Varfarin these days."

Elgan shrugged. "Don't look to me for a defense of Derwen. I told Cormor he'd destroy the Varfarin, but Cormor said that wasn't the point and the Varfarin would recover under its next Esalfar." He hesitated, then added, "What is your quest that it brings you here?"

"I've been mapping Tamar and locating teleport points in all the areas I've mapped," Ashe said. "The idea is that, eventually, I'll be able to get to any point on Tamar in only a few days, instead of the weeks or months it would take by sea."

Elgan's eyes widened. "That sounds like an immense and very valuable project indeed. How much of it have you completed?"

"All of the continents of Noia and Cibata, the archipelago of islands leading down from Noia to Kandorra, most of Kandorra, the north polar region and the northern part of Macosia. I need to finish Kandorra, explore the south polar region and the southern half of Macosia. Then I'll be done. I'm sure I've missed a few islands, but most of those are probably too far from any other point of land to be accessed by teleportation."

Elgan whistled. "You've almost finished the whole planet. Are you willing to share your mapped loci?"

"Yes," Ashe said, "but I'd really like to trade them to you for that trick with the pocket universe. I've never seen anything like it and I've been living in a tent I can carry on my back. A few amenities in a pocket universe would really help."

Elgan laughed. "I'll bet it would. You could, if you wanted to spend enough power, carry a whole house around on your back. I don't recommend it however. The initial power is only the start. There's a continuing drain. I prefer to have several small pockets. The initial outlay is still fairly major." He paused and looked at Ashe. "You do know how to access ley lines, don't you?"

Ashe nodded. "Yes. Kaaremin taught me that."

"Pocket universes take a lot of energy to start up," Elgan said. "After that, though, the permanent drain is variable dependent on their size. The thing you have to remember is that there are a lot more dimensions than what we can see. The universe goes in a lot more directions than north, south, east, west and up and down. Our normal senses, even in the high sight, just don't register those extra directions unless you create a gateway and tag and shape it clearly. Once you have the gateway open you can put things inside. Those things aren't in this universe anymore, so they have no weight here, but you can reach them and draw them out at any time."

Elgan paused. "That's another thing. You have to be specific about time, too. If you aren't, your small universe will age much faster than this one and your perishable things will turn to dust in just a few days. That happened to me with the first universe I created. Cormor was kind and transformed the dust back into what I'd lost, as it was still in the range of time that it had a memory of what it had been, but he warned me that it was possible for enough time to have passed in a pocket universe for the dust not even to have memory."

Ashe considered this burst of information and said, "This was a creation of Cormor's, wasn't it?"

"Yes," Elgan said, "and before you ask I'll tell you that, no, he didn't share it widely."

"I can understand why. I'll do my best to conceal my knowledge."

Elgan said, "I'll show you how to conceal the gate. If I'd known you were coming, you wouldn't have seen mine, but I've gotten careless being out here without any other wizards in the vicinity. Magra doesn't have high sight yet so she can't see it."

MAGRA LISTENED AVIDLY AS ASHE entertained with stories of his travels. Valanta had arrived that morning with four other wizards and Magra was finding the interactions between them all fascinating.

There was Astil, whose name meant "Little Worm," a short, stocky man with light brown hair, Eldana, even shorter with dark brown hair and a puckish grin, and Vitry and Basel, who seemed to be a couple, although they weren't linked. Vitry was blonde, her hair paler than Valanta's and her build slighter. Basel was tall and gaunt with shaggy brown hair and cataracts on his eyes. Magra didn't question the cataracts. Having lived with show people all her life, she understood the value of visual aids and knew that, as he was a wizard, he could heal himself if he wished.

Rather than crowd them all into his caravan, Elgan had chosen to hire one of the carnival tents and partitioned it up to give private quarters to his guests. The main part, however, was set up for Magra to take her oath. She felt more than prepared for that, however, and was enjoying the festivities in the meantime. Ashe seemed to be in an unusually talkative mood.

"So you changed your form to match whatever people you were among to do this mapping?" Valanta asked. "Wasn't that strange to you, changing your form so often, changing your form at all?"

"Yes," Ashe said, eyeing Basel warily, "I have, over the years, assumed the form of every type of lar, even a fallar, although that was hard," he added, looking rueful.

"I thought the fallar warrens were very comfortable." Eldara said.

"Oh, yes, even luxurious, but there's no light except occasionally some phosphorescent fungi. They see entirely in the infra red. After a time, I'd get desperate to see the sun."

"Why would you need to live with the fallarin?" Elgan asked.

"I wanted to locate all of their major warrens in my maps, determine good locations near them, and I'd lived as every other type of lar so I was curious," Ashe said. "After all, no one assigned my project to me, so it has no timetable. Anyway, it was a fascinating experience, but not one I'll willingly repeat."

"Changing your shape like that. It's not something to be done lightly," Basel said.

"I know myself very well," Ashe said to Basel, "and I never change my form lightly."

"I think it's time," Elgan said, "for us to hear Magra give her oath." There was a chorus of assent.

Elgan turned to her, "Magra, you understand that training in wizardry has a price. The things I ask of you will not always be easy and you must swear to obey me until you reach the status of journeyman wizard."

Magra licked her lips nervously and nodded.

"I know you're a worshiper of Jehan," Elgan continued. "Are you prepared to take your oath in his name?"

"Yes," Magra said.

Elgan turned to the assembled wizards. "You've all had time today to meet and talk to Magra and her mother. Do any of you here know of any reason why I shouldn't take the oath of this apprentice?"

Magra looked around the room, knowing that none of the wizards here would question her ancestry although many in other places might. It gave her a faint sense of conspiracy.

Elgan thought, *"Then we shall link minds."*

Magra reached out to link with Elgan. Then she was not simply linked with Elgan, something she had done many times before, but floating naked in space, her mind wide open, with eyes looking into her brain.

"Will you, Magra, honor your oath given to Jehan?"

"Yes."

"Then give your oath, and we shall bear witness."

Magra took a deep breath and remembered the word images she had rehearsed, *"I swear that I shall be guided by the laws of the Council of Wizards."*

"And what is the first law?"

"I will not use the knowledge I gain from my training to act against the interests of the Council, the Varfarin, or my master."

"The second law?"

"I will not teach, or transmit in any way, the knowledge I gain from my training to any being who has interests opposed to those of the Council, the Varfarin, or my master."

"The third law?"

The ceremony continued as Magra swore to each of the complex laws with the wizards in rapport to witness both her sincerity and her understanding. When she had sworn to the last law there was a moment of silence. Then Elgan thought, *"You have witnessed this oath?"*

The assembled wizards replied as one, *"We have."*

"Do you accept Magra as an apprentice with all the rights and responsibilities that entails?"

"We do."

Magra felt the linkage dissolve and was alone again in her head. She was exhausted.

Eldana came up and hugged her. Magra felt enveloped by the strong arms. "I'm the youngest wizard here, so I went through that most recently. My sympathies. I slept for a week."

Magra managed a weak smile, hoping she would soon be able to imitate Eldana and retire. The long period in the multiple linkage had drained her more than she had expected and she knew a headache was coming.

Elgan sensed her discomfort. "Go on back to your caravan, Magra. You need to sleep now."

Magra nodded. "Thank you, rai," she said, and left.

When she was gone Elgan looked at Valanta. "You've been bursting with news all day. What is it? I take it Magra's too young to hear."

Valanta looked at Ashe.

"Oh, he's all right. He may be a member of the Varfarin, but I think Eldana and Basel are too, and it hasn't kept any of you from assisting me even though you're well aware Derwen would disapprove," Elgan said.

Eldana grimaced. "The mapping sounds so like something the Varfarin should have commissioned." She looked at Ashe. "I'm glad to hear you're doing it."

Ashe grimaced. "It's an excuse to wander. I spent twenty-four years stuck on a small island the last time Derwen found something for me to do. I don't even want to consider what he'd assign me next. I'm hoping his successor develops quickly."

Elgan looked around at the faces of the visiting wizards and nodded, "Ah, it's something to do with Derwen's victim, and, hopefully, his eventual replacement. So what has happened to Jerevan Rayne now?"

"The bearer of Lyskarion gave him the ability to shapechange to a dolphin and has given him the freedom of the seas," Basel said. "We're all afraid that he won't come back, that he won't want to be a man again. Particularly given the tremendous handicaps he faces in his human form."

"I wouldn't worry too much about that," Elgan said, feeling his usual distaste for Basel's emphasis on form. "From all I've heard, he's no saint. He'll have to come back to land to take his revenge on Derwen."

XL

4662, 467TH CYCLE OF THE YEAR OF THE EAGLE
MONTH OF DIRGA

"It is the practice today in many of the nations of Tamar to put children to death merely because they are born without were-sight. This practice must be stopped..."

"Another of the paramount purposes for which the Varfarin was created is the elimination of infanticide in every nation on Tamar."

— EXCERPTS FROM *ILVARFARIN: THE OPEN ROADS* BY THE WIZARD CORMOR

"I APPRECIATE THAT you supported me for my current position," Timaru said, "but the situation is an impossible one." He was visiting Mazilek's office in Feshi.

"In what way," Mazilek asked.

"In every way," Timaru said, turning to face Mazilek, who was frowning with concern. "The military commanders accepted the need for new weapons, but felt they could be designed by the same people who made the old. They refused to countenance the expense of importing rifle-makers from the Thallassean region, or from Gandahar. The result is large, clumsy rifles that one man can barely handle. They'll be extremely awkward in the field."

"Most of them also accepted the fact that, if maliks are to be used in future at all, they must be conditioned to ignore rats. However, they refused to start breeding rats. Therefore, they've been sending teams of men out to catch them. The result is that the slums of Azrak and Feshi have never been freer of rats, but we've only caught enough to train some fifty maliks in two years."

"But you're the commander," Mazilek said. "You can simply order it done."

"So I thought when I took this position," Timaru said, "but that doesn't seem to be the reality. I issue an order, and someone comes back and says, 'I'm sorry, amtamrai, but that can't be done.' I ask, 'Why not?' Then I'm given an endless list of reasons, all carefully orchestrated so that there's no one person I can blame."

"Have you thought of simply retiring all the current commanders under you and elevating a whole new officer corps?" Mazilek asked.

Timaru shook his head. "You know I can't do that. They'd just protest to Dekese, and he'd remove me and put Kaya in my place. I think the reason many of the old commanders supported me was that they knew they'd be able to limit my effectiveness in changing the system. They don't want to be modernized. Most of them still feel their losses to Cassinga were all Bashan's fault."

Mazilek frowned. "I wouldn't have encouraged you to take the position if I hadn't been sure that many of the officer corps really want to make changes."

"Many of the younger officers do want to modernize, but they don't dare go against their superiors, and all but one or two of the top rank of officers are still fighting the Dragon Wars. Take Tamrai Khetav, for instance, high commander of the malik divisions, with only three fingers on one hand and two on the other from the days when he actually rode the creatures. He's convinced that it's the fault of the current riders that their maliks go off after rats. 'That would never have happened in my days as a rider,' he says whenever the subject arises. He claims that accustoming the maliks to rats is the same as coddling the current crop of riders. Therefore, what rats we do manage to capture, are used to train the scrub ranks, never any of his elite troops."

"I hear that Kaya has been made your sub-commander," Mazilek said.

"Oh, yes," Timaru said. "Dekese's just waiting for me to fail so he can put Kaya in charge, but in the meantime, Kaya's getting to commiserate with all the old timers regarding my unreasonable demands. Nevermind that, if he does get control, he'll just kick most of them out. While I'm in charge, he's all sympathy."

"WHAT WILL YOU DO IF YOU MEET our son on the battlefield," Atira asked, her voice carefully controlled.

"I will let him kill me," Timaru told his mate. "I didn't want this job, and I'm not going to succeed in achieving the goal for which I accepted it. But I'll not be forced into killing our son."

"And that's supposed to make me feel better, that should you meet our son will kill you?"

"Nothing about this war is supposed to make either of us feel better, Atira."

MONTH OF INGVASH

JUBA WAS ENJOYING HERSELF. She had loved the pomp and ceremony of being crowned Ahar of Cassinga, riding in the open carriage through the streets and hearing the people cheer. They had never cheered for Mamfe.

But now, back in her royal suite of rooms, she could enjoy an even greater pleasure. She could actually exert some control over her daughter.

She looked around her at all the new bed hangings and curtains, purple and gold as she had specified, and inhaled the incense she had ordered to scent her rooms, a hint of cinnamon and musk, and grinned.

"Mother, you know I love you, but you really don't have any idea about how to rule Cassinga."

"I'll listen to the wizards, Pala. I sure won't do any worse than Mamfe."

"It isn't enough to be better than Mamfe. He scraped the bottom of the barrel. Cassinga needs real leadership."

"We've won our last few rounds with Senanga," Juba said. She loved it when Pala was passionate.

"Thanks to the Wizard Arrun," Pala said, "but he's from the North. He's got no permanent ties to Cibata."

"Of course, you're right, dear," Juba said smiling. Despite being Pala's mother, she had rarely been able to exert any authority over her daughter. Keeping the throne might not be the best thing for Cassinga, but she wanted grandchildren. "You'll make a much better ruler for Cassinga than me."

"Then why won't you abdicate?" Pala asked.

"I will, child, just as soon as you find yourself a mate and give me grandchildren," Juba said with relish. "I'll be off this throne as soon after that as I can arrange it, but not before. So you better get out there and find yourself a mate."

Pala stared at her mother.

Juba nodded with satisfaction. "That's right, Pala. This time you won't get what you want, unless I get what I want from you first."

Pala sighed and Juba was shocked to see a hint of defeat in her daughter's posture. "Oh, I found myself a mate," Pala said. "He just won't acknowledge I've grown up yet."

Juba eyed her daughter. She'd suspected for years that Pala had never grown out of her childhood adoration of Nathan, but she was glad to have the suspicion confirmed. "You have your eye on Nathan?" She laughed.

"What's so funny?" Pala demanded.

"Oh, you got your work cut out for you with that one. He's modeled himself after his master. He's a virgin, child."

"So am I," Pala said. "I don't see that as a problem."

Juba paused and studied her daughter. "I'm not saying Nathan's consciously chosen celibacy. I doubt he's even thought about it, but unconsciously he's always avoided thoughts of sex because that's the example Balek set. You're going to have to seduce him. He'll never ask you to bed with him."

"And how do I do that?" Pala asked.

Juba grinned. "You're a female. You should be able to figure out a way. I doubt he's totally immune to you."

MONTH OF CERDANA

The Wizard Arrun arrived back in Cassinga on a grey, rainy day in Cibata's fall. Nathan was wet and irritable when he went down to meet the ship.

"We expected to hear from you before now," he said pointedly as Arrun came down the gangplank. "No one has known where you've been."

"Not even Senanga's spies," Arrun said cheerfully, "so isn't that a good thing?" He examined Nathan carefully and added, "I heard you graduated to being a full wizard while I was gone, so why are you standing around sopping wet, an example of a good student not permitted to make himself comfortable?"

Nathan glared, noticing the almost invisible energy shield that was keeping Arrun dry. "Because I never thought of doing that," he said, analyzing the shield and copying it for himself. He smiled ruefully and added, "Making oneself comfortable is not something Balek would consider relevant."

"Whereas Ashe was a master at that art," Arrun said.

Nathan looked beyond Arrun to a group of four well dressed gentlemen accompanied by several crewmen with large baggage carriers.

"Who are those men?" asked Nathan. It was unusual for groups to move to Cassinga, particularly wealthy ones, as these men appeared to be.

"Cassinga's new arms industry," Arrun said. "They're experienced gunsmiths and they have the detailed plans and the license to produce long range Khykar rifles here in Candith." He grinned. "After some research and tours of all the major weapons producers in the Thallassean region, I determined that Khykar would serve our purpose best. What's more, for the license fees and a percentage interest in the business, the Khykar Company was willing to put up twenty percent of the cost of establishing the production facility. Each of the gunsmiths will put up another five percent of the costs of construction."

Nathan gaped. He had thought of Cassinga producing its own weapons, had even suggested it in the Council, but he'd never actually believed such a thing would happen, or done anything actively to start such an operation. Yet here was Arrun with gunsmiths and capital, the whole enterprise almost a fait accompli.

"Where will the rest of the capital come from?" he asked weakly.

"I'll put up some of it myself. Kaoda and Selene promised to put up some before I left and I believe the Uleins will put up the rest," Arrun said. "I made it clear to them, however, that they'd never get a controlling interest. The arms industry is a necessary evil at this point in time but it's one that needs careful watching. Down the line, we don't need wars started merely so that shareholders can make a profit."

IN THE WEEK FOLLOWING ARRUN'S RETURN to Cassinga Pala noticed an almost infintesimal easing in Nathan's habitual tension. She decided that, if she was ever going to try to seduce him, it should be now.

It still disturbed her that she was seriously considering taking her mother's advice. That wasn't the way their relationship had worked, not even when she had been a child. On the other hand, she had to admit that the realm of male-female relationships was one area where Juba had much more experience and might know what she was talking about.

There was a vale near Tibati where a small stream fell down a cliff into a circular pool. It was not a large waterfall, just a constant trickle and splash. She had seen her mother and Rovan there once. They had been sunning on the flat rocks at the outer edge of the pool when she came upon them, but she had known what they had been doing earlier. She remembered that the grass beyond the rocks was one of the soft varieties, dark green and fine textured, edging into moss around the rocks. It was autumn, the air would be cool but not cold. Yes, the vale would be a perfect place to lose her virginity, but how could she get Nathan there?

Nathan often sought her out, particularly if they'd been arguing. It was one of the things that made her believe he really did care for her. She could always pick a fight. She loved him, but he had some annoying habits. As Juba had noted, he modeled his behavior too closely after Balek.

She usually restrained herself from criticizing Nathan, but, come to think of it, there were a number of things she had been aching to say. She should be able to generate a really good fight, if she put her mind to it.

Then she could run away to Tibati. It was a natural place for her to go. She'd grown up there, and she'd been meaning to make a visit to inspect the Fort sometime in the next few months anyway, so the trip wouldn't even come under the heading of dereliction of duty.

Then, if Nathan sought her out, she'd arrange for him to find her in the vale, naked and oiled and posed on one of the boulders at the edge of the pool. If she couldn't get him to make love to her in that setting, then there was no hope for them.

NATHAN AND PALA WERE TOURING the schools, looking for talent. This had become an annual routine. The trained eagles were having eaglets of their own now and every year more children needed to be found.

Cassinga was now exporting journeymen to man telepathic relays all over Tamar. They were producing more than Sussey, which had previously been the major source for such journeymen.

It was a gray, fall day and all the children were assembled on the playground. It started to rain, a thin, fine drizzle. Nathan hunched his shoulders and examined the next child.

"*Have you no consideration, Nathan?*" Pala demanded in the intimate mode.

He looked up, startled, and saw that the children at her end of the playground were protected from the rain by a thin shield of force, like the one Arrun had shown him on the day he returned.

Nathan hurriedly erected a matching shield over the children on his side of the field. "*Sorry,*" he thought, "*it's not something I think of automatically yet.*"

"*I really don't care if you get wet,*" Pala thought, "*but you should have considered the children's welfare immediately. This is cold season, after all.*"

"*I'm drying them now,*" he responded, forcing moisture out of the air inside the shield and warming it.

"*But it takes much more energy to do that than it would have taken to erect the shield quickly in the first place. You have to learn to think, Nathan.*"

"*It's my energy,*" Nathan thought, annoyed that Pala would criticize him so harshly.

"*But it's Balek's pattern,*" she accused. "*You know perfectly well that he's often wrong, but you imitate him anyway.*"

"*He's my mentor,*" Nathan defended himself. "*And much of what he's taught me is good and right.*"

"*You're a full wizard now, Nathan. You have to learn to think for yourself.*"

"*I do,*" he thought, nearly missing the bright talent in the small girl he was passing. He stopped and turned to the child. "What's your name?"

"Nedra Charn," she said.

"Would you like to train an eagle?" he asked.

The child's eyes brightened. "Oh, yes," she said. "My cousin showed us hers and me and my brother got to feed him and stroke his feathers. I'd love to have one of my own."

Nathan marked her name on his crystal, relieved by her chatter. With a cousin already in the program, the parents of this child were unlikely to object to her being trained. When Arrun first started the program, a lot of the parents were hostile to their children learning wizardry. That happened less often in these days, but it still happened.

"*Keep an eye out for the brother,*" Nathan thought to Pala. "*Talent often runs in families.*"

"*I've already found the brother,*" Pala thought. "*He's just as talented and as eager, and I do understand genetics. I've been doing this nearly as long as you have.*"

Nathan took a deep breath, shocked by the anger in Pala's thought. "*I know you have,*" he thought, "*I was just...*"

"*Just condescending to share your elevated wisdom to the neophyte,*" Pala thought. "*But I'm not a neophyte. I haven't been for years and I don't like being treated like one.*"

Nathan wanted to defend himself, but realized that he was guilty as charged. He'd been doing it in self defense, he knew. If he kept thinking of her as a child, as someone to be instructed, he could control his desire for her. Why should he need to control it? He'd been blocking his desire for her for years out of pure habit. She was a journeyman wizard now. There was no reason at all for him to hold back.

He eyed her across the field, proud and beautiful and furious with him. This was obviously not the right moment to propose they go off somewhere and have passionate sex. But they'd had fights before. She always forgave him. He grimaced, realizing that he'd almost always been the one in the wrong.

Well, when she'd had time to cool down, he'd seek her out and see if he couldn't solve the problem.

Except the next day, when Nathan tried to find Pala, he discovered she had left suddenly for Tibati.

PALA LAY POSED ON THE FLAT ROCK LISTENING to the water splash gently into the pool behind her. There was a scent of mint in the air from where it grew at the edge of the pool. She thought it blended well with the citrus oil she had spread on her skin. The rock was warm.

She knew Nathan was coming. She had felt his mind when he came within range of her telepathic ability. He had teleported to Tibati. There had been no trace of him, then he'd suddenly been close, and now he was coming closer.

She had expected him to teleport, which was why she had spent the whole morning by the pool. But now she was having all kinds of doubts and second thoughts. Was the oil too much? Would he laugh when he saw her spread naked on the rock?

Then he was standing at the edge of the grass, staring at her. She stiffened and said defiantly, "I think it's about time you stopped treating me like a child."

She saw him swallow. "Yes," he said, "I think so too." Suddenly he was as naked as she was and leaning over her on the rock. Their lips met. He kissed her. She was surprised when his tongue parted her lips and entered her mouth, but soon lost herself in the thrust of tongue on tongue.

Then she felt his hands caressing her breasts. He pulled back, though, and she felt bereft.

"Don't stop."

"I won't," he said and she was surprised by the breathless quality of his voice. "I just think we should continue this on the grass. It's softer." He picked her up and she felt him lay her on the spongy turf. Then he was lying beside her. His lips replaced his hands on her breasts and his hands explored lower. She burned wherever he touched her.

She reached out to link her mind with his, but he broke the linkage. "Not yet, Pala. If we link while doing this, it could become permanent."

"Don't you want it to be permanent?" she asked.

"I love you, Pala, but I don't think either of us is ready yet to form a lifetime linkage. Lets just enjoy each other for a while first."

"Very well," she said, but the bright edge of the joy she had felt when he kissed her was blunted.

NATHAN FELT HER DISAPPOINTMENT and applied himself to making her think of other things. He might not ever have done this before, but he'd been studying the subject for years. He started to apply the knowledge with his lips and fingers on Pala's body. Then her hands were exploring his body as well and he almost lost himself in the spiraling fire of passion.

He felt her body contract and knew that she was moist and ready for him. He kissed her again and began to enter her. Maera's mercy, he thought, her hymen was still intact. He dissolved it with his mind so not to bring her pain and drove himself into her fully. She gasped, but asked "What did you do?"

She'd felt the invasion of his mind altering her flesh. "Later" he said. She was so warm and tight he thought he would explode right away, but held himself back and started to move inside her. The urge to link and and share with her his feelings and feel what she was feeling was powerful, but he held it back. His hands explored her driving her higher, and then she was over the edge and he followed her into an explosion of ecstasy. His mind blanked out. All he could do was feel.

When he felt able to speak, he said, "I do love you, you know."

"I suppose I understand. You thought you loved Lagura for years. You're afraid this may be an illusion as well."

"No," Nathan said. "That's not it at all. I'm afraid that you'll change your mind down the line. You're still very young."

"Old enough to know my own mind, but I'll let time convince you," Pala said, then rolled over until she was leaning over him. "I warn you though, I enjoyed my first experience of physical passion. I'll expect repeat performances on a regular basis"

"No problem at all," he thought, reaching up to pull her down on top of him and kiss her. *"We can start right away."*

XLI

4664, 467TH CYCLE OF THE YEAR OF THE TIGER
MONTH OF ANOR

> *"Where does responsibility end? It is not enough to say, 'I did not commit an illegal act.' If one knows a crime is going to be committed, one is responsible for preventing it. But if one only suspects? Must one then investigate, or be equally guilty? If that were true, then one might spend half one's life pursuing chimeras of guilt. No. Only if one has good cause to be at least halfway certain does one have the responsibility to act."*

— EXCERPT FROM *PURSUIT OF JUSTICE*, BY OREN CARSEGAN OF ILLWHEIRLANE, 4531

TIMARU SAT ON HIS HORSE on a hilltop and eyed the jungle across the river bank warily. He and the Senangan commanders supposedly under him had at least agreed that another assault on the well-defended pass would be unwise. Therefore, they were mounting a two-pronged attack across the Kipembawe River.

He had also managed, over many objections, to choose two lesser known sites to cross, and sent feints to the better known ones. As far as he knew, only he and two other commanders had known the crossing points in advance.

The Senangan forces would, as usual, outnumber the Cassingan, so he should have felt confident. He did not.

Maliks would still lead the forces, and those maliks had not been familiarized to rats. Timaru had insisted on a wider buffer space than usual between the malik troops and the foot soldiers, but still feared the worst.

Still, he had no choice at this point but to command the attack. He gave the signal and the maliks charged across the ford.

Then, as he had expected, the maliks were met by rats. The shallow stream erupted into chaos and he signaled to the foot soldiers to hold back. Their commander ignored him as archers in the trees on the opposite bank began to pick off any malik troops making it to the far shore.

Riderless maliks struck the oncoming line of foot soldiers and his offense lost all organization. He told his aide to order a retreat.

"No, Timaru, I'm sorry, but I can't allow that."

"What do you mean?" Startled, Timaru turned to face the voice he recognized, the voice of his cousin who should have been commanding the other prong of the attack. "What are you doing here Kaya?"

Timaru looked around and realized that he was alone with his sub-commander. All the other commanders and aides who had been on the hill with him had apparently been sent out with orders while his attention had been across the river. He hadn't even noticed.

He stared at the man he understood was going to try to kill him. "Why?"

"You were too vocal in your protests of this attack. If you live, you'll be able to remind everyone that you said this wouldn't work. If you die, all that can be forgotten."

Timaru nodded. "Jadne suggested this, didn't she?"

Kaya frowned. "I can think for myself. Anyway, it's time for you to die." He thrust a knife into Timaru's chest.

Timaru was a wizard. He could have struggled, fought, healed himself. But Kaya was also a wizard and Timaru found in that final moment of his life that he had no desire to struggle anymore. He did not want to live with such betrayal, or in a world where such betrayal was possible.

NATHAN SAW HIS FATHER MURDERED. He was high in a tree, well back from the line of scrimage, watching the fighting and sending reinforcements where he saw a need.

Arrun had insisted that they place observers at every crossing this time, and hold the bulk of their troops back until the major attack points could be determined. This ford would not have been a place anyone would have guessed the Senangans would use in advance, but Nathan had gotten his troops ready to defend only moments before the actual assault had begun.

The maliks had performed as usual, however, and Nathan had looked up the hill to see how Timaru would respond just in time to see one of Timaru's sub-commanders put a knife in his chest. The killer had then turned and run down the hill.

Nathan had taken in the location almost automatically. He hadn't realized he was going to teleport until he found himself kneeling beside his father on the ground.

He reached out to heal the wound. His father was not quite dead yet.

"No," Timaru thought. "Let me die."

"Why? Why did one of your own officers do this?"

"*It was Kaya himself,*" Timaru thought. Then answered Nathan's un-spoken question as to whether Timaru recognized him. "I'm a Kamrasi, related to the Royal House," he said and his eyes focused on his son, "as are you. I didn't want to command this army, but was persuaded that it could be a path to peace. That was a lie. Remember this, Nyunze; there'll never be peace with a Kamrasi on the throne of Senanga." He died.

Nathan heard soldiers coming up the hill and realized how exposed he was. He managed to teleport back to a clear spot on the far bank, but then he passed out from shock and exhaustion.

When he came around, Balek was leaning over him back in the field camp. "What happened? Why were you found unconscious on the bank with not a mark on you?"

Nathan blinked and put his hand up to his eyes. His head hurt more than it had since he'd been a beginning student. "I teleported," he said, then added, "twice. I saw my father murdered. Kaya Kamrasi murdered him as he was about to sound a retreat. I could have saved him, but he wanted to die."

Nathan looked around and found Pala hovering in the doorway. His mind went to hers.

That evening he came to her and she was able to ease his pain.

4665, 467TH CYCLE OF THE YEAR OF THE DOLPHIN
MONTH OF ANOR

Magra extended her sight deep into the ground and sensed the veins of minerals, the streams of water. She mapped them on her crystal and showed the map to Elgan.

They were deep in a cave in the Alerby Hills, the southwest reach of Kandorra. There was no light and Magra went to light one.

"No, Magra. No light. You can see in the dark. Find the way out."

Magra heightened her sense of the infrared and found there were enough heat traces for her to make out her location and see the way they had come. Still, it took her over an hour to retrace their steps as she had not marked the path on their way into the caves. She was relieved when they emerged in the valley outside.

"Now count the needles on the tip of the third branch of the tree to the right at the top of the ridge," Elgan commanded.

Magra refocused her inner eye, extending her vision over the green meadows and rolling, forested hills up to the ridge line to the south. She found the stand of trees and focused on the one on the right, bringing the cluster of needles into fine focus and counting them. "Sixteen," she said.

Elgan grabbed a beetle off the ground and handed it to her. "Read its genetic pattern to your crystal and show it to me."

Magra again adjusted her sight until she could see all the way into the beetle's cells, and then deeper into the spiral helix of the genetic code. She examined each gene and chromosome and recorded the information on the crystal.

"Very good," Elgan said when she showed it to him. "You have now seen with the sight of every one of the werefolk. Do you know what that means?"

"No, rai," she said. "Just that I can see as well as any of the werefolk."

"But each of the were races see slightly differently," Elgan said, "All you have to do is see with all their talents at the same time and you have the high sight. Do you understand? You have all the elements, you just need to combine them. Then you will be an apprentice wizard, not just a journeyman."

"But you've never shown me the high sight. I thought I wasn't ready yet."

"I've shown you all the elements. I'll give you one glimpse of them all together, then you should be able to do the rest for yourself." He held out his hand to her. "Take my hand."

She linked their fingers and then she was seeing with his eyes everything at once, the whole world large and small. It was all there, just a matter of focusing on what she particularly wanted to see. She flinched and the vision was gone.

"Is this how Cormor taught you the high sight?" she guessed.

Elgan nodded. "He wanted me to always remember that the high sight is not something unique to the eslarin. Jehan always intended it to be the heritage of the werefolk as well. They were his children. He hadn't originally understood that their differences would make them divide so drastically. He created the larafarin to get them to interbreed, but that was too slow.

"It was Jehan and Maera who brought humans to Tamar. Maera told him that they would solve his problem, and they have."

"Because humans have interbred with all the races?"

"Precisely," Elgan said.

Four days later Magra managed to combine all the different ways of sight Elgan had taught her and saw with the high sight on her own.

"Good," Elgan said. "Valanta and Ashe should be here tomorrow to help you celebrate your new status."

"Do I need to take another oath?"

"No, Magra, no more oaths until you become a full wizard, just a celebration and a few toasts. I believe tomorrow is also your eighteenth birthday."

She was startled that he had remembered. He didn't usually seem to register such things as dates. "My mother will be coming."

"Yes, I know. I'll check Temen to see if he's learned to see. He lacks your power, but should make a decent journeyman."

"But not Keth," Magra said sadly.

"No," Elgan said. "Keth inherited a blocker gene from your stepfather. He has no talent for the sight."

4668, 467TH CYCLE OF THE YEAR OF THE MOLE
MONTH OF TORIN

SARANITH FINISHED THE DELICATE GENETIC manipulation she had been making on the tropical fish she kept in a large tank in her cabin. She had found them so beautiful when she saw them swimming amid the coral reefs, and the chemical balancing and genetic manipulation gave her ample practice at using the high sight. She could now hold that vision for over ten minutes; long enough, she knew, to qualify her as a journeyman wizard by the human ratings.

There was a knock on her door and her first farail Tabrik Masse called her. He had replaced Kaltos in that position when Kaltos became an arrai. "Arhan, a message just came from Ammarai Mazilek. He wants to see you."

"Thank you, Tabrik," Saranith responded, wondering why Mazilek would summon her to the Amarraite again so quickly when she had just spoken with him the day before.

Twenty minutes later she entered Mazilek's office. "Some change in my orders, rai?"

Mazilek looked up and frowned. "No, Sara, just some new information that I thought you ought to hear in private."

Mazilek looked away from her toward his window. "You've always been fond of your cousin Kaya."

Saranith stiffened. "Yes, but I've become increasingly aware that he's now more Jadne's puppet than the man I used to know."

"Then I hope it won't shock you to hear that there's a rumor it was Kaya who killed Timaru, not the Cassingans."

"A Cassingan wizard was seen standing over Timaru's body and then teleporting away. I interviewed the man who told me that myself, and he wasn't lying."

"No. That part is true, but the Cassingan wizard was Timaru's son, who was smuggled out of Senanga when still an infant. Nathan is his name, you may have heard of him. He knew that Timaru was his father. Apparently Timaru gave him a crystal." Mazilek shook his head, "I don't know all of the background, but Nathan would have no reason to lie about not killing Timaru. He was a legitimate target of war."

"Where did you hear this?" Saranith demanded.

"The story is going the rounds of the Jehanites at the University of Kobala. Perhaps it's only been planted to create antagonism to Kaya's succession. I don't know. But I thought you should hear about it in private, before it got sprung on you."

"Timaru would have wanted to call retreat as soon as things started to get bad, wouldn't he?" she asked.

"He was always a cautious player in the war games. He didn't like to lose men."

"There were a lot of high ranking old timers in command of those troops," Saranith continued.

"An unprecedented number of senior officers, in fact," Mazilek said, eyeing her carefully. "It was why we both checked out the story of Timaru's death at the time."

"Dekese challenged them personally, I believe," Saranith said.

"So I've heard."

"I wonder why the rumor took so long to circulate?" Saranith asked. "It's been almost four years since the battle."

"Perhaps there was no real effort made to circulate the information. Perhaps it just leaked," Mazilek suggested.

"That would tend to refute the charge of propaganda, wouldn't it."

"Not necessarily."

Saranith looked at Mazilek and smiled, her mouth crooked. "Thank you, old friend."

Back at her ship that evening she was restless and her eyes fell on her helmsman Rethen. It had only been ten years, but she could qualify as a journeyman wizard now. Why not try?

Saranith went up to Rethen and examined him, finding the spell trace easily. She reached out with her mind and broke it apart.

Rethen moaned.

"I'm sorry, Rethen," Saranith said, suddenly realizing that she hadn't even asked if the man still wanted the curse broken. He'd seemed quite content over the past years as her helmsman.

"What did you do?" he asked. "My feet hurt."

"Your roots are turning back into toes," she said, examining him and noting that the changes were already starting.

"You really did it. You really broke the curse? I'll be a man again? But why now?"

She thought for a moment. Then said, "Because I was feeling helpless. You were there, and I suddenly realized that curing you was something I could now accomplish. So I did."

"You were feeling helpless..."

Saranith wished she had not long ago fixed her face not to show emotion. She wanted to laugh. "All things are relative, Rethen. Even the powerful can have problems that are too great for them at times."

Book IV

CORMOR'S LEGACY

"There was a time when wizards ruled the world,
And in that Golden Age the wizards made
Eight living crystals. So, while wizards die,
The karionin live and never fade."

— EXCERPT FROM "ILKARIONIN: THE LIVING CRYSTALS" FROM *LEST WE FORGET: A BOOK OF TEACHING RHYMES* BY WILTON WIRRAMARETH OF ILWHEIRLANE, 4207

XLII

4670, 467TH CYCLE OF THE YEAR OF THE OX MONTHS OF AGNITH TO ILFARNAR

"And never, ever turn your back
Upon a linlar or you'll lack
Some part of your anatomy,
A fatal risk, you must agree."

— EXCERPT FROM "THE WEREFOLK" PUBLISHED IN *A CHILD'S GUIDE TO THE LARIN AND OTHER BEASTLY TAILS* BY ENOGEN VARASH OF ELEVTHERAI, 4557

"YOU WANT to go to Ilwheirlane?" Magra said, stunned.

"We'll be leaving within the month, Magra," Elgan said in the tone of voice he used when there was no arguing with him.

Magra's mind reeled. She was so happy traveling with the carnival. Since she had become an apprentice wizard she had taken over the "see as the wizard sees" performances. Her life was just as she wanted it. She saw no reason to uproot herself and travel halfway around the world. "I don't want to go," she said.

"Remember when I first took you as an apprentice, I told you there was a cost, Magra. That being a wizard was hard and required sacrifice."

"But leave my home?"

"All of Tamar is moving toward a great struggle, Magra. In Kandorra you've been shielded from the conflict. But you're in training to be a wizard, and therefore you have a duty to take your place in the trenches." He sighed. "I should have taken you away from here years ago, but you're precious to me. I wanted to protect you as long as possible, but it's past time I returned to the lands about the Thallassean Sea. Aavik of Gandahar has great ambitions and his strength is growing. The Varfarin has grown weak under Derwen. Every wizard is needed."

Magra glared at him. "I swore an oath to obey you until I graduate to being a journeyman wizard, so I must come with you now if you insist, but I want no part of your human wars. As soon as I graduate, I'll come back here to my home."

Elgan nodded slowly, his expression wry. "Of course, that will be your right when you reach that level. I hope that new experiences will change your mind, but it may be that I've protected you too long. Nevertheless, you'll need to start to plan what you want to take with you. We'll visit your mother before we depart. I'm sure she'll store your caravan and furniture for you."

"What about the carnival? What's it going to do without a wizard?"

"A journeyman will be coming from Cassinga to take our place. That's all a carnival really needs."

"So you've planned this for months."

"For years, actually, Magra, but you're not taking it as well as I had hoped. I'd thought you would want to see new lands and new people."

"I see all the new lands and people I want to see traveling with the carnival," she said.

"You may occasionally see new people, but they're mostly the same type, and the carnival follows the same route every year, Magra."

"It's enough for me," she said and deliberately turned her back on him and marched away.

ELGAN WATCHED MAGRA stare out over the railing at the Jevac Lessar, the Eastern Ocean. The *Lomling*, the Sweet Fish, was in the southern reaches, just north of the Petalwan Archipelago.

Even after four days at sea Magra was hardly speaking to him. He hoped she would get over it, but her reaction was much stronger than he'd anticipated. He'd thought he understood her, but obviously he had missed some vital element in her makeup. It worried him. So much would depend on the young wizards of this new generation. Perhaps he was too old to train someone so young.

He glanced back at the island, wondering if it was one of those mapped by Ashe. He had the whole world grid Ashe had made recorded on his crystal. Ashe had finished Kandorra and the southern polar region and was now somewhere in Macosia with his own little pocket universe concealed in a backpack, but the teleport grid had made it easy for them to visit each other. Elgan hadn't expected to make such a close friend so quickly, but he enjoyed the gamlar wizard's company.

Despite his age, Elgan realized, he didn't have many real friends. There were many acquaintances, but those didn't count as true friends. He knew it was mostly his fault, although a little of his isolation had been caused by having Cormor as his grandfather. It still made the almost instant friendship he had formed with Ashe all the sweeter.

He brought up Ashe's map of the Petalwan Archipelago in his mind and located himself on it. The island he could see was, indeed, the northernmost point in the Archipelago and had merited a teleportation locus. He looked that way then scanned the horizon as he had been doing regularly since they had entered these waters.

This time he saw a ship to the southeast, almost directly in their wake. It was still far distant, the lookout in the crow's nest hadn't seen it yet, but Elgan's vision was far better than a man's.

He focused on the following ship fearing what he would see. Pirates were a danger in these waters and he saw immediately that his fears were justified. It was a Senangan vessel, thus undoubtedly a pirate, and it had already seen them and was on their trail.

He went and warned the captain.

"PUT ON ALL SAIL," the captain ordered, but he looked back at Elgan with a frown. "This is a merchant ship and from what you say, yon ship's a schooner. She'll run us down, if that's her pleasure."

"Can this ship defend itself?"

"Got a few small cannon, but that won't help with a Senangan pirate. Most of 'em got wizards aboard, can stop the shot from hitting 'em."

"I can stop their shot from hitting you," Elgan said.

"Reckon they might shy off when they see that," the captain said. "Depends who's chasing us."

"Then head for the nearest safe harbor," Elgan said.

The captain nodded.

Through the day the Senangan ship gained, and Elgan soon saw that there were two more ships behind the first, so he was facing not a simple arrai, but an ilarhan, or even an arhan. Such an officer in the Senangan navy was bound to be a wizard. Elgan cursed.

When the ships drew close, Elgan boosted a cannon ball far beyond its normal range and power and took out the mast of one of the chasing ships. He knew it was a feat he was unlikely to be able to repeat. The officers of the remaining two ships would now be on the alert for another attempt. Indeed, he tried to take out another ship a few minutes later, and the cannon ball was deflected with ease.

Later, when the two remaining ships drew closer yet, Elgan reached out and stopped the heart of the helmsman of the lead ship, slewing the wheel so that ship would cut off the ship behind, but the wheel was wrenched from his control almost immediately and the next helmsman was shielded from him.

His heart sank once he recognized the name on the bow of the lead ship: *Ningand*, the *Black Dragon*. He fought the pursuing ships as long as he could do so and still have the strength to get away himself, but it was clear from the beginning that he had no chance of defeating the pirates. Aketi Kamrasi, the commander of the *Ningand*, would have strong wizards under him. He was, after all a member of the Senangan royal family and his sister was the Estarharil of Senanga.

Magra had come and lent her strength to his in the struggle and she recognized as soon as he did that it was hopeless.

"I can reach the island to the south," he said, "but I can't teleport you as well."

She nodded. "But you can see where I'm taken and arrange to rescue me."

"I hope so," he said. "As you're a hailar, Aketi may not take you as a prisoner. The linlarin have no quarrel with the hailarin."

"But I've been trained by a human wizard," she said. "The fact that I'm part hailar will probably not offset that fact."

"If they take you prisoner I swear to you, Magra, I will find a way to rescue you."

"I know you will, Elgan. Get away now, while you still can."

He nodded and teleported to the locus from Ashe's map.

AKETI WAS FURIOUS when he realized the wizard who had killed his helmsman and dismasted one of his ships had teleported himself to safety. A wizard who could teleport could not be caught by ship.

The *Lomling's* cargo didn't even hold much of value and the *Lomling* itself was just a fat merchant tub. Ordinarily he wouldn't even have bothered taking it, just sunk it, but he'd need to salvage some value from this fiasco. Therefore, he was pleased when his second farail reported that there was a second wizard aboard, a young female.

"An apprentice, I'll wager, not up to the master's tricks," Aketi said, grinning, "but he'll come after her."

"It's a funny thing, though. If we hadn't been looking for a wizard, I'd never have spotted her shield. She's a hailar, got feathers instead of hair. Never heard of a hailar wizard before."

"No, nor have I," Aketi said. "I wonder why our escaping wizard was training a hailar, but there can't be many mixed blood hailarin with talent. If he was training her for a reason, that means he's even more likely to come after her. I think I'll keep this little wizardling somewhere very safe indeed."

ELGAN WATCHED FROM THE HIGHEST point on the island as the Senangan ship *Ningand* took over the *Lomling*. The second ship had turned and was going back to the ship he had dismasted. He felt Magra's mind cut off from him when she was capped. She was still alive, however.

He watched as most of the crew of the *Lomling* were executed. He would have felt guilty that his resistance had caused their deaths, but he knew that Aketi always killed those from whom he could expect no ransom. The *Lomling's* captain and a few of the other officers were not killed he noticed, only imprisoned.

Ningand headed back through the Archipelago with the *Lomling*. He'd been afraid that it might continue out to sea where he couldn't follow, as the other two ships seemed to be doing. He was determined to find out where Magra was being taken so he could arrange for her rescue as soon as possible. The thought of Magra in Aketi Kamrasi's hands appalled him.

With the Senangan ship sailing through the islands, however, Elgan had no trouble keeping it in sight. He just skipped from island to island after it. He had some bad moments when the ship reached the south-western edge of the islands, but Aketi apparently felt there was a better chance of prey if he stayed close to the coast.

Elgan was able to teleport along the south coast of Noia, with the *Ningand* never quite out of range of his sight. This was a primitive part of the world with no cities and few towns. He knew from Ashe's map that there were villages and a few fallarin warrens, but they would be no help to him. He ate clams he could dig from the sand, or mussels he could pry from the rocks, supplemented by the occasional roots, berries and edible plants.

After over a month of sailing, the *Ningand* turned due south and out of reach of his sight, but he came to the Strait of Eketaba that evening and crossed over to Cibata, catching up to Aketi's ship early the next morning where it was sailing south along the coast of Akasha. He took a leaf from Ashe's book there and changed himself into a linlar. He also exchanged his now ragged clothes, for clean clothing off someone's laundry line in one of the villages. Then he came to the end of the Cape of Daloa and lost the *Ningand* again.

He was pretty sure Aketi was headed for Senanga by then, but he wasn't sure whether Aketi would sail to Feshi or one of the other ports. He hopped back and forth between Kumba, Abaji and Feshi for almost a week before seeing the *Ningand* pass Kumba and sail up the Zamfara River. He actually teleported on board that night to confirm that Magra was still there.

He found her capped but awake, tied up in a cabin. He assumed from her bonds that she was putting up a resistance. Her eyes found him as soon as he materialized. "Can you get me out of here?"

"I can't teleport with you," he said, "but I'm following and will organize a rescue as soon as I know where Aketi's taking you."

"Hurry," she said. "He hasn't done much to me yet, despite the fact that he was furious that you got away. Still, there's something about him that scares me."

Elgan swallowed, but didn't tell her that she was in the hands of one of the most notorious sadists on Tamar.

He continued to follow the *Ningand* all the way to Azraq and watched as Magra was brought ashore there and taken into Cinkarrak. After that his vision was blocked by the Tower's defenses and he could see no more.

It would be Cinkarrak, he thought, knowing that he would have trouble mounting a rescue to take someone from the Red Tower, the heart of Senangan strength. He couldn't imagine himself how it could be done.

XLIII

Madom ba ral ga e sabat.
Madom sav rem.

*"Hatred is a strong and hungry beast.
Hatred eats thought."*

— ESLARIN PROVERB

MAGRA STARED UP at Aketi, her eyes bright with defiance despite the ropes that tied her hands and feet to the bedposts. She might be a prisoner now, but Elgan would come for her. And this linlar who had captured her was evil. Even with the cap on her head shutting out her wizard sense she knew evil when saw it.

Aketi smiled. "You look as though you'd like to kill me," he mocked. "But there's nothing you can do. Shall I demonstrate?" He reached down and untied one of her arms.

Magra froze, watching him.

He untied her other arm. He was leaning over her. Before he could straighten she lunged up, clawing at his face. Her finger nails caught his cheek just missing the eye before he jerked back.

His will threw her flat on the bed. "That was unwise," he said. "You're my property now, and I punish rebellion."

She couldn't move her body, but she still managed to spit in his direction.

Aketi shook his head. "You're only making yourself more uncomfortable. You can't hurt me. But I think you deserve a lesson. You tried to claw me, so I'll remove your claws."

Magra felt her hands burn. She looked in horror at her right hand and saw that it was melting, the flesh from it moving up her arms. She looked to her left and that hand had also disappeared. She felt the flesh migrate up her arms and across her chest to her breasts.

"I prefer my women buxom," Aketi said. "You were a trifle flat chested for my taste, but now you look better."

She stared at him. "I'll never submit to you."

Aketi laughed. "Yes you will. In fact, there'll come a day when you'll beg to submit to me. But right now, I rather enjoy your hatred."

Still holding her to the bed with his will, he took off his clothes and raped her. When he finished, he said, "Tomorrow when I come I'll expect you to smile. If you don't, I'll have to punish you again."

She glared at him until he left. Later two women came in and untied her. Her dinner was a stew she slurped out of a bowl, using the stubs of her wrists to hold it up.

On the second day of her captivity Aketi didn't visit her until late in the afternoon. She had explored her cell. It had smooth walls, but one section was transparent and she could see that she was high in a tower. A park surrounded the tower and there was a wide river beyond the park, the widest she had ever seen. She decided, remembering the geography lessons Elgan had given her, that she was in the Red Tower in Azraq, the capitol of Senanga. She hoped Elgan would be able to find her. She was lying on the bed, thinking of Elgan, when Aketi entered her cell.

"Do you have a smile for your master yet?" he asked.

She glared at him.

"I told you I'd punish you," he said, crossing the room to the bed. "if your attitude didn't improve."

She waited until he stood right beside the bed before she launched herself at him. Her body struck him at hip level, knocking him backward.

He fell, but regained his feet quickly.

She was slower. The stumps of her wrists hurt when she tried to use them to push herself back to her feet. Before she managed to stand she felt herself lifted and then she was flat on her back on the bed again, held down by Aketi's will.

"I warned you about rebellion," he said.

The burning she had felt in her hands the day before now attacked her arms. They seemed to melt and her breasts and hips started to swell. Terror claimed her as she felt her body change again, altering to his will.

"There," he said, some minutes later. "I think this form is much more amusing than your original one."

Magra looked down at her inflated breasts and the stubs ending just inches from her shoulders where her arms had been. She hated him, but there was nothing she could do to him.

She watched as Aketi fondled her enlarged breasts, pinching the nipples cruelly to cause her pain. She lay there, helpless beneath him as he raped her.

When he had finished, he released her so she could sit up on the bed, although she found her movements awkward without her arms and with the new bulk of her breasts.

"Remember," he said, "you must smile for me tomorrow, or I'll punish you again."

Then he left her. A servant brought a bowl of soup to her that evening. She had to lap it up like an animal.

The next day her breakfast arrived in a tall glass with a straw. She had to stand up and bend over the glass to drink. At one point she nearly knocked the glass over because she misjudged the thrust of her enlarged breasts.

Aketi came to see her just before noon. "Do you have a smile to greet your master yet?"

Magra glared at him from where she stood next to the window area of the wall.

"Then the least you could do would be to get into your proper place," he said viciously.

She felt her body lifted and thrown onto the bed. He held her down while he again tied her legs. Then he held her head and started to kiss her. She tried to bite him.

He smiled and she felt the burning sensation in her mouth, felt her teeth change, soften, and her jaw muscles weaken.

"Now if you bite me," he said, "it won't hurt at all. In fact, it may be rather titillating." He stuck his tongue in her mouth, but her teeth were now soft, spongy pads and her jaw had no strength. Her attempt to bite was, indeed, more a caress. She lay still and passive as he raped her again.

Afterward, the servants untied her, bathed her and dressed her. They brought her food in another tall glass with a straw. Without her teeth all she could do was suck. With her weakened jaw, she had to swallow quickly not to drool.

On the fourth day of her captivity Magra was again standing by the clear section of the wall staring at the ships when Aketi came.

"Have you learned your lesson yet?" he asked. "Will you smile for your master."

Magra forced her face into a smile and turned to face him.

He smiled smugly and crossed the room toward her. She kicked him in the groin when he was still two paces from her.

He doubled up in agony, but she felt herself thrown across the room to the bed by the force of his will. "You'll regret that," he said, between gritted teeth.

He held her flat on her back on the bed while he healed himself. Then he walked over and looked down at her. "I've never had a slave as rebellious as you before," he said. "But you won't kick anyone again."

Again Magra felt her body being altered. This time her feet, ankles and lower legs melted and the flesh migrated up to swell her thighs, hips and buttocks, some going higher to expand her breasts even more. When he was done, her legs ended with her thighs.

He rubbed her enormous breasts which had become more sensitive, as though he had also added nerve ends. Then he pinched them and raped her yet again.

When he left she looked down at herself. She was a doll that he could mold however he wished. With her plump thighs, rounded hips and hugely enlarged breasts she looked like some sort of primitive human fertility symbol. And now she couldn't even walk to pace her prison. Without arms or legs she was totally helpless.

When Aketi came the next day, she smiled and didn't try to attack him. She didn't want to find out what further punishment he could impose, and he had left her no way to hurt him anyway.

He watched her as he played with her breasts. "You still hate me, but you fear me now. That's good. You should be afraid. I can change your body further. I can do anything I want to you. But I won't, as long as you behave. And if you're a very good slave, I may even reward you. Would you like me to reward you?"

"I'd like my arms and legs back," Magra said.

Aketi smiled. "You'd have to be very good, for a very long time, but if you are, who knows? I might even be persuaded to restore you completely. Are you going to be good now?"

Magra swallowed. "I'll be good."

"Then spread your thighs and smile," Aketi said, mounting her.

This time Magra smiled while he raped her.

XLIV

4670, 467TH CYCLE OF THE YEAR OF THE DRAGON
MONTH OF ILFARNAR

*"The ultimate goal of the Varfarin, and Jehan's ultimate
purpose in having me create this organization, is to bring
peace to all the races of Tamar.*

*"While it is obviously absurd to claim that all sentient beings
are equal, all such beings are loved equally by Jehan and
Maera.*

*"No matter a being's degree of sight, wisdom or will, all self-
aware beings should enjoy equal rights.*

*"The Varfarin shall not be disbanded until every self-aware
being, no matter that being's degree of sight, wisdom or will,
shall be considered equal in rights before the laws of every
nation on Tamar."*

— EXCERPT FROM *ILVARFARIN: THE OPEN ROADS* BY THE WIZARD CORMOR

P ALA ENTERED BALEK'S CONFERENCE ROOM arm in arm
with Nathan. Their being a couple was taken for granted now,
but he still would not agree to a permanent linkage.

"It's too soon, Pala. We're both too young to think in terms of a
lifetime commitment."

"You mean you think I'm too young."

He had his classic "you're right, but I'm not going to change my
mind" expression on his face, so she pulled him down beside her on
one of the couches and changed the subject before he could say anything. "Do you know what this meeting is all about?"

"Balek said something about a visiting wizard with an absurd
request, but I don't know anything more."

"Well, given that evaluation by Balek, I'll root for the visitor," Pala
said.

She caught sight of a man standing in the doorway, and said,
"Great Jehan, that must be the Wizard Elgan. He looks like Cormor
come back to life."

As though the strange wizard's arrival were a signal, Balek banged on his desk and said, "Very well, Elgan, I've assembled the Council; make your request."

"Thank you, Balek," Elgan said, still standing in the doorway. He looked around the room and said. "For the last fifteen years I've been training a new apprentice, a very promising apprentice who happens to have hailar blood. We were on our way to Ilwheirlane when our ship was attacked by ships commanded by Aketi Kamrasi. I was able to teleport away, but Magra, my apprentice, is not advanced enough to teleport so she was taken prisoner. I followed Aketi's ship to Azraq and determined that Magra is imprisoned in Aketi's suite in Cinkarrak. Obviously, I cannot rescue her from that location by myself, so I've come here to the Council of the Varfarin in Cibata requesting assistance."

"I should say now," Balek said, "that as the Wizard Elgan is not a member of the Varfarin, he has no valid right to request this organization's aid. Furthermore, the apprentice he wishes to rescue is not a human apprentice and, therefore, aiding her is against the old Council's laws. And finally, Cinkarrak is impregnable, if I had agreed to his request I would be sending wizards to their deaths. On all of those grounds, I denied his request, but he insisted on this public forum anyway."

"As he should have done," Arrun said, from one of the chairs by the table. "Aketi is a known sadist. Maera have mercy on a young woman, an apprentice wizard, in his grasp, and no place, not even Cinkarrak, is impregnable. What's more, the laws barring those with mixed blood from Council training were cast down and no longer stand. I myself have ingvalar blood, and you haven't refused my aid over the past years."

"The Wizard Derwen accepted your oath to the Varfarin," Balek said, "therefore your status was out of my hands. However, if you wish to aid this wizard, you will do it on your own. The Varfarin in Cibata will not help you while I am still its head."

There was a stir and Balek looked around the room. "Does anyone wish to question my leadership, or my right to make this decision?"

Pala stood up. "I think your decision is outrageous."

Nathan said, "Pala, you can't take part in an expedition to Cinkarrak. It's too dangerous and your life is too necessary to Cassinga."

"I know I can't go," she said, "but you can and I support his position that we should help him." She walked over and took up a position beside Elgan, facing the rest of the room.

Arrun said, "Perhaps another question is called for here. Elgan, would you please explain why you left the Varfarin after your grandfather's death?"

Elgan snorted, "Gladly, Cormor told me to quit. He wanted me to do things of which he knew wizards like Balek here and Derwen would disapprove. I was ordered to find hailarin or fallarin wizards and train them. So far I've found precisely one and she's now a prisoner in Cinkarrak."

"Then," Arrun said gravely, "you have my promise of whatever aid I can personally give." He looked at Balek. "I hereby resign from the Varfarin in Cibata as it no longer represents my beliefs." He rose and crossed the room to stand beside Elgan and Pala.

Nathan said, "Balek you can't do this. Don't you see, what you're doing is opposed to the very values you taught me."

Balek said, "Even if everything you've said is true, I won't let wizards under my command take a suicide mission into Cinkarrak just to save a single apprentice."

Nathan rose and said, "Then I must take the side of Elgan, Arrun and my future mate." He crossed the room to the doorway and stood by the others, then turned back. "I've known you to be wrong before, Balek, but never so terribly wrong as this. Won't you reconsider even now."

"No, Nathan. The risk is too great for too small a reward."

Kaoda said, "I agree that the risk is too great to rescue one apprentice, but I gravely regret the divisions being exposed here. We're supposed to be opposing the linlarin who wish to purge Cibata of humankind, not fighting among each other. I hope you'll reconsider Nathan, and you, Arrun. One apprentice is not worth this."

"I'm afraid you're wrong," Arrun said, "but we will see." He ushered his companions out the door.

"So what do we do now?" Nathan said when they'd left the Palace.

"I'm fairly certain I can stage a rescue from Cinkarrak, but it would require at least twenty-two to twenty-five people, all of them apprentice or journeyman wizards," Arrun said. "An actual assault on Cinkarrak would be impossible. The Senangans far outnumber any force we might assemble and the Tower is impregnable. I'd use trickery to get us in and out before the Senangans even know we're there. That should serve to rescue a single prisoner."

"Can you teleport?" Elgan asked.

"Yes," Nathan and Arrun said as one.

"I can't," Pala said, "not yet. I know I can't actually go to Senanga, but I can arrange for arms and so forth."

"To assemble the size of force Arrun has described, I'll need to go to Sussey," Elgan said.

"Jerevan Rayne," Arrun said. "He was once Aketi's prisoner himself."

"Yes, I know," Elgan said. "I have kept up with some of the major events in the world outside Kandorra. He should be getting close to the point where he'll be able to break his curse. In any event, everyone knows he's Derwen's successor. If he backs our expedition, we'll get support from the Thallassean. With that, we can come back and face down Balek to get the rest of what we need."

"It'll take over a year to get to the Thallassean and back," Nathan protested.

"It will take less than a week to get to Sussey," Elgan corrected, "if we teleport. I'm afraid we'll have to come back by ship as Jerevan won't be able to teleport, but I can't think of any other way to get the wizard power we need."

XLV

4670, 467TH CYCLE OF THE YEAR OF THE OX
MONTH OF MINNETH

*"History is like a great river. Most lives flow smoothly down
the center of the current. Some drift into stagnant shallows.
A few are born to be caught up in the rapids or plunge through
the whirlpools.*

*"Quiet lives leave no mark upon the shores of time. Violent
ones may rise so high they shift the course of the stream."*

— FROM *THE ART OF GOVERNMENT* BY VYDARGA V OF ILLWHEIRLANE

JEREVAN RAYNE HEARD THE TONE of the summoning gong
amid the myriad other sounds that made up the song of the sea. For a
moment, as usual, he wanted to ignore it, to swim away in his dolphin
form and never go back to the land.

But he couldn't take that path. He had responsibilities, and, in any
event, the sea was no permanent solution. Being a dolphin had slowed
his growth, brought his appetite more under control, but he was still
growing.

Still, it was with great reluctance that he turned and swam toward
shore, being careful to eat his fill from a school of fish on his way in. He
had arranged his affairs so that ordinarily he need only take his human
form once every other month to review documents and sign papers
relating to his estates. He had done that less than two weeks before.
This summons had to be something else.

Handicapped on land as he was, Jerevan had still taken missions for
his wizard friends on several occasions over the past years when the
sheer power of his will could make a difference. But he had come to
hate being human.

He maneuvered himself as close to the shingle beach as he could
come without grounding. As the bell had been rung, there was already
a crew ready with a harness to help him to shore. He changed back to
human form and was immediately helpless, his vast bulk out of his
control.

The crew of six men grabbed him and got him upright so he could
breath while they attached a harness around him. When they had the

harness firmly buckled around him, four of them worked the hoist and the rest maneuvered him onto the great wheeled tilt bed they'd brought. Two of them pulled a sheet over his body so they wouldn't have to look at the obscene mass of his flesh as they wheeled him up the long sloping ramp that had been built solely for the purpose of making it possible for his weight to be hauled up the hill.

When Errin Anifi had first enabled him to change to a dolphin, Jerevan had been staying at the Anifi estate. He had purchased this estate just down the coast after his first year in dolphin form. He had not wanted to impose on the Anifis any longer for his visits ashore, when it became apparent that he would be spending many years at sea. The house and the ramps at this location had all been constructed to his design. There were no narrow doorways and the floor plan was level except for the ramp down to the shore.

He was a strong enough wizard that, on level ground, he could move the wheeled bed himself. But his present weight was over three thousand pounds. There was no way he could push himself up a hill. Even the great wizards had never been able to raise more than a thousand pounds and he had only been training as a wizard for twenty-two years.

When the men got him to his bedroom, Otto was there to bathe him in fresh water and instruct the men in using the hoists necessary to get him out of the harness and dressed like a man. He couldn't be lifted up all at once. His mass was too great for that now. Each leg had to be lifted individually and his pants pulled on. Then his middle was raised just enough to pull the pants all the way up around his belly. Then his upper body was raised so a shirt could be put on. He could still raise and lower his arms by himself, but he couldn't raise his upper body off the bed by himself or raise the mass of even one of his legs. On land he was totally helpless, a prisoner in his own flesh. Without the wheeled bed he wouldn't have been able to get around at all.

When Jerevan was decently covered, Otto said, "A group of wizards have come requesting your help, your grace. One of them is the Wizard Arrun who assisted in your rescue from Ravaar."

Jerevan sighed. He owed Arrun for his sanity, if not his life. This was a petition he would have to hear. "Very well," he said. "Where's Marion?"

"She went into Ruffin today before the wizards arrived. She should be back soon though. Do you need to eat?"

Jerevan shook his head, hating the way his multiple chins rippled with the motion. "No, I ate on the way in. If the meeting takes more than an hour, though, you better bring me a meal," he said, sensing the partial emptiness of his stomach. It always horrified him how quickly the hunger grew on land.

He started shifting the weights with his will, fifty pound weights now, sliding them one at a time until he'd moved enough to adjust the fold of his bed until the upper part of his body was as upright as he could manage given the mass of his belly. Once he was positioned as best he could manage, he propelled himself out of his bedroom and down the hall to what he referred to as his audience chamber.

Arrun and two other men were standing near the window that looked out over the Bay of Aelos.

"I thought you were living in Cibata now," Jerevan said.

"So I have been," Arrun said, turning from the window. "Jerevan, I'd like you to meet the Wizards Elgan and Nathan." He indicated the two men with him. "There is an apprentice wizard we need your aid in rescuing from Cibata. She is being held prisoner by Aketi Kamrasi."

"Aketi," Jerevan said, remembering his own experience as Aketi's prisoner, and realizing that Arrun brought that memory up deliberately. Arrun loved to manipulate.

"I thought you might feel some sympathy for a delicate, young girl in Aketi's hands," Arrun said.

Jerevan frowned. "Why should an apprentice wizard be considered delicate?" he asked.

"Mentally she's quite strong, but she is physically delicate due to her hailar blood," Elgan said, looking a little annoyed with Arrun. "Her bones are partly hollow."

"Hailar blood," Jerevan repeated. Then he remembered that he'd heard the name Elgan before. "You're Cormor's grandson."

Elgan nodded. "I hope you don't hold that against me. It's not something I had any control over."

Jerevan laughed. Feeling his fat jiggle, he stopped. "No, I don't suppose you did. Did he make life very difficult for you?"

Elgan smiled. "At times."

Jerevan looked at the third man. "So what's your concern in this?"

"Only that my one-time master, the Wizard Balek, refused his aid, or the official aid of the Varfarin in Cibata," Nathan said. "I've broken with the Varfarin in Cibata over the issue."

Jerevan considered the three men before him. His eyes went finally to Elgan. "I suppose the apprentice with hailar blood has something to do with one of Cormor's visions."

Elgan nodded, his expression wary.

"As a matter of curiosity, do you know where she's being kept?" Jerevan asked.

"Yes," Elgan said. "In Cinkarrak."

"In the Red Tower itself," Jerevan said, feeling a moment of real dread. "You know I won't be able to see into the Tower."

Arrun said, "If you help, others will help. Otherwise, Balek and Derwen can block Magra being rescued at all."

Jerevan studied them for a time and thought of what he could do and the cost. Finally, he sighed and thought, *"My price will be that you each assist with my training during the journey. As I'll travel to Cibata as a dolphin, you'll each have to swim in the sea with me. Do you all agree to that?"*

"Certainly," Elgan responded in the mind speech, making it a binding oath.

Nathan nodded. *"So will I. Errin Anifi taught me the form, but I haven't used it often."*

Arrun thought wryly, *"I haven't indulged my ingvalar blood in many years, so I'll undoubtedly enjoy it all too well."*

4671, 468TH CYCLE OF THE YEAR OF THE DRAGON
MONTH OF DIRGA

JEREVAN SWAM AROUND *NIKASHA*, the ship that would take the wizards and Otto to Cibata. It had been specially fitted to his specifications so that he would be able to live on it when they got to Senanga. No changes could be made once they left Sussey, so if changes needed to be made they would have to be made now, which meant he would have to test the hoists and the facilities. There was no point in his swimming all the way to Cibata if he couldn't get aboard the ship when he got there and live in it for a week or more. He couldn't just swim up the Zamfara River. A dolphin his size would be too noticeable. He was as big as an orca.

He could see the sailors in the water with the harness. He swam up to the ship and allowed them to position it around him. Then he changed to his human form. They hurriedly tightened the straps and he felt himself being lifted out of the water. The ropes strained, but held. The crane lifted him up over the railing and the deck and down into the hold. Part of the cargo hold had been partitioned into a room for him. Men came forward and maneuvered him onto his bed. As he had feared, it was a tight fit and he would only be able to move the bed a couple of meters forward and back. There would be no turning it around.

Otto, Marion and the Wizard Jao came forward. Jao had come back with Marion the day he had agreed to this venture and, surprisingly, had said she needed a vacation from the wizards school she helped the Wizard Delanan to run

"The facilities are limited, your grace," Otto said, "but they seem adequate for a short period of time."

Marion said, "You'll need to spend time keeping your weight down on the trip. We won't be able to get you another bed, if you grow out of this one."

"I'm aware," he said, keeping his head as still as possible to keep his chins from jiggling. He always hated his human form more when Marion was looking at him. She reminded him that he had once been a normal man capable of loving her.

Marion smiled at him. "I've been telling you that you need to work on getting back on your feet again. You're strong enough now to spend time on reshaping your body as well as healing it. Reducing the mass is a good start, but only part of the problem."

He smiled back at her, knowing she really cared, but smarting at her words. He had been trying, trying hard for years, but he couldn't alter his human form while he was a dolphin. When he was human, it was all he could do to heal himself and keep up with whatever need had forced him to assume his human form. Still, he was growing stronger as a wizard. How could he help but grow stronger when he had to use all his talent to keep up with his curse? At least he was winning that battle now. He no longer needed the help of other wizards just to survive in human form.

And someday he would be strong enough to break the curse. Jerevan hoped he might manage it in thirty years. Then Derwen would need to look out and maybe Marion would look at him again with something besides pity and concern in her eyes.

"Put me back in the sea," he said sharply, angry with himself. Such thoughts did him no good under the current circumstances.

"Shouldn't you eat first, your grace," Otto asked.

"No. I'll find a school of fish quickly enough when I'm back in the water," Jerevan said, but he managed a smile. "I'll be fine."

Back in the sea he circled *Nikasha* once more before finding a school of fish and filling his, by then, aching stomach. The ship had been named after a poisonous, spiny sea creature in the hope it would bring them luck in their endeavors. The next day it would sail and he would swim after it all the way around the world. He realized that he was both dreading and looking forward to the experience.

XLVI

4671, 468TH CYCLE OF THE YEAR OF THE DRAGON
MONTHS OF REDRI AND ILFARNAR

Tamar po latwe qua less et ling,
kulrheod pa amse lithla.

*"A world can be seen as large or small,
depending on one's viewpoint."*

— FROM "THE WRITINGS OF THE WIZARD CORMOR"

SARANITH APPROACHED CINKARRAK with great misgivings. Had Kaya learned of her knowledge of his betrayal of their cousin? There had been nothing overtly threatening in the summons; she had simply been required to report to the Estahar for a new assignment. But as a naval officer all her assignments in the past had come through the naval chain of command. What assignment would Kaya need to give her personally?

Perhaps her fears were without cause. She was Kaya's cousin. Members of the royal family were occasionally drafted to perform personal services. Maybe she was seeing shadows simply because she knew in her heart that her loyalty to Kaya had died with the almost certain knowledge that he had killed Timaru. And that was part of the problem. She wasn't quite certain that Kaya was guilty. There was still doubt, and while there was doubt she could not act.

So she had determined to wait. She would do nothing to either support Kaya or attack him until she could determine whether he had become totally Jadne's creature or still maintained the ethical values that he had espoused when he taught at Fethi.

Saranith entered Kaya's office with all her emotions securely in check. She had no intention of giving away her feelings to Kaya. She walked up to his desk and saluted him formally, with full military acknowledgement of his rank.

"Saranith," he said, rising and coming around the desk to embrace her in what she thought of as the generic family hug. "It's good to see you again. Gracious, I haven't actually seen you since Nema's naming ceremony. That's eighteen years."

"What can I do for you, your majesty? Your summons said you have an assignment for me."

He stepped back. "Call me Kaya, Sara. We are cousins after all."

"Very well, Kaya."

His oddly crooked face twisted in a wry grimace. "This is outside your naval duties. I've already talked to Naval High Command and they're willing to release your services for the next two years. I need you to be the new Ambassador to Akasha."

"I thought Mekari Kamrasi, your great uncle, was filling that position."

"He went and died at a critical moment in the drawing up of a new treaty. They're very status conscious there. As he was a relative of the royal house, they'll feel insulted if I don't send someone with equal connections."

"I have no diplomatic training or experience," she protested.

"But you were bound to start getting it sometime, Sara. All members of the royal house get dragged into this sort of position at some point in their lives."

"I see," she said, her mind whirling. "What will my duties be?"

"Well, as you said, you have no diplomatic experience, so you can pretty much leave the actual negotiations to the diplomatic staff already in place there. They're fully familiar with the details of what we want in the treaty, and what the particular hang ups are likely to be. You just need to attend all the meetings and look royal and official."

"For two years?"

He looked somewhat sheepish. "I'm sorry, Sara, but that's pretty much the official tour of duty. I promise I'll find someone to replace you at the end of that time."

"It's a promise I'll hold you to," she said. "Otherwise, from the sound of it I may die of boredom. What did my predecessor die of, by the way?"

"I believe he slept with the wrong nobleman's daughter and was assassinated," Kaya said. "The diplomatic staff said that it was a purely personal vendetta, not an official act of hostility toward Senanga."

"I see," she said. "Is assassination common in Akasha?"

"I believe it is among the nobility."

"I thought the pure-blooded linlarin abhorred violence?"

"Organized violence," Kaya said. "They don't approve of wars, but they quite like personal challenges. It's a sort of game as I understand it."

"Very well." She thought of two years to work on mastering Cinkarion and the high sight with none of the distractions that usually plagued such efforts and almost smiled. But it wouldn't do for her to look too pleased with the assignment.

"Thank you, Sara. I'll make sure it doesn't lose you seniority in the Navy. There's some sort of provision for equal duty, I believe."

JEREVAN SMELLED THE EFFLUENT in the water that meant a major city was near. So the *Nikasha* was about to arrive at Candith, the capitol of Cassinga. He would have to go ashore, which meant he would have change back to human form once again. He felt the dread of being helpless claw at him and repressed it.

He had tried to reduce his mass on the journey, but his dolphin form wasn't fat, so it wasn't a matter of removing fat as it was when he was human, but removing mass: muscle mass, flesh and skin, and that was very hard to do while swimming in the body he was changing. What's more, it was painful.

Therefore, while he had offset all growth caused by his constant intake of food, he had only reduced his size by a few hundred pounds during the six month journey. He was well aware that Marion was disappointed in him. Moreover, he was now going to be put on display to a group of strange wizards.

"They'll want to meet you," Arrun had told him in the mind speech. *"They'll want to hear you say that you support the rescue of a potential hailar wizard. Balek has told them that he's opposed to the rescue. They know that as soon as you break your curse, you'll be the new head of the Varfarin. They want to hear you take a stand."*

Jerevan heard the ship's bell ring the signal for him to come aboard. He swam up to the ship and let the straps be put around him. Then he changed his shape, felt the harness tighten and was lifted into the air.

He had a brief glimpse of ships and buildings and crowds of people and then he was being lowered into the hold of the ship. He was again a prisoner of his portable tilt bed. It had to stay tilted. If he lowered it to the point where he could lie flat on his back, the tremendous mass of his flesh impeded his breathing. So he had designed the bed like a tilt table, its surface conforming to his shape, but inclined at an angle that enabled him to breathe and with a bend in the middle, so he was half sitting and wouldn't slide off. He could adjust the bend and the angle of the bed by moving weights on sliding bars and then locking them in place. Changing the angle frequently slowed down the breakdown of his flesh under the constant pressure of his mass. The bed could even be tilted to raise him into a completely erect position, although for safety reasons he couldn't do that on his own. He could not sustain a standing position without a harness to support most of his weight.

His hands, in what was a deeply entrench habit, kneaded the upper portion of his mountainous belly. They found a point of discomfort and pressed, releasing trapped gas. He belched loudly. As if that were a signal, Otto appeared with a rolling tray.

"I thought you might want to eat before your bath, your grace," he said.

As though he had a choice, Jerevan thought, feeling the emptiness of his stomach and the way his mouth filled with saliva at the sight of the food.

"Thank you, Otto," he said.

When Jerevan finished his meal, Otto cleared away the tray and six men came in to lift him off the wheelchair for a sponge bath. First they tilted the chair all the way up until he was almost erect, four men supporting each of his arms to relieve the strain on his legs. When he leaned forward with their assistance, the other two men passed the rear straps of the harness down his back and under the great, flabby masses of his buttocks. Next, they arranged the front of the harness under the mountain of his stomach and tightened the straps. Then, with all six men at the end of the harness cable taking up most of his weight, he managed to stand and step off the tilt table. His legs trembled at the strain of holding him up even partially. They tied the harness cable off and four of the men again took his arms, helping him to lean forward, which brought his belly in contact with the floor. The harness cable was then relaxed and Jerevan pushed himself forward onto his stomach striving for the position that would have been described as being on his hands and knees if his mass had not grown so great that, when he achieved a face down position, only his fingers and feet touched the floor.

Otto brought water in a large basin and bathed his back and sides while Jerevan healed whatever pressure sores, lesions and broken capillaries had developed since he had come out of the water. With that part of his bath finished, the men rolled him back to a kneeling position, tightened the harness cable, again relieving him of the bulk of his weight, and helped him to regain his feet and step back onto the tilt bed. They then angled the bed back to take the strain off his legs and removed the harness.

Otto then bathed the front portion of his body and legs, and Jerevan did a deep scan and found whatever else he needed to heal. That went more quickly, as the skin on the front of his body was not subject to the same pressure.

When they had finished bathing and dressing him, Jerevan said, "So what's the schedule for this carnival I'm to perform in tomorrow."

"I believe that Arrun and Nathan have arranged the use of the dock crane to lift you, bed and all, to shore in the morning. From there you'll be taken to the Palace. I believe you're to have an audience with Juba, the ahar, and then meet with the Council of the Varfarin in Cibata, which, I understand, takes place in Balek's quarters in the Palace."

"I presume food will be served at these events," Jerevan said.

"I'll make sure you have a good meal before you go ashore and both Arrun and Nathan are aware of your condition. I'm sure it will be taken into account."

Jerevan suddenly felt an immense weariness. "Let me rest now, Otto. I'm too tired to think. Tell the wizards I'll talk to them tomorrow, but no more tonight."

Otto nodded. "Very well, your grace. Does that order include the Wizard Marion?"

"Yes, Otto. It particularly includes Marion. Keep them all away from me until morning."

PALA LOOKED AROUND BALEK'S ROOMS at all the familiar cast of characters and wondered what was causing the guilty excitement on their faces. Then there was a stir and they all turned to the doorway. Pala watched in amazement as a massive form propelled itself into the room on a rolling bed. This had to be the new wizard from the North.

No wonder they were all feeling guilty anticipation, she thought with distaste. The figure on the bed was more deformed than any carnival freak. While the hugely swollen body was covered with balloon like clothing, the face with its massive rolls of receding chins and bulging cheeks was exposed. There was a short fuzz of thin blond hair on the top of his head and she realized the hair looked thin because even his skull was covered in a thick rolls of fat spreading the hair folicles far apart. How could anyone get so fat and still be alive? How could he endure being so helpless?

Balek was also staring at Jerevan. He said suddenly, "So you're to be the next head of the Varfarin? I'm supposed to take orders, and allow my people to risk their lives in Senanga, because a lump of lard says so. Excuse me, I should have said a mountain of lard."

"No," Jerevan replied. "I've issued no orders. I came here at the request of the man to whom you've trusted Cassinga's strategy for the last twenty-two years. He and the man you've raised to be your aide both agree that the Wizard Elgan's request for assistance to rescue his apprentice is important to the future of the Varfarin, its long term goals and Tamar itself."

"It's opposed to the oath I took to the Council for me to aid in the training of a hailar," Balek said. "Besides, it's a suicide mission. She's being held in Cinkarrak itself."

"It seems to me," Jerevan said, "that you can swallow an elephant, but choke on a gnat. No member of the Varfarin protested when the head of the Varfarin placed the curse that made me as I am, although that act was clearly against the Varfarin's laws as well as those of the Council of

Wizards. Yet you cite laws that were altered and no longer stand, laws of a Council that no longer exists, to prevent you from rescuing an innocent child from a known torturer. I think your ethics are questionable."

There was silence in the room. Pala had never before heard that assembly so still. Finally, Kaoda said, "I believe our guest from the North has made a valid point, Balek. I think we must offer what aid we can to Elgan's expedition and allow anyone to volunteer who wishes to do so."

"THANK YOU JEREVAN. I realize it was difficult for you, but we'll get all the help we need now. I have nineteen new volunteers. We should be able to leave for Senanga tomorrow."

"Then you can take me back down to the shore tonight," Jerevan said.

"It's only a four or five day sail to Senanga, depending on the wind," Arrun protested. "I thought you'd stay in human form so we could go over our plans."

"You can't make any real plans until you know more about the situation where Magra is being held," Jerevan said. "I'm not going to lie helpless in the hold of your ship any longer than is absolutely necessary."

Marion said, "You've said yourself that you can't really lose weight or change your human form while you're a dolphin, Jervan. You're going to have to spend some real time as a human soon. You're strong enough now that, if you worked at it, you could get back control of your form. You need to do that. I know that you've avoided being human for years because it's so uncomfortable for you, but to change that you're going to have to face the discomfort."

"I'm well aware of that, Marion," Jerevan said quietly. "But crammed into a small room in the hold of a ship is not the best place for me to practice being human. You're right, I am stronger now. I should be able to remove the fat and reshape myself if I stay human for a few years. I'll even promise to do that when I get back to Sussey. But at least on Sussey I'll have some freedom of movement even while I remain a monstrosity. In the hold of a ship, I have no freedom at all."

She nodded her head. "I understand. I'll hold you to your promise when we get back to Sussey."

"I will, Marion. I give you my word."

"Aren't you strong enough now to break the curse?" Nathan asked. "I mean, I've met Derwen. He isn't a strong wizard. In fact, I doubt he could qualify as a wizard if he tried to take the test now. He's been letting himself go for years." He looked around at the other wizards in the room. "Jerevan is much stronger. He should be able to break the curse now."

Arrun nodded. "You're right, Nathan. Jerevan probably could break the curse now, but he'll kill Derwen if he does it from here. I advise him to go back to Ilwheirlane and break the curse there as soon as we've rescued Magra. It will take him much less time to reshape himself once the curse has been broken."

"You actually think I can break the curse now?" Jerevan asked, his expression lightening. "Derwen told me it would take forty to seventy years when he cursed me."

"I think he underestimated both your talent and the motivation he gave you," Arrun said wryly.

Marion said, "I hope you'll break it as Arrun says, in front of Derwen. I hope you won't kill him to gain your freedom. Although what he did to you was cruel, he's not really an evil man."

Jerevan shook his head, feeling his rolls of fat ripple. "I've been thinking I still had years, decades, to go before I could break the curse. I have to think about this." He turned to Arrun, "But that doesn't change my mind about wanting to go back into the sea for the journey to Senanga."

Arrun nodded and looked around the room. "Agreed. Marion and I can find some strong apprentices or journeymen to get you back to the docks."

JEREVAN ROLLED HIS SHOULDERS back and turned his head left and then right as far as it would turn, trying to ease the constriction in his back and neck. The rolls of fat hindered the effort, but he did feel some relief. He would need to work on healing himself soon, but the effort of farseeing had taken too much energy for him to manage anything else for the present. He'd been back aboard the Nikasha for five days now and the confinement was getting to him.

"Did you find out anything, your grace?" Otto asked, entering with the food trolley.

"I know where Magra's being kept in the Tower. The guards were talking about it."

"How heavily is she guarded," Marion asked, coming up behind him. Her hands came down on the rolls of fat on either side of his head, and he felt her healing the broken capillaries and sore muscles. For a moment, feeling her touch, he remembered what it had been like to make love with her and felt a stirring far down in the mass of his flesh.

He closed his eyes on the bittersweet memory. "There's at least a full division stationed in the Tower compound," he said, "and ten linlarin, a full kam, stationed in the hall outside the room where Magra is kept. I'll try again tomorrow to get more of the guard changing routine."

Marion nodded, "I'll tell Nathan what you learned. We'll have a meeting after you've eaten and had a bath and a rest." She left.

WHEN JEREVAN WOKE and had eaten, all the senior wizards crowded into his room in the hold. It was a tight squeeze and Marion and Jao perched on the foot of Jerevan's bed. There were no chairs so everyone else had to stand.

Arrun said, "We know Aketi's suite in the Tower is guarded. Jerevan said we should expect a kam. The guards, however, don't live in the Tower itself. They live in dormitories inside the walled compound. As I understand it, the guard troops muster in the courtyard in front of the dormitories and march to the Tower and inside as a unit. If we can take down the guard unit assigned to Aketi's suite between the courtyard and the Tower, we can take their places, impersonate them and just march into the Tower. We'll need at least twenty wizards to acheive this. First we'll have to get twenty of us inside the compound without being seen. Then we'll have to take down the guard unit. Ten of us will then each carry a body out of the compound and conceal them somewhere secure. The other ten will pretend to be the guards. When the bodies are concealed, Elgan and at least one of the other non-guards will have to enter the tower and remove the prisoner. The guards should remain as guards until they're relieved of duty. Only after they've marched back out of the Tower should they disband and disappear."

Arrun turned to face Jerevan. "Jerevan, this is where your contribution will be vital," he continued. "Very few of the apprentices and journeymen who've volunteered for this expedition are capable of holding an illusion for eight hours. You're going to have to hold the illusions for them for a good part of that time. Can you make yourself invisible and hold the illusions from inside the Tower?"

"How can you get me in this," Jerevan thumped his wheeled bed, "inside the Tower?"

"If you can pretend to be a wagon load of something, we can just wheel you into one of the storage rooms off the kitchen," Arrun said. "Down there you shouldn't be disturbed."

"I'll have to eat during that time," Jerevan said. "I can't go eight hours without food. I'd start having cramps and be unable to function at all."

Arrun stared at him, obviously frustrated.

Nathan said, "But you could take food with you. Someone would have to be with you anyway to pretend to push the wagon. Whoever it is can help feed you. The pretend guardsmen would have to hold their own illusions while you eat as well as when they first enter the Tower, but everyone going in should be able to hold their own illusion for at least two or three hours, especially if those hours are broken up into two segments rather than one long stretch."

"I wouldn't have to hold the illusion for all of them, or for any of them for the full eight hours, is that right?" he asked finally.

"No," Arrun said. "I can hold an illusion that long. So can Nathan. We'll try to pick the strongest at holding illusions to be guardsmen."

"The people smuggling the bodies out will need to be able to hold illusions as well," Marion said, "a couple of us who are good at illusions should be with them to back them up if anyone has a problem."

Arrun sighed, "You're right, Marion. He turned back to Jerevan. "Can you do it?"

"If you and Nathan can take care of yourselves and all the other guardsmen can hold for at least three to four hours on their own, broken into shifts, I believe I can hold the illusions the rest of the time," Jerevan said, "assuming that once in the Tower, I'll be able to reach through several floors to Aketi's apartment. I don't know that the Tower doesn't have internal barriers as well."

"Does Ninkarrak?" Arrun asked. "I've never been inside the Black Tower."

"I sensed no internal barriers in Ninkarrak," Jao said, "when I met with Vanda some years ago."

Arrun nodded. "There's no guarantee that all the Towers are alike, but as they were all supposedly constructed at the same time by the same techniques, we'll have to take that as an acceptable risk."

"Will you be able to wheel yourself back out?" Nathan asked.

Jerevan hesitated. "I think I'll be able to manage that if the serving yard is level, but how will I get back down to the river. I can't control this bed on a slope by myself."

"There's a stock pen inside the compound," Nathan said. "Maybe we can hitch Jerevan's bed to a horse. He'll be making it look like a wagon, after all. Whoever is with him can unhitch him before he enters the Tower and hitch him back up to get him away."

"Isn't there any security around the kitchens," Jao asked. "I'd have thought that was a major site for potential sabotage."

"There are guards," Nathan said, "but they don't pay much attention to kitchen drudges."

"But wouldn't they wonder about a wagon being removed."

"Can you look like a load of full boxes on your way in and empty ones on your way out?" Arrun asked.

Jerevan sighed. "The more energy I have to use to disguise myself, the less I'll have to project the illusions for others. I think you better find out just how long every member of your party can hold an illusion. When I know that, I'll tell you if what you want is possible or not."

Jerevan moved the weights on his bed to change the angle at which he was sitting. The pressure sore on his rump was getting worse and a new one was forming. He shut the pain away and turned to face Arrun. "There are passwords you'll need to know to be accepted as guardsmen. I'll see if I can find out what they are."

"Good," Arrun said. "I think we can make this plan work. We just need to iron out a few details."

XLVII

4671, 468TH CYCLE OF THE YEAR OF THE DRAGON
MONTH OF ILFARNAR

"No matter how well one's battle plans are laid out,
One can never discount the element of chance."

— EXCERPT FROM *THE COLLECTED WRITINGS OF VYDARGA THE RED*

NATHAN CROUCHED behind the hedge with Arrun, Marion, Lagura, Bella and fifteen other volunteers watching as the Senangan guard unit formed up. They were all camouflaged to match the ground and no one was having any problems so far. It reminded him of his first rescue mission, deep in the Senangan jungle when they's saved Evran, Rainal, Marion and Lagura. Pala would never have been born if that mission had failed. He hadn't been surprised to see Lagura among the volunteers either.

The guards finally finished their muster and started marching toward the Tower. Arrun held off giving the signal until the first guards were almost past their group.

Then the signal came and Nathan lunged through the hedge. He crushed the throat of the guard in front of him and the one just beyond, turning to see if anyone else needed help, but all the guards were down. They'd had no notice, no reason to be shielded doing what amounted to a ceremonial guard duty, so they'd died quickly and quietly.

Nathan dragged the body of the first guard he'd killed back through the hedge and stripped him, donning his uniform. It was tight across his shoulders and a little short on his legs, but it would have to do. He fixed the image of the guard in his mind and stepped back through the hedge. Other guards were forming up around him. The whole procedure had taken less than two minutes.

"We're ready then," Arrun thought to them all. *"Start on three: one, two, three."*

They stepped out together and from what Nathan could tell they looked like the guards they'd replaced. They marched right up to the Tower and through the entryway and the guards at the door just nodded to them.

"Cochlea," Arrun said the day's password to the ganha in charge. It had taken Jerevan almost a week of constant surveillance to determine when and where the password was issued each day, but after that it had just been a matter of listening at the right time.

"You're late," the ganha said. "Better get upstairs right away before Nefru ruptures something."

Arrun nodded and they marched up the stairs.

Arrun didn't even have time to say the password when they reached the door to Aketi's suite. The head guardsman there just said, "About time," and commanded his own troop to depart.

JEREVAN FOUGHT TO CONTROL HIS FEAR as the journeyman led the wagon through Azraq to the gates of the park around Cinkarrak. The journeyman's name was Leto Morvil. He was one of the last to volunteer in Candith and couldn't hold even a simple illusion long, so Arrun had assigned this job to him as all he'd have to do was dress like a country boy or a kitchen drudge.

Jerevan would have felt more confident with someone a little more skilled. Still, when they got to the gates, the guards didn't see through Jerevan's illusion of crates and waved them through and the journeyman led the wagon up the curving drive to where it divided, taking the right fork to the kitchen courtyard. Then the wagon was at the loading dock, the tailgate was lowered, and Jerevan had to think quickly at Leto, *"You have to wheel out the bed. The guard is watching."*

"I can't pull that weight by myself," Leto objected.

"It's on level ground, you don't have to lift it and, anyway, I can propel it. It just can't look as though the load of crates is moving itself."

"Oh, right," Leto said out loud and moved around to push at the bed.

The guard gave him a funny look but then was distracted by something across the courtyard and Jerevan propelled the bed, with Leto hanging on, out of the wagon onto the dock. From there he maneuvered into the kitchen and across it toward one of the larger pantries.

"Whatcha got?" asked one of the kitchen drudges.

Leto swallowed nervously. "S'supplies for C'Chef C'Costen," he stuttered. Choma had assured them that Chef Costen was very particular about his ingredients, but would not be on duty that day.

The drudge nodded and turned away. Jerevan propelled himself into the pantry and to a back corner out of sight of the door. *"You'd better go and move the wagon,"* he prompted Leto.

"Okay," Leto thought.

Jerevan gritted his teeth. *"Remember to park the wagon in the back of the courtyard next to the other vehicles there,"* he thought, striving for patience, and wondering if the man's incompetence was caused by fear or stupidity.

Leto nodded.

"And remember to unharness the horse and put him in the paddock. Then come back here with the sacks of food. Can you remember all that?"

Leto suddenly looked indignant. *"Of course I can. I'm not an idiot."*

Jerevan bit his tongue and restrained himself from communicating his real reaction—then stop acting like one—and thought instead, *"No, of course you're not, but you are under a lot of stress."*

Leto nodded and thought, *"I can do it."*

When he was gone Jerevan reached out to find Arrun.

"Thank Jehan you're finally here," Arrun thought and gave him the images he needed.

Jerevan braced himself and took over the illusions for seven of the guardsmen, remembering to maintain his own illusion of crates. Then he settled himself into a semi-trance, relaxing his mind and thinking of nothing but holding the illusions.

ELGAN WALKED UP TO THE ENTRANCE to Cinkarrak with the forged papers Choma had given him and smiled at the guardsmen as they let him pass. Despite being the strongest of all the wizards in the rescue party, he was not acting as a guardsman, because he would have to be the person to get Magra out. She would recognize him, even disguised as a linlar. He was dreading what he would find. Magra had been prisoner now for over a year.

He nodded as he passed the guards. He was fully capable of seeing through the illusions Arrun, Nathan and Jerevan were maintaining, but they looked solid enough to pass any ordinary inspection.

He entered Aketi's suite. The first room was a sitting area with two doors. He went to the one on his right first and knew immediately that he need search no farther. The armless, legless sex doll on the bed was almost unrecognizable as Magra, but he knew it had to be her and when he went closer he saw the feathers on her head.

"Magra?"

"Elgan," she said, her voice like a small child's and strangely slurred, as though she couldn't work her mouth properly. "Is 'at really you? I'd begun to be afraid you weren't coming."

"It took a little longer than I'd hoped," he said quietly, "but I'm here now."

How was he going to get her out of here? he wondered. She couldn't walk and he wasn't going to be able to reform her all at once. Too much of her had been altered.

"Don't be afraid, Magra, but I'm going to have to bundle you in those sheets, pretend you're a load of laundry, to get you out of here."

"I understand," she said, her eyes very wide, "but the cap, can you take the cap off?"

"As soon as I get you to the ship," he said. "I don't want to have to hide your awareness while we're still in Cinkarrak."

She closed her eyes then and seemed to withdraw into herself as he bundled the sheets around her and lifted her up. When he left Aketi's rooms he was disguised as servant with a sack of laundry.

Arrun took one look at the sack and stared at Elgan in horror. *"How will you get her out of here like that?"*

"The laundry rooms are near the kitchens. If I can get her down to that part of the Tower, hopefully I can make her look like trash and smuggle her out through the kitchens."

"You can load her on the wagon Jerevan came in. I'll tell Leto to show you the horse. There should be time to get Magra to the ship and have one of the others who disposed of the bodies bring the wagon back for Jerevan."

Elgan nodded. It took great effort, however, to disguise his nausea as he carried what Aketi had made of his apprentice down the Tower stairs.

JEREVAN ROUSED HIMSELF out of his semi-trance when he sensed Elgan and was appalled by what Elgan carried. *"Maera's mercy,"* he thought, *"I knew Aketi was a monster, but this?"*

"Arrun said I could borrow your wagon to get her to the ship," Elgan thought.

Jerevan did the calculations in his head, and thought, *"He's right. There should be no problem if someone brings it right back. Remember to hold the illusion of it being empty on the way out, though."*

"I'll see to it," Elgan thought.

"Leto," Jerevan thought, *"help Elgan with the wagon."*

Leto nodded and followed Elgan out of the pantry. Jerevan resumed his semi-trance state.

MARION WAS STARTLED WHEN she saw the wagon heading down to the dock. Jerevan wasn't due back until evening, after everyone else was safely out of the Tower.

She was relieved when she saw Elgan and realized Magra's condition, until she saw that Leto was with them. Then she looked in the wagon and saw that one of the sacks of food she had packed was still in the wagon.

"What are you doing here, Leto? And why is that sack of food still in the wagon?"

"Jerevan said to help Elgan with the wagon," Leto said.

"But why is the food not with Jerevan?" Marion asked. "He'll need to eat his second meal in the Tower within the hour, and it looks like most of the food is here."

"He has what was left in the first two sacks," Leto said.

"Why doesn't he have it all?" Marion yelled.

"I couldn't carry all the sacks in one trip," Leto said.

"Then you should have made two trips. Jehan grant me patience," Marion said and turned to Elgan. "Get Magra out of the wagon so I can start back with it now, and pray to Maera as well that I get there in time."

Elgan nodded and lifted Magra out right away. "I didn't even notice the sack. I'm sorry Marion."

"It's not your fault," Marion said, starting to turn the horse and wagon around.

Leto blocked her way. "He told me to help with the horse and wagon."

"Get out of my way. You're either an idiot or an enemy and at this point I don't care which."

Leto stepped back and Marion finished turning the wagon around and headed back for the Tower, but she knew Jerevan's schedule as well as he did, and she knew she was going to be too late.

JEREVAN REALIZED HE WAS IN TROUBLE when he roused himself from the semi-trance to take his next meal. Leto wasn't there and nor was most of the food he needed. He warned the guardsmen for whom he was holding illusions that they would have to hold their own for a time. Then he levitated what there was in the sack up to his bed and ate it. It wasn't nearly enough to hold him until the end of the guards' duty period.

"*Arrun,*" he thought, "*I can take up the illusions again for a while, but I won't be able to hold them for long.*"

"*Why not?*" Arrun thought. "*We still have two hours of duty time to go and the two apprentice wizards are already pretty exhausted.*"

"*Leto's disappeared. I think he went with Elgan back to the ship, and apparently he never brought in the last sack of food. I've eaten what was here, but it won't hold me for long. I'll probably start having cramps within an hour to an hour and a half. I'll hold the illusions as long as I can.*"

"*Agnith's furies,*" Arrun thought, "*and I can't reach through the Tower barrier, or I could get someone to bring you food easily enough. Leto wasn't supposed to go with Elgan, just help Elgan get the horse harnessed to the wagon.*" He hesitated, then added, " *As soon as we get out of here, I'll come back for you.*"

"*I'll be here,*" Jerevan thought wryly.

Jerevan put himself back in the semi-trance. Time passed and he grew aware of discomfort, but he suppressed all consciousness of self and focused on the illusions. Then the guards were out of the Tower and he could let the illusions go, except for the one around himself. But now he couldn't hold even that illusion because his stomach cramps were no longer mild but severe. He was close to the point where he would black out, and all he could do was try and keep himself from thrashing from the pain and calling attention to himself.

Then Marion was there and thrusting food into his mouth. He ate.

"I'm sorry. I'm sorry, but the streets we used this morning were closed. Some kind of market and it took me forever to get the horse and wagon back here."

"Not your fault," Jerevan managed after a time, when his stomach was no longer cramping so violently. He was so tired he could barely keep his eyes open.

Then Arrun and Nathan were there as well, looking like kitchen drudges.

"We need to get out of here," Arrun thought. *"The guards will be missed soon."*

"Can't hold illusion any longer," Jerevan thought. *"Make sure..."* He lost the ability to project his thoughts, said "empty" aloud. Then he was unconcious.

"I can hold the illusion of the crates," Marion thought. *" I haven't been holding any other illusions for hours."*

"The horse and wagon are still at the dock?" Arrun asked.

"Yes," Marion thought and reimposed the image of the crates of fruits and vegetables over Jerevan and his bed.

They wheeled Jerevan and his bed back onto the wagon and started leading the wagon toward the gates. They were halfway down the drive when the guards in the kitchen courtyard started yelling about stealing vegetables.

"Great Jehan, Marion," Arrun thought, *"the crates were supposed to look empty when he left. The guards think we're stealing Chef Costen's precious produce."*

"That's what Jerevan meant when he said 'empty' before he passed out. I just duplicated the illusion I saw him use this morning."

"What do we do now?" Nathan asked.

"I'll take an illusion of this wagon for a jaunt across the park," Arrun thought quickly. *"You, Nathan, can make this wagon invisible and Marion can lead it through the gate, making herself invisible. Hopefully, they'll chase the visible wagon and I can try to lose them on the other side of the park."*

Arrun levitated to the height of the wagon seat and they saw a wagon head out across the park. Nathan hurriedly made himself and the real wagon invisible as the new one ceased to be imposed over the old.

Marion's image started to fade, but then Nathan heard the sound of gunfire and saw Marion's chest erupt with blood. The blood was a vivid red and he could see her clearly as she fell to the ground. She died instantly, he thought, fighting shock.

He hurriedly pulled the horse and wagon further down the drive, creating a fierce keep away field to go with the invisibility. Fortunately, all the guards were chasing the image of the wagon being pulled by the galloping horse across the park. He got through the gate, down the street and into an alley. Then he checked that no one was watching before letting the wagon and horse become visible again. He formed an illusion of empty boxes over Jerevan and hurried as fast as he could to the ship, praying that Arrun would meet him there.

ARRUN SAW MARION DIE, but managed to keep the illusion of the horse and wagon crossing the park until he felt that Nathan was through the gate. Then he abandoned the illusion and tried to make himself invisible, but there were suddenly three wizards too close to him for the illusion to hold.

"Immobilize him," one of them said.

Arrun felt himself held. He tried to teleport, but they were holding him with their wills and he was too tired after all his earlier exertions to overcome them.

"Got him," one of the wizards said. The voice was female and Arrun looked up and saw that Jadne Kamrasi, the Estaharil of Senanga, was one of his captors. It hardly surprised him when he saw that the man who would cap him was Aketi Kamrasi. He passed out with the pain of the cap being forced into his skull.

XLVIII

4671, 468TH CYCLE OF THE YEAR OF THE DRAGON
MONTH OF ILFARNAR

Lomcaul borwe a nik bar quesa esk
a farin jercet ab remrak.

*"Taking pleasure from pain is a classic symptom
of twisted pathways in the brain."*

— EXCERPT FROM *FARIN A GAB*, "THE PATHWAYS OF INSANITY" BY THE ESLARIN
SCHOLAR MIKALA

"**S**O THIS IS THE WIZARD ARRUN, our cousins' scourge," Aketi
said, looking down at the unconscious, capped man. "One could
almost feel gratitude for his efforts. He certainly put an end to the political
ambitions of Djema Kamrasi's line."

"Yes," Jadne said. "It would be a pity to just kill him."

Aketi frowned. "He stole my toy. She was beginning to get a little
tiresome, but he still had no right to steal her."

"I'm not sure how he managed that," Jadne said. "But one of the
other wizards was killed and this one was captured and, quite frankly,
this one is worth much more than your little toy."

"Yes, he is," Aketi agreed absently. "Calls himself a jester," Aketi
added, pursuing his own train of thought. "I think we should make him
a toy. Just think of the possibilities. Then we could give him to Saranith."

Jadne's eyes widened and she smiled. "Oh, wouldn't she hate that.
Any other wizard she'd just let escape, but she wouldn't dare release
Cassinga's great military strategist. And if he stays capped long enough,
he'll die of it."

"And she'll have to watch," Aketi said, grinning.

"Yes," Jadne said. "I've always felt that her stony, insectile face was a
mask."

"Oh, she's soft as whipped cream inside, Jadne, look at the way she
always protected Luri. Bet I'll get at that soft center after she's had to
watch this wizard die."

"You want her?" Jadne looked startled.

"She's got secrets," Aketi said. "She's learned the high sight, too."

"No one in Senanga taught her," Jadne said quickly. "I'd have learned
of it. I've always had her watched when she's here."

"You haven't been able to watch her at sea, though," Aketi said. "I've never understood how she gets such loyalty from her crew. She can't have sex with them all."

"You think too much with the thing between your legs," Jadne said disgustedly. "She doesn't use sex at all. She never loses her temper and she takes care of all her crew. Now, I'm counting on your help in reforming this wizard. What shall we do first?"

Aketi was distracted and looked down at the prisoner. "Well, first of all, if he's going to be a toy he needs to be shorter. Let's shorten him down, make his body thicker so we don't have to dispose of mass."

The second day they worked on him Arrun was conscious and had to watch as his flesh melted and flowed into a new configuration.

Aketi, enjoying himself, said early in the process, "We can't leave his penis either, if he's going to look like a child's toy."

"But we want him to suffer. I think we should just shrink it down so he can't use it but has all the nerve endings. Maybe make it so small it can't even be seen if we give him long hair, like a child's stuffed animal."

"That's a wonderful idea, Jadne. We can make him a little bear. Bear's can walk like men so we won't have to bother changing his hip joints."

"You're both very sick," Arrun said. "You know that, don't you."

"Oh, that's another thing we'll have to change," Aketi said. "Toys shouldn't be able to speak."

So after that, Arrun couldn't speak.

By the end of a week Arrun did look like a short, stocky brown bear.

"There's something missing," Jadne said. "He doesn't look whimsical enough. He needs to look cuddly, but there should also be something unreal. I know, he needs to be blue. We need to make all his fur and his skin blue. Can you make it so it will grow that way?"

"I think I can," Aketi said. "I'll just need to make a trip to the zoo. I think I've seen just the color you want on one of the parrots. I should be able to adjust the genetic coding from that."

So two days later Arrun watched as his skin and his new fur coat turned blue. After that they tormented him physically for a while and Jadne made a point of rubbing him repeatedly between his legs and laughing at the way it made him pant.

Jadne surprised Arrun, however, when she said after a time. "We should stop now. We don't want to do any real damage to him before we give him to our cousin. It would spoil the effect."

Aketi nodded, and eyed Arrun. "We wouldn't want to spoil Saranith's fun." He smiled. "I believe you humans call her "the eater of souls.""

After that Arrun was truly afraid.

JEREVAN WAS STILL SUFFERING FROM SHOCK complicated by exhaustion three days later. He ate when Otto fed him, would answer direct questions, but initiated no conversations.

"He's healing himself, but that's all he's doing," Otto told Nathan, who had taken over command of the expedition as Elgan was too busy dealing with Magra to do anything else.

Nathan came to see Jerevan for himself the moment the *Nikasha* reached open sea away from the Senangan shore.

"We're in open water now," Nathan said to Jerevan. "Do you want us to hoist you back into the sea?"

"No," Jerevan said, with the most emotion he'd shown since being told of Marion's death. "If I'd done what Marion has wanted me to do for the past five years, stayed human and fought my weight back down, she'd still be alive. I'd have been able to walk out of the Tower all by myself. There'd have been no need of a last moment rescue that got her killed and Arrun captured."

"Don't flay yourself because a stray bullet killed Marion," Nathan said. "We should all have erected shields, but it didn't occur to any of us. That was our stupidity and nothing to do with you."

"The fact remains you wouldn't have been at risk if you hadn't had to come back for me."

"And we wouldn't have had to come back for you if the man Arrun chose to accompany you wasn't an idiot. I can't blame it on Leto, because he apparently can't help but be an idiot, but Arrun should have interviewed him more closely before assigning him that position."

"Do you think they'll kill Arrun?"

"No," Nathan said. "Not Jadne and Aketi. They won't kill him when they can torture him instead."

Later that day Elgan came to see Jerevan. "I hear you've declined to return to the sea?"

"Yes. I'll remain human now until I reach Ilwheirlane and break the curse. I intend to have Otto book passage on a ship as soon as we get to Candith."

"Then you'll be traveling with Magra and myself."

"How's she doing? I saw what Aketi did to her."

"I've restored her physically, of course, but she seems to have retreated in her mind. It's as though she's gone back to being a small child. She had an abusive father. That may be part of the problem. I don't know."

"Her mind wasn't damaged by the cap?"

"No. The paths atrophied somewhat from lack of use, but I detect no real damage. Her problem seems to be something else, something I don't really understand."

BALEK HAD CALLED A MEETING in his chambers to be held within an hour of *Nikasha's* docking in Candith, as soon as he learned from the telepathic relay when they would be arriving.

"So you've come crawling back, and your expedition was a disaster, just as I warned," Balek said, when Jerevan's wheeled bed rolled into the room.

Pala had gone to Nathan the minute he appeared in the doorway and simply hugged him then pulled him down beside her on their usual couch.

"It wasn't a total disaster," Elgan protested. "We did retrieve my apprentice and she seems to be starting to recover from what Aketi did to her."

"But to gain back an apprentice you lost two full wizards," Balek said. "That's not even close to an even exchange. What's more you gave up an effective method of penetrating Cinkarrak that we could certainly have used for intelligence gathering. But they'll tighten their security now."

"Not necessarily," Choma said. She had teleported in as soon as she learned Balek had called the meeting. "The Senangans still don't realize the Tower itself was penetrated. Their current theory is that one or more of the guards were bribed into smuggling the girl down to the kitchens. Frankly, I was amazed at how well Arrun's plan worked, except for the small problem at the end."

"Losing two wizards is not a small problem," Balek said.

"No, it isn't, but frankly Balek, that was your fault. If you'd agreed to the rescue expedition when Elgan first asked, Arrun would have had time to iron out the details. His plan only developed problems because Leto is an idiot and Arrun never had a chance to talk to him so he could realize that."

"I stand by my position that the mission was an unmitigated disaster and an act of defiance of duly constituted authority, and all members of the Varfarin who took part in it should be reprimanded," Balek said.

"YOU KNOW, ELGAN, BEFORE LISTENING TO BALEK rant the other day, I hadn't planned on coming back to Cibata for a long time," Jerevan said.

"But now?"

"Now I'll return as soon as I've become Esalfar. I can't leave Balek as the chief representative of the Varfarin in Cibata. Replacing him will be a priority."

"There are others like him," Elgan warned.

"But I haven't yet been personally exposed to the venom of the others," Jerevan said. "If I don't do something about Balek, after being forced to listen to him, I'll seem to be condoning his policies."

XLIX

4672, 468TH CYCLE OF THE YEAR OF THE EAGLE
MONTH OF ISKKAAR

Jasod a remlan ba mek a benisa qua ma rham.

"The linkage of minds is an act of intimacy like no other."

— EXCERPT FROM THE *MEMOIRS OF THE WIZARD ANOR*

A FTER NATHAN HAD SEEN JEREVAN and Elgan off, he went in
search of Pala. *"I want to go back to Tibati with you,"* he thought.
   "Why Tibati?" Pala asked. *"You come to my rooms in the Palace
almost every night."*
   "But I want to get it right this time, Pala. I want to link with you."
   Pala's eyes widened. *"What happened in Senanga to make you change
your mind?"*
   Nathan snorted. *"I can always count on you, Pala, to see right through
me. It's funny because I don't think I'm that transparent to everyone else."*
   "Ah," Pala thought, *"but the others haven't made a lifelong study of you.
I have. So tell me what happened."*
   *"I saw Marion die, and I realized that I could die, you could die, anyone of
us could die at any time."*
   She smiled at him ruefully, *"Most people come to understand mortality
at a much younger age, Nathan."*
   He nodded. *"I realize that, but I never did."*
   Pala went up to Nathan and hugged him. "I love you," she said
aloud and sounding slightly exasperated, "but sometimes you're the
most impractical man alive."
   "What do you mean?" Nathan asked.
   "It's summer, Nathan. What's the vale in Tibati going to be like in
midsummer?"
   "Oh!" His face fell with dismay. "The grass will be brown and dry."
   Pala nodded. "What's more the rocks will be so hot you can barely
touch them."
   "So not Tibati," he thought, trying to reestablish the feeling of intimacy.
"I still want to make love to you someplace special."
   "What about the water gardens?" Pala thought. *"It's cool there and I can
get some of the spider silk bedding."*

"Isn't that a bit public?" Nathan protested.

"What's the point of being the daughter of the Ahar of Cassinga if I can't order everyone out of a section of the palace for the rest of the day?" Pala asked.

"Then the water gardens it will be."

The water gardens were walled and roofed with thick adobe bricks. The ceiling was high for coolness and skylights highlighted beds of flowers. Pipes ran from the river to fill pools, some deep, some shallow, all around the garden, and other pipes drained the water back to the river downstream so the water was constantly flowing and never became stagnant. Pala had arranged for a proper bed where there were usually lounges.

They swam together in one of the deeper pools as they were both hot and sweaty from the temperature outside, but the water gardens were cool. There was the same sound of moving water that Nathan remembered from Tibati.

He remembered that Pala's skin had been scented with orange oil that day in Tibati and he had found the scent intensely erotic, so he had brought some and when they came out of the pool and lay on the bed he reached out to link with her and started to spread the oil on her skin.

He had, of course, linked with her before and with others to complete some task that took more than one, but that was a different level of linkage. This would be a much deeper, more intimate, the type that, once formed, would always be there between them. This form of linkage was the marraige ceremony of wizards.

The link felt natural, comfortable, although it heightened the sensation of the oil spreading on her skin, as he felt the feel of his fingers, slightly rough, as well as the smoothness of her skin.

They had been lovers now for some time. They knew each others pleasure points, but knowing that pressure on a certain point brought your partner pleasure and feeling that pleasure were two entirely different things. Nathan tried to go slowly, to spread the oil and explore every point with hands or tongue, but the pleasure escalated and then he was inside her and lost himself and all control in a mounting surge of ecstasy.

When the surge died down and left him lying tangled with Pala on the bed, weak and slightly stunned, he felt her smile and snuggle. *"I'm glad we're going to live a long time,"* she thought.

"Why?"

"So I don't need to be angry with you for wasting so much time before you got around to this," she thought. She reached out with her will and pulled the cord to summon servants.

"What are you doing?"

"Ordering food so you can fortify yourself and we can do this again," she thought. *"Don't think that now that I have you at my mercy I'm going to let you go easily."*

Nathan laughed. *"I hope you won't."*

She turned and looked at him more seriously, *"You do know that my mother will abdicate in my favor as soon as I'm known to be with child by you?"*

Nathan shook his head. *"She's told you this?"*

Pala nodded and grinned. *"The same day she told me that, if I ever wanted to have you, I'd have to seduce you."*

Nathan gaped, but saw a faint reflection of the scene in her mind and laughed.

"Remember, she seduced Rainal when she was young. It's the one thing she's quite good at."

"Do you want to have a child right away?"

"I don't know," she thought. *"I don't want to plan a child. I want any child between us to be the product of the fates. We take no action to prevent or cause. Just let it happen or not. Do you understand?"*

"Yes," he thought, understanding her meaning completely. *"Wizards are too prone to take control of everything. Some things should be left to chance and nature."*

L

4672, 468TH CYCLE OF THE YEAR OF THE EAGLE
MONTH OF ISKKAAR

*"A good diplomat needs to be able to lie well.
Honest men make bad diplomats."*

— FROM *THE COLLECTED WRITINGS OF VYDARGA THE RED*

S ARANITH STROLLED OUT ONTO THE VERANDA of the old
house that was hers for the two years she would represent Senanga
here in Akasha. She extended her sight in a wide sweep. The structure
of the building was solid mahogany on a foundation of cut granite
blocks. The wizard who had built it had built for the ages.

She had felt his signature of power in the mortar between the stones
and the bonding of the paint to the wood from the first day she had
come to this place. Just examining the house, she had learned about the
things that wizards could do. She also admired the bright blue paint.

The house was set on a knoll three hundred meters from the shore.
The jungle came to within ten meters on either side, but the area
between the house and the beach had been cleared. She looked out on a
vista of ordered flower beds and well tended lawn. Her wizard vision
detected the falin runs under the grass near the jungle on both sides.
The lawn ended with a smooth, sandy beach running down to a small
line of debris marking the high tide.

There were living things all around her. She studied the complexity
of a flower down to its genetic structure. Then did the same with a
mosquito. The mosquito flew and for a moment she followed it, but it
was hard to focus on something that small when it moved. She focused
farther out toward the sea.

There was a frigate anchoring next to the *Cinhai*, Aketi's ship,
Ningand. She saw him in his cabin. He looked pleased with himself.

Saranith strolled along the veranda to a group of lounges. Then she
lay back in a lounge chair, letting go of her vision. She needed to rest
for a moment, if she was going to have to deal with Aketi. Her head
ached from the strain of maintaining the high sight for over ten minutes, long enough to qualify her as a full wizard by the old Council
standards. She'd been right to take this assignment. As Ambassador to

Akasha she had much more free time than she'd ever had at sea. She needed to concentrate on being a wizard.

She sighed. Of course, the drawback was that everyone knew where to find her. If Aketi didn't block her promotion, she would be named Ilamrai when she went back on active duty. She smiled. Her commands had been more successful than his, her prizes richer. He hated her, but he also wanted her, or wanted her secrets. He had been actively pursuing her since she got back from the Petalwan Archipelago.

It amazed her that he believed he could make her want him after the history between them. But, of course, his ego was colossal. He might not yet know of Cinkarion, but she couldn't keep the secret much longer. She would have to tell Kaya soon, should have done so already. As soon as Kaya knew, Jadne would know and then Aketi would know. He would want to link with her then, believing he would be able to overpower her in the linkage. He would never believe that her will could be stronger than his.

She considered the strategic advantage of confessing to possession of Cinkarion as she heard Aketi on the path. Then she stiffened. He had two junior officers with him and one of them led a short, blue creature with a head vaguely like a bear's. It had a cap on its head. Kyra's furies, she thought. It had to be a wizard he had capped.

She stood up. Her mental shield was impenetrable. Lifelong habit kept her face immobile, and the jewels could never hold expression as eyes might have done. "Aketi," she said. "How nice to see you."

"Sara," he said. "I've brought you a present." He turned to the blue bear, taking its paw. "Bow to your new mistress."

The blue bear stared at him.

Aketi smiled. "He still needs a few lessons in obedience," he said, knocking the bear off its feet. He then stepped on the bear's back and pushed its face in the gravel of the path. "That's right, Arrun, kowtowing is better than bowing."

Saranith watched Aketi, thinking that he was the same nasty bully he had been when he used to pick on Luri. Anything weaker and Aketi would torment it, but she was no longer weaker. Aketi had learned the high sight as a child, but did not have the patience for long practice sessions. His will was strong, but he had no finesse. He wasn't growing stronger as he grew older. No, her cousin was too complacent for such discipline.

Aketi pulled the bear to its feet. "His name is Arrun, your own private jester," he said. "We captured him trying to rescue another prisoner."

"His form is intriguing. What inspired you?" Saranith asked.

Aketi grinned. "If he calls himself a jester, he ought to entertain, shouldn't he? Jadne and I considered several forms, but I thought this would be the funniest. I knew you'd appreciate it. It took us a week to get all the details right."

"What did you do to the other prisoner?"

Aketi frowned. "One of the other wizards was killed, but the prisoner and the rest of the wizards got away."

"What a pity," Saranith said. "Would you like to come in and have something to eat?"

"I wish I could but I'm supposed to rendezvous with the fleet in two days. I really shouldn't have stopped here at all, but I wanted to give Arrun to you myself." He pulled a large, oval crystal on a chain out of his pocket. "This is his crystal. I'll keep it to be sure he doesn't get hold of it." He eyed her slyly. He knew she might aid the wizard to escape if she had the crystal, despite the political repercussions. Then he added, "Remember, he is Cassinga's vaunted military expert."

"I'll keep track of him for you," Saranith said, carefully suppressing all emotion but boredom from her voice. She watched Aketi back to the ship's dory, and then while he was rowed out to the *Ningand*, not taking her eyes off him until *Ningand* raised anchor. Only then did she look at the blue bear.

ARRUN GROANED SILENTLY. Surely Aketi and Jadne Kamrasi had been bad enough, but now he was the property of Saranith Kamrasi. The one who controlled Cinkarion. The one who killed when she linked.

If Aketi was a sadist, which he certainly was, what would she be like?

Arrun felt his fear intensify. Aketi's sadism he had expected, understood. But with Saranith he had no idea what to expect. She looked pitiless. Of course, the jewels in the eyesockets helped. They gave her face an inhuman, insectile look. But it was more than that. Her whole body remained still. She had no nervous mannerisms, no motion at all that was not precise and deliberate. She'd put out her own eyes at the age of twelve, for Jehan's sake. She might be capable of anything, things he couldn't begin to imagine.

When Aketi left, she stood and watched him go. Arrun wondered if she cared about Aketi, she watched him so intently.

When she finally turned to him she asked, "Can you talk?"

He stared at her. Aketi had removed his vocal chords and most of his tongue, but he wouldn't have answered her even if he could. He'd determined on passive resistance as his best bet to retain his sanity.

"No," she said, "well, it doesn't matter. I imagine you're hungry, if you've been with Aketi long. Would you like something to eat? A nod will do."

Her voice was calm, indifferent, but it wasn't threatening. He nodded.

She offered him her hand. He stared. Frozen.

She shrugged and climbed the stairs, and he realized that the stairs were steep for his new body. What if she really had only meant to assist him up them?

He climbed after her with difficulty. First one knee up, then the other. Pull himself to his feet. Then repeat the process. He felt very tired and weak. Aketi hadn't fed him more than once a day on the journey, but had arranged for him to be roused at regular intervals.

Saranith led the way to the door of the blue house and opened it, holding it for him. There was a guard on duty by the door, but he didn't seem to think it strange that she should hold the door. He hadn't moved to open it for her. Arrun swallowed and went into the house.

Saranith passed him and led the way to the kitchen. There was a tall, cadaverous woman standing by a large wood-burning stove.

"Greva, what do you have on hand for our houseguest?" Saranith asked.

Arrun blinked. Houseguest?

Greva stared at him. "What's he eat?"

Saranith looked at him, then said, "I believe anything that you or I could eat would do. His current form was enforced on him by my cousin Aketi. You shouldn't hold him responsible."

Greva grunted. "Aketi's been here?"

"He's gone back to his ship."

Greva looked at her sharply. "What did he want?"

"He just brought me this present," Saranith said, nodding toward Arrun, her voice as expressionless as her face.

"Present, huh," Greva said.

Arrun, braced for torture, felt disoriented. He watched Saranith leave with disbelief.

"Let me see those paws," Greva demanded.

Arrun held out his paws, no longer possessing opposable thumbs.

"Can't handle a spoon," Greva said with disgust. "Have to get Sara to fix something for you tomorrow. If Aketi's been here she won't be up to it tonight. You'll have to eat from a bowl."

Moments later he was sitting on the floor with a large bowl of some meat and grain dish that tasted delicious. He had to stick his snout in and lap like a dog, but his tastebuds hadn't been altered and he was hungry. He ate every bite.

"You want more?" Greva asked when she saw he had finished.

Arrun shook his head. He felt full and exhausted.

"Then we'll go see if Sara's fixed a place for you," Greva said, reaching down to help him to his feet.

This time Arrun didn't hesitate to accept the assistance. If this was all a softening up procedure before they started torturing him, well, it had worked. He could be passively resistant later when someone attacked him. For now he was tired and would take whatever help and nourishment he could get.

The next day he woke in the small blue room Greva had said would be his. The bed had been too high for him to climb into, so Saranith had removed it and put the mattress on the floor. She had also found a child's toy chest for him to keep his things in and moved and altered the handle on the door so he could open and close it himself if he used both paws.

Saranith and Greva had made him as comfortable as he could be given his present shape. He didn't understand why. The linlarin were known for their sadistic treatment of prisoners. Aketi had supplied what he'd expected. Granted, the imposition of the form of the blue bear had been more creative than what he had imagined experiencing, but it was certainly torture. Yet Saranith, who was known to the Varfarin as the ultimate symbol of linlarin ruthlessness and cruelty, was treating him like a guest?

He rose from the bedding and waddled over to the chest. He pushed it open and pulled out the jumper Aketi had given him. It was dirty, but it was his only garment. His paws were clumsy and gave him no grip, so it took several minutes for him to pull it over his head and get his arms in the sleeves.

There was a knock on the door. Then it opened. "I know you can't answer," Saranith said, "but I thought the knock would at least give you warning I was coming. Would you like to join me for breakfast? I usually eat on the veranda. I fixed some tools that should make eating easier for you."

Arrun nodded and waddled over to the door. She took his paw and led him out onto the veranda, opening the door for him as she had the day before.

A table had been set a few meters down the porch from the door. One of the chairs had been raised on blocks so that when he sat in it he would be able to see over the table. He wondered how she expected him to get up to it, but then she leaned over, picked him up and sat him in it.

Her head tilted slightly afterward though, and she said, "You must have been a tall man."

Arrun didn't respond. His heartbeat had accelerated when she lifted him, but the emotion he had felt had not been entirely fear. Her hands had been strong and sure and being so close to her he had felt something stir inside him.

He had not noticed the day before. He had been too tired and too frightened. But Saranith was beautiful, in a strange, barbaric way.

A maid brought a tray with their breakfast dishes. When she had served them she withdrew. Arrun looked around the veranda. There was a guard by the door, but he wouldn't be able to hear any conversation at the table. There were more guards at the foot of the garden near the dock.

"We're alone, but I've studied your form enough to know you can't speak," Saranith said. "You needn't be afraid. I'm not Aketi. I'm not going to torture you. But I can't break the shape he's put you in, nor can I remove the cap and let you go. Technically, you're a prisoner of war and you've been put in my custody. At least, that's how my cousin Kaya, the Estahar, would look at it if I were to free you. So, for the moment, I can't. Do you understand?"

Arrun watched her intently as she spoke. He nodded. His mind reeled. Her words implied that she would free him, were she able to do so without damage to herself. This had to be some trick. He stared at her, trying to find some reason for her words.

"Never mind." She sighed. "I can't expect you to understand. Still, while you're here, you'll be treated as a guest in my home."

Arrun watched her. The sigh and the wistful note in her voice were the first sign of emotions he had seen in her. What if she were telling him the truth? What if this strange, passionless creature truly did mean him no harm? She was the bearer of Cinkarion. Elgan had once said that they should trust the crystals to pick their bearers, that the crystals were tools of Jehan. But they'd all been appalled when Cinkarion had chosen Saranith.

Saranith had been eating her breakfast while he thought so furiously. She looked up and saw he wasn't eating. "Do you need help putting the cuff on? I thought utensils would make it easier for you to eat."

Arrun looked down at the table and saw a metal cuff he could slide over his paw. There were several attachments with it that could be snapped on: a hook, a spoon, a fork, and a knife.

"I realize you'll need help changing the attachments for now, but I've designed a magnetized one. If you keep that one on your left paw you should be able to change the attachments on the right one yourself. It should be ready this afternoon." She reached out and slipped the cuff on his right paw, snapping in the spoon. "There, now you should be able to eat more comfortably."

Arrun had gone beyond amazement. He dipped the spoon into the bowl of fruit in front of him and found he could eat more or less normally with it. His bear snout was a problem, as on his first try he poked it with the spoon, but that was a matter of adjustment to his new shape.

In the weeks that followed Saranith proved to Arrun that she truly meant him no harm, yet as that time passed he began to suffer in a way he had never expected.

He felt stunned the first time she sat him across her lap. They had been sitting on the porch swing, side by side. She had been talking to him, as she often did. Then she had twisted around to sit sideways on the swing with her legs up, and she had picked him up and positioned him across her lap in the same gesture. Her breasts cushioned his head.

"There. I hope that's as comfortable for you as it is for me?"

He nodded, but comfortable was not what he felt.

"It's so peaceful here," she said, and stroked him absently.

That was when he began to understand what true torture was. He had braced himself for physical torture, but had never expected the kind of mental agony he began to suffer.

He wanted her. Under the form of the blue bear, he was still a man. She was a woman he found infinitely desirable. What was worse, she enjoyed petting him.

It hadn't taken him long to realize that she'd had a deprived and miserable childhood. He was her first toy, her first thing to cuddle. If he'd protested in any way, she would have stopped immediately. She knew he wasn't a toy, but it made her feel good to cuddle him. She hoped he enjoyed it too.

And, of course, it was the most agonizing mixture of pleasure and pain he could ever imagine!

LI

4672, 468TH CYCLE OF THE YEAR OF THE EAGLE MONTH OF INGVASH

> Theocan al Ingva ba end a lodisa ab tolon
> e government. Noben netwe ab no end
> so poborisa less quen dom e vada.

> "The Year of the Dolphin is a time of creativity in arts
> and government. Those born in this year
> have a great capacity for love and joy."

— FROM THE *BOOK OF YEARS*

PALA SAT NEXT TO HER MOTHER IN THE CARRIAGE taking them to her coronation which had to move slowly due to the cheering crowds. Even with guards along the way people were breaking through. Some of them threw flowers and there was a strong scent of broken blossoms.

Juba thought, *"The people never cheered for my father. They cheered for me, but nothing like this. You and your friends have given them hope. They believe, as do I, that, even if Arrun is lost to us, you and Nathan together can keep Cassinga safe."*

Pala nodded. *"I think so too,"* she thought, *"but I didn't realize you even remembered mind speech. You've never used it with me before."*

"I practice with Rainal sometimes. I did take some training as a child, before my father stopped it." She hesitated, then added, *"I was never strong enough for Rainal to link with me. I resented that and, spiting myself, I gave up the mind speech for many years. But I've grown up a little in my old age, and seeing you with Nathan."*

Pala smiled. Just Nathan's name made her smile. She thought, *"It's a wonderful thing, being linked with someone you love. I've always loved Nathan, but even loving him I never imagined this closeness."*

Juba smiled at her daughter. *"You were born in the Year of the Dolphin. I always thought that was lucky, and Jehan knows you've proven to be more than I ever dared to wish. I told you when I took this crown,"* she tapped the jeweled tiara on her head, *"that all you had to do to take over from me was get yourself a mate and get pregnant. Now you've done both those things."*

"Nathan and I haven't announced the pregnancy."

"I've had Rainal watching you ever since you linked. It's the right of parents to be the first to know."

"I imagine Balek objected to the abdication."

"He didn't say much at all. Just that it was my decision, if I wanted to hand over my rule to a child."

Pala laughed.

"THERE WERE TWO SKILLS CORMOR achieved that no other wizard ever has," Elgan said during one of the many conversations he'd had with Jerevan on the long sea voyage from Cibata.

"What were they?" Jerevan asked, absentmindedly massaging his still massive belly.

"The sybil trance where he could see alternate futures, and the ability to teleport another lifeform with him."

"How many others have tried."

"Oh, many. Both Rav and I have tried to transport other lifeforms. I quit after trying with a beetle. It arrived with me, intact but dead. I believe Rav tried many times with people."

"Did Cormor ever discuss those talents with you?"

"He told me that, if the Varfarin were lucky, you'd learn both skills, that you and your mate would truly become his equal."

"So I'm to have a mate?" Jerevan asked, just as his fingers found a pocket of trapped air and he belched. He looked significantly down at his body.

Elgan shook his head. "You've lost over a thousand pounds so far on this journey and we've over a month to go. It's not going to take you long to be back to what you were before the curse, once you've broken it. I think I'll reserve my pity for the members of the Varfarin who stood by when you were cursed."

"I thought of your name as well as Myrriden's when I was cursed, but I had no idea where to find you. Would you have helped me?"

Elgan considered Jerevan. "I wouldn't have broken the curse or killed Derwen. I believe, I'd have brought you to Derwen and then, while monitoring him, moderated the curse to the point it was only a mild annoyance. No blackouts, no comas, and you would have been able to keep your stomach a normal size. I have thought of the problem, you see."

Jerevan nodded. "I could have lived with that."

"And when you'd proved conclusively that you were striving to become a wizard, I'd have removed the curse entirely. Of course," Elgan added, "you can do that yourself now, and the problem still remains that it must be done in Derwen's presence to spare his sorry existance."

"You aren't fond of Derwen?"

"I detest the nasty little fathik," Elgan said. "I detest Balek, too, for that matter, for many of the same reasons. They're both narrow-minded old bigots."

Jerevan laughed. "What percentage of the Varfarin would you say shares their views?"

"Oh, probably thirty or forty percent," Elgan said. "Fortunately, they aren't the ones who've been training the new apprentices. Delanan on Sussey and now Arrun in Cassinga are where the new wizards are coming from. I've trained a few in Kandorra, but not nearly as many as I'd like to train."

"You'd like to set up a school?"

"Yes. In Lara, or on the Nyali Coast. Actually, schools should be set up in both places."

"Why those places particularly?

"Because I still haven't found a fallar apprentice," Elgan said, "and those are the places I'm most likely to find mixed blood with talent."

He paused then added, "I know you have no reason to love or respect Cormor, but his visions have often come true."

"To the contrary, I respect him quite highly," Jerevan said.

"He believed that the gods will stack the deck. There will be, or already are, extraordinarily strong wizards being born with mixed blood. Either we find and train them, or the chances are they'll get their training from the isklarin and end up fighting against us."

"What's more," Jerevan said, "they'll end up carrying karionin."

Elgan eyed him, "Yes, so I believe."

"That wasn't difficult to guess," Jerevan said. "Look at the bearers of the karionin that are currently active. Errin Anifi and Elise Adun, both with ingvalar blood, and Saranith Kamrasi, a linlar. They've been shown to have volition. I imagine they're hunting as hard as we are for those mixed blood bearers."

LII

4672, 468TH CYCLE OF THE YEAR OF THE EAGLE
MONTH OF ANOR

Zand amvalod loadetwe, nalorin rut.

"When the universe was complete, the gods laughed."

— ESLARIN PROVERB

Nikasha docked in the great harbor of Ninkarrak near noon early in the month of Anor. Magra and Elgan came to say good-bye to Jerevan while the seamen were removing the frame from around the door to his cabin so he could leave, as neither he nor his wheeled bed could get through otherwise. The cabin doorways were particularly narrow.

That had limited his mobility, but the captain had been firm, "Demolition at the beginning and the end of the voyage will cause quite sufficient damage to my ship."

Magra came up to the side of his bed and said, "I hope I'll see you again when you've broken your curse. I didn't really believe Elgan when he told me a man had been cursed into becoming a wizard."

Elgan said, "I look forward to seeing you again, also. When you're Esalfar of the Varfarin I'll rejoin and retake my oath. There's a great deal of work to be done if you plan on restoring the organization to what it was in Cormor's time."

Jerevan nodded. He didn't have as many chins as he'd had when he left Cassinga, but their ripple effect still annoyed him. "I've seen first hand just how badly Derwen has managed the Varfarin. I have a number of changes in mind, but my first duty will be going back to Cibata and removing Balek from office. I'll want to retrieve Arrun, too, if he hasn't already been rescued by the time I get back."

"You won't tell us what you're going to do to Derwen?" Magra asked.

He looked at her soberly. "It's not that I won't, Magra. I can't tell you, because I'm not entirely sure myself. I have a number of ideas, but the final decision will depend on Derwen and how I feel when I actually face him again."

"I hope you do something really nasty to him," she said. "I plan on doing something awful to Aketi."

Jerevan's mind touched Elgan's, *"She will recover. She's just repeating her childhood, but she's gotten steadily better during the voyage."*

Elgan's response was rueful, *"You mean she sounds like an eight-year-old instead of a four-year-old? Yes, I know she'll recover. It's my patience I'm worried about in the meantime."*

When they had left and the doorway was wide enough, Jerevan wheeled out onto the deck. His will had grown steadily and nothing during the voyage had distracted him from working to prepare his body to walk again. He was as ready as he could make himself until the curse was broken. And that, of course, was the whole purpose of the journey. He was down to under a ton for the first time in sixteen years. Of course, he hadn't been able to exercise his new muscles so they weren't as strong as he would have liked.

Jerevan propelled his wheeled bed to the top of the gang plank, but there he stopped.

"I'm going to walk ashore," he said, looking out over the bustling harbor of Ninkarrak for the first time in over twenty years.

"Is that wise, your grace?" Otto asked, and though his face was expressionless as usual, Jerevan heard the worry in his voice. "You should save your energy today with what you have planned for tomorrow."

"I'll be all right, Otto, if I have someone on each arm to assist me. This is what I've been preparing for and I won't roll ashore in Ilwheirlane like a ton weight of lard. One of the sailors can help."

"Very well, your grace." Otto gestured to a sailor who had been watching by the rail. "Come here man. I'm going to tilt his bed up all the way. Stand on the other side of him and hold his left arm."

Otto unlatched the safety bar and turned the wheel that controlled the angle of Jerevan's conveyance. When the angle was steep enough, Jerevan's mass slipped down and his feet touched the ground. Otto was quick to take his arm, but Jerevan's legs supported his weight.

He pushed himself off the bed and stood erect. He felt the strain in the muscles in his legs and back, but he was standing on his own for the very first time since he'd been a prisoner in Ravaar. He forced the memories back. Now was not the time. He was on his own two feet again. He eyed the ramp and gripped the sailor's arm feeling Otto's firm grip on his other arm. Then, one step at a time, he descended the short distance to the bottom of the ramp.

The step to the ground, however, proved to be too much. His legs buckled under his weight and he fell, dragging Otto and the sailor down with him. He released them quickly and they scrambled out of the way as he landed on his belly, spread out over the cobblestones in a quivering mass.

"Help me to my feet again," Jerevan gasped.

The sailor who had gone down on his knees grimaced, but joined Otto. It took the two footmen from his carriage in addition, however, to get Jerevan back on his feet and by the time they managed it an audience had begun to gather.

"Never seen a whale in clothes before," some dockside wit called out.

Ignoring the catcalls, Jerevan gripped Otto and one of the footmen, waving the others off, and waddled across the street to where his carriage and his specially designed curricle were waiting. He had sent orders by a courier ship before he left Cibata that the curricle be brought from Sussey to Ilwheirlane. He could not imagine living on land without the means to get around in something other than his wheeled bed.

Getting into it without a hoist was a problem though. It took both footmen, Otto and the sailor to get him into the seat. Still, despite the laughter of the crowd, and the fact that he was breathless and exhausted from the effort, Jerevan smiled while he waited for his wheeled bed to be loaded on the back. His luggage and Otto would travel in the carriage. He was back in Illwheirlane and he could get around on his own. He was home.

JEREVAN HAD TAKEN THE SCENIC ROUTE to the Inn of the Sleeping Dragon, enjoying the freedom after being confined to the ship's cabin. Two ostlers managed to assist him to get out and onto his feet once more. Getting down was easier than climbing up. Then, with only one ostler's support, he managed to shamble up to the door of the inn.

Jerevan leaned against the wall next to the door as the ostler hurried away. Eyeing the entry to the inn, he could see that his girth was greater than the doorway. He opened it with his will and wedged himself in. The rolls of his flesh were pliant enough that he was able to push himself through.

Once inside he leaned against the wall to catch his breath. The hall was wide, two meters at least, and posed no problem to him. The taproom itself appeared to have an arched entry and thus it, too, would cause no problem. As his legs were starting to tremble from the strain of supporting his weight, he heaved himself erect once more and lumbered down the hall toward the archway.

There he had to stop. The archway itself was broad enough but there was no path through the tables that filled most of the room beyond. He swayed and again subsided against the wall, panting from the exertion.

"Otto," he called, between gasps.

Otto came charging down the hall from the rear of the inn with the landlord beside him. "I've arranged for a private parlor, your grace," he said, going straight to Jerevan's side and supplying him an arm to lean on.

"Which way," Jerevan asked.

"Back down the hall, your grace. Through the first door you passed," Otto said.

Jerevan felt the landlord's amazed eyes on him as he managed to turn himself around and, leaning heavily on Otto, return down the hall. When he reached the door Otto had indicated, he backed against the opposite wall so Otto and the landlord could get past him. The landlord, who was portly, had to squeeze to get through and the contact with Jerevan's soft, voluminous flesh flustered him.

"Your pardon, your grace," he muttered as he opened the parlor door. "There's a bench inside that I had brought in for you."

The parlor door was narrower than the front door had been and Jerevan required Otto's assistance pushing and pulling to get him through, but as his rolls of fat were anything but firm he made it. After that, it was all he could do to waddle to the bench and lower himself onto it.

He could hardly remember a time when he had been able to sit in a chair. Even benches were often too narrow and therefore uncomfortable. This one was wide, however, and set out far enough from the wall to allow him to get support from it.

His leg and back muscles were in agony from the prolonged strain of standing, he was bathed in sweat and his breath came in gasps.

Otto removed Jerevan's boots and began to massage the spasming muscles of his calves. He couldn't reach the massive thighs as they were buried under the mountain of Jerevan's belly.

As Jerevan caught his breath and Otto's fingers eased the worst of the muscle pain, Jerevan began to feel the ache of hunger. He said, "I hope the landlord is planing on bringing me something to eat soon. I can feel an attack coming on."

Otto rose, alarmed. "I've ordered a meal, of course, your grace, but you should have had enough in the carriage to have kept you comfortable."

"I stayed out too long enjoying the freedom of movement," Jerevan said, and grimaced as the first hunger cramp gripped his stomach.

Otto saw the telltale ripple across Jerevan's belly, and rose. "I'll see to your dinner immediately, your grace."

When Otto had gone, Jerevan settled himself against the wall and panted in a way that helped him to ride out the pain. Otto returned with the landlord and several serving boys carrying a whole baron of beef, four roasted and stuffed sulcaths and the rest of what he needed to fill himself. When Jerevan had eaten all of it down to the last crumb, and his stomach was tight and comfortable again, he thought, "Never again. Once the curse is broken, I'll never again eat just to fill my stomach."

When Jerevan started to rise, Otto said, "There's no need, your grace. I told the landlord that you would require your bed to be set up for you down here after your first meal."

Jerevan flushed. "You don't think I can make it up the stairs."

"Your grace, be reasonable," Otto said sharply. "You've already undergone a tremendous strain today. Have you even attempted to check on the damage done to your system?"

Jerevan sighed. "No, and you're right. I probably couldn't have made it up a staircase. I converted fat to muscles on the ship, but they aren't strong enough yet to support me for long. I'll have to work on them more tonight. After all, I wouldn't want to fall down in front of Derwen."

"You'll break the curse, your grace. Everyone's told you that you're strong enough now."

When he was undressed and had performed all his natural functions, Otto bathed him, put his night robe on him and assisted him back onto his tilt bed.

The next morning Jerevan looked at himself in the mirror, something he usually avoided doing. His fat cheeks were rosy from the exertion of being dressed. His multiple chins expanded in rolls until hidden by the collar of his shirt and the shirt sloped only shallowly over the mountainous expanse of his stomach. His breeches were held up by suspenders as what had once been his waist was now by far the widest part of him. His legs splayed out awkwardly, forced to that angle by the massive circumference of his thighs. His boots were vast and the calves of his legs were as thick as a good sized tree.

Yet what he saw in the mirror was recognizably a human form. Moreover, he was able to stand again, even walk a short distance. It was time to face Derwen.

JEREVAN SAT IN HIS SPECIALLY DESIGNED curricle and studied the nondescript brownstone across the street. He had truly wished that he could be back in his own form before he faced Derwen. He'd always imagined their confrontation that way, but he wasn't willing to wait the year or more it would take him to fight the curse and reduce his size at the same time. He wanted the curse to end now. He signaled the two footmen on the back of his curricle to help him to the ground. Then he shambled across the street and leaned against the doorframe.

He used his will to pull the bell rope by the door. Derwen was at home. Jerevan sensed his presence.

Several minutes passed. Jerevan sensed movement and then heard a shuffling on the other side of the door. It opened.

Derwen had changed. He looked older and sloppier than Jerevan remembered him.

"Hello, Derwen," he said. "You'll need to open the door all the way if you intend to let me in. Even then, it looks like I'll have to squeeze through."

Jerevan smiled at Derwen's appalled expression.

"Well, are you going to let me in, or shall we conduct our business in the street?"

Derwen gasped and swallowed, stepping back hurriedly. "Of course, come in. I wasn't expecting..."

"No, you weren't expecting me. Or was it that you weren't expecting the size of me." Jerevan stepped into the doorway, pushing the door wide. The space was indeed too narrow for him to simply step through. He had to press his bulk against the frame, first one way, then the other, squeezing through as he had with the inn door the day before.

Jerevan pushed himself free of the door into Derwen's entryway, a somewhat dingy space with a stairway going up to the second floor some three meters ahead and an archway into a sitting room to the left. He headed for the sitting room, one laborious step at a time. The muscles in his legs and back ached with the strain, but he had strengthened them since the day before. He wasn't going to fall down in front of Derwen.

Derwen was walking backwards in front of him, staring at him as though he was some form of apparition. Well, he supposed he was.

Jerevan made it to a couch. I looked fairly sturdy and was fortunately fairly deep. He sat down, grateful that, while it groaned in protest, it didn't collapse under him. "Sit down, man," he said to Derwen, who was still hovering in front of him.

Derwen sat down in the chair opposite. The sitting room was brighter than the hall with windows facing a nondescript yard.

Jerevan waited a moment, catching his breath from the physical strain of walking so far. Then he felt for the spell strand of the curse. Derwen's eyes went wide with fear and Jerevan knew he sensed the contact. Jerevan explored the spell. It was like a psychic vine, connecting him with Derwen. It had no substance though, and it had stretched all the way to Cibata. He couldn't simply break it. He examined the way it attached, and sensed the first weakness. It had tendrils that permeated his body, but they could be broken. He broke one.

Pain seared through him and the tendril regrew.

He searched them all out and wrenched at them all at once, uprooting them and tearing them away from his body. Agony lanced through him but he focused the pain into tearing every piece out and hurling them all back at Derwen. Then they were gone. The pain eased.

Derwen gasped and paled, his hand going to his chest. Jerevan waited until his own pain had completely gone and he managed to catch his breath. He had been panting with exertion. Then he reached out mentally and examined his nemesis. The wretched man was having a heart attack. Jerevan reached in and healed him. Then he started examining Derwen in detail and healing him more extensively.

After the exertion of ending the curse, he couldn't do much for Derwen, but he made sure the man would live. Then he sat back and waited. Derwen had passed out early along in the healing process, but he recovered consciousness fairly quickly after Jerevan stopped healing him.

He was very still when he first regained consciousness. Jerevan guessed he was examining himself. "Why did you spare me?" Derwen asked, looking up suddenly to meet his eyes. "I was sure you'd just let me die when you broke the curse."

"Oh, no, Derwen, you don't get out of your duties that easily," Jerevan said. "You've made a mess of running the Varfarin, a mess that I'm going to have to clean up. That will mean my traveling all over Tamar, so I'll need you here, running the head office, so to speak."

"You want me to keep on representing the Varfarin in Ninkarrak?" Derwen said, sounding dazed.

"Not as Esalfar, at least not after I've qualified as a full wizard. That will probably take me several months. After that you'll be publicly named my aide. I have a number of projects that need to be started here and you'll supervise them, as well as providing a conduit to me. What's more, Derwen," Jerevan said, smiling, "I get to determine your form this time."

"What do you mean?" Derwen asked, stiffening.

"I'm staying at an estate I've purchased in the hills outside of Ninkarrak, Tormor House. I'll expect you there tomorrow by ten o'clock and I'll continue the healing I started today. When I've finished with you, you'll not only be fully healed but reshaped to a form pleasing to me. Do you understand?"

Derwen nodded slowly, his expression indicative of dread. "Oh, yes. I understand."

"And while we're speaking of forms, I would like the image you took of me before you cursed me. I assume you did record it?"

"Of course I did," Derwen said.

"Then show it to me," Jerevan demanded.

Derwen fumbled in his pocket and drew out a crystal. He mentally highlighted a point on the crystal and Jerevan copied the exact cellular image of himself at twenty-one, before the curse, onto his own crystal. He had made an image of himself later that year, but he'd already gained over forty pounds by then and he wanted to restore himself as he had originally been.

"Then I'll expect you tomorrow," Jerevan said, looking directly at Derwen. "Don't be late."

He paused and studied the fearful, cowering wizard across the room for a moment. Then he said, "Now go outside and call my footmen. I need them to help me to my feet. I can't get up off this sofa without some help."

Derwen gaped at him and then went and did as he'd been told.

His expression alleviated all the pain Jerevan felt as he retraced his steps back out of Derwen's house and across the street to his curricle. Getting back into the curricle without a hoist was an ordeal. Derwen was ordered to supply two more servants and it took all four to boost him up into the seat, but Jerevan still laughed as he drove himself to his new estate.

Otto would be there ahead of him and Tormor House would be ready for his arrival. He would get to torture Derwen for weeks before Derwen realized Jerevan wasn't going to turn him into some horrible monstrosity. He would simply remake Derwen to a form Jerevan found attractive. After all, he'd have to look at the man for centuries. But every time Derwen looked in a mirror he would know that the young, slender, handsome man he saw was not his own form, but one Jerevan had imposed on him. Most people would not see it as a punishment at all, and wonder how Jerevan could be so generous with the man who cursed him, but Derwen would know.

WHEN HE WOKE THE NEXT MORNING, after having slept through an entire night for the first time in over twenty-five years, he remembered what he had accomplished. His body ached and his stomach felt empty, but there was no cramping and no pain from the hunger. The curse was really broken.

LIII

"All men wear masks.
Only some can be removed."

— SAYING OF THE PLAYER'S GUILD

O TTO CAME IN WITH HIS JACKET and helped him into it, perfectly tailored and fashionably tight. Jerevan eyed himself in the mirror with satisfaction. His waistline was now precisely what it had been all those years ago. His legs were a little more muscular, his shoulders slightly broader, but he was older and had seen no need to make himself an exact replica of what he'd been. He was ready to face the wizards of the Varfarin, and after today they would answer to him.

This morning he would meet with the Council of the Varfarin in Ninkarrak. He would take the tests that showed he was a full wizard and then be elevated to the rank of Esalfar of the Varfarin. He smiled. Then they would be in for a surprise.

He arrived in the hall by teleporting. He had realized, after practicing the other skills required to qualify as a wizard, that teleportation was really no more difficult than shapechanging and required the same skills.

The wizards standing around the hall, several of them grouped about the new Derwen, stiffened at his sudden appearance.

"Impressive," one of them said, "that's usually not something attempted by new wizards."

"And you are?" Jerevan asked.

"The Wizard Hulvar. I was an apprentice of Derwen's."

"My condolences," Jerevan said. He looked around at the others. "Are you ready to proceed?"

"A new wizard must not only pass the tests that confirm his skill, but take an oath as well," Hulvar said agressively, obviously unhappy about Jerevan's words.

"I'm aware. Shall we get on with it," Jerevan thought. *"I'm currently seeing with the high sight. I suggest that someone start timing me and we can proceed to the roof. I understand there's a platform there and a straight run to the nearest telepathic relay."*

He went through the demonstrations quickly and ended up by transforming himself into the tiger form of a linlar. When he changed back to human form, he asked, *"Have I performed the tests satisfactorily?"*

"Yes," a chorus of voices agreed.

"Then I'm ready to take my oath."

They linked minds and the oath was administered, in Eskh as it always was for a wizard. When Jerevan had completed the oath, he asked, still linked, *"Is there any other requirement I need to complete before becoming Esalfar of the Varfarin?"*

"No," Derwen thought, *"I now appoint you Esalfar of the Varfarin."*

Jerevan nodded slowly, *"Now, then, I've some requirements of my own. Anyone who wishes to remain a member of the Varfarin must now retake their own oaths linked to me. There will be no more exceptions to the oath that wizards not abuse their powers, and it will also be understood that it is the purpose of the Varfarin to aid all the races of the larin to achieve wizardry, to recreate a Council of Wizards that will, this time, not consist solely of humans, but represent all the races of Tamar. Any of you not willing to so swear should leave now. I will record your resignation from the Varfarin effective immediately."*

There were a number of gasps, but one wizard applauded. Jerevan checked his mental images of the minds he'd been linked with and identified the wizard clapping as the Wizard Rand.

"I take it you approve?" he thought.

"Oh, yes!" Rand thought, *"and about time. If Delanan were here he'd be clapping too."*

Jerevan hesitated then asked, *"Is there anyone who wishes to leave?"*

There were more grumbles, but in the end all the wizards relinked and retook their oaths.

"That went better than I hoped," Jerevan thought to Rand at the end.

"All of this group at least cares," Rand thought, *"or they wouldn't have been here. The ones you'll have real trouble with are the isolated ones who've been doing their own thing for centuries. Some of those will just quit."*

"I was prepared for a loss of up to thirty percent of the membership," Jerevan thought.

"No, I'll wager it'll be no more than fifteen percent," Rand thought.

MONTH OF DIRGA

SARANITH SAT DOWN ON THE FLOOR next to Arrun. He was trying to play pick up sticks with his clumsy paws, moving the whole pile for every stick he picked up. He turned to look at her with his green gold eyes.

She didn't meet his gaze and he felt a stirring of unease.

She looked down at him and then ran her fingers through his long blue fur and rested her forehead on his shoulder. "I never missed having something to cuddle, until Aketi gave you to me." She swallowed. "I know Aketi didn't mean for me to enjoy having you, and I know you'll die if I keep you." She shook her head. "Maybe I underestimate Aketi but your form was probably Jadne's idea. She's much subtler than her brother. She might have guessed that I'd grow to care about you, that your death would make me suffer." She swallowed.

He stiffened under her hand.

She squeezed his shoulder. "But you won't die. There are human wizards off shore and more in the strip of jungle behind the house. The guards haven't detected them, but they will if your friends approach the house as I'm sure they're planning to do once they think we've gone to bed. It would be better if we went for a walk in the garden, and you slip off into the bushes." She felt his body twitch and she gripped his fur more tightly. "Not yet. Aketi hasn't drunk enough yet not to notice when we go out. Give him another half hour. He's feeling very pleased with himself."

Arrun relaxed and hugged her with his short blue arms. Then he put his paw under her chin and turned her face toward him. Where her eyesockets had held rubies, they now held eyes, bright green-gold eyes.

Saranith smiled at him. Her cheeks were wet with tears. "These are my eyes," she said, "and this is my true face. No one but Luri, and now you, has seen me since I turned twelve. I know I'll never see you again, and that I won't recognize you even if I do, but I want you to remember me as me."

Arrun made the gesture that meant Aketi followed by a question mark.

Saranith shook her head. "He can't harm me. He won't even live to realize you've disappeared. He wants the power of Cinkarion. He's been pushing me to link with him ever since he learned I bear it. Tomorrow I'll let him." She looked away from his eyes. "I almost let my mind die when I felt Luri's mind burn as we linked. I had nightmares about it for years, but I won't be sorry when I feel Aketi's mind shrivel and burn."

"Jadne will be furious. I think she's actually fond of Aketi, as fond as she's capable of being. She'll also want to know what happened to you. But I think I'll be able to explain that you escaped in the shock and confusion of Aketi's death."

Deliberately she changed her eyes back from flesh to rubies. The tears vanished with her tear ducts. "Aketi has just fallen asleep. It's time." She rose and helped Arrun to his feet. Then she took his hand

and they walked through the house and out the back door, across the verandah and down the steps into the garden. Arrun, as usual, had trouble with the steps and she had to help him. She nodded at the guards as they passed.

When they reached the edge of the woods she took a clear crystal from her pocket and tucked it into one of the pockets on his jumper. "You may need this. Aketi never noticed when I made the exchange."

He made the gesture that meant time between them.

"Six months ago," she said. "I've always known I'd have to give you up. At first I dreaded the day, but lately I've been worried. It's taken your friends so long. I don't want your stay here to have done you permanent harm. You must go now." She bent down and hugged him one last time. "Good bye."

Arrun slipped through the first line of trees and then looked back. Saranith still appeared to be walking in the garden with her blue teddy bear. He shut his eyes for a moment, then turned away and started walking deeper into the woods. He had only been walking five minutes when Nathan and Ashe stepped out into his path. "Arrun?" Nathan asked.

Arrun nodded and lifted his clumsy paw to the cap.

SARANITH WAS UP EARLY THE NEXT MORNING having her breakfast on the veranda when Aketi joined her.

"So," he said, "have you made up your mind." His tone was aggressive.

She tilted her head, knowing that gesture irritated Aketi and stressed the insectile impression of her faceted "eyes."

"Well?"

"You realize," she said carefully, "that Cinkarion killed Luri."

He frowned. "What do you mean? I've always wondered how the little muloplen died? The only one of your crewmen I could get to talk said you were alone with him in the cabin."

Only a lifetime of self-discipline kept her face expressionless, but she couldn't stop herself from some response. "And he didn't stay my crewman after talking to you. How disappointing for you."

Aketi snorted. "Your crewmen always have been a closemouthed bunch. Not sure how you manage it."

"It's called loyalty, Aketi. It has to work two ways, which is probably why you don't receive much from your own crew."

He nodded, pleased with himself for forcing the reaction from her. "So how did the Heart of Fire kill him? I thought you controlled it?"

She waited until she had herself back under control. Then she said, "When I first linked with Cinkarion, the linkage forced me to relive Agnith's last moments as she died in the Bane. I suppressed the pain immediately. I didn't realize that anyone else linking with Cinkarion would have to experience the same thing. The Heart of Fire has real fire inside it, Aketi. It destroyed Luri's mind. Are you sure you want to take such a risk?"

"Luri always was a weakling. I'm not surprised he couldn't bear being linked to one of the karionin. You were a fool to try it with him. But then you always were a fool, weren't you, when it came to Luri."

Again, control only came with effort. Aketi had gotten clever over the years at identifying her weak spots. Still, he had risen to her bait.

"Perhaps," she said, allowing him his victory. "But under the circumstances, I'll need to have witnesses if you want to link with me. If you aren't as strong as you believe and Cinkarion burns you, I don't want to be accused of murdering you, or trying to. Jadne would want me executed and, as she's Estaharil of Senanga, I'd have little defense."

Aketi's eyes brightened. "Then you agree to the linkage?"

"If you can supply impartial witnesses with the high sight."

"Done," he said, his voice full of satisfaction. "My first farail has the high sight. He's House Katharti's heir. And I have Yocastim Nehu as a passenger. I'll be taking him to Kavarna to be our new Ambassador to Gandahar. I'm sure he'll be glad to act as a witness and, like Katharti, he has no special ties to my faction."

"That will be satisfactory," Saranith said. "When do you want to schedule the linkage? Next week?"

"Oh, no, Saranith," Aketi said. "Now you've agreed to it, I'm not giving you time to change your mind. I'll go aboard now and bring the witnesses back within the hour."

She took a deep breath, allowing him to see the reaction. Then said, "Are you sure you don't at least want your breakfast first?"

"The food will taste better afterward."

"Very well, Aketi. It shall be as you wish."

He grinned. "Oh, yes, Saranith, and I'll hear a lot more of that phrase from now on." He headed down the steps toward his ship.

Saranith took another deep breath and released it. She had done it. The witnesses would feel the fires themselves. They wouldn't be burned, but they wouldn't be surprised if she were prostate afterward. When someone finally realized that Arrun was gone, it would be easy to claim that he'd been here this morning and, after that, she had no knowledge of what might have happened to him.

There would be another benefit as well. The witnesses would witness the price that Cinkarion demanded for the link. They would tell others that most minds could not survive such a link. That might well cut down the attempts on her life. After this, only the strongest wizards would dare to try to take Cinkarion or link with her.

WHEN ARRUN WOKE he was lying on a bunk in the cabin of a ship on its way out to sea. The cap was gone, but he was still a blue teddy bear. He examined himself carefully. He was naked. He sat up and looked around the cabin. His blue jumper hung over a chair nearby. He levered himself to the edge of the bunk and jumped down onto the floor. Then he waddled over to the jumper and took his crystal out of the pocket. Whoever had restored his skull had replaced the crystal where he found it. His paws were clumsy, but using both he managed to hold it.

Then he examined himself again. He was very weak. There was no way he was going to be able to simply turn himself back into a man, but there was no permanent damage to his mind. He'd been careful not to strain against the cap. In all the cases where he'd encountered permanent damage, the wizards around the victim had described a constant struggle. He had never struggled, never fought. His care seemed to have paid off. He looked at the imprint of himself in the crystal and restored his throat and larynx.

"Arrun, what are you doing?" Nathan said, coming through the door. "We thought you'd sleep for hours yet. You shouldn't be out of bed."

Arrun cocked his teddy bear head and said, "I was tired of being without a voice. I may not be up to much, but that, at least, I could accomplish."

Nathan shook his head. "You're incredible. You wear a cap for over a year and six hours after it's removed you're up to altering yourself?"

"Just my throat," Arrun said. "If you'd been a mute for a year, I assure you, you'd find a way to do something about it as soon as that was even remotely possible."

Nathan frowned. "We still haven't figured out how you knew to escape into the woods at the right time."

Arrun bared his teeth. "I had some inside assistance."

Nathan gaped at him. "Someone in Saranith's own household was willing to help you?"

Arrun shut his eyes, feeling an unexpected pain at Nathan's disbelief. He said, "It was Saranith herself."

"She made a mockery of you by turning you into a little blue bear, and then helped you escape?"

Arrun shook his head. "Saranith didn't capture me. What made you think she turned me into this form?"

"I don't know," Nathan said, looking confused. "I suppose because you were her prisoner and it seemed like something she'd do."

"No," Arrun said. "Saranith would never do something like this. Saranith understands the pain of humiliation far better than most people. Aketi and Jadne, her cousins, designed my form as a joke and gave me to her. They thought it would cause her pain to watch me die."

Nathan stared. "That's the truth?"

"Oh, yes, but Aketi will be dead by tomorrow. Saranith is going to allow him to try and link with her." He swallowed. "She believes that linking with her will cause the death of anyone who tries. In Aketi's case, I'm sure she's right. She's much more powerful than he is, and she hates him."

Nathan's eyes narrowed. "But you don't think she's right in all cases?"

"No," he said. "And some day I'm going to prove it."

"Maera's mercy, but you're in love with her."

Arrun grunted. "Ironic isn't it. I've always boasted that I'd know when I met the right woman. But I didn't. I'd heard so many dreadful things about her, it took me almost a week to realize that none of the rumors described who she really is at all. Yes, Nathan, Saranith Kamrasi is the woman I'm destined to mate with someday. It's strange the way fate works. I'm descended from Ilfarnar and Agnith. I have Ilfarnar's talent. The wheel turns and history repeats itself."

"Have you considered how you're going to court her? I don't think you'll have many chances to even see her again."

"It may take years, even centuries, Nathan. But wizards live a long time. And now that I know my fate, I'll work on the circumstances. After all, haven't I been acclaimed as a brilliant tactician?"

"I don't know whether to wish you luck, or pray to Jehan that you fail."

"Wish me luck, Nathan. Then imagine the world reformed in such a way that a member of the Varfarin can mate with the Estahar of Senanga. Isn't such a world, after all, our ultimate goal?"

LIV

4673, 468TH CYCLE OF THE YEAR OF THE LIZARD
MONTH OF CERDANA

So sime quen zara ua ife.
Ba acadend reba wen oa pon.

"Be careful for what you wish.
There's always a chance you may receive it."

— ESLARIN PROVERB

"**Y**OU WITNESSED this linkage, both of you?" Jadne demanded of the two men in front of her. They were in the sitting room of her suite in Cinkarrak, lavishily decorated in crimson and gold. The colors became her, setting off her dark bronze skin and black hair. Her eyes were only a faintly paler shade of gold than the giltwork.

"Yes, your majesty," Yocastim Nehu said. "Aketi asked us to bear witness when he linked with Saranith. We thought it a strange request..."

"Get to the point? Did Saranith burn out Aketi's mind?"

"Oh, no, your majesty. That isn't what happened at all. Cinkarion sent out flames. I was burned myself, before I could break contact, but from what I saw before I escaped the linkage, Saranith tried to shield Aketi, but joined as she was to Cinkarion she couldn't get between them."

"She did warn Aketi of the danger," Soren Katharti said. "That was why she insisted on witnesses. She told us that she tried to link with her lifemate through Cinkarion and the crystal burned out his mind. That she had been unable to stop the pain. She warned Aketi that Cinkarion bore the memories of the deaths of all the wizards who died in the Bane and that the price for bearing it is experiencing those deaths. We felt only a faint touch of those memories," Yocastim said. "The wizards burned, Jadne. They burned."

"But Saranith endured the pain."

"She was pale and shaken," Soren said. "She said it was the third time she had felt Cinkarion's fire and it never got easier. She cannot cry with those jewelled eyes, but we felt her distress."

Jadne sighed. Later that night in their bedroom, also decorated in crimson and gold, she told Kaya. "She's clever. She knew that Aketi would never give up trying to get a linkage to Cinkarion. Eventually he would have killed her and given the crystal to me, if she hadn't given in to his requests that they link. She had to have known that. So she demanded witnesses, eliminated Aketi, and demonstrated that Cinkarion has a sting of its own all at the same time.

She smiled wryly, "I've always hated her, but she's your ally and Cinkarion gives her significant power. As I know of no one else who could bear that kind of pain, I think we should give up all thoughts of taking Cinkarion for ourselves."

"Is her talent for taking pain so extraordinary?" Kaya asked. "Aketi liked to inflict pain, but he didn't like to experience it himself. I've always thought that personally he was a bit of a coward."

Jadne frowned. "Sara put out her own eyes with a poker when she was twelve. Now, I can imagine someone determined to gain the high sight managing to poke out one eye, but she then suppressed that pain and poked out the other. I can't imagine anyone else who could achieve that. In the name of Kyra the Destroyer, she was just a child then.

AS THE WIZARD ARRUN insisted on restoring himself and was weakened by the months under the cap, he didn't report to Balek until over a month had passed since his escape. When Arrun finally appeared, however, he seemed unaware of Balek's irritation and merely greeted everyone as though it were an ordinary meeting.

"I've been hearing strange things about your escape," Balek began.

"Saranith Kamrasi was a surprise for me too," Arrun said, "but as Nathan may have told you, she's the woman I will one day link with."

"That's absurd. She's a known pirate, a relative of the Royal House of Senanga," Balek said explosively.

"Yes, she's all of those things," Arrun said, "but by the laws of her country she's a naval officer, not a pirate, and no one can help who they are born."

"The time in the cap must have damaged your mind," Balek said. "You're unlikely to ever see her again."

"No, Balek, remember that my strength is strategy. I'm well aware that I'll have to change both our worlds before we can stand a chance of being together. But I'm a wizard; I have time to change the world, and I know that others wish to see it changed just as I do. The telepathic relay has reported that the Wizard of Leyburn is the new Esalfar of the Varfarin, and the Wizard Elgan is now a member of that organization once again. Change is coming, Balek. Be ready for it, or get out of the way."

Balek nodded then and said, "Very well. I've seen this coming for some time. It's time I retired. My opinions no longer represent the majority of this Council. Nathan," he turned to him, "I hereby name you the new Esalfaril of the Varfarin in Cibata, until the new Esalfar appoints someone himself."

He looked around and said, "I will, of course, continue to assist the Varfarin in any way I'm able. I'm fairly good at training children. I trained you, after all!"

NATHAN LOOKED AROUND the dock, where the message had said he was to meet the new Esalfar of the Varfarin, the Wizard of Leyburn. The time was right, but no ship had arrived at this dock on this day and the only person present was...he blinked and focused his sight.

Jerevan thought, *"You might have recognized me more easily if you used your sight more often. It's lazy of you to use your physical eyes."*

"Jerevan?" Nathan's eyes widened in amazement, looking at the tall, slender man in front of him, immaculately clad in the latest in fashionable clothing.

"The Wizard of Leyburn now, and Esalfar of the Varfarin. I'm here to make changes and take oaths."

Nathan was startled by the icy tone of this new wizard's mind. He was not as Nathan remembered him at all. "Balek has already resigned as head of the Varfarin here in Cibata. He named me his successor," Nathan said aloud.

"That will be satisfactory to me, if you are willing to retake your oath linked to me. In fact, I'm requiring that every member of the Varfarin retake that oath, linked to me," he paused and added with emphasis, *"with particular emphasis on the abuse of wizard power. I believe it goes, 'As a member of the Varfarin I will not tolerate the altering of any sentient being in any way without that being's consent.'"*

Nathan drew a deep breath. No. This was not the man he remembered. This was an altogether new being. The power had always been there, but it had seemed softer when Jerevan had been huge and confined to his bed. Now there was a knife sharpness to him and the power was more refined. Nathan had wondered about Jerevan becoming Esalfar of the Varfarin. He had no doubt that the Wizard of Leyburn was up to the job. He thought carefully, *"I will have no trouble taking that oath."*

"Then as the new head of the Varfarin in Cibata I suggest you arrange for every wizard, journeyman wizard and apprentice wizard in Cibata who wishes to remain a member of the Varfarin to visit Candith in the next two months. Anyone missing me during that period will not be considered a

member of the Varfarin until they find me back in the Thallassean region and take the oath there. Is that understood?"

"Yes, rai, I understand, and for what it's worth, I fully agree."

The Wizard of Leyburn nodded. *"Very well, Nathan, it seems as though I'll be able to work with you. I've arranged for a house near the Palace, the Aldecante Estate off Kingfisher Lane. Be there tonight by six o'clock to take your oath, along with anyone else currently in Candith who you feel will be important to your administration. Make sure that Balek attends if he wishes to take any further part in the Varfarin."*

Later when Nathan found Pala, Balek was with her. "Well, what did the new Esalfar want?" Balek asked.

"He commands that all members of the Varfarin in Cibata retake their oaths linked to him, or else they will no longer be considered members," Nathan thought.

"Retake my oath to that fat slug," Balek said. *"I won't do it."*

"He's no longer fat," Nathan thought. *"I think you'll find him,"* Nathan paused, thinking of the right way to describe the new Wizard of Leyburn, *"formidable,"* he finished finally.

Balek's eyes narrowed. *"This is not a joke."*

"Oh, no," Nathan thought. *"Cormor found no one he thought suitable to succeed him among the wizards who survived the Bane, so he saw to the creation of someone suitable. And he made sure that his successor would have great power and no respect for the members of the Varfarin at all."*

"What do you mean?"

"I worked with Jerevan for months on the trip back to Cibata and while he was here, but I never saw, not for one moment, how much anger there was in him," Nathan thought. *"I don't believe even he was aware of the depth of the anger he had buried in order to survive his curse. But he has survived the curse. He's now one of the most powerful wizards on Tamar. If I were you, Balek, I wouldn't cross him in any way. I've already told the telepathic relay to convey his summons to every member of the Varfarin here in Cibata. I'll be retaking my oath this evening."*

Nathan turned to Pala. *"Pala, as Ahar of Cassinga you don't have to be a member of the Varfarin, but you did take the oath originally. I'd appreciate your accompanying me tonight and taking it again."*

"Of course I will," she thought, but her face showed concern. *"But why is he so angry?"*

"Because every member of the Varfarin broke his or her oath when Derwen's curse was allowed to stand and Derwen was not instantly removed from the Varfarin," Nathan thought. *"Is that not so?"* he asked of Balek.

Balek frowned but nodded slowly. *"Yes. I'd not thought of it in that light, but you're right. We all are foresworn."*

"But it was Cormor's will..." Pala said.

"So we thought," Balek said, *"and therefore we put what Derwen told us was Cormor's will ahead of our oaths. Nathan's right. We should not have done that."*

Balek turned to Nathan and said, *"But an angry wizard is not going to make a good leader either."*

Nathan shook his head, *"Not angry as in raging, Balek. Angry as in ice. The Wizard of Leyburn won't act without thinking or out of simple malice, but I suspect that many members of the Varfarin will not be entirely comfortable for some years to come."*

Balek snorted. *"I can't argue with that. I've thought a number of us deserved a swat now and then myself."*

THERE WERE, THEREFORE, almost a hundred people assembled in the ballroom of the Aldecante house that evening. The Wizard of Leyburn administered the Journeyman's oath first, as that was appropriate to the largest part of the crowd. The journeymen, apprentice wizards and journeyman wizards all took their oaths, linked together and were then dismissed. Pala, however, stayed with Nathan.

Jerevan looked around at the remaining wizards: Nathan, Balek, Evran, Rainal, Choma, who happened to be visiting Candith that day, and Lagura and Bella. He chose to address Balek first but broadcast his thought so all present could hear, asking, *"So you're willing to take your oath again to me?"*

Balek eyed him keenly, and thought, *"Nathan brought it to my attention that I was foresworn. I admit I'd not thought of my actions in that light, but once I did, I was willing to retake my oath with the belief that nothing will cause me to be foresworn again."*

"You understand that Cormor's vision included all races of the larin on a Council of Wizards? If you pledge to the Varfarin now you will be dedicating yourself to that goal?" Again, Jerevan included all the wizards present.

"I still have some difficulty with that concept, but I'm coming to accept it," Balek thought. *"I've always striven for peace. The old Council of Wizards envisioned a peace enforced by human wizards and that has always been my vision as well. But it hasn't worked, and I've begun to see that it never will. We were all appalled when Saranith Kamrasi linked with Cinkarion, but Arrun claims that she is also one who desires peace..."*

He broke off and shook his head.

"Did you speak to the hailar child, Magra?" Jerevan asked.

Balek nodded. *"Yes. I saw how badly she was damaged, but that her potential was strong."* He sighed. *"I'll pledge myself to your new vision, although how it can be brought about I can't imagine."*

"You should have spoken longer with the Wizard Elgan while he was here. He was with his grandfather for the entire last year of Cormor's life and

Cormor shared many insights with him. I benefited greatly from them on my journey back to Ilwheirlane," Jerevan thought.

He looked around the room. *"Do all of you agree to retake your oaths with the goals of the Varfarin as I've restated them?"*

They all indicated assent.

"Then we should link minds," Jerevan thought. They all did and the oaths were given.

Nathan said, when they were done, "That was a lot easier this time round."

There was general laughter.

Jerevan looked at Balek. *"If you've been brought to see the new course the Varfarin must take, I have much greater hope for all of Tamar."*

Balek thought, *"I've always known the karionin belong to Jehan. I tried to ignore the fact that the bearer of Lyskarion was an ingvalar, the ingvalarin have always held a special place since Luth taught them."* He shook his head. *"Then Cinkarion chose a linlar, Saranith Kamrasi. I thought that had to be a mistake, but Arrun, whom I've come to trust, tells me it was no mistake, that she wants peace as much as any member of the Varfarin."* He paused and looked at Jerevan. *"Yes, I'm an old man and set in my ways, and even in my youth I was never flexible. I've been proud of that. But I worship Jehan. If his karionin are giving power to the larin how can I object? They are his children. The old Council forgot that, but I've been reminded and I'll not forget again."*

"So be it," Jerevan thought.